Doubleday Canada and colophon are registered trademarks of
Penguin Random House Canada Limited

Library and Archives Canada Cataloguing in Publication

Title: Known to the victim / K.L. Armstrong.
Names: Armstrong, Kelley, author.
Identifiers: Canadiana (print) 20240301943 | Canadiana (ebook) 20240301978 |
ISBN 9780385697705 (softcover) | ISBN 9780385697699 (EPUB)
Subjects: LCGFT: Thrillers (Fiction) | LCGFT: Novels.
Classification: LCC PS8551.R7637 K56 2024 | DDC C813/.6—dc23

This book is a work of fiction. Names, characters, places and incidents are
products of the author's imagination or are used fictitiously. Any resemblance to
actual events or locales or persons, living or dead, is entirely coincidental.

Cover and text design: Matthew Flute
Cover photo: wilpunt/Getty Images
Typesetting: Sean Tai

Printed in Canada

Published in Canada by Doubleday Canada,
a division of Penguin Random House Canada Limited,
and distributed in the United States by Penguin Random House LLC

www.penguinrandomhouse.ca

10 9 8 7 6 5 4 3 2 1

Penguin
Random House
DOUBLEDAY CANADA

K.L. Armstrong is the pseudonym of a popular author.
She lives in Ontario.

T0007246

Also by K.L. Armstrong

The Life She Had
Every Step She Takes
Wherever She Goes

KNOW
TO TH
VICTII

K.L. ARMSTRO

DOUBLEDAY CANADA

KNOWN
TO THE
VICTIM

PROLOGUE

The day my mother was murdered wasn't the worst day of my life. I didn't even find out she was dead for twenty-nine hours. Sometimes, the guilt over that crushes me, as if I should have heard the sonic boom of my life exploding. Instead, I'd gone to classes and then hung out with friends that night while we tossed back shots and moaned about midterms. Some nights I'll jolt up in a cold sweat, remembering myself perched on a campus barstool, saying that if I didn't get a B in chem, my life would be over.

No, my life was not over. My mother's was. And I had no idea.

I'd texted her that morning, as I always did, and she'd popped back a quick "Good morning, sunshine!" and "Busy day. Talk tomorrow?"

I'd sent a thumbs-up, pocketed my phone and moved on with my day. As I'd learn soon enough, she hadn't sent those texts. She couldn't. She was already dead, stuffed into her killer's trunk. He'd flipped through her messages to see how she talked to me, and replied with something that would buy him time to dispose of her corpse and possibly even buy him an alibi.

Why no, she couldn't have been dead already—she was texting her daughter.

Those texts didn't raise any red flags. Nor did the ones she sent her law partner, Dinah, saying she had "some kind of bug" and would be "sleeping it off." The red flags were noticed by a trucker who spotted a car down a side road, the driver struggling with something in the trunk.

Struggling with my mother's body.

The next day, the police showed up at my dorm to tell me Mom was dead. But that wasn't the worst day of my life, either, because I was too numb to react. I spent the next few days in shock, propelled along only by Dinah, who led me through all the appropriate steps because there was no one else to do it. My parents had split before I was born, my father remarrying within the year and exiting from my life. I had half siblings on my father's side, and I'd never met them. My mother was an only child, so I had no aunts, uncles or cousins on her side. By the time I was in college, both her parents were gone, and I'd never had any contact with my father's side of the family.

It was just the two of us. Kim and Amy. "The Gibson Girls," Dinah always joked, and it wasn't until I was nearly twenty that I realized that was a reference to an old TV show. When I watched it, I understood the allusion: a mother and daughter who adored each other, just them against the world. Of course, in our version, Mom wasn't nearly so flighty, and I wasn't nearly so sensible, but it was a cute name, nonetheless.

Dinah guided me through the funeral arrangements, but after that, I insisted on going back to school, and when I took her daily calls, I pretended everything was okay. Eventually, I answered her calls less and less often, but I always texted saying I was just busy. She took me at my word. I was back to school, immersing myself in it, and I didn't need my mom's friend hovering.

That was a lie. I needed Dinah. I needed *someone*. But I didn't know how to ask for help, and I didn't want to be a burden, so I played the role of a young woman who was grieving but okay.

I was not okay.

The worst day of my life wasn't the day I had to choose my mother's casket. It wasn't the day I buried her. It wasn't the day I cleaned out her closet for charity. It wasn't the day I returned to school and had to explain my mother's death to classmates who wondered where I'd been. With each passing marker, people swore things would get better. They lied. It got worse.

The truth was, there was no "worst day"—just an unending blur of worse. I stopped going to classes and spent my days locked up in my dorm room, watching that damn mother-and-daughter TV show as I cried.

My father didn't come to the funeral because I hadn't bothered to let him know that Mom had died. He'd never been part of our lives, so screw him. I did, however, make one inexcusable mistake: I didn't tell my brother.

Oliver was ten years older than me. His parents split when he was five, and our father got custody of him. That meant, for the three years of my parents' marriage, he'd been my mom's child.

Mom always hoped that Oliver and I would have some kind of relationship once I was old enough to stop letting my anger at my father spill onto my half brother. For the few years that she'd been part of his life, she'd loved him like a son, and she always said that losing Oliver had been the worst part of the divorce. Not being his mother by blood or adoption, she'd had no right to see him, and she never had again. I should have called and let him know she was gone.

Oliver reached out a few weeks after Mom's death. He must have read about her murder in the news, which was a shitty way to learn it. Oliver asked whether we could talk, and I dodged and weaved until he sent me an invitation to a video chat.

It took me three days to prepare. I spent the first one working up to showering, which I did on day two, and then on day three, I finally left my dorm room and washed the clothing I'd been wearing since Mom's funeral.

Right up until the moment of the call, I had to fight myself not to cancel it. I wrote the email three times. Wrote the text a dozen. But I didn't send them, and when the call came, I took it, and it was . . .

It was wonderful. And it was horrible because it was wonderful. Does that make any sense? For years, I'd had this mental image of Oliver. I knew he'd taken over our father's business—some company whose exact purpose was so dull I couldn't keep it in my mind longer than it took him to explain it—and I knew that the business was one of the leading employers in Grand Forks, where they lived. I also knew that my father was one of those assholes who could afford to pay the bills for a thousand underprivileged kids but didn't even pay child support for his own daughter.

I can hear Mom's patient sigh at that. I'm not saying I was deprived by my father's neglect—emotional or financial. I was a loved and privileged kid with a mother who'd decided to raise me on her own significant income. My point is that's the kind of guy James Harding is—he once bought a yacht and let it rot in the marina for a tax deduction. I assumed that Oliver would be Dad 2.0. In other words, Corporate Asshole 2.0.

Except he wasn't. The guy on that video call reminded me of my mom. He was sweet and patient, and he never once said "I'm sorry for your loss," because that was obvious. Instead, he talked *about* her.

"I have so many good memories of your mom," he said. "She was so much *fun*. That's what I remember most. Hey, did she still make those cheesecake brownies?"

My eyes teared up, and all I could do was nod.

"I love those brownies," he said. "One time, she put them out to cool, and I asked if I could have a piece . . ."

"And you took a whole row and blamed the dog."

"She remembered?" His smile is surprised, but also pleased.

Of course. She remembered everything about you. You'd been her child, once upon a time.

But I didn't say that. I could only imagine what stories our father had told him about Mom.

"Your mom was awesome," he said. Then he rolled his eyes. "Yeah, that makes me sound about twelve, but she really was. I remember, one night Dad was working late, as usual, and I had a math test the next day. I was freaking out. Your mom spent *hours* working with me, and then we went for ice cream. That's who she was. Work hard, play hard, and I really . . ." He cleared his throat. "She was awesome."

Pain stabbed through me, but for the first time in weeks, it didn't feel like a fatal blow.

"She was," I said.

"And I'd say my dad made a huge mistake leaving her, but honestly, I always figured she dodged a bullet there."

I choked on a laugh.

Oliver's voice lowered. "Our dad is an asshole, Amy. I hate what he did to you and your mom."

"What he did to all of us," I said before I could stop myself.

His voice cracked then. "I used to beg to see your mom again, and he said she didn't want to see me." Before I can protest, he hurries on. "Which is a lie. A few years ago, she reached out, now that I was an adult, and my father couldn't interfere. She probably never mentioned that."

"She didn't." I wasn't surprised, though. Now that I think about it, I'd have been more surprised if she let him go and never contacted him again.

"We even had lunch a couple of years ago. You were in your senior year, and she was so proud of you, Amy." He was quiet for a moment, then he said softly, "I know you weren't ready for a relationship with me. You were understandably angry with our dad. So your mom and I decided to wait a bit. And then . . ."

My eyes filled. "I'm sorry. She was right. I was angry with him, and I shouldn't have let that spill onto you."

"I understood. Our father—" He cut himself short abruptly. "Enough about him. He doesn't deserve it. Let's talk about her. Is that okay?"

Was it okay? God, it was *so* okay. Talking about Mom and sharing good memories was exactly what I needed, and that video call was the best thing to happen to me since the "before" times.

That should have turned everything around for me, right? Back on my feet, determined to start the uphill climb and find my new normal?

No. In fact, it was the opposite.

I'd psyched myself up for the call with Oliver, and it had gone better than I could have dreamed, and somehow that sent me crashing even deeper into the pit. I became racked with guilt for not contacting Oliver when Mom died. Guilt for letting him see it in the news. Guilt for presuming he'd be an asshole. Guilt for not telling him, during that call, that Mom had loved him. That's what depression does: people think you just need something to cheer you up, and sometimes, your brain takes that "good" thing and weaponizes it against you.

I bottomed out after that. At least before the call I'd been forcing myself to eat and finding temporary solace in that TV show. After the call, I stopped both.

And no one noticed. Dinah presumed if I ducked her calls with texts, I was just busy. My back-home friends all presumed I was drowning my grief in schoolwork, and they didn't want to interfere. My new college friends presumed I'd gone home after I'd dropped out. No one wanted to bother me, and that only made me feel more alone.

I won't say I was ever suicidal. That would require action. I just . . . stopped. It was as if I shut down, and even the most fundamental parts of life seemed like too much effort. I had to force myself to eat and drink, and otherwise, I lay in bed and existed. I existed, and that took all the energy I had, with days where even that seemed like too much effort.

Mom was gone. Dead. *Murdered*. With her went the center of my universe, the only person who truly cared about me.

Then came the knock at my dorm door.

"Amy?" a man's voice said. "It's me. Oliver." A pause. "Your brother."

I didn't move. I stayed in bed, staring at the ceiling. Even processing what I was hearing seemed like too much effort. My brain was empty.

The knock came firmer. "I know you're in there, Amy. I know you dropped out of college, and I know you didn't go home. You haven't been returning my texts, so I got worried and made some calls. No one's seen you in weeks."

Another pause. Then he said, "Maybe I should be breaking this door down, presuming the worst, but I'm hoping I don't need to do that. I realize you don't know me from a stranger, and I'm sorry for that. I misunderstood the situation. I realize that now, and I want to make up for it."

Silence.

"Come stay with me," Oliver said. "I have a guesthouse." A short laugh. "It's not as fancy as it sounds—the former owners built it for their parents, and it's tiny—but it has a bedroom and bath and kitchen. Come stay with me until you're back on your feet." He cleared his throat. "Or we can figure something else out. Please, Amy. Just open this door." Another pause. "I owe your mom. Let me help you. For her."

I lay there for two seconds. Then I whispered, "Okay," rolled out of bed and padded to the door.

ONE

EIGHT YEARS LATER

I'm standing at the front of an auditorium, looking out on a packed room. My first sold-out show. I try not to get too excited about that. This is a library, not a thousand-seat auditorium. But it's the central library, with a two-hundred-and-fifty-person-capacity auditorium, and every seat is taken by someone here to listen to me, Amy Gibson, host of the true crime podcast *Known to the Victim*.

After Mom died and Oliver helped me back to my feet, I switched my major to sociology with a minor in psychology. Intimate partner violence became my focus. I wanted to understand what happened to my mother and how to help others, the survivors of such violence and the families the victims left behind.

That led to volunteer work in shelters and on helplines. Then, as part of my master's degree work, I started the *Known to the Victim* blog, devoted to cases where, as the title suggests, people were killed by those they knew.

Intentionally seeking out cases like my mother's isn't easy. It's a reminder of how she died, but also a reminder of the injustice and the commonplaceness of that injustice. My mother's story should be unique in its horror, and it is not. Her killer should be unique in his monstrosity, and he is not. They are just two actors playing out an age-old drama, where one partner leaves a relationship and the other kills them for it.

My coverage of one Toronto case gained me a guest spot on a Canadian true crime show, where the host convinced me to turn my blog into a podcast, which I did. I won't say the podcast is a runaway success. Podcasts can fill arenas with live shows, and I'm in a library, an hour from where I now live in Grand Forks. But in the last six months, I've been on over a dozen lists of up-and-coming podcasts, with my numbers increasing exponentially month by month. These days, I divide my time between the podcast and part-time doctorate studies, where my thesis is on how familial factors impact the reporting of domestic violence.

I've been doing live shows across Ontario for about a year now. Not many, but it's a huge and exciting step. The people that attend are here to see *me*. To listen to *me*, Amy Gibson. That's both exhilarating and daunting.

I stand behind the podium and introduce myself, thank everyone for coming and thank them for their support, hoping they can see how much I truly appreciate it. Then I start the presentation.

"This was my mother," I say as her photo fills the large screen behind me. "Kimberly Louise Gibson. Lawyer, daughter, mother, world's best brownie baker, world's worst driver, world's biggest Scrabble cheat."

A soft round of polite laughter.

"She died on October 2, 2015, while I was in my second year of college. Strangled to death. Murdered."

I walk beside the big screen, wireless mic in hand. "Next, I should explain how I singlehandedly tracked down her killer and how that launched my podcast, right? That's not what happened. The police arrested my mother's killer the next day. Should I say that the case was tossed out on a technicality, and I found the evidence they needed to convict him? Nope, that didn't happen, either. My mother's killer was tried and convicted and sentenced to life in prison. I did nothing to find my mother's killer or bring him to justice. The system worked exactly as it should."

I look out at the crowd, allowing a beat before saying, "But that doesn't change the most important thing: that my mother is dead. That she was murdered by someone she knew."

I pace the stage, still talking. "I did nothing to help catch her killer, so maybe I started the podcast out of guilt. I failed to see the danger signs, and *Known to the Victim* is my attempt to keep others from making that mistake. But it isn't that simple, either."

I turn back to the audience. "I started *Known to the Victim* for a thousand reasons, all of them about my mother and what happened to her. Were there more things Mom could have done? Warning signs she missed? Things I could have done? Signs I missed?" I shrug. "I don't know. You can decide that. I can tell you this much—when you stand in my shoes, everyone judges what you did, the choices you made, and no one judges them as much as you. My mother was murdered by a man she went on three dates with."

I press the remote in my hand. Another picture fills the screen. It's a man in his early fifties, heavyset, broad shouldered, with a lazy left eye. A murmur goes through the audience. A few women relax. See, they wouldn't have made the mistake my mother did. They can *tell* this man is trouble.

"William Levy," I say. "Twice divorced. At twenty, he spent a year in prison for assault. Got out, joined the army for a few years, then went into private security and finally became a long-distance trucker."

I turn to the screen. "Bill is the reason my mother's killer was caught. He noticed a man parked near a pond, taking something from his trunk. Bill snapped photos of the man and his license plate. Then he called the police. He showed up for court even when it could have cost him his job. I exchange Christmas cards with Bill and his wife, and whenever he comes through this way, we go for coffee. He's a good man, and I owe him so much."

I click to the next photo, of a man in his early forties, smiling and pleasantly handsome. "This is Grant White. College professor. Married his high school sweetheart, who died of cancer a decade later, leaving him a widower with two young children." I look out at the audience. "This is my mother's killer."

I turn away from the photo as fast as I can, pretending to casually stroll across the stage. "My mother didn't meet White in a bar. She didn't meet him online. They were introduced. He was friends with a longtime client of hers. Afterward, that client told police the charges against White were a terrible misunderstanding, that clearly something happened, a tragic accident, and White panicked and tried to dispose of my mom's body. When she—yes, the client was a woman—discovered that White had strangled my mother, she declared it rough sex gone wrong. When she discovered my mother had reported White for stalking her, she declared my mother had always been"—I air-quote—"'a little high-strung.' White was upset over the breakup and only trying to get Mom back, and Mom overreacted, and yes, it obviously looked bad, in light of her death, but it had to be a misunderstanding . . . or maybe my mother did something that sent him over the edge, because Grant White was not that kind of man."

I turn to the next slide, which shows a quartet of official complaint reports, the victims' names and all identifying information redacted. "These are four students White taught in college. They all accused him of unwanted sexual advances. He lost two jobs as a result, but as part of the negotiations, the details were not on his employment record, which means they weren't passed on to future employers. If four women filed complaints, studies suggest there would have been more who didn't. Two ex-girlfriends also testified at his trial that he had threatened them. One had even taken out a restraining order."

I turn to the audience, and I focus on the ones whose eyes are on me, those who nod, react, give me their full attention. There will always be some who fuss or play with their phones, but I'm beginning to recognize that implies discomfort more than boredom. I let them have their quiet moment, unobserved, while I shore up my confidence with the others.

"The warning signs were there," I continue. "My mother saw them by the third date. White called her during work hours when she'd asked him not to. He wanted to talk about their future even after she said it made her uncomfortable. He grumbled when they couldn't go out one night because she had plans with me. After that last one, she ended things, and I made her promise to be careful, to stay away from White, and to use her home-security system."

My throat seizes with old rage and grief, but I push on. "She did all that. When he wouldn't stop calling and showed up at her work twice, she also reported him. She saved troubling messages and was consulting with a lawyer on next steps. That's when White grabbed her in the secured-entry parking garage of her law firm. At eight in the morning. In broad daylight."

I flip to the next slide. It's my mother's headstone. "My mom did all the right things. Had she known of this man's past, though—if she'd had any way to access that, if the police had found the previous restraining order—she'd have done more than just consult a lawyer."

I look out at the audience and pause. "White was a serial predator, and it was only a matter of time before he killed someone. That someone happened to be my mother. This is why I started *Known to the Victim*. Predators rarely *look* like predators. Many of them are men, like White, who will have their friends swearing—in all sincerity—that there's been a mistake, that the woman is to blame. There will be a pattern of behavior—"

"Like with your brother," a voice calls from the audience.

I go still as I squint, trying to pinpoint the speaker. A woman stands. She's a few rows from the front, and my mind immediately catalogs everything I can see about her. There are many ways my mother's murder changed my life, and this is one of them: I am perpetually hyperaware of threats. Sometimes, I feel like my brain is one of those cybernetic eyes in science fiction movies, scanning even the most minor potential threat and spitting out the data, just in case I should ever need to make a police report.

Is this healthy? Probably not, though it has helped with my podcast. I notice everything, and I analyze and store the data. In this moment, I take in this woman. She's in her early forties, brown hair past her shoulders, glasses so unfashionable they might be coming back *into* fashion. About five foot three, a hundred and thirty pounds—though it's hard to tell in the oversized sweater she's wearing. She's in the fourth row, third seat from the middle aisle.

"Your brother is Oliver Harding, yes?" she calls.

"He's my half brother, actually," I say. "Ten years my senior. We have different mothers." Ever since *Known to the Victim* started seeing a modicum of success, I began clarifying that, because more than one person had made the connection and offered condolences to Oliver on the murder of his mother.

"Oliver Harding," the woman continues, "whose first wife died under mysterious circumstances."

There's a murmur in the audience, a shift of discomfort. My heart picks up speed, but I force myself not to jump into defense mode. Bigger names in podcasting have warned me about this. It's the reason I keep my online comment section moderated—always a good idea when you're public about a personal tragedy—but the trolls know they can have their say at a live show.

"Oliver's college *girlfriend* died by suicide," I say calmly. "It's one reason . . ." I swallow. "I fell into a pit after my mother died. Oliver hauled me out, and that's one of the reasons. He knew the danger signs for suicide from personal experience. He also knew what it was like to lose someone and feel as if you hadn't been there for them. I was at university when my mother was killed. He was in the US with friends when his girlfriend died."

If I expected that to shame the woman to silence, it proves I don't have nearly enough experience with trolls. She plows on as if I haven't opened my mouth.

"Then there was his second wife, who drowned under equally suspicious circumstances."

"Laura was his first and only wife," I say with all the calm I can muster. "She drowned three years ago while they were out boating."

My words send another rumble through the audience, followed by the hiss of people whispering to their neighbors. I might stiffen at that, but I get it, too. Laura's death was a classic suspicious death, but the circumstances meant that the police didn't do more than half-heartedly investigate, mostly because they didn't want to be accused of failing to do so. Witnesses saw Laura dive off the bow to swim, my brother at the stern. They heard her teasing him about not joining her. Then they saw her duck underwater . . . and not come up, while my brother was still visible on the boat.

I could say all that, but my producer has taught me not to feed the trolls.

"If you're interested," I say, keeping my voice even, "it was fully reported in the local papers."

"*Fully* reported?"

I maintain eye contact with her. "Yes."

"And what about his new girlfriend?" the woman continues. "What about her accusations against him?"

My whole body tenses, and I don't have time to school my features. "Accusations?"

Stop feeding the trolls, Amy!

"I don't know what you mean," I continue, "but since you seem to have concerns, maybe you should speak to the police."

I'm sorry, Oliver. That's a shitty thing to say.

On the other hand, I know it's exactly what he'd want me to say. After Laura died, before all the facts came out, there were plenty of whispers. Rich guy's wife disappears while they were boating? Convenient . . .

At the time, I'd just started my podcast, and I had so few listeners that no one asked me about it, but Oliver said that if they did, I should refer them to the police. Don't defend him. That only makes things worse. Steer people in the proper direction for answers.

"Oh, there's no need to tell the cops." The woman's lips twist in a smirk. "They already know. That's why your brother is sitting in the Grand Forks police station right now, answering their questions."

I blink. She's lying. She must be.

But what if she's not? What if something's happened, an argument between Oliver and Martine that turned into . . . I don't even know what.

Something *could* have happened, and Oliver *could* be answering questions at the police station, and if I deny it—without being certain—then I am no better than every bystander I talk about in my podcasts, the people who denied that their friend, sister, brother, child, parent was a predator.

"If something has happened," I say slowly as I bite back the urge to qualify it as a misunderstanding. *I'm sorry, Oliver. I'm so sorry.* "Then I'm sure I'll hear about it later. Right now . . ." I look straight at her again. "Was there a question in that comment?"

The woman fixes her gaze on me, defiant. "I just thought everyone should know."

I stand there, channeling Mom in the courtroom, the way she sometimes paused after a witness had spoken, as if waiting for them to say more, as if whatever they'd said didn't make sense, so clearly couldn't be *all* they'd meant to say, and she'd hate to cut them off.

I wait, my gaze on the woman, and eventually, she shifts, as if uncomfortable.

I wait to the count of five, then move my gaze from the woman.

"All right then," I say. "Now, where were we . . . ? Right." I click the presentation slide. "Let's talk about gaslighting. As you may know, the term was popularized by this 1944 film." I wave at the screen. "*Gaslight.* In it . . ."

TWO

An hour later, I'm in the parking lot, and I'm shaking. I have my windows rolled up despite the warm May night. When I notice a trio of women watching, I recognize them from the show and wave my hand in farewell. Then I start my car and back out.

I did well. That's what everyone said, from the guests who'd come up to me afterward to the librarians who'd been watching from the dressing room.

You handled that so well.

I don't know what that woman thought she was doing.

Some people . . .

After the show finished, I'd gone to the seat I'd noted earlier—fourth row, third from the center aisle—and marked down the number. 4J. The woman herself was long gone, having left after she interrupted my show.

Why had she done it? I couldn't wrap my head around that. It was a sold-out show, meaning she'd bought her ticket well in advance with the intention of doing this.

Was she an old friend of Laura's? She seemed about the right age. Maybe she was a friend who'd been furious when the police hadn't pressed charges. But they'd investigated and found no reason to believe Oliver had done anything wrong.

The boat trip had been Laura's idea. Swimming off the side was her idea, too—she always insisted on it, and Oliver always worried that swimming in such open water wasn't safe. A group of men fishing a bit away had spotted an attractive woman in a bikini balanced on the bow of a boat, and two had picked up binoculars to watch. They saw Laura dive in while Oliver stayed at the stern, well out of reach. They'd then seen her swimming and calling back to Oliver, laughing and teasing before ducking under the water. When Laura didn't resurface in a few minutes, Oliver frantically flagged them down.

The case was so cut-and-dried that even tabloid media only lured people in with clickbait headlines before acknowledging that it'd been a tragic accident.

There will still be people convinced that Oliver got away with murder. That obviously includes the woman who accused him tonight. And she'd thrown in Oliver's college girlfriend had died, for extra ammo.

Oliver told me about Greta shortly after we connected, when he confessed how worried he'd been that I might have been suicidal myself. Oliver and Greta had been students together in Vancouver. He'd known she was struggling with the pressures of school and parental expectations, but he hadn't realized how bad it'd gotten until it was too late. While he'd been in Seattle with friends, she'd downed her whole bottle of antidepressants. He will never forgive himself for not being there that weekend.

And Martine?

The troll hadn't even said Martine's name; she'd just thrown out a wild accusation about Oliver's girlfriend filing a complaint with the police.

Oliver has been seeing Martine for six months now. He's wild about her, and what I've seen of her, I really like. She's quiet, apparently more like Greta than Laura. She's smart and sweet and good for him, encouraging him to step off the corporate treadmill, slow down and breathe.

I can't imagine Oliver doing something to Martine. He is frustratingly even-tempered, and she is so quiet I have to lean in to hear what she's saying. No fight between them would have escalated to a screaming match that brought the police.

Still, having spent my adult life studying intimate partner abuse, I know I can never say with absolute certainty that someone is incapable of it. Just because Oliver has never been that way toward or in front of me does not mean I can absolve him of guilt or even suspicion.

What I need to do now is speak to Oliver. Warn him in case he's in danger from this woman. Another person might argue she was just some troll causing trouble, that she's hardly going to show up on his doorstep tonight with a gun. But anyone who thinks that hasn't had a loved one murdered by a stalker. And anyone who thinks that doesn't listen to my podcast. Even if it's an overreaction, I don't ever want to be looking back wishing I'd warned him sooner.

I call Oliver's number over Bluetooth, and my brain mentally adds a hatch to this week's tally: the number of times I've contacted Oliver versus the number of times he's contacted me. Yes, I keep track, and I like my tally to be always just slightly lower than his. He's my only family, and I am terrified—*terrified*—of clinging too tight. Terrified of losing him and terrified of relying on him so much that I suffocate him. I measure everything, and I know that's not healthy, but it keeps me calm and steady.

I know I am not a burden in any way—Oliver reaches out more often than I do. He invites me out more often than I invite him. Despite his offers, I don't work for his corporation. I no longer live in his guesthouse. I don't even accept the money transfers he sends when I have an unexpected expense.

The trust fund from my mother's estate covers tuition and rent while I slowly finish my doctorate. Right now, with advertising and promotion—and paying Raven, my producer, her cut—I'm not exactly reeling in millions with my podcast, but I have started clearing a very low four figures a month, which covers daily expenses and allows for some savings. Even if my growth pattern slows, I predict being able to take care of expenses and rent in a few months. So, in other words, I'm doing just fine financially.

I turn onto the highway as the phone rings three times before going to Oliver's voice mail.

"Hey," I say. "It's me. Had a weird thing happen at the show tonight, and I'd like to talk to you about it."

I sign off and then check the car clock. It's nine thirty. Not late enough for him to be in bed, but late enough that I won't have caught him working late.

Could he be out with Martine? No, I remember her mentioning a Tuesday book club, because I've been trying to work up the nerve to ask whether they take new members.

So why do my fingers itch to hit the Redial button?

I switch lanes and go to turn on a podcast, but only drum my fingers against the wheel instead, as I think about my own podcast and whether I'll need to address tonight's interruption, maybe with a note on my website. My fingers move to the screen to place another call, this one to Raven Kwan, my producer. She's on the West Coast, so it isn't too late. I should also warn her what happened.

Except if I phone her, I might miss Oliver's return call.

I'll email Raven later instead. A few minutes pass. Oliver still doesn't call back.

I mentally replay my message to him and curse myself. I made it sound as if I just needed to vent or cry on his shoulder. If I were him, I'd quietly pretend I didn't get that message until morning.

I call him.

"Hey, it's me again," I begin when I get his voicemail for a second time. "The short version is that a woman interrupted my show to ask about Laura, and she seemed a bit unhinged. I wanted you to know right away."

I sign off again and disconnect.

He doesn't call back.

After I get home, I text Oliver the woman's description, acting as if I'd just forgotten to mention it in the call. I write a note on everything I remember about the woman: her seat number, her age and appearance and exactly what she said. Then I make myself popcorn and load up a streaming show on my laptop . . . watching exactly twenty minutes of it and remembering not a single scene because I spend more time watching the status of that text.

Unread.

Maybe Oliver has an early morning meeting and is already in bed. He sometimes does that. Martine also could have stopped by after book club, and maybe they're in bed and *not* sleeping.

It's fine. Drop it, Amy. Seriously, drop it.

But I don't drop it. I look up the number of the Grand Forks police department and script what I'd say if I called.

Hi, so, uh, I have reason to believe my brother may have been brought in for questioning, at his girlfriend's behest . . . No? He's not there? . . . Am I concerned about her safety? Why, no. Not at all. Why do you ask?

Yeah . . . I can't call.

Instead, I look up Martine's number, and again I script what I could say.

Hey, Martine. It's Amy. Weird question, but have you and Oliver had a fight lately? Possibly one that could have led to you calling the police and him being taken in for questioning?

I groan. I have to stop this. There is nothing I can do that won't make me seem as if I need more therapy, nothing I can say that won't make trouble for my brother.

Oliver is fine.

Everything is fine.

Go to bed, Amy.

I don't go to bed.

THREE

I eventually drift off on the sofa and wake flailing at the sound of the lobby buzzer. I tumble to the floor hard enough to set me cursing. The buzzer sounds again, and I scramble up and run into the front hall.

Even after four years, my tiny apartment still has that new construction smell. Personally, my tastes lean toward older architecture, and I'd been eyeing lofts in the city's grand Victorians, but Oliver had asked me to consider this place for one reason . . . that is on full display as I approach a small video screen.

My building has state-of-the-art security, and Oliver's insistence that I consider that is proof I'm not the only one affected by the circumstances of Mom's death. Would this system have saved her? No, but it does protect me. Oliver found this apartment—with its double-locked doors, umpteen security cameras, well-lit outdoor parking and a list of safety features that make it ideal for single female residents—and convinced me to rent it.

Do I hate living in a world where solo women in need of secure housing is an actual marketing demographic? Yep. But being angry about it doesn't mean I'll insist on living in a loft with a door that can be broken with a swift kick.

I tap the screen, which lets me view my visitor without letting them know I've responded. When I see Oliver, I blink, as if thinking about him conjured him up. Then I remember why I fell asleep on the sofa.

I press the lobby buzzer as fast as I can. When Oliver reaches my apartment a few minutes later, I'm at the open door, waiting for him.

"Coffee?" he says, lifting a cardboard cup. He's trying for a smile, but his face is haggard, his cheeks covered in stubble, and his always-perfect dress shirt looks as if he found it balled up in a corner.

"Oliver?" I say.

"I was tempted to go home and clean up before I came over, but then I remembered who I'd be seeing." He offers a wan smile as he steps into my apartment. "You wouldn't buy the act . . . and you're the one person I'm not afraid to look like this for."

Oliver sets the coffees on the hall table before locking the door and deadbolt behind him. "I got your messages," he says, then takes the coffees and waves me into the living room.

"What happened?" I finally ask, hovering next to the sofa.

He passes me a cup as he sits. I put the coffee down and perch on the edge of the recliner. When he stays silent, my heart pounds.

"Oliver . . . ?"

"The police took me in for questioning."

For a moment, I can't breathe. "What?"

"The police came to my house. They said they wanted to ask me some questions at the station. They didn't say what it was about, and I didn't push. After Laura ..." He takes a deep inhale. "After Laura, I don't like to argue with the police."

"Why? Dinah says there was never any possibility of charges. Zero evidence for prosecuting you and a ton of evidence against it."

He leans back. "I know, Ames, but I'm still a rich guy whose wife drowned swimming off their private boat. No matter how much Dinah reassured me, I was certain I'd be charged based purely on the circumstances."

Oliver lifts a hand against my protest. "Yes, I know that's not how it works. I just mean it's how I felt. I know it had to be an accident, but I'll always wonder whether I did something or failed to do something. After Greta ..."

I reach to lay my hand on his. "So the police invited you in for questioning but didn't tell you why? Is that legal?"

"They gave some vague reason, and to be honest, I wasn't even listening. I had two officers at my door saying they needed to speak to me. I didn't register anything after that."

"Okay. Then what happened?"

"They took me to the station and put me into a room for questioning. I was in there, alone, for over an hour. Eventually, they came in, started asking about what happened to Laura, and I thought someone had called in a tip again."

"Again? This has happened before?"

He sips his coffee and then grips the cup with both hands. His hands shake, and he fists one as if to ward off the trembling.

Signs of anxiety or nerves make him uncomfortable. That's not who he wants to be—not who our father raised him to be—and I have to bite my tongue against comment.

Oliver often jokes about me being lucky, not growing up with our dad, but it's not really a joke. Our father is one of those guys who put on the face others want to see. For my mother, that face was serious and ambitious, but it was also the face of an open-minded modern man who considered women his equals and saw nothing wrong with men showing emotion. Both were lies.

Not that Mom ever said an unkind word about James Harding; I've just gotten to know him better through Oliver. Our mothers and James's current wife put up with—or, in the first two cases, *didn't* put up with—controlling and psychologically abusive behavior.

As for Oliver, he experienced the toxic masculinity that often goes along with sexism and spousal control. I'm the only person Oliver confesses his fears and worries to, but he reins in the emotional displays that go along with that. Except now. His shaking hands tell me exactly how freaked out he is by what happened, even if he tries to put a good face on it. He has to, and I have to let him . . . and be there for him when that dam breaks.

"Oliver?" I say. "Has someone called in tips before?"

"A few times. I haven't ever mentioned it because . . ." Another swig of coffee. "You never questioned what happened to Laura. You might be the only person who didn't."

"Because I was at the marina. I saw how frantic you were. I knew she liked to swim off the boat, and I knew it made you nervous."

His lips twist in a sad smile. "You knew I was telling the truth, and you have no idea how much I appreciated that. I also know how upset you get when people think I had something to do with it. What happened at your show last night . . . I never wanted you to have to deal with that."

He shifts, looking uncomfortable. "But it's not new for me. It's died down in the last couple of years, but there are still people who think I must have been involved with Laura's disappearance. It's a classic setup. Husband takes wife for a boat ride, and she"—he air-quotes—"'goes swimming' and drowns."

"Except *you* were the one with the money, and your marriage was fine," I say. "You didn't get together with Martine until more than two years later, so you didn't kill your wife to be with a girlfriend. You had *no* motivation."

"It doesn't matter. To armchair detectives, I obviously did it. The police have had people call with allegedly new information. They even brought me in once. That's why I didn't question it this time, and it's also why I didn't complain. This is a line I tread with great care."

"I'm sorry," I say. "I had no idea."

"Which is how I wanted it." He fusses with the lid on his coffee. "You're making a career out of helping people in the exact situation some people think I put Laura in. I am so . . ." He makes a face. "I'd say I'm proud of you if that didn't sound patronizing, but you know what I mean."

He lifts his gaze to mine. "You're making a difference, Ames, and I will not do anything to jeopardize that. After last night, I can see that's not just me being paranoid. My history is a threat to everything you're working for."

I shake my head. "No, Oliver, it was *one* person in all the time I've been doing this. A minor ripple. I'm concerned about *you*. You say the police questioned you about Laura."

Oliver nods. "And then about Martine. I told them to call her, see whether she had any concerns. I should have notified Dinah. I know that's the right thing to do, but asking for a lawyer always suggests a person has something to hide."

"It doesn't. It's just in law enforcement's best interests to make you feel that way."

"I know." He sets the coffee aside. "They kept looking at me like I was something they scraped off their shoe. Like I was someone who'd murdered his wife and had gotten away with it. It wasn't until I got your messages that I realized their questions about Martine might have actually been *why* I was called in."

"Because she filed a complaint?"

He throws up his hands. "About what? That's what I keep coming back to. It makes no sense. The obvious answer is to call her and find out, but . . ." Another of those strained smiles. "I listen to your podcasts. If a woman feels you're harassing her, absolutely do not reach out to discuss it. Get a third party to intervene."

I take out my phone. "I can do that. I'll . . ." I stop as I realize the problem.

"Yep, that's not a good idea, either," Oliver says, shaking his head. "The third party needs to be disinterested, right? Or someone connected to Martine but not to me. Since I can't imagine what I might have done, though, what if I'm wrong? What if she didn't do anything, and I have a third party ask whether she reported me to the police?"

He runs his hands through his hair. "I really need advice, Ames, and you're the closest thing to a domestic-conflict expert I know."

I lift my hands. "Whoa. No, I'm definitely not. I can put you in touch with someone who is, though."

"I might need that, but not yet. You know what I mean. You have more background in this than the average person. I would appreciate your advice."

"I don't think it was Martine," I say. "If she filed a complaint, the police would have told you. I need to find out more about the woman who interrupted my show. She *knew* you were being questioned by the police. That's significant."

"You think she called in a tip?"

"That's the only thing that makes sense. She calls in a tip about Laura and expresses concern for Martine. The police follow up, but they don't find anything worth pursuing. As awful as that was, I have to give them credit for bringing you in."

"Following up on a domestic violence concern with immediate action, rather than just phoning me in the morning."

I nod and take my laptop from the coffee table. "I don't have any classes today. Let me follow up on this. In the meantime, if this was any other day, when and how would you reach out to Martine?"

"Usually over breakfast. Just a quick text to wish her a good morning."

"Do that then. I don't see any way it could be interpreted as harassment. If she doesn't reply—or says anything that suggests she'd rather not speak to you—cease all contact."

"I will."

———

After Oliver leaves, I spend a lot of time sitting and thinking about everything he's gone through. Is it horrible to admit I also sift through my memories of his marriage to Laura looking for signs of trouble? Or that I regret not getting to know Martine better so I could evaluate her relationship with Oliver?

Laura and Oliver had their rough patches—Oliver always confided in me and asked for advice—but they'd been normal marital issues, like arguing over him working too much or her drinking too much at a party, getting loud and, well, obnoxious.

To most, Laura was the fun kind of extrovert. With me, though, she'd been abrasive and dismissive. I never admitted that to Oliver because he only saw her sparkle and wit and joie de vivre. When she got drunk at parties, he was never embarrassed—he only worried about how much she was drinking. They had a solid and loving marriage, with no obvious danger signs.

As for Martine, we've met for lunch once and dinner once, and what I remember most is how she and Oliver looked at each other. It made me so damn happy for my brother . . . and maybe a little envious that I'd never found someone to look at that way.

I let myself dwell in those thoughts for a while before I put them aside in favor of another question. Who sat in 4J last night? It might seem simple enough to pull up the seat map of ticket holders, but the problem is that I didn't actually manage the event. The library invited me and paid me half the proceeds, with the remainder going to a local women's shelter. That meant zero expenses and zero extra work for me. It also means I don't have the booking information.

I know libraries take privacy very seriously. If there were a clear threat, I could ask them who sat in 4J, but there isn't. Not yet.

While I use a private investigator for my podcast, contacting her seems like an overreaction. Last night's police visit was hard on Oliver, but it doesn't justify me pulling out all the stops to find this woman.

Maybe I can find something online. Not her identity, per se, but more information in case I do need to track her down.

I start by scouring the internet for anything about last night's disturbance. This is usually part of Raven's job—she gives me feedback by reading reviews of my podcast and events. I sent her an email last night about the event, and I'm hoping to discuss the incident today. That's show-related. Finding the troll is *personal*, which means I need to wade through the online comments myself.

I quickly find a Reddit thread. *Hey, did you know the* Known to the Victim *podcast chick has a brother who drowned his wife? It came up in her live show last night.*

Uh, no, his wife drowned and police investigated and didn't even charge him. Here's why . . .

This is the thing about online true crime aficionados. They love research. Give them a case they've never heard of, and within hours, they could practically testify as expert witnesses. Overnight, armchair detectives dug up the case of Laura's disappearance and laid out the facts, concluding that there was never any evidence to support charging Oliver.

Another thread on a true crime forum is almost identical. Same with the comments on a forum devoted to the podcast. Reading all that, I breathe a sigh of relief. The issue has been raised and dismissed.

The last place I check is my website forum. Because it's on my own site, and because people know I frequent the forum, it's the place where I'm least likely to see a negative opinion. If a newbie criticizes me, the fans pile on in my defense, no matter how clear I am that everyone has the right to an opinion.

I do find a mention of last night's event, a fan saying how well I dealt with the troll, which leads to others asking what the troll said and then a quick and vigorous defense of Oliver that makes me more uncomfortable than those dispassionate dismissals elsewhere. That's what I expected, though, which is why I came here last. Fan forums are great for the ego, but not the place to receive constructive criticism.

I quickly find a thread about last night's show—one for people who were going. I skim it, expecting nothing, when a post from yesterday morning catches my eye.

> VAWSurvivor3: Hey, fellow KttV fans! Does anyone have a ticket they can't use for tonight's show? I'll pay double! I'm such a fan, and I can't believe I didn't realize she was having a live show so close to me.

VAW stands for Violence Against Women, and I run the kind of podcast and forum where women feel comfortable identifying as survivors. Many use #VAWS in their signature lines. This username wouldn't normally catch my eye if not for the reply to it.

> Momof3: I have one. My babysitter called in sick this morning, and I'm not having any luck finding a new one. My seat was 4J.

VAWSurvivor3: OMG! Thank you! DMing now!!!

4J. That's where the woman had been sitting. I click the user-name. The account was created yesterday and has only those two posts.

She came on, created an account, pretended to be a superfan and offered double the seat price.

It was a setup.

The troll coordinated her police tip with my live show. She must have expected to cause a greater stir than she did. I almost laugh. Guess she figured I was a much bigger name and imagined it'd be like standing up in a theater full of people, with reporters on the sidelines.

That solves the mystery of how someone who apparently bought tickets back before the show sold out knew Oliver would be taken in for questioning. But it doesn't identify the woman herself because her account is set to private, and I've set up the forum so even I can't access that. I could make a new account and contact her through it, but if anyone discovered me using a fake name on my own site, it'd be a publicity nightmare. Also, since I could easily tell that she was a brand-new member, she could tell that the person reaching out to her was equally—and suspiciously—new.

The fact she bought that ticket at the last minute erases any doubt that she called in that tip. This woman has targeted my brother, and I need to know who she is, in case she continues her vendetta.

It's time to call in the big guns.

FOUR

Having a private investigator on retainer sounds much fancier than it is . . . and that's part of the reason the partnership works. On the podcast, I make liberal mention of "my investigator, Ioana," which lends an air of professionalism to my research. In return, Ioana gets the constant name checks plus the cachet of being the investigator for an up-and-coming podcast.

Ioana and I met through that true crime TV show host who convinced me to reinvent my blog as a podcast. Soon after I started, I realized I needed to do more than just rehash old cases.

My podcast might focus on people killed by a partner, but it still falls under the umbrella of true crime, and I need to keep it there if I want an audience. I'd bristle at the suggestion that I'm adding sugar to the medicine, because that would imply women are in need of medicine and too foolish to take it without the sugar. What I do is teach by example without victim blaming or shaming.

Women are the primary consumers of true crime, especially crimes against women. They joke that it's like a self-defense class—studying how they can avoid the same fate. It's a joke that's not really a joke.

Raven has been dating a woman with an off-the-grid cottage in northern British Columbia, and Raven says that her news feed shows her every bear-attack story because the algorithm knows she'll read it. Why does she read it? For tips. What prompted the attack? How did the person deal with it? Did they survive? Women live in "bear country" every day of their lives. Most encounters with our "bears" are uneventful or even positive. But we still need to be ready for the meeting that goes wrong. That is one reason why women consume true crime. To prepare for the encounter with a man that goes wrong.

Being a true crime podcast means I can't just regurgitate what's in the news. I need to dig deeper. That's where Ioana comes in. I find the cases and do my preliminary work, and then I turn them over to Ioana for additional investigation. In the beginning, I tried to do more investigating myself and screwed up. I learned my lesson, and I leave the detective work to her.

Normally, I'd just text Ioana and ask her to call when she's free. I'm overly cautious now, though—paranoid, even. If Oliver is the target of this mystery woman, I need to be as discreet as possible.

I make the fifteen-minute drive to Ioana's office, which is in one of those old downtown-area Victorian homes where I'd once fantasized about living. This particular house has been turned into offices, and hers is on the third floor.

As I pull in, I admit that Oliver was right to dissuade me from taking an apartment in one of these houses. Parking is around back, the rear yard having been paved for vehicles. There's an eight-foot solid wooden fence and hundred-year-old trees, and even at midday, the lot is dim and shadowed.

From the lot, I enter through the back door. The grand old house has been gutted in the most cost-effective way possible. The stairwell is cramped, with a bulb that barely illuminates the stairs.

There's zero security. No lock on the back door. No camera in the stairwell. Anyone can walk into Ioana's office. Her only protection is . . . Well, it's the guy sitting at the first desk.

If I were asked to picture a private eye, my Hollywood-tainted mental image would be of someone who could slip about unnoticed. The kind of person who blends in a crowd. I wouldn't imagine Ioana Balan, who looks like a corporate VP. Nor would I imagine her business partner, Dean Castillo.

In fact, if I ever spotted Castillo tailing me, I'd get to a public place, fast. He's well over six feet, bulky in that way that's 75 percent muscle and 25 percent "big guy mostly stuck at desk job." His left cheek is badly pitted with what looks like acne scars, but I know it's from shrapnel. Castillo spent his young adulthood in the US military, before an explosion sent him home and made him decide on a career change.

All that makes Castillo intimidating, but what slides him over the line into "wouldn't want to meet in a dark alley" is his permanent scowl.

Okay, fine. The scowl isn't permanent. Or so I've heard. I wouldn't personally know, because that scowl is all I ever see.

"Hey, Dean," I say, as brightly as I can.

He doesn't look up from his computer. "Ioana's not in."

"Do you know when she'll be back?"

"Your phone not working? That's how people communicate in the twenty-first century, Gibson. They text. They email. They call. They don't just show up and expect people to be there, ready to help them."

Yep, Castillo is a *delight*. He analyzed the minimum amount of data about me—lives off a trust fund while playing podcaster and half-heartedly pursuing a doctorate—and spat out a box designed to fit me, and everything I do is interpreted within the confines of that box.

Forget that my "trust fund" comes because my mother was *murdered*. Forget that my podcast has loftier goals than fame or fortune. Forget that my doctorate is taking longer than usual because of my podcast and the time I took off school after my mother's death.

I'm accustomed to Castillo's rudeness. I'm also aware that I've given him reason to dislike me—50 percent misunderstanding and 50 percent justified—but that's another story. Mostly, I deal with it by staying out of his way.

"Okay," I say. "Sorry for bothering you. I'll text Ioana—"

"She's busy. Important case in Toronto."

"Do you know when she'll be back?"

He still hasn't looked up from his work. "No idea. I only know it's important, and she doesn't have time to play research monkey for you."

Breathe. Just breathe.

"I understand," I say, as calmly as I can, while reaching for the doorknob. "I'll find someone else—"

"That a threat? Taking your business elsewhere because Ioana isn't at your beck and call?"

I keep my jaw clenched to the count of three and fight for the same calm tone. "You just said Ioana was busy, and I have something urgent—personal, not professional. That means I might need to hire someone else, for this one thing only."

"What about me?"

I give a short laugh. "You wouldn't do it."

"Did you ask?"

I cross my arms and stare at him, hoping it's just a stare, though I suspect there's a hint of a glower in there, too. "Do I look like Charlie Brown?"

His brows twitch up at that.

I wave at my jeans and sweater. "Note that I am not wearing a yellow shirt. Therefore, I am not going to fall for the trick where I try to kick the football and you pull it away. Or where you goad me into asking whether you're available and then sneer that you wouldn't work for me if I paid you double."

"You're offering to pay me double?" Castillo leans back in his office chair, boots on the desk. "That's mighty generous of you, Gibson. You don't need to go that far, though. I'd do it for fifty percent above the standard."

I want to walk out, but I hesitate for two reasons. One is the fear that if I do, I'll look like the snotty socialite swanning off with her nose in the air. The other is that I don't want to insult Ioana by taking any business to another agency.

"Twenty-five percent above standard," I say.

"Thirty-five."

I do a quick calculation. "I can afford ten hours at that. Will you warn me if you expect it to take longer?"

He grunts something that sounds like assent.

"It's about my brother," I say.

"I know." He takes out his phone, flips to a screen and shoves it across the desk at me. "We run automatic search alerts for our clients. Ioana sent that this morning."

I read it where it lies on the desk, and then I really do glower at him while wishing I were the kind of person who could whip a cell phone at someone's head.

I read the text aloud. "Hey, seems Amy had a problem at her show last night, and it might not be a run-of-the-mill troll. If she comes by, can you squeeze her in, please?" I lift my gaze to Castillo's and then read Ioana's final text. "Oh, and don't be an ass and overcharge her."

"Huh," he says. "I missed that part."

"Whatever," I say. "I can afford it, and judging by those ragged-ass boots, you need the money more than I do."

I shouldn't stoop to his level, but the pang of guilt is out-weighed by the satisfaction of seeing how fast his boots vanish under the desk.

"You deserved that," I say. "Now, if we can put aside the schoolyard shit and talk, please."

"You shouldn't swear, Gibson. You sound like a five-year-old saying a bad word."

"Last shot goes to Mr. Castillo," I say. "And I concede."

I pull up a chair and explain what happened last night at the show. Then I tell him about Oliver's questioning and what I found on the woman who sat in that seat.

Castillo doesn't interrupt. He even takes notes, jotting them on his phone faster than one would think possible for fingers his size.

"You think this woman called in a tip to the police," he says when I finish.

I shrug. "It's a theory. Otherwise, she'd need to work for the police and know they planned to bring Oliver in. She bought the ticket that morning, and he wasn't questioned until evening."

He leans back in the chair and props his boots again. "Yeah, most likely scenario is that she called it in. You didn't recognize her?"

"No, but I can give a description."

He lifts his phone and waves for me to go on. I read aloud the notes I took on my own phone.

"Thorough," he says.

"I always get a good look at any potential threat."

I expect a snarky comment, or at least an eye roll that says I'm overreacting. Instead, he mutters, "Good," and I'm not sure what to do with that.

"I can try convincing the library to give me the booking info," I say. "But the troll isn't the original seat holder."

"The original seat holder might be able to help, but I doubt the troll communicated with the seller using anything traceable. I'll see what I can do with that." He pockets his phone. "Tell me about your brother."

"He didn't kill his wife," I say immediately.

Now I do get a roll of those dark eyes. "No shit." He taps a pen on his desk. "I looked into it once. Clear-cut case of accidental drowning."

Okay, that was not what I expected.

"What can you tell me about the college girlfriend?" he says. "I looked that up after I saw her mentioned in the stuff about last night, but there wasn't anything online."

I relax a little. "Her name was Greta. It happened in Vancouver, where they were both going to the University of British Columbia for business. I wasn't part of Oliver's life then. He's my half brother, on my dad's side, a decade older than me. My parents divorced before I was born."

"You didn't see Oliver when your dad had custody time? He lived with his mom?"

I shake my head. "Oliver lived with our dad. My father didn't . . ." I clear my throat. "My father remarried shortly after I was born. We . . ." Another throat-clearing. "There was no custody time."

Castillo stares at me. "He didn't get to see you?"

I keep my voice as level as I can. "He didn't *wish* to see me."

He grunts, and it almost sounds apologetic.

I continue, "Greta died long before I came back into Oliver's life, so I can only tell you what he told me. She was struggling with school. An MBA was her parents' dream, and that's part of what brought Oliver and Greta together—both were in the program because of their parents. Oliver tolerated it, but he had an aptitude for it. Greta hated it. Her gifts were in the arts—she was a skilled sculptor. She'd been struggling, and Oliver thought it was just . . . normal stuff. Problems with parents, school, whatnot."

I tense, realizing what I've said can open me up to sarcasm. Rich-people problems. But Castillo just keeps listening.

"She took pills," I say. "Oliver wasn't even in Vancouver that weekend, which he blames himself for. She was found by her roommate, and he'd been in Seattle since the day before."

"And the new girlfriend? What's their relationship like?"

I pull my legs up onto the chair, sitting cross-legged. "While I never met Greta, my sense is that Martine has more in common with her than with Laura. Martine is quiet and introverted. She's a music teacher, and she plays flute in their city orchestra. She'd been married once. Her husband died of cancer. That's how she met Oliver—in a therapy group for widows and widowers."

"This woman at the library suggested there was an issue between Martine and Oliver. Abuse? Physical? Psychological?"

"She didn't specify, and I . . ." I rub the back of my neck. "I want to say that I can't believe Oliver would do that, but I can only see him as a brother. What a girlfriend might see could be very different. However, I can say categorically that I've never noticed anything that's caused me concern. Martine might be very quiet, but it's not because Oliver speaks over her or controls her interactions. He does most of the relationship planning—where to go, what to do—but he's told me that makes him uncomfortable. It makes him *feel* controlling, even when it's her choice. He'd like her to be less . . ."

"Passive?"

I nod. "They've only been dating for six months. My sense is that she's not comfortable taking the lead yet. That might be learned experience."

"Her husband?"

"I got the feeling, from Oliver, that there were some . . . danger signs in that relationship. Oliver suspects Martine is still getting used to a more equitable partnership, and he's trying to give her space to do that."

"Okay." Castillo swings his feet down. "So this troll gave the cops some tip about your sister-in-law's death and feigned concern for the new girlfriend's safety. That put the cops in an awkward position. They had to follow up, but there wasn't enough evidence to do more than question Oliver. The bigger issue comes if this troll doesn't drop it."

"She might try again."

He nods. "Yes. I have a contact at the department. I'll get what I can and work on identifying her. It'll be four hours' work, maybe five."

"Thank you."

He makes a dismissive gesture, clearly uncomfortable with the gratitude.

"I'll text you when I have something," he says. "And don't try playing detective again. Go home and . . ." He waves a hand. "Study or whatever."

FIVE

I don't "go home and study." Instead, I work a bit on my dissertation and then edit the script for the podcast episode I'm taping tonight. I also text Oliver, asking whether Martine has been in touch. Eventually, I hear back from Raven.

"What bullshit," she says when I pick up the phone. I don't answer, and she sighs, "Fine, fine. As the producer of a show focused on violence against women, I shouldn't automatically side with the guy here and say he's innocent."

"As the producer of my podcast, you should know it's not about violence against *women* per se."

"You're a pain in the ass, you know that?" she mutters. "I don't know why I keep you on."

"Because I'm a rising podcaster who might actually make serious money at this someday, and you like money."

"Fuck, yeah. But fine, I shouldn't say your podcast is about violence against *women*, even though it mostly is, because that opens you up to all the assholes whining 'What about the men killed by their wives?' All five of them."

I make a noise in my throat.

"Fine," she says. "It was more than five. I also know it was infinitesimal compared to the women killed by partners, but you need to acknowledge that they exist. Otherwise, men will feel left out. Because they're always being left out."

"Do you know why I love talking to you?"

"Because I say the things you can't?"

I smile. "Because you're a ray of happy sunshine in my darkest days."

"Damn straight. So I acknowledge that men are also killed by partners. I also acknowledge that I can't say your brother is definitely innocent and this woman is a pathetic loser looking for attention."

"You just said it."

"Made me feel better to get it out there. Okay, so I got your email, obviously, and I am here to advise, as your older and wiser producer."

I snort. "You're two years older than me."

"I'm a prodigy. It's a burden, but I bear it well. Okay, so you're concerned that this woman might be a problem for your podcast. I say no. She's a troll who dragged her soapbox to your show, clearly thinking her pronouncement would have more impact. You handled it like a champ."

"So it's over?"

Raven's voice drops, going serious. "I hope so, but considering she almost certainly was responsible for the police questioning your brother, she isn't just a garden-variety troll."

She takes a deep breath before continuing. "I don't know Oliver well, but based on that time he picked me up from the airport, I liked what I saw. What's happening to him sucks, and I'm hoping it just all goes away. But if it doesn't, this woman might swing back to you. You have a platform she can use to attack Oliver, and she obviously doesn't mind making you collateral damage."

"The little sister so oblivious to his crimes that she has a podcast exposing men like him," I grumble.

"I don't know what's going through her head. The point is that you don't need to address it on the show right now. But you might *want* to, as an example of a case where public opinion condemns an innocent party."

I wince, and she sighs. "And that's a shitty idea. You're helping women develop the predator-radar. Discussing a case where a supposed predator is innocent will only reinforce hesitancy."

I have to smile at her language. When she first took me on last year, she'd been clear that social justice podcasts were not her thing. But since then, she's clearly been listening.

She continues, "Okay, so let's put a pin in this. If Oliver's accuser comes at you again, we'll revisit our response."

I'm barely off that call when Oliver responds to my text asking about Martine.

OLIVER:
Everything's fine

I quickly type back.

ME:

Whew! What did she say about
the police interview?

OLIVER:

We're going to talk about it later

OLIVER:

So what have you been up to
today?

Worrying about you is what I want to say, but that'll just make
him feel bad. So I lie without actually lying.

ME:

Talking to my investigator about
a case. Chatted with my
producer about the show

OLIVER:

It's still Raven, right?

ME:

It is

OLIVER:

Good. I like her. Scares the shit
out of me, but you need
someone like that on your side

ME:

LOL yep, she's a force of nature

OLIVER:

Did you talk to her about the
troll?

ME:

I did. She said there's nothing
to worry about

OLIVER:

Excellent. I was concerned, but
I didn't want to say anything
and make it seem like I thought
it was a problem

ME:

It's not. So how was your day?

He answers, and we chat like that for a while. When we're done, I relax for the first time since the show last night.

I'm preparing dinner when I get a text from Castillo, who is apparently just as charming in writing as he is in person. "Nothing. Still digging." I think of texting back to tell him to pause the investigation now that everything is fine.

Castillo might consider me a "rich girl," but I have better ways to spend my money. Still, it's only a few billable hours, and it might prove important if this woman doesn't back off. Also, I don't want to seem like the flighty client who asks him to take a job and then drops it halfway through.

I know what Castillo thinks of me ... and I know he partly has good reason. When that talk show host suggested I dig deeper into cases, I got a little overeager and leaped at the chance to be an investigative reporter, despite having zero qualifications. Ioana updated me on a podcast case, and I didn't think she'd gone hard enough with a witness, so I followed up myself. I pissed off the witness, who called the cops, who showed up at Ioana's office with a complaint about their new investigator, who apparently did not have a license ...

Ioana recognized I was just overeager, even a little starry-eyed with the possibility of playing private eye. We had a long talk about what my role was—and was not—as her client, with a gentle but firm warning against doing it again.

Castillo had been furious. He didn't see an enthusiastic young woman; he saw a spoiled brat accustomed to doing whatever she wanted, a client who hadn't trusted Ioana's expertise and had endangered her career. He wasn't entirely wrong.

Then, a few months ago, Castillo's second cousin was murdered. He emailed me, asking whether—as someone who had a loved one murdered—I might speak to his cousin's wife. But I never got the email.

When Ioana mentioned it a couple of weeks later, I searched madly. No email in my inbox. No email in my trash. No email in my spam.

Ioana believes me when I say I never got it. And really, why the hell had Castillo emailed instead of just picking up the phone? Because, I realized, asking someone like me for help was the last thing he'd wanted, and an email made it less painful. When I didn't respond, it seemed to prove that I was exactly what he'd expected: a self-centered young woman who was milking her mother's murder for podcast fame, only pretending to care about victims.

I've offered to speak to his cousin's family, but he brushes it off with "Wasn't important" and "Whatever."

So I can be angry at how he's typecast me, but I have at least partly earned it—through one real mistake and one miscommunication—and so I really don't want to fire him halfway through this job.

I text a bit more with Oliver before I go to bed. He hasn't heard from the police, and I haven't seen any sign of the troll trash-talking either of us online. She made her play and failed. For now, all is quiet, and I can get some sleep.

When my phone rings a few hours later, I roll over in bed. I have ringtones for everyone I know well enough to talk to on the phone. This is the one for those who don't fall into that category.

I open one bleary eye to peer at the clock. 1:37. With a groan, I bury my face in the pillow. A moment later, my text chime sounds.

I glance at my phone on the charger.

> CASTILLO:
> It's me, Gibson. Pick up.

The phone rings again. I reach for it, hit Talk and manage a groggy hello.

"I'm in the parking lot," he says, by way of a greeting.

"What parking lot?"

"McDonald's. I felt like fries. Thought I'd call and let you know." A beat pause. "I'm in *your* parking lot."

I lift my head. "My parking lot?"

"Yeah, it's one thirty in the morning, but we need to talk, and it needs to be in person, and it can't wait until morning. Tell me how you want to do this."

I blink, replaying his words and struggling to parse the meaning.

He says, slower, "How do you want to do this, Gibson? The ball's in your court because it's the middle of the night, and a guy you barely know wants to speak to you. We can talk outside. We can talk in the lobby. Hell, we can actually go to McDonald's for fries if you like."

"Uh . . ." I make a face, knowing how clueless I sound. I clear my throat. "Come on up. It's fine."

There's a long pause. Then he says, "I'm going to presume you're just too tired to think straight, because I hope you—of all people—*wouldn't* actually be fine with that. And I sure as hell hope you aren't saying it because you don't want to seem like you don't trust me. You barely know me. You shouldn't trust me."

I rub my face to be sure I'm awake. I'm not sure which seems more like proof that I'm not: Castillo in my parking lot, or Castillo being concerned about my safety precautions.

"There's a twenty-four-hour Tims on the corner," I say finally. "We can go there."

"I'll be on the sidewalk."

—

The moment I step from the safety of my building, my brain assesses my surroundings, looking for danger. It's a quiet neighborhood, on the southeastern edge of the city, a planned community with a cluster of amenities. There are no trees near the door, and that feels intentional—no place for someone to lurk. The trees are all closer to the road but spread far enough apart that the road is visible . . . and residents exiting the building are visible from the road.

During the day, there's steady traffic—that road leads into the subdivision behind the apartment complex. At this hour, it's so quiet that I can hear traffic on the busier ring-road artery a few kilometers away.

I spot Castillo immediately. He's made sure I can—he's not only on the sidewalk; he's firmly under a streetlight. He has his leather jacket bundled under one arm, even though it isn't nearly warm enough tonight for short sleeves. His light-gray T-shirt makes him easy to spot, and I suspect that's the point—so he's not in head-to-toe black lurking outside an apartment at 2 a.m.

He's scanning the road as I approach. When a lone car passes, the driver slows, as if peering at Castillo, trying to decide whether his presence warrants a call to the police. When the car speeds off, Castillo snorts.

"Guess I need to work on being scarier," he says.

"Nah," I say. "If they call the cops, they'd need to stick around and give a statement. Better to post on the neighborhood forum and warn everyone about the guy seen lurking . . . directly under a streetlight."

Another snort. Then he starts walking without a word. I jog to fall in beside him.

"Martine was shot tonight," he says finally.

I stop so fast my running shoes squeak on the pavement. I say, "What?" but he's still walking, and again, I have to jog to reach him.

"She's fine," he says, as if he didn't notice I'd fallen behind. "She's in surgery now."

My heart hammers. "In surgery? That is not *fine*."

"She's alive, and whoever shot her hoped otherwise, so I think she'd consider herself fine."

"I—I need to call Oliver," I say.

"He already knows," Castillo says with a quick glance at me. "He's been arrested."

My heart seems to stop. I stand there, frozen, barely able to draw breath, panic rising. This time, Castillo notices and circles back.

"Shit, I did that wrong. You want to go somewhere else and talk?" he asks, and his voice is uncharacteristically low, even gentle.

I glance up and down the empty street. I'd like to go back to my apartment—this feels too exposed—but I know better than to suggest that. Castillo waves me to a more private spot along a fence dividing the road from a strip mall.

"I got the call a half hour ago from my contact in the department," he says. "I'd been talking to them earlier about your brother, so they reached out as soon as they heard about this."

I struggle to focus on his words.

He continues, "It happened around eleven. Martine saw your brother's car in her driveway as she was getting ready to go to bed. She went out to see why he was there. Window rolls down. Two shots are fired. One goes wide, the other hits her in the shoulder. The shooter must have thought it was fatal and drove off. Luckily, Martine had her phone and was able to call 911 before she passed out."

I struggle to breathe as I reach out to lay my hand against the fence, the wood cool under my fingers. "You said *surgery*? She's in surgery?"

"Emergency surgery. Expected to survive. That's what I have. Before she passed out on the 911 call, she said Oliver shot her. In the ambulance, she regained consciousness long enough to confirm that."

"Wh-what?" I stare up at him as if I've misheard. "She identified him? But he wouldn't—He couldn't—" I squeeze my eyes shut. "I'm sorry. I . . . I shouldn't say that."

"You're talking to the guy you hired to investigate, Amy. Not the cops. Not a lawyer. Not a reporter. Yeah, I get it, with your podcast, you don't want to claim your brother couldn't have shot his girlfriend. But this isn't that kind of conversation."

I want to say the words. *Oliver didn't do this.* But everything I've devoted my life to tells me I cannot say them. I cannot even *think* them. And that feels like the worst betrayal imaginable.

"I can't imagine how or why Oliver would do this," I say instead. "He doesn't own a gun. He doesn't know how to shoot."

"Neither did whoever pulled that trigger."

"But this? Shooting Martine?" I shake my head sharply. "You said she identified him as the shooter. She saw his face?"

"I don't know."

"She said it was his car in her drive. The same make and model or his exact car?"

"I don't know." He shifts his weight, hands going back into his pockets. "This is what I have right now. Martine is in the hospital, and she says Oliver shot her, so he's been arrested. Oliver should be able to explain everything to you himself tomorrow. I just wanted you to know as soon as I did. Otherwise, you might wake up to reporters on your doorstep."

"Reporters . . ." I remember my mother's murder, and my gut clenches.

"Hell, I don't know. Maybe they won't make the connection between you and him for a while. To be safe, though, I'm going to suggest you go home, pack a bag and go stay with someone."

When I don't answer, he says, "You have family. Other than your brother, of course."

"I don't have—" I shake my head. "I'll be fine. You've warned me, and I appreciate that." I look up at him. "I really do appreciate that you came out here to tell me in person."

He glances away and shrugs it off. Then he says, "You shouldn't be alone—"

"I'm fine. I have a very secure apartment, which I will stay in until morning, and then I'll find out what's going on."

He scratches his cheek and says, "I could find out more tomorrow," with all the enthusiasm of someone offering to undergo elective dental surgery.

"No need," I say, a little more curtly than I intend.

He shoves his hands deeper into his pockets, rocks back on his heels and mutters in Spanish.

"Thanks," I say. When he glances over, I add, "I took Spanish."

He has the grace to murmur something like an apology.

I shrug. "Not like I don't already know what you think of me." I walk away, but he strides to catch up to me.

"Ioana says you feel like you owe your brother something," he says. "For helping you when you were in a bad place."

I start to answer, but he continues, "Well, I owe Ioana, and she wants me to help you."

"You helped me yesterday, and you brought me this information personally, which I really do appreciate. As you said, I'll find out the rest from Oliver tomorrow. If he needs an investigator, I can give him your number. Or not. It's up to you."

"I'll find out what I can and bring it to you in the morning."

"You don't have to."

"Ioana wants it," Castillo says.

I stop and turn to look at him. "Do you have any idea how awkward that is? Knowing someone is only helping me to repay a debt to another person?"

"You'd rather I pretended otherwise and let you find out later that I'm only doing it for her?"

I shake my head and resume walking. He doesn't try to keep up, but I can hear his footsteps as he escorts me within sight of my building. I pretend I don't know he's there and head inside.

SIX

After that, all I can think of is Martine. I want updates about her surgery, but I know I'm not entitled to them. I keep imagining her walking out to her driveway, being shot and thinking it was Oliver. Then I think of Mom and what it was like for her, walking through a secured parking garage, her mind zipping ahead to all the mundanities of the day, when Grant White approached her.

Did he talk to her? Was her first reaction annoyance, seeing him showing up at her work again? Or did she know she was in trouble the moment she saw him? Did she think she could escape? Talk her way out of it? At what point did she realize she couldn't?

And that has nothing to do with Martine, which sends me into a spiral of guilt along with the grief. Hours pass where

I'm curled up on the sofa, crying for both of them. It's only then that I can even think about Oliver.

There is no way he shot Martine. I don't mean it's impossible to believe he'd ever hurt her under any circumstances. Years of research ensures I will never say that about anyone.

My point in defending him here is that the setup is ludicrous. He sits in her driveway and shoots her when she comes out? That makes no sense.

Someone must be framing my brother for murder. Is it the troll from my show? That would be the obvious answer, but shooting Martine is a million miles from phoning in an anonymous tip.

Martine will wake up, and she will admit she only saw a car that *looked* like Oliver's. That she never saw the driver's face. If she says anything else, she's mistaken.

I pause. Mistaken? Or lying?

I don't want to even consider the latter, and I can't—that's victim blaming. I also don't see any reason for her to lie. If Martine says she saw Oliver pull the trigger, she must be mistaken.

I text my brother.

> ME:
> Thinking of you. We'll figure
> this all out.

I know he won't have his phone in jail, but I want him to get that text of support the first moment he can. Then I start searching online for any traces of the story. Finding none yet, I set up alerts to notify me of anything with my brother's name or Martine's.

The next obvious step is to email Raven and warn her that Oliver's been arrested. I get one line written before I trash it. My brother has been charged with attempted murder, and I'm worrying about my damn show?

The truth is, I'm not worried. I'm just preparing. Still, it looks bad to be doing it now, when Oliver is in jail. It *feels* bad. I will need to notify Raven, but it can wait until morning.

Instead, I try to distract myself. I surf the net. I watch five minutes of a TV show. I read two pages of a book.

Then I'm back to Martine and Oliver, jotting down questions. What did she mean when she said it was Oliver's car? Was it the same model and color? Or just the same color? And how well could she have seen?

It was after dark. How bright is her outdoor lighting? She lives in the bungalow she'd once shared with her husband. I was there, briefly, when Oliver picked her up for our lunch, and I remember an old residential area with lots of trees. How easy would it have been for someone to sit in a car similar to Oliver's and wait for her to notice?

The gun is another avenue of investigation. In Canada, legal handguns are rare. While I can laugh at the image of my brother buying one in a back alley, the possibility has to be addressed. I suspect, though, that it's impossible to prove he *doesn't* have one.

Before I know it, my morning alarm is going off. I check my search alerts. Nothing. I run the searches myself, just in case. Nothing.

When a text comes in, I jump, certain it's Oliver.

CASTILLO:

Heading over at eight. No
updates. Just planning

ME:

Thanks. Don't eat. I'll make
breakfast

The news hits at seven on the dot, as if media outlets held off until people might actually be awake. Within ten minutes, my alerts are coming in faster than I can read them. I turn them off, pause, and—feeling like a self-centered bitch—start them up again but add my name or the podcast name. If I am linked, I need to know that. Thankfully, nothing pings. Yet.

Despite the sheer number of alerts, I learn nothing new. In fact, I know more than they do. According to the news, Oliver Harding is under arrest for the attempted murder of his girl-friend, Martine Dupont, who is in stable condition. That's literally the sentence on nearly every mention.

Oh, they pad out their articles, mostly doing so by talking about who Oliver is. CEO of one of the biggest local employers, one started by his father, who retired three years ago. Oliver has an MBA from UBC, where he graduated top of his class. He was the headliner in Grand Forks's Most Eligible Bachelor charity auction last year. There's his photo from the auction, where he looks handsome and polished, if a little sheepish.

And Martine? She's a music teacher. No mention of the school where she teaches, no mention of the orchestral position she holds, and no photograph. Just "Martine Dupont, local music teacher." I am furious on her behalf, but I'm not surprised.

What I *am* surprised about is that they don't mention Oliver's marriage to Laura . . . and the very newsworthy conclusion to it. They'll get around to it. In the meantime, I add an alert for Oliver plus Laura. I'm finishing that when the lobby buzzer sounds. I hurry over and then see the clock and slow. 7:45. I hit the screen to activate the video. Castillo stands there, looking impatient despite the fact it's been literally three seconds since he buzzed.

"It's me," he says when I respond. "I'm early. If you aren't ready, I'll wait down here."

I buzz him up, but I don't hold the door open, as I did for Oliver yesterday. I wait for the knock, and then I check the door cam to be sure it's Castillo.

I let him in. He kicks off his shoes before I can tell him he doesn't need to.

"Coffee?" I say. "I haven't started breakfast. I forgot to ask what you like."

"Food."

"Good, because that's what I have. You can choose between eggs and French toast. Or don't choose, and I'll make both."

He walks past me without a word, which I presume means both. As I start the French toast mixture, something inside me relaxes. Does it seem weird to say that I relax around someone who doesn't like me much? This is solid ground, though.

"Bacon okay with the eggs?" I say.

"Anyone ever say no?"

I don't point out religious restriction. He seems testy. I glance over to see he's at the window, looking out.

"Lousy view," he says.

"Thank you."

Still in the living room, he looks around as I make his coffee.

"Tiny apartment, lousy view, lousier location. What's the attraction? It's not near the core. Not near the university. Your brother live close?"

"North of the city."

"So, no." He paces through the kitchen and through to the hall. Then he grunts. "Security. New construction. Hyper-secure. Built-in system for the door and windows. Video camera. The works."

"Cream or sugar?"

"Both."

I add a splash of cream and stir some sugar into a mug of coffee and then put it on the counter. "If you're done assessing the value of my apartment, your coffee is ready."

"I'm sure it's overpriced."

"Nah, I'm not charging you for it. Just taking five bucks off your bill."

He shakes his head. "The apartment. You could get something better and install your own system. But I guess you wanted the controlled entry."

"It was Oliver's—" I cut that off.

"The security is your brother's idea?" He studies my face. "Yeah. Okay. That makes sense." He takes the coffee and lowers himself into a kitchenette chair. "After what happened to your mom, if you were my kid sister, I'd want full-blown security for you, too."

"Speaking of my brother," I begin, wanting to steer this back on track, "you said you didn't have any updates?"

"Only that Martine pulled through, but if she hadn't, I'd have let you know right away."

He sips the coffee. "The story has hit the news."

"I saw. I set up alerts, and they went wild at seven. It's just basic information, though. Nothing even on Laura. I turned off the general alerts but added ones that include her name."

"Same here. I also added ones that mention you or your podcast. You should set those up, too."

"Also done," I say as I start cooking the French toast.

"The next step is bail. The only way he won't get it is if the judge worries he'll go after Martine again, but she won't be out of the hospital for a few days. My contact will let me know how that's proceeding." Another sip of his coffee. "There is another way to get information, but you can't misuse it."

"Can you try phrasing that another way?" I say. "One intended for a grown woman and not a misbehaving child?"

"I'm not worried about you Nancy Drew-ing it again. I'm worried about you getting in the way by bugging the person I'm about to mention."

My hand tightens on the spatula. "Has Ioana ever said I've bugged her for updates?" I meet his gaze with a level stare. "No, she has not. Because I don't."

"This is different. It's your brother, and you're worried, but you need to let the professionals—me or anyone else—do their jobs and get him out."

"If you're telling me not to pester Oliver's lawyer, I know better. My mom was an attorney, remember?"

"On that note, do you know who Oliver is using? I know he has a lawyer—a woman—but I don't have a name."

"It's probably Dinah Umar, my mom's old law partner. That's who represented him when Laura disappeared. She semi-retired to Kitchener after Mom died, but made the drive in for

Oliver, even used a temporary office at a local law firm. That's who he'll want. But she's even closer to retired these days, and she might not take the job." I pick up my phone. Then I stop. "May I reach out to her?"

"Yeah, see if it's her."

I pop off a quick text to Dinah. I've barely turned back to breakfast-making when she replies.

> DINAH:
>
> You're up. Good. I was planning to call at nine. Yes, Oliver contacted me last night

ME:

And you took the case?

> DINAH:
>
> Of course

> DINAH:
>
> I'm sorry, Amy. I know this is all a shock. I'm sorry you had to hear about it from someone else. I wanted to call last night, but Oliver asked me to wait until morning

> DINAH:
>
> It was still my decision, and I apologize if I made the wrong one

I have to smile at those three texts. I can see her sending the first, the simple "Of course," and then realizing it might sound abrupt and sending the second. Then she must have realized the second could sound like blaming Oliver for her not notifying me, and so she'd taken responsibility.

Some people show their consideration with warmth and sympathy. Dinah shows hers with action and loyalty. The fact she took this case tells me how important I am to her.

ME:
No worries. I heard about it
from someone in person, so it's
all good

DINAH:
I'd talk now, but I'm on hold
with the jail, checking in. Can I
call you in thirty minutes?

ME:
Whenever you get a chance.
I'm not going anywhere

"Dinah's already taken his case," I say to Castillo. "She'll call me in a half hour."

"Okay. Wait for her call then. No point planning anything until we know more."

———

Dinah phones in *exactly* thirty minutes, just as we're finishing breakfast. She tells me Oliver is doing as well as can be expected, but there's not much more she can say right now.

"I will keep you posted." Her voice lowers, that brisk business tone giving way to something softer. "How are you holding up? And if you say 'fine' this time, I'll know you're lying."

I twist to hide my wince from Castillo. I would have preferred Dinah never knew about my post-Mom breakdown, but of course she had found out, and I hate that she still blames herself for missing the clues.

"I'm okay," I say. "I'm with someone right now, but if we can talk later, that would be good."

"We can definitely talk later. I'll hold you to that, too. I'll be at Oliver's house in an hour. Can you join me there?"

"Ten o'clock at Oliver's house. I'll be there."

Castillo waves his fork to get my attention.

"Right," I say. "Before you go, Dinah, I have an investigator from a local firm that does work for me. He's the one who gave me the heads-up on Oliver's arrest. I know you have your own investigators, but if you need anyone local . . ."

"Who is it?"

"I'm with Ioana Balan, but she's out of town. This is her partner, Dean Castillo."

"I know the name. Can you bring him with you? My investigator retired last year, and I've been using another firm, but local would be better."

I quickly ask Castillo, who nods, and I tell Dinah we'll meet her at Oliver's house.

SEVEN

We arrive at Oliver's place five minutes early, and Dinah is already on the scene. Her car is in the driveway, along with a police cruiser and what I presume is an unmarked police car. The only people in sight are Dinah and a plain-clothed officer. They're in rapt conversation on the front porch.

Castillo warns that we shouldn't approach. I agree. If the suspect's sister gets too close to the search scene, the police will wonder whether she's trying to tamper with evidence. I text Dinah that we're here, waiting in the car.

"Nice place," Castillo says as he peers out at Oliver's house.

I tense. Here we go . . .

"I expected some kind of mansion," he says. "The house is small. But the value's in the property. That's gotta be worth a small fortune inside the city limits."

I only nod, still braced. He's right. Oliver's brick ranch seems unassuming compared to the mansions on either side. It looks like the lone holdout of a real estate boom, where every other house was bought and bulldozed, and these homeowners remain, some crotchety old couple declaring they'll leave in caskets, and not a moment sooner.

In reality, this might be the most expensive property in the neighborhood. It's two acres of land well inside the city borders, a private sanctuary of hundred-year-old oaks and maples.

"Personally, if I had that kind of money, I'd be outside the city," he says. "I rented a place in the country once. Quiet. No nosy neighbors. Room to walk the dog. Liked it."

"You have a dog?" I perk up. I eye puppies the way some women my age eye babies. My apartment doesn't allow them, though.

"Had one," he says. "Passed a couple years back. Figure I'll get another when I can live outside the city again."

"Regretting the move to urban living?"

"Not really my choice. Guy who owned the country place sold it to developers. My house is now a field of condos."

"Oh. Sorry."

He shrugs. "The place was old. If there'd ever been insulation, the mice made nests of it years ago. Cost a fortune to heat and cool, and utilities were on me. Next time, I'm buying, even if it means a helluva commute."

Castillo peers at Oliver's house. Again, from the outside, it doesn't look like much. Just a pleasant one-story ranch house, built a half century ago. But a closer eye can tell that the gardens are professionally tended, and there's no sign of wear—

everything from the roof to the windows has been replaced in the last five years.

"Didn't Ioana say you used to live here?" Castillo says.

"In the back. There was an in-law cottage there when Oliver bought the house. It isn't any bigger than my apartment now, but I loved it. There's a city park with trails in behind, and the cottage is set far enough back for privacy, with a line of trees between it and the house. Top-notch security, of course, with that around the property"—I motion at the wrought-iron fence—"and a secured gate leading into the park, so I felt safe."

I stop short, realizing I've slid into nostalgic gushing.

"Then your brother got married," Castillo says.

I shrug. "The cottage was a perfect office for Laura, so I decided it was time to move out."

"You decided? Or she did?"

I try not to squirm. "It was time," I say firmly. "If I was paying rent, I'd have stayed. But it felt like mooching, and it wasn't fair to Laura. No newlywed wants their sister-in-law living out back."

Castillo's gaze scans the property again. Seeing Dinah heading over, I slip out of the car and walk to her as Castillo ambles along behind.

Dinah Umar was Mom's best friend in law school. After years of working for different firms, they eventually formed their own. I've known Dinah all my life, but it's been a few years since I've seen her. I notice there's more gray in her close-cropped dark hair, and I might spot a wrinkle or two on her dark skin, but it could also be a trick of the light. As always, she's dressed in a power suit perfectly tailored to her tiny form.

We hug, and I introduce Castillo.

"Is it okay for me to be here?" I say. "I don't want to cause trouble for Oliver."

"I told the police you were coming, under the excuse of having a former resident here in case they have questions about the house. Mostly, I'm just here to make sure they don't exceed their warrant. It doesn't cover the cottage yet because they didn't realize it was here."

I bite my tongue. The civilian in me worries that would seem suspicious. It's like Oliver not wanting a lawyer when he was brought into the station for questioning. From my mom, though, I know that Oliver absolutely should have "lawyered up" and that Dinah is right to not let officers into the cottage without a warrant. In the meantime, they can guard it to be sure no one sneaks in and tampers with evidence.

"How's Martine?" I ask as we walk into the shade. Castillo silently trails along, still surveying the property.

"Stable. She's spoken to the police, but she won't meet with me."

"She really does think Oliver did this."

Dinah waves me to a bench under an old maple tree. We sit, and she motions Castillo to the adjoining bench, but he stands watch instead, his back to us, close enough to listen to the conversation.

"How much do you know?" she asks.

"Pretend it's zilch and walk me through it."

"All right then. You're aware that Oliver was taken in for questioning the other night, on an anonymous tip about Laura and concern for Martine?"

"Yes. And he didn't seek legal counsel, even though he knows better."

She leans back. "Oh, believe me, we have had that conversation. He should never have gone with the police in the first place. It should have been an at-home interview with me present. As a lawyer, I want to give them shit. As a woman, I'm happy they acted on a tip."

"Yep. Do we know what the tip was? Oliver was never told."

"Another reason to have me there. The caller claimed to have been a friend of Laura's. She said Laura had told her that Oliver was getting increasingly controlling and gaslighting her. He'd canceled her credit card and insisted it was a bank error. They'd argued over her workload, and she'd mysteriously lost clients. Oliver said they'd left because she was overextending herself. Laura feared Oliver was interfering and somehow cost her clients."

I stare at her. "He canceled her credit card?"

Dinah lifts a hand. "According to this unknown caller. I'll speak to Oliver today. It doesn't sound like him, but of course, it has to be investigated. Even if this woman *is* a friend of Laura's and Laura *did* tell her that, we're taking Laura's word for it. This woman even admitted she dismissed it at the time. She said Laura was 'high-strung' and dramatic."

I make a noncommittal noise.

Dinah continues, "This woman believed Laura's death was clearly an accident. Slowly that turned into guilt—what if Laura had been telling the truth? Then she realized Oliver had a new girlfriend and became concerned."

"But why would the police bring Oliver in for questioning without speaking to Martine first?"

Two seconds of silence. When I can't read her expression, dread seeps in.

"They did," I whisper. "They spoke to Martine, and she said . . . What did she say?"

"She lost her credit card a few weeks ago. She canceled it right away . . . and wasn't able to get a new one. According to the bank, it was a clerical error. However, when the police were speaking to her, one of their questions was about finances, and the missing credit card came up."

I struggle for breath. "And it sounded uncomfortably close to what this anonymous caller claimed Oliver did to Laura."

"That's why they questioned Oliver. None of it was actionable, but it was enough to bring him in, mostly as a warning."

"Okay. But Martine and Oliver straightened it out before she was shot."

Dinah is silent.

I meet her gaze. "Oliver told me everything was fine."

"Can you . . . elaborate on that?"

When I don't answer, my thoughts racing, Castillo turns and finally speaks.

"Amy told Oliver it was okay to reach out to Martine as if nothing happened, just his usual good morning," he says. "Nothing more. He agreed to do that. Amy later asked how things went, and he said fine. I'm guessing that's not what happened?"

Dinah sighs. "Not exactly. Oliver reached out, and Martine didn't answer. He tried again, and she said she was busy. He sent five texts total, trying to find out what was going on, while she continued to insist she was busy and then stopped answering."

I curse under my breath.

"Yes," Dinah says. "I understand he was worried, and I understand he didn't want to tell you he'd ignored your advice. At least they were only texts."

"But she would have been braced in case he showed up," I say. "Which is why when she went outside, she thought she saw his car in the driveway last night."

"It *was* his car."

I go still. "Martine identified Oliver as the shooter?"

"No, she identified his car, which was also caught on a red-light camera two blocks from Martine's house. It was undeniably his. There's a dent in the front fender from a couple of weeks ago."

"Right. A parking lot hit-and-run. He hasn't had time to get it fixed."

"Martine recognized that dent before she went outside."

"And the shooter?" I say, heart hammering.

"The person's face was covered. Martine was almost to the car before the window went down. As soon as she saw the driver was wearing a balaclava, she turned to run. That's when the shots were fired."

"You say the car was caught on a red-light camera," Castillo says. "Which only goes off if you run a red."

"Yes."

Castillo snorts. "Yeah, if I'm going to kill my girlfriend, I'm definitely running a red on the way, with the camera in plain sight. Did it get a picture of the driver?"

"Wearing a balaclava."

"Better and better. Because that wouldn't be suspicious at all, driving around with your face covered. The shooter pulled it down when they ran the red, and then again to shoot Martine."

"That would be my theory," Dinah says.

"Where does Oliver say he was during this?" Castillo asks.

"Sleeping. He went to bed just after ten."

"That tracks," I say, carefully, hoping I don't sound as if I'm defending him. "He's an early riser, and he especially wouldn't stay up after spending the night before with the police."

"Where's his bedroom located?" Castillo asks, looking at the house.

"At the back," I say. "Which means he wouldn't see or hear anyone taking the car. When he's there alone, the gate is set to automatic. He hates having to fuss with the code. It's finicky."

"Any other security?" Castillo says. "Cameras and such?"

"Oliver usually parks in the driveway during good weather, and there's a camera right there." I point to it. "It's on a motion sensor. The recording will show someone taking the car from the drive last night. There's also a full security system on the house, and he does use it when he goes to bed. It should show that he didn't leave the house."

"That's what we expect," Dinah says. "The police jumped the gun. A force this size only sees a few murders a year. If Martine identified Oliver as the shooter—and that red-light camera puts his car in the area—they're going to make an arrest. I suspect there was also a bit of a misunderstanding. They seemed to be under the impression she'd seen his face and was making a complete ID."

"Now that they know better, will they drop the charges?"

"After they see the security logs and camera footage? Yes."

EIGHT

Castillo leaves Oliver's house shortly after the conversation. I stay with Dinah while the police finish their search. As much as I'd love to see Oliver, that's not possible. Instead, Dinah drops me off to get my car and then grabs takeout and meets me at her temporary office, where we hang out while we await news.

Dinah and I talk a bit, catching up, but it's hard to focus on anything except Martine in the hospital and Oliver in prison and what happened to my mother. I don't want to think about Mom. I want my full attention and sympathy to be with Martine. But being here with Dinah takes me back eight years to when she sat with me at home, waiting for news about Grant White.

Now I'm waiting to hear whether my brother will be charged with attempting to kill his girlfriend, and Dinah is with me again, and those two cases swim along the same stream in my mind.

Martine and my mother. Oliver and Grant White.

Is there any chance Oliver did this? Logically, it makes no sense. But then I think of White's children and friends and loved ones, and all the waiting they'd done at each stage, still in shock that he had been charged with my mother's murder, still thinking there'd been some mistake.

Am I doing the same thing?

I really hope not.

It's nearly five by the time the call comes. The police have finished with the security logs and footage. I wait for the news that they found no evidence of Oliver leaving last night. That they have security-tape evidence of someone stealing and then returning his car.

That is not what they found.

"I don't understand," I say to Dinah. "There's nothing?"

"Nothing between nine last night and one this morning. Someone turned the system off."

"Or maybe Oliver never turned it on."

Dinah shakes her head. "It was on after he returned from work. Then it goes offline for four hours."

I consider that. "Could someone have hacked it?"

"That's my theory," Dinah says, "but of course the police are going with the simpler solution."

"That Oliver turned it off to hide him leaving."

"Yes."

"The charges won't be dropped then."

"I'm going to speak to the prosecutor and see whether they have anything substantiative enough to warrant the charge.

Worst case, they'll string us along for a few days. Either way, your brother will be out—on dropped charges or bail."

Before heading home from Dinah's office, I go to start the map app and realize my phone is turned off from this morning. Both Castillo and Dinah had been with me—and Oliver in prison—so there was no one I needed or wanted to hear from.

When I turn it on, I have so many message notifications that I'm tempted to shut it down again. Most are from people and numbers I don't recognize. One, though, makes me wince, and I sit in the law firm parking lot as I return the call.

"What the fuck is going on?" Raven says when she answers.

"I'm sorry."

I tell her the whole story, and I relax a little as the edge falls from her tone.

"So someone stole Oliver's car and is framing him for murder?" Raven says.

I tense. "I know it sounds ridiculous."

"Hell, no. It sounds great. For a true crime story, that is. Not so great if your brother is in the middle of it, though."

I roll my eyes. "You think?"

She sighs. "Fine. I'll turn my producer brain off. Halfway off anyway." She pauses. "Someone seriously hates your brother, Amy."

"You think?" I say again.

"At least you haven't lost your sense of sarcasm." A rustling, as if she's walking while talking. "Oliver's lawyers will handle this. We need to concentrate on podcast damage control, because either way, this is damaging."

I fight a spark of panic. "How damaging?"

"If your brother was somehow convicted, you'd have two choices. Either close shop or turn him into an example."

"Fall on my sword and use myself as an example, too. How even those close to a predator might be blind to it."

"Yes, even if you still thought he was innocent. But the trial isn't happening tomorrow. The problem is that, if it *goes* to trial, you need to address it in a way that doesn't condemn him . . . but doesn't support him, either." A moment of silence, and then her voice drops. "You can*not* publicly support him or defend him in any way."

"I know."

"You could do that?"

"I'm hoping it won't come to that, but if it does, then I agree that either I'd need to do it or I'd need to end the show."

"You have something here, Amy. Your growth rate is one of the best I've seen. This could be a career for you . . . if the podcast doesn't get derailed by what's happening to Oliver."

A bird calls in the background, and she pauses, as if waiting it out.

Raven continues, "I'll fight like hell alongside you if that's what you want, but if you decide it's not worth it, you'd damn well better let me know. I don't want to look up and realize I'm the only one bailing out the ship."

"I understand."

"There's more. You lost two sponsors today, Amy. Henderson Berry Farms and Old Crone Brews."

My hands tighten on the steering wheel. "Shit."

"It's not a huge deal. They're both local, and they weren't exactly shoveling money into your coffers. But if this story goes national, you're going to lose more." She pauses. "Maybe all."

Objectively speaking, that won't affect my bottom line. Right now, I make 90 percent of my podcast earnings from advertising and Patreon. Sponsorship at this stage is mostly free website hosting, discount show merch, and—in the case of Old Crone Brews—a monthly tea shipment that I've been giving away online because I'm more of a coffee drinker.

But small-scale sponsorship is a stepping stone to the big bucks. It's also a stamp of validity. If my podcast has sponsors, it's not a vanity project. When those names disappear, it'll be noticed.

"I have an idea, though," Raven continues.

"Okay . . ."

"Don't sound so enthusiastic."

"I'm bracing," I say.

"Yeah, yeah. Seriously, though, I think we could turn this into a real growth opportunity."

"Switch my show focus to people who've been wrongly accused of killing a loved one?"

"Hey, if you meant that, I'd be all for it." A pause. "Strike that. My money-grubbing soul would be all for it. Ethically, I like where you are now. And I know you only want to be where you are now, which is the quandary."

"Yep."

"Do you remember when I first reached out to you? What had you done that caught my attention?"

"Quintupled my subscribers in a week."

She snorts. "You went from a hundred subscribers to five hundred. Not exactly hitting the big leagues. It wasn't the numbers that caught my eye—it was the growth."

"Isn't that what I just said?"

She ignores me and continues, "Most podcasts can trace that kind of spike to an outside element. They're recommended by someone big. They get media coverage for a specific show. You did it organically. That's what put you on my radar. You added something to the format, and it spiked subscribers and kept them. Then you continued growing because you continued adding that new ingredient."

"I started investigating cases rather than just regurgitating them."

"*Exactly.* And that's how you can not only weather this storm but ride these winds to where you want to be."

I hesitate. "If you're suggesting I investigate Oliver's case, I can't do that. I only dig into completed cases so that I don't interfere with the prosecution and defense's work."

"I'm not suggesting you investigate. I'm suggesting you *report*, as only someone in your position can. I'm suggesting you cover the case."

"Cover a case about my brother as an attempted-murder suspect? While remaining completely neutral and not shaping the data in any way, because that would be unethical?"

"Yes."

"So you want me to be the kind of cold-hearted bitch who'd use a tragedy in her family to increase ratings?"

She sighs dramatically.

"What?" I say. "That's what I'd be doing, right?"

"No. Someone else might do that, but you are one of the few people I know who could cover this dispassionately. It's not milking a family tragedy. It's acknowledging what is happening and proving your commitment to the podcast by not sweeping it under the rug."

I say nothing.

"Think about it," she says. "See what happens."

"I wouldn't do it if Oliver objected," I say.

"Understood."

"And I wouldn't do it if Oliver's lawyer objected."

"Understood."

With any luck, those charges are going away, and this will all be moot, because I don't want to cover my brother's case . . . and I really don't want to ask whether that'd be all right with him.

I get two texts from Dinah that night. Short and sweet.

DINAH:

Nothing to report

DINAH:

Stay offline

If it were anyone other than Dinah, I'd worry that telling me to stay offline meant something had happened and she didn't want me to see it. I know better. She's saying that there isn't any news, and so anything I see online is either speculation or outright fabrication, probably with some slander thrown in.

My mother's murder taught me the wisdom of Dinah's words. I'll be the first to know of new developments, and surfing will only keep me awake at night. I need to sleep, and I think—with a little chemical help—I can manage it.

Martine is alive and in stable condition.

My brother didn't shoot her.

This will all be cleared up soon.

Do I really believe that?

I'm not sure.

I do sleep, though the pill means I wake up groggy to incoming texts. I hadn't bothered to set an alarm, and when I open my eyes, I see it's almost nine. That has me scrambling up, reaching for my phone.

The texts are from Dinah.

> DINAH:
>
> Picking you up at 9

> DINAH:
>
> Charges not dismissed

> DINAH:
>
> Oliver is fine and wants to talk
> to you

> DINAH:
>
> STAY OFFLINE

I read her texts twice, hoping to see something that I'm missing, some nuance that says my twisting stomach is an overreaction.

If she's picking me up and taking me to Oliver, something has happened. A development that's more than "charges not dropped."

I must resist the urge to go online. No good can come of it, not when Dinah will be here in ten minutes and I'll get the facts straight from her.

I yank on clothing, and I'm washing my face when the buzzer sounds. I make sure it's Dinah, and then get my hair brushed before she's there.

"I overslept," I say as I open the door.

"Good. You needed it."

"Just let me grab a coffee and an apple."

"We'll hit a drive-through on the way."

NINE

When we're in the car, she says, "They're not dropping the charges. The police are convinced that Oliver turned off the security system himself. Dean is investigating. The system is connected to WiFi, which means it *can* be hacked. Dean says that model is known for security breaches, and Oliver hasn't updated the software or the firmware."

"Hasn't updated either *recently*?"

She nods. "Excellent question." Over the car's Bluetooth, she sends a voice text to Castillo asking whether he knows how long it's been since Oliver updated. The response comes back in seconds, and the system reads it aloud.

"Good," Dinah says. "Not updating it is an established habit, and therefore not suspicious. We need to prove either that it was hacked or that it could have been, if proving or disproving hacking is impossible."

I force myself to wait until we're out of the drive-through before I say, "There's more, isn't there? A development that isn't in Oliver's favor?"

"The Crown is considering reopening the investigation into Laura's death."

"What?" I twist to look at her. "Based on an anonymous call?"

"No, though that doesn't look good, either. It exposed a potential pattern of behavior."

My heart gallops, and I have to focus on my breath before I can continue. "So Oliver did something? With Laura's and Martine's credit cards?"

"He's asked me to let him explain it to you."

Dinah's voice is calm, but everything in me explodes in gibbering panic.

Oh God, Oliver. What have you done?

"How . . . how bad was it?" I manage.

She meets my gaze. "He'll explain it, Amy. He does have an explanation, and while I would not condone his actions, if I thought it indicated abusive control, I'd tell you."

I take two deep breaths. "Okay."

"There's also this."

She pulls up something on her phone and passes it over. It's a news article from the local paper.

NEW EVIDENCE IN LAURA HARDING DROWNING?

When my heart stops, I inhale deeply and focus on that question mark. It's a significant bit of punctuation, saying that the paper is raising a possibility rather than stating a fact.

The opening paragraph mentions Martine's shooting, along with "This is not the first time Harding Enterprises CEO Oliver Harding has been accused of trying to kill a romantic partner. Three years ago, Harding's wife, Laura . . ." It goes on to succinctly sum up Laura's drowning. Then comes the bombshell.

One of the two witnesses, Dale Cranston, is now retracting part of his statement. At the time, he told police he saw Laura Harding dive into the water, of her own accord, while her husband was at least two meters away. Now Cranston admits he didn't see where Oliver Harding was standing, because he was fully focused on Laura Harding.

"It was a hot chick in a bikini," he is quoted as saying. "I wasn't looking anywhere else."

According to Cranston, it was his friend, Keith Landry, who saw where Oliver Harding stood, and Cranston did spot someone else on the boat, so he echoed his friend's version of events.

"Even if he was too far away to push the lady," Cranston says, "that doesn't mean she couldn't have jumped into the water to get away from him. He might have been holding a gun on her or something. Like I said, we were watching the chick in the bikini."

In Landry's statement three years ago, he had said he heard Laura Harding laughing to her husband and trying to coax him into the water, which indicated she'd jumped in voluntarily. However, Cranston says he never heard anything, and Landry died last year, leaving Cranston as the only witness.

Harding was never charged in his wife's death, which means if Cranston recants his story, this may open the door to more trouble for Oliver Harding.

The first sip of coffee churns in my gut as I reread the article. Then I look over at Dinah.

"Is this grounds for reopening the investigation?"

She hesitates. "Yes," she says finally. "The eyewitness accounts are what halted further investigation in its tracks. Combined with the lack of evidence, it meant there was no reason to think it was anything except a tragic accident."

"Now there is?"

"If it was purely this guy changing his story, then no. He's not saying he saw anything suspicious. Only that he lied to police, which he seems to think is no big deal."

"Yeah, he's going to find out what they think of that."

"He is, and my hope is that Cranston will revert to his original version and blame the media for taking his words out of context. Witnessing Laura's accident was the biggest thing that ever happened to this man. Suddenly, he was a key witness in a major news story. Now he sees the chance to be relevant again. We need to hope he realizes his mistake and backs down."

"But now that the possibility has been raised, it's a problem. The other witness is dead, and this mystery woman has linked Greta and Martine with similar allegations against Oliver."

"It means they can reopen the investigation, Amy," she says gently. "It doesn't mean the police will find enough for the Crown to charge him."

I stare out the window until we're nearly at the county detention center. Then I say, "This isn't going away, is it?"

Dinah squeezes my arm without answering.

"You expect it'll go to trial?" I ask.

"I hope not. We know Oliver is being framed. We know the woman who came to your show has something to do with that, and now that she's a person of interest in a criminal case, Dean will find whatever he needs to uncover her identity."

"Do you think she's the one who shot Martine?"

"If not, then she is a link to the person who did, because there's very little chance the accusation and the shooting *aren't* connected."

As we turn into the parking lot, Dinah says, "Have you considered how this might affect your podcast?"

I pass her a wan smile. "I should say that's the absolute last thing on my mind."

"No," she says firmly. "You are a young woman finding success in a passion project. You can be worried sick about Oliver while also being concerned about how his arrest affects your livelihood. Don't let anyone make you feel otherwise."

"My producer wants me to cover the case," I blurt. Then I pull back into my seat, tugging my sweater tighter around me. "I know that's not important right now—"

"If it's about your life, Amy, then it's important to me. Tell me what she's thinking."

"That I need to get ahead of this," I say. "I've already lost local sponsors, and that's just the beginning of a downhill slide. My focus is people who kill intimate partners . . . and my brother is accused of murdering his wife and attempting to murder his girlfriend. I have to address it, and Raven thinks the best way to do that is to dispassionately cover the case."

"Because you'll have an inside track on information. From me."

"I wouldn't—"

Dinah lifts a hand. "You would, and that's what she's hoping for. You become the expert on this case, and combined with the personal connection, you're better than any traditional news source." She drums her fingers on the steering wheel. "It could work."

"In Oliver's favor, you mean?" I say. "But that's only if I filter the data and slant the angle, which I can't do."

"He doesn't need that. I do not, for one moment, believe Oliver parked in Martine's driveway and shot her. If a man like Oliver wanted to kill someone, he'd hire a professional." She pauses. "No, Oliver would know better than that. A professional killer means a wild card. He'd plan something far more foolproof than pushing his wife off a boat or shooting his girlfriend in her driveway—and leaving her alive to identify him."

When I don't answer, she waves a hand. "I'm not saying I can imagine Oliver killing anyone. But if he did, he'd be smarter about it. So would I. So would you."

I still say nothing, and she curses under her breath. "That was insensitive. Other people might speculate about things like that, but it's not a parlor game for you. I'm sorry."

"I understand what you mean," I say, "though I think Oliver would rather his defense was something other than 'He'd have done a better job of it.'"

"Unfortunately, that may be an angle, if it comes to it, though never so bluntly. For now, I'll talk to him about you covering the case on the podcast. I see advantages. There's one roadblock, though. You can't have Dean back. I need him."

"I know. I'd find someone else."

"Hold off on that. I can't promise to give you everything Dean uncovers, but I will give you everything that will also be passed on to the Crown." She opens the car door. "We can discuss that more later. Oliver is waiting."

I've never been in a prison visiting room. I certainly wasn't going to visit my mother's killer, and since then, even when convicted killers have reached out to the show, wanting to give their version of events, I've never even been tempted to go.

This is the county detention center, where the accused await their bail hearings or their day in court if bail was denied or inaccessible. It's a sterile government building, and a fence behind it indicates a yard for exercise, but from where we enter, that's hidden.

It's a Canadian jail, and most of my expectations have been shaped by American television, but there are no surprises in the experience. We have to show ID and leave our valuables and pass through a security check.

After that, I presume I'd normally be shown into a common area with security shields, but I'm here with Oliver's attorney, and we're accorded the privilege of a private space that reminds me of a TV cop-show interrogation room, with the bare minimum of basic office furniture.

Dinah tries to distract me with small talk that I barely hear. My gaze is fixed on that door, ready to burst into a welcoming smile the moment the knob turns. I've taken extra care with my appearance—including layers of cover-up for my under-eye circles. I want Oliver to know I'm concerned, but I don't want him thinking I'm on the brink of another breakdown while he's in here and can't help. His focus needs to be on his own situation.

We've been waiting about ten minutes before Oliver is escorted in. He's not wearing handcuffs, and he's dressed in a T-shirt and jeans, as if he's spending the weekend at home, doing yard work. What I notice most, though, is how tired he looks. He'd been exhausted when I'd seen him two days ago. Now it looks as if he hasn't slept since. He's made the effort of shaving, though it's a haphazard job, with more than a nick or two. His hair is still wet, as if he just showered, but he hasn't done more than finger comb it.

I want to jump up and hug him. I want to be the kind of little sister who rants that she can't believe this is happening to him, it's so unfair, how dare they think he did this. But I'm not, and it'd only make him uncomfortable, so I settle for a gentle smile, and I try, very hard, not to think of what he must be going through, because breaking down in tears won't help, either.

"Hey," he says as he slides into a chair across from me. He reaches over the top, takes my hands and holds them tight. "I'm sorry, Ames. I'm sorry about all this."

I manage a choked laugh. "I think that's my line."

"You know what I mean. I'm sorry to be putting you through this." He releases one of my hands to rub his face. "They'll get the charges sorted, but someone *shot* Martine. She's in the hospital, and she thinks I put her there, and I can't . . ." He runs a hand through his hair. "I can't even process that. I understand why she thinks it—the shots came from someone driving my car. I'm praying she'll be fine, physically, but she's not going to be fine completely. You understand what I mean."

"I do."

"And even when it's proven that I didn't pull that trigger, she's always going to remember thinking it was me. We aren't going to get past that. I'll get out of this mess, but that won't change the fact that she was shot and that I'll have lost a relationship with someone—" He clears his throat, eyes misting. "Someone I cared about very much."

"I'm sorry."

He straightens, reaching for my other hand again and holding both on the tabletop. "The important thing is keeping her safe and putting this bastard behind bars. That's why I asked Dinah to bring you here. I've made a decision, and I didn't want you to hear about it secondhand." His hands tighten on mine. "I'm not seeking bail."

I stare at him, thinking I've misheard. "What?"

"At this time," he adds quickly. "I'm not seeking bail at this time."

"I don't understand." My heart picks up speed. "You can't stay in jail, Oliver. It's not safe."

"Someone is using Martine to get to me," he says. "They shot her for the sole purpose of putting me in prison, presumably to pay for whatever they think I did to Laura. Martine is nothing more than a pawn to them. If I'm out, what's to stop them from killing her to frame me? What's to stop them from coming after *you* to frame me?"

When I open my mouth, he cuts in, "I know you'd say you'll be fine, so we'll focus on Martine. I want to be certain no one can hurt her. And from a selfish standpoint, I don't want them framing me for it. As long as I'm in here, we're both safe."

I glance at Dinah.

"I agree with the strategy," she says. "For now. I'll make it clear why we aren't seeking bail and that we may do so at a later time."

"There's more," Oliver says. "I don't want anything that comes out to surprise you." He shakes his head. "No, I don't want to disappoint you, and this might do it, so I want you to hear it from me."

"Okay," I say, my voice tight, suspecting he's going to talk about the credit cards.

"The woman who called the police said Laura believed I'd canceled her credit card. Then Martine lost hers, which makes it sound as if I might have taken it. I didn't. At least . . ." He inhales. "I didn't touch Martine's credit card. She legitimately lost it and the bank has confirmed that any problem she had reinstating it was a clerical error. But . . . I did cancel Laura's. I told her it must have been a bank error, after I instructed my banker not to reissue her one based on my credit rating."

I start hiding my shock and disappointment, and then I decide I can't pretend that was okay. So I just look at him and let him see what I'm feeling, and when he flinches, I try not to feel guilty.

"I made a mistake," he says. "Laura was . . . You remember how she was with money. She liked to shop, and most of it never left her closet. That bothered me. A lot. We had the money, but your mom taught me fiscal responsibility and charity. Whenever I talked to Laura about her spending, she'd spend more. I should have confronted her more strongly. Instead, I did the cowardly thing and canceled her card on my account, leaving her with her old personal one, which had a low credit limit."

He watches me expectantly, as if waiting for me to say I understand.

"You canceled her card and pretended it was an error," I say. "When she suspected what you'd done—which she must have, because she told a friend—you stuck to your story, making her feel like she was overreacting. We call that gaslighting."

He slumps, and I can't keep looking at him or I'll dial back my censure. I turn to Dinah, who's pretending to be busy with a notepad.

"They'll use that against him, won't they?" I say.

"They will." She meets his gaze. "It was a terrible thing to do, but I'm glad he confessed before it came out. He told me last night, and I'm already on top of it."

"And the other accusations?" I say. "The caller said you interfered with Laura's business."

He shakes his head vehemently. "Never." He meets my eyes. "I'll be blunt here, Amy. I was worried about her spending my income, so I certainly wouldn't have cut into her ability to make her own. But she was having business problems. She really was taking on too much and—I hate to say it—losing clients who felt she wasn't giving them her full attention."

"Because she wasn't."

"Yes. I offered to help her get better organized, and she took offense at that, so I left her to it. According to this caller, I was also driving wedges between her and her friends. That's not true. Again, she was dropping balls, missing lunch dates and coffee meetings."

"Can confirm," Dinah says. "Dean has already been in touch with one friend who says Laura didn't show up for lunch twice, and a client who dropped her for blowing deadlines. We'll keep digging and get more stories."

"Laura was pushing herself too hard," Oliver says. "I've always blamed myself for that. I convinced her she had the talent to start her own business. I bankrolled it, too. I thought I was being helpful, and now I realize it might have made her feel like she'd traded a boss for an investor. I made mistakes. But I loved her and absolutely would never have hurt her. I only wish we'd had the time to work it out."

TEN

I've been home for an hour, and I haven't moved from the kitchenette chair. I managed to get that far and slumped into it, and I've just sat here, unmoving and unthinking. My brain is blank in a way it hasn't been since Oliver came and pulled me from the abyss that day eight years ago.

My brother is in jail for the attempted murder of his girlfriend. The murder of his wife may be added to the charges. He's innocent of both—I know he is. He's being framed.

That isn't his loving sister spinning wild conspiracy theories. It's a near-certain fact, and I only say *near-certain* because I've been conditioned not to ever be absolute in cases of potential domestic abuse.

Did Oliver drown Laura? No. What we have is a witness

retracting a statement because, as Dinah says, he wants another
fifteen minutes of fame.

Did Oliver shoot Martine? No, because the way it happened
is ridiculous and screams "Setup!"

Did Oliver gaslight Laura?

Yes.

Oliver took away Laura's credit card, lied about it, and then
made sure she couldn't get a new one while lying about *that*.
He made her feel as if she was overreacting and imagining a
problem when he'd caused the problem himself.

If he'd continued down that line, it could have spiraled into
psychological abuse. As it stands, it was the first step on a slip-
pery slope, and I trust that he would have realized it and pulled
himself back from that edge.

Either way, it's going to impact his case.

As for not seeking bail, I hate the thought of Oliver spending even an extra hour in prison, but I understand the sacrifice
he's making. It's the right thing to do because it means Martine
is safe.

When the lobby buzzer sounds, I ignore it. Dinah has warned
me that the press is going to track me down very soon. The only
reason they haven't is that I don't share a surname with Oliver.

I've been through a media onslaught before, when Mom
died. I say her murder was an ordinary one, shockingly com-
monplace, but that doesn't mean it wasn't noticed. Canada had
554 homicides that year—yes, I memorized the stats. Of them,
my mother was one of 460 people killed by someone they
knew, and one of 89 killed by an intimate partner. Cases like
my mom's—successful lawyer grabbed in secured parking

garage by a guy she dumped—still pick up their share of press.

I'd only wanted to grieve in peace, and if I couldn't do that, then I wanted to bring my mother to life, show the world what they'd lost. But the press just wanted photos of her sobbing daughter, sound bites of that daughter shouting for justice, details on the murder that weren't in the official press releases. That is a large part of what spurred me to change the direction of my life. I saw how my mother's death was treated, and I wanted better.

Back then, Dinah stepped in and shielded me. I won't ask that of her now. If the media comes for me, I'll deal with it, but mostly, I'm just going to make myself unavailable.

Here's where I'll be especially grateful for my secure apartment building. No one can show up on my doorstep. They can't ambush me leaving for work or school, either, because I don't need to go anywhere. Being a part-time doctoral student means I'm only on campus a couple days a week. Any meetings with my thesis advisor can be done virtually. I don't plan to hole up indefinitely, but I'm grateful to be able to hunker down for a day or two.

The buzzer sounds again. I continue to ignore it.

When a text comes in, I glance down at my phone.

CASTILLO:

Answer the door, Gibson.
Your car is in the lot. I know
you're there.

I frown and let him in. As I walk to the door, I catch a glimpse of myself. I'd gone out this morning with a neat ponytail, a flick of mascara and a pop of lip color. Now my ponytail is askew, tendrils having escaped from running my hands through my hair. That "flick of mascara" has smeared from crying. The lip color is long gone. I resist the urge to at least comb my hair. It's Castillo. Maybe if I look sad and bedraggled, he'll take pity on me.

I open the door at his knock, which is really more of a pound.

"Hey," I say. "Were you trying to get in touch with me? I must have missed your texts."

He waves me back, steps in, shuts the door, locks and dead-bolts it.

"Did you even look out to be sure it was me?" he says.

"No," I say honestly. "I should have. It's been a long day." I check my watch. "And it's barely noon."

"I didn't text," he says as he stalks into the living room.

"All the better to sneak up on me," I murmur under my breath. Then I raise my voice so he can hear. "Anytime you want to talk, you can call. I'm screening, but I'll answer yours."

"I hate talking on the phone."

"Too easy for people to hang up on you?" This time, I forget to say it under my breath. Or maybe I just don't bother.

"In this instance, yeah. What's this about you covering the case on your podcast?"

I fight against tensing and lower myself into a chair. "I'm considering it."

"Well, stop."

"I may not have a choice."

"You always have a choice, Gibson."

I look up at him still standing—*the better to loom, my dear.* "Maybe, but I'm in danger of losing my podcast. My brother is accused of the very thing it stands against. I need to address it."

"Why? You aren't your brother."

I shake my head. "It's optics. I'm already losing sponsors. Using my brother's case to keep my podcast afloat seems cold, but the show means something to me. It means a lot, and if I can keep it without hurting Oliver or his case, I'd like to do that."

Castillo doesn't answer, and I don't dare look at him.

When he walks to the patio door and looks out, I say softly, "I never got your email."

"I said I didn't message."

"I mean about your cousin's murder. I know you think I ignored the email, which would make me a hypocrite. I use my mother's death to start a podcast pretending to care about victims and their families, and when someone actually asks for help, I show my true colors. It's all performative."

He sighs as he turns to face me. "I don't think that, Amy. I overstepped. You barely knew me, and I wasn't exactly friendly after your little Nancy Drew stunt."

I stiffen. "The 'Nancy Drew stunt' was a mistake."

Another sigh. "I know. You screwed up, and you didn't do it again, but in case you haven't noticed, I can hold grudges, especially against those who threaten people I care about."

I nod. "I endangered Ioana's career, and your firm's reputation."

"It's Ioana I care about. I can take care of myself. But, yeah, you did, and I held it against you for longer than I should have. Then I came asking for a favor, expecting you to do something you aren't comfortable with. You're not a therapist. I just wish you'd been honest with me instead of pretending you didn't get the email."

"I *didn't* get the email, Dean."

"I sent two."

"And I didn't get them." I meet his gaze. "When my mother died, I came damn close to following her. I would never, *ever* ignore someone in need. I would have talked to your cousin's wife and suggested resources."

He turns back to the window.

"I'd like you to leave," I say.

He sighs again, deeply this time, still looking outside. "Let's not—"

"I am asking you to leave, Dean. This is my apartment, and I don't need to put up with your bullshit. Not here. Not now."

He turns. "I didn't come here to fight."

"Really? Then I'd hate to be around when you do. You came *spoiling* for a fight. Accusing me of exploiting my brother. Accusing me of lying about the emails. I don't give a shit what you think of me, Dean Castillo. I do not have the bandwidth for you right now."

"I admitted I was still pissy about the Nancy Drew shit and that I shouldn't have been. I don't think that's spoiling for a fight. As for the emails, *you* brought that up, and I admitted I overstepped asking for your help. And I never said you were exploiting Oliver. I came here because obviously your brother and his lawyer are too wrapped up in this case to realize you're about to do something stupid."

"Stupid . . ." I say.

"Not *stupid*. *Foolish*." He gives his head a firm shake. "No, not *foolish*, either. *Dangerous*. We aren't dealing with a run-of-the-mill troll who tried to ruin your show and made an anonymous call to the police. This person *shot* your brother's girlfriend. Tried to *murder* her."

"And I'm the silly little girl who thinks this is some movie-of-the-week plot she should cover on her silly little podcast."

"Don't put words in my mouth, Gibson. I did not say that about you or your podcast. I don't think that, either. I'm concerned that you haven't thought this through enough. I know I'm not explaining this well, but stop reading between the lines, please, and listen to me. If you put Oliver's case on your podcast, you make yourself a target for the psycho who shot Martine."

"Do you really believe that?"

"Yes."

"You think I'd be a *possible* target? Or a serious one?"

"You want to start playing the odds now? Exactly what are the chances this psycho will kill you?"

I glance toward the kitchen. "Is it too early for a drink?"

He snorts.

"Seriously," I say. "We both have our backs up. We're both stressed. If you want to have this conversation, we both need to chill, and I could really use a drink."

"Go ahead."

I walk into the kitchen and take a beer from the fridge.

When I notice him looking, I lift it. "Oh, that's why you said no. You didn't figure I'd have anything you'd want. This isn't mine. It's left over from my last boyfriend. I only drink canned cocktails, the fizzy ones in pretty colors." I open the beer and take a sip as I head back into the living room.

"I like canned cocktails," he says. "Especially the blue ones. But I'd take a beer."

I point to the kitchen. He goes in and finds another beer in the fridge.

When he sits down with his bottle, I say, "I'm not sold on the podcast idea, but I see my producer's point. It would undo damage that's only going to get worse. Dinah thinks it could help Oliver's case, which I obviously want, as long as it doesn't cost me my integrity. But I'm not comfortable with it, and yes, I hadn't considered I might be making myself a target. But what's the alternative? Put the podcast on hiatus and hope for the best? That could look like his own sister doesn't believe he's innocent, or it could look like I really am a hypocrite—happy to fight for this cause unless it impacts me personally."

Castillo fingers his bottle, gaze down, looking very uncomfortable. Okay, so I tried honesty, and that wasn't what he wanted, either. Message received.

I set my beer aside. "Sorry for rambling. Like I said, it's been a long day. You've delivered your warning, and I'll figure out my next move."

He exhales. "You're in a tough spot."

"I'll get myself out. I'm not looking for advice." I stop and make a face. "That came out wrong. I mean that I'm not expecting advice. I know I need to figure this out for myself."

"I'm shit at giving advice," he says, "but I can help you work out a solution, if you need someone to bounce ideas off."

I hesitate.

"Okay, I'll get out of your hair." He stands, beer in hand. "Just remember what I said."

"No, I—" I take a deep breath. "We're both tiptoeing around, and it doesn't suit either of us. I would love to bounce ideas off you, but I don't want you to feel obligated to listen."

"You really think I ever feel obligated to do anything?"

"You felt obligated to take my case while Ioana was out of town."

"Obligated to her, not you." He lowers himself back onto the sofa. "Done right, I agree that this might be the best way to save your podcast. Yeah, I don't think it should be at risk in the first place. You're not your brother. Your podcast is all about people missing the signs and predators hiding in plain sight, and if Oliver did this, wouldn't that just prove your point? It's not like you're setting yourself up as an expert who can always read the signs. No one can. You're studying this and using what you learn to help others."

I blink. He's right. That's exactly what I'm doing. I'm just surprised to hear this from Castillo.

"What did you have in mind?" he says. "How would you handle this?"

I could say I haven't thought about it. I almost want to, as if admitting I have plans negates my claim that I don't want to cover Oliver's case on my podcast. Both can be true—I'm just not sure Castillo will understand.

No, that's unfair. He's smart and shrewd and very capable of understanding it. I just don't want him leaping to conclusions and judging me for them.

I take a deep breath. Then I explain what I'm considering.

"That could work," he muses, leaning back into the sofa. "Report on the case. Just the facts, ma'am. No editorializing."

"Mmm, no editorializing regarding Oliver's guilt or innocence. I'll need to add my own thoughts in general, though. Otherwise, it really is just a cold recitation of facts. They can listen to the news for that."

"Reasonable."

"I'll need to mention my connection to Oliver in every episode introduction," I say. "Or people will accuse me of hiding my bias."

"Yeah, people are assholes." He stretches out his legs. "If you want to stay ahead of the media, you're going to need insider information."

"Dinah said she'd make sure I get everything she's passing along to the Crown. I can't report on it before they have it, but I can tape an episode and be ready to launch."

"Cops won't like it. Prosecution won't like it. But I can help make sure you don't say anything they can shut you down for. I'll pass on tips, too, right after Dinah gives the thumbs-up. There are things that wouldn't concern *her*, but might help *you*."

"She already warned me that I can't use you as an investigator."

He waves a hand. "I'll talk to her. I know what I'm doing."

"I'd appreciate that . . . but I'm not sure I can afford it."

"We'll work something out." He stops. "Payment, I mean." He makes a face. "*Fees*. Just to be clear."

I lift a brow. "I don't expect you to work for free."

"No, I just meant that when I said we'd work something out, that could sound creepy."

"I wouldn't have inferred anything."

"Maybe, but if you wouldn't consider the possibility that a guy might be hoping for something else, then you need to listen to your podcast more."

"I just mean I didn't misinterpret *your* meaning. Yes, if Dinah agrees and we can work out fees I can afford, then I could use some help. I'll tape the first episode today."

He glances around. "You record here?"

I nod. "I'm not at the professional-studio stage yet. I have decent equipment and a closet big enough for a makeshift studio."

"Good. Better not to go anywhere. So what's the next step?"

"I write the script and let you and Dinah see it."

He stands and takes the beer bottle into the kitchen. "I'll leave you to that. Send it over when you have it." He pauses before setting down the bottle. "Email it, but also text so I know you've sent it."

So there are no misunderstandings over emails gone astray.

"You'll have it in a couple of hours," I say.

ELEVEN

It's been over a week since Martine was shot. I can't say things are going well, because the charges against Oliver haven't been dismissed. I can't say they're going well while he's still in jail, not seeking bail. Otherwise, though? I hesitate to consider *otherwise*. It seems flippant.

Everything is going well here, except for the fact my brother is in jail, having been framed for shooting his girlfriend.

Martine is fine and being released in a couple of days. Sources say she's going to stay with her parents in Toronto. She hasn't made contact, and I know better than to reach out. Dinah has tried speaking to her again, but Martine still refuses.

Her story remains firm, which is actually to Oliver's benefit. We know it was his car in that driveway. Our fear would be that, on recovering, she'd claim she saw something about her shooter that proved it was Oliver. I won't say she'd lie, but she's been through a trauma, and if she is absolutely certain Oliver shot her, she might misremember details or mold the narrative to ensure he goes to prison. But she doesn't. So between that and her refusal to speak to Dinah, we can interpret that she is no longer convinced it was Oliver, but she's not sold on the frame-up theory, either. In her shoes, I'd think the same.

The police have reopened Laura's case file, but all Dinah hears is that they're still reviewing it along with "new" evidence. She suspects that they only have that one anonymous tip and a witness changing his story, and it's not enough to lay charges.

Castillo hasn't been able to track down the woman from my event yet. He did contact the person who sold her the ticket, but the transaction was small enough to go through an anonymous money transfer service, and the buyer sent the tickets to an email account that seems to have been opened just for that one purpose and closed right afterward.

Castillo also managed to convince the library to share security-camera footage, and with my help, he found the woman. His hope was to match it to a photo online, but it's too grainy for a simple plug-and-play reverse image search. He's still working on that.

I've recorded two podcast episodes on Oliver's case, but the second was little more than a "nothing new" non-update. If Dinah has any leads, she's not sharing them, and I know better than to ask. Same with Castillo.

The episodes have done exactly what I needed them to do. The first went live the night I recorded it . . . and just in the nick of time. The connection between me, my podcast and Oliver hit the news the next morning, thanks to an anonymous tip. By then, my podcast episode about it had been live for nearly twelve hours, which meant the connection wasn't much of a scoop.

My favorite part was when the article claimed that I tried to hide my connection to Oliver by using my mother's surname. Dinah got in touch, and there was soon a correction, stating that I had never used Harding—my birth certificate surname is Gibson. Then there was the article that claimed I hadn't said a word about my brother's arrest on my podcast site . . . which was taken down soon after commenters pointed out that I'd already posted an entire episode on it.

In the end, news articles linking Oliver with me and *Known to the Victim* only served to direct people to my podcast, where they got insights into the story that the regular media lacked.

I spent two days dealing with an explosion of calls and texts. Then it went quiet. Yesterday, I even went out to coffee with my thesis advisor, and no one recognized me. The media coverage of Oliver's case was already petering out, a fire that dies from lack of oxygen.

I visited Oliver earlier today. He's struggling in jail but holding firm to his commitment to remain there. Dinah and I went to dinner afterward, and she told me that Castillo has proof that Oliver's security system had been hacked. With any luck, charges will now be dropped.

Buoyed by that, I spend the evening surfing my podcast forum. There's a section for Oliver's case, which Raven is monitoring, but she's sent me direct links to a few questions I can safely address. I'm doing that when a username lights up in the list of members currently online.

VAWSurvivor3.

That's the username of the woman who bought that ticket. The one who stood up at my show.

I click it to be sure. Yes, it's her—as I noted before, she'd signed up on the forum the day of the show, with only two posts from when she bought the ticket. She hasn't posted since.

My admin panel shows she's currently in the subforum devoted to my coverage of Oliver's case. The same subforum I'm in, along with a dozen others.

My username is AmyGibson, and I'm showing as "active" right now—always set that way when I'm answering posted questions. Otherwise, it looks as if I'm sneaking in and answering when no one knows I'm there, so they can't—God forbid—speak to me.

I hesitate. Then I click the link on her profile to send a chat message.

```
AmyGibson: Hello! It's Amy. I see you're new to
the forum, and I wanted to reach out and say
welcome!
```

I hold my breath and watch the green dot beside her name. It stays green. She didn't immediately log off. Nor did she answer, though. I count to five. Still green. Still no reply. Then I reread my message and wince.

```
AmyGibson: That sounded auto-generated, didn't it?
Sorry! I just popped in to post, and I've been
trying to say hi to new members. We have a lot
lately lol
```

Five seconds of silence. Her green light stays on. Then she answers.

> VAWSurvivor3: That's really you? Not some intern?

> AmyGibson: I'm not at the intern-hiring stage yet.
> Or the assistant-hiring stage or the social-media-
> manager-hiring stage. It's me

> VAWSurvivor3: Prove it

I try not to be taken aback.
Remember who this is. Not an actual subscriber. A woman who got up and confronted you in front of a room of people.

> AmyGibson: You want to see my ID? ;)

> VAWSurvivor3: Where were you living before you got
> your apartment?

A chill touches the back of my neck. *Stay calm, Amy.*

> AmyGibson: I grew up in Toronto, went to Montreal
> for school, and then I lived in my brother's
> guesthouse for a few years

> VAWSurvivor3: When did you move out?

> AmyGibson: After Oliver got married

VAWSurvivor3: Why?

We've been theorizing that the person framing Oliver knew Laura. An old friend. Whoever called the police did know things only a friend might. This is also something a friend might know. A test, yes ... and proving that she's not some random forum member.

AmyGibson: Newlyweds don't need anyone living in their backyard lol

I watch that dot. It stays green.

She's on the hook, and she has no interest in wriggling free.

Do I have her? Or does she have *me*?

With a jolt, I realize something I should be doing, and I quickly dial Castillo's number.

VAWSurvivor3: Your choice? Or his?

AmyGibson: I think I'd rather have shown ID. This feels a bit like therapy :)

"You okay?" Castillo says as he answers.

"Yes," I say. "Sorry for calling."

"It's only eight thirty, Gibson."

"I meant that I know you don't like talking on the phone."

"I'll survive. What's up?"

The woman types something. I resist the urge to read it and instead quickly fill him in.

"What?" he says, his voice sharpening. "You're talking to her online?"

"Hold on a sec."

I read her message.

```
VAWSurvivor3: Fine, you're Amy


AmyGibson: In the cyber-flesh. Now that we've
established that, did you have a question for me?
```

I glance away from the screen to focus on Castillo. "My producer has an ID set up to be incognito—it won't show when the user is online," I say. "I have the login info. I never use it—feels unethical. Do you want it? You can join the chat."

"She won't know I'm there?"

"No." I open my email and click a few more keys.

"So it lets someone eavesdrop on private conversations?" he says. "Yeah, 'feels unethical' is right."

"Which is why I don't use it. I've just sent you the login."

"Got it. Signing in now."

I turn back to the screen.

```
VAWSurvivor3: I remember you. Oliver's kid sister


AmyGibson: Wait, we've met?


VAWSurvivor3: Long time ago. You were a stuck-up
little bitch
```

I reread the line, as if I might have misinterpreted that. As if it might be a poor attempt at humor.

```
VAWSurvivor3: Everyone else buys your sweet-
little-sister act, but I never did. Just like I
never bought your brother's nice-guy act
```

"She's goading you." Castillo's voice makes me jump. "Yeah, I'm in. Just keep her talking. I'm trying to get her IP address."

I turn back to the screen. Before I can come up with something to say, she messages again.

```
VAWSurvivor3: You must have been delighted when
Laura was gone. Got your brother all to yourself
again. There was something creepy going on between
you two. You were sooo close. Still are, I bet
```

"She's still goading," Castillo says. "Keep acting confused."

"I *am* confused," I say. "No, I'm disgusted *and* confused."

"Yeah, that's the point. She's trying to get a rise out of you. Once she does, she'll sign off."

```
AmyGibson: I don't understand
```

```
VAWSurvivor3: Oh, I think you do, but in case you
don't, Sweet Innocent Amy, here's a tip. Your
brother is a little too interested in your
welfare. It's unnatural
```

AmyGibson: Unnatural for a brother to be interested in his sister's welfare?

VAWSurvivor3: On that podcast, you talk about predators, but you don't see the one circling you. You think the sun shines out of his ass. "Oh, he's staying in prison to protect me. How sweet!" Is that what he told you?

AmyGibson: Why would he need to protect me?

VAWSurvivor3: He doesn't. He just wants you to feel like he is. Big brother, looking out for you, sooo sweet. Whatever excuse he gave for not seeking bail, it'll end tomorrow

AmyGibson: ???

VAWSurvivor3: I'm using my crystal ball to foresee the future. Tomorrow, he'll decide you're safe. Or maybe he'll decide he can better protect you from the outside. He'll request bail. Mark my words. Within twenty-four hours, your brother will try coming home

The green light next to her name goes red.
"She's gone," I say to Castillo.
"I see that."
"Do you understand what she just said?" I ask.

"The bullshit about you and Oliver? She's trying to make you doubt him by creeping you out. As for the bail shit? It's an educated guess. Martine is due to be discharged from the hospital in a day or two. Dinah has been trying to convince Oliver that once Martine is safe at her parents' place in Toronto, there's no reason for him to stay in prison. Right now, he's resisting. I get it. It's shit inside, but it's safe—no one can do anything and frame him for it. Whoever you were talking to expects he'll go for bail as soon as Martine's safely away."

"Which is why she's saying that nonsense about him being in there to keep *me* safe. Diversion. If she says it's about Martine, I'd make the connection and realize it's an educated guess."

"Right. Because Martine is being released, she expects he'll try for bail soon. That will make it seem like she predicted it. As if she knows him."

A clicking of keys. Then a grunt.

"You couldn't track her IP," I say, interpreting that sound.

"No, I just got it."

So apparently, Castillo-grunts work for everything from disappointment to contempt to disbelief to success. That's helpful.

"You have her IP address?"

"Yeah, she tried to hide it, but she did a shit job. She obviously researched how to disguise her IP, but she used a program that was hacked months ago, with the hack readily available online."

"Short version being that you have her IP address."

"And her rough actual address." There's no change in inflection. His voice is its usual gravelly tone, somewhere between bored and "Why are you talking to me, and can we stop now?"

"That's great."

"Mm-hmm."

"It's not great?" I try. "You don't sound excited."

"This is my excited voice."

I choke on a half laugh. "I can tell."

"Excited would be waking up to realize I've won the lottery. Never happens."

"I'm sorry."

"Would help if I bought tickets," he says.

"In other words, the bar for exciting is set so high you never have to worry about reaching it."

"Yep. This is fine, but it's not case-breaking. It's just a lead." More tapping of keys. "You want to come with?"

"Come with . . . ?"

A snap, like the closing of a laptop. "She lives in St. Anthony. I'm going to scope it out. All I have is your description of her and a shitty photo."

"Hey, my description is good. You said so yourself."

"You got a good look at her, which is why I'm giving you the option of coming along. If I spot her, you can make an ID. Oh, no, wait. It's almost nine. Wow, when did it get so late?"

"Ha-ha." I close my own laptop. "Yes, I want to go. Should I meet you there?"

"You're on the way out of town. Give me twenty minutes, and don't come down to the lobby until I've texted."

TWELVE

I'm in Castillo's pickup, heading out of the city. The IP address is taking us to St. Anthony, a smaller city about a half hour from Grand Forks.

The region between Toronto and the Detroit border is a densely populated corridor, with Grand Forks being one of the largest cities along it, though it doesn't have much in the way of tourist attractions. There's no particular industry bent, as much as the city council tries to stake a claim on one or another. It's a university town, and all that goes with that, but in this region, nearly every large city is one of those. What Grand Forks offers is what most midsized cities offer: convenience. World-class hospitals, lots of green space, transit and an endless array of restaurants, shops and services. Want a city with more character, culture and attractions? Look elsewhere. Grand Forks is a fine place to live, but as with most cities, it's never going to top anyone's dream destination list.

St. Anthony is about a tenth of the size of Grand Forks. It'd been a working-class city until the factories moved out and the Grand Forks commuters moved in.

The address takes us to the courtyard area. There are gorgeous old homes here, like the ones I dreamed of in Grand Forks. Some are businesses and some are private residences, but a lot have been converted into apartments, and not exactly luxury accommodations at that.

Castillo stops in front of a variety store with barred windows and a sign advertising XXX video rentals.

"They don't get the internet in St. Anthony?" I ask.

Castillo follows my gaze. "Apparently not."

I can't tell whether the store is open. It's lit, but I suspect those lights stay on at all hours. Together with the metal bars, it looks as if it belongs in a much seedier part of town. We're only a couple of blocks from the downtown core, though, which means the security is to warn off desperate addicts more than armed robbers.

"Where's the address?" I ask.

Castillo waves north.

"Helpful," I murmur. "Why are we parked here?"

"The place we're going to is a quiet street. Too easy to look suspicious at this hour."

"It's nine thirty."

"Yeah, and if it was much later, we wouldn't even park this close. You see traffic?"

He has a point. One car has passed since we started talking. The street isn't deserted, but there are few people driving and even fewer walking.

"Come on," he says.

As I exit on the sidewalk side, he stands by the driver's door, as if considering. Then he roots around in the back seat. A moment later, he's trading his black hoodie for a navy windbreaker. Then he takes off his ball cap and runs a hand through his hair. A glance at the window, as if checking his reflection. A grunt and a shake of his head says he isn't satisfied with the results.

He adjusts the windbreaker, tugging it open and hooking his thumbs into his pockets, trying for a more casual look.

"No one's going to mistake you for an addict, if that's what you're worried about."

"Last time I did recon work in this damn city, someone called the cops on me. I was walking along the sidewalk. Might be better in this neighborhood but . . ." He shrugs.

When I frown, he says, "City's too fucking white. Like ninety-five percent, and that's no exaggeration—I checked the last census."

"Ah. Got it. Walk with me then. When you look like this"— I circle my face and give a big smile—"you can be caught breaking in and just pretend you got the wrong house."

He mutters and shakes his head. It's not only my skin color. It's my overall look. Fresh faced and cheerful, even when I feel neither.

Castillo falls in beside me.

"I'm going to take your arm, okay?" I say.

His eyes narrow, but he nods consent. I put my hand on his elbow.

"There," I say. "Now you're just out for a nice walk with a nice girl."

"Instead of kidnapping her at gunpoint?"

I roll my eyes. He leads the way down a side street and points out the address with a jerk of his head. It's one of the houses that's been converted into apartments. An upper floor and a lower, from the mailboxes at the front. Lights illuminate both levels.

Castillo keeps walking until we're around the corner.

"Next step?" I say.

He pulls out what looks like a single-eye scope from his pocket. "Talk to me," he says.

I blather nonsense as he uses the scope to look over the low fence into the upper windows of the target house.

"Kids," he says. "A couple even younger than you with a little one."

"Wow. Babies having babies. Someone should call child services. For the record, I'm twenty-eight."

"You sure?"

"Wanna see ID?"

He checks the scope again.

"How old are you?" I say. "Forty?"

That makes him startle in the most satisfying way. His glare is lethal . . . until he sees my smirk.

I'd peg him at early thirties, though the scarring on his cheek makes him seem older. I calculate his approximate age by knowing he was in the army for eight or nine years and Ioana saying something about him going straight into the service from high school.

He lowers the scope. "Definitely twentysomethings in the upper apartment. Can't tell with the lower one."

"I could knock on the door," I say. "Pretend I'm looking for a friend."

"Yeah, because if it's our target, she'd never recognize you."

"Er, right."

"I'll knock," he says. "You stay on the sidewalk near the front window. Curtains are open. Check whoever answers the door and try to see anyone else inside. First, though, I'm getting license numbers from the cars in the driveway."

We walk back. When we round the corner, he pauses, as if peering through the dark at the house number. When he does the same at our target house, he also snaps photos of the license plates for both cars in the driveway. Then he shows me where to stand, in a spot where I can see through that big bay window, but I'm also half-hidden by a fence between this lot and the next.

He rings the doorbell. A moment later, a man answers. My brain automatically collects data: white, dark haired, clean shaven, lean build with a bit of a stomach. He's not much older than Castillo, shirtless, wearing sweatpants, a beer in hand. Castillo consults his phone, as if reading something from it. The man shakes his head.

Through the window, I see another figure moving into the living room to see who's at the door. It's another guy around the same age. Someone sits up on the sofa. A third guy.

Castillo chats with the guy at the door, and everything is cool. There's even a laugh that seems to come from Castillo.

"Thanks!" Castillo says as he trots back down the steps. "Appreciate the help. Sorry to disturb you."

"No worries," the guy calls after him. "You sure you don't want a beer? It's the good stuff."

Castillo throws back an actual smile. "Nope, got my girl waiting." He waves toward me.

"Bring her," the guy says. "We've got plenty."

I don't catch what Castillo says, but it's good-natured, lots of smiles and laughs from both. As soon as he reaches me, that smile is gone, and he rubs his face, as if the performance was painful.

"I could only see two other guys about the same age," I say when he reaches me.

"Yeah. I spotted them. He says there's a woman living across the street, couple doors down, could be our troll."

When I raise my brows, he lifts his hand. There's a woman's necklace in it.

"I said I found this on the sidewalk," he explains, "right after I'd seen someone matching the description of my target. When I came back around the corner to ask if it was theirs, they were gone, suggesting they live nearby. If there's someone at home fitting the description, they'll call them to the door."

"They'll say it's not their necklace, and you leave, having made the ID. Nice."

"Didn't help here."

"But the IP address led to this physical address. Wait! It's connected to the WiFi address, right? You have a way of tracking the IP to a WiFi address, and maybe to a physical device, which is coming from that house, but the signal could be used by a neighbor."

"Yeah." He squints along the road. "Guy said the woman neighbor is in that narrow house over there. The redbrick one with the porch swing. Lives alone. We'll get a closer look."

We continue down the road. Across the street from the house, he turns me so my back is to it and then talks as he peers through a lit window.

"TV's on," he says. "But if she's in there, she's out of my line of sight. Guess I'm going over."

He takes out the necklace and finds a spot where I can watch the door while out of sight.

"Remember she might have been in disguise," he says. "Wig, loose clothing, and so on. Look past all that."

"Got it."

He approaches the house. When he rings the bell, a woman rises from the living room. The sheers are drawn, making it hard to see. She disappears into the front hall. When she doesn't open the door, Castillo knocks again. I know she must be there. When I squint, I can make out a peephole. She's looking through it and deciding she's not at home. It's past nine, and there's a big guy—a stranger—on her front porch ringing her bell.

After a third knock, Castillo comes back to me.

"She's there," I say.

"Yeah, I know. Got a look at me and decided not to open the door."

"So what do—?" I stop. "Don't turn around. She's pulling back the sheers to get a better look at you."

"Can she see you?"

"I don't think so. She can only tell that you're talking to a woman." I smile up at him and touch his arm. He tenses.

"Sorry," I whisper. "Just trying to look cozier."

He grunts.

"She's still watching and . . ." I exhale. "That's not her."

"You sure?"

"She's closer to seventy than forty, shorter and heavier than the woman I saw."

He shakes his head and mutters, "Fuck." Then he shoves his hands in his pockets and starts walking.

I jog to keep up with him. "So what does this mean?"

"That I screwed up." He takes a few more steps. "I was smug, wasn't I? Getting her IP address so easily. She made it easy."

"She's using misdirection."

"Yeah."

We get into the truck. A few minutes later, as we're driving along the main street, country music blares from a tavern. It's the kind of place that boasts having the best wings in town, despite a decided lack of competition.

I glance toward the restaurant, and I'm struck by the urge to ask whether Castillo wants to grab a beer and wings before I return to the confines of my little apartment.

"You need to get back?" Castillo says.

I jump at that, my gaze going to the tavern. I pull it away fast, but he says, "You got time for a bite?"

"Uh, yes. Sure." My laugh sounds a little forced. "I'm starting to get cabin fever in my apartment."

"Yeah . . ." The word trails off, and there's a note of something like reluctance in it. "I need to discuss something with you. Business."

My cheeks heat, and I'm happy for the darkness. "Of course. That's what I figured. I just meant that I'd love a quick bite someplace where I can relax."

He's quiet, and I replay my words.

"This might not be the most relaxing . . ." He trails off. Then he clears his throat. "It's an . . . ethical . . ." He shakes his head sharply. "Forget I mentioned it. We can talk tomorrow. You want a snack. Let's get you a snack."

THIRTEEN

I don't press Castillo for details before we're in the restaurant or he might decide to take me home. I wait until I've ordered my beer and wings. It's the two of us at an indoor table, the only occupied one, everyone else outside despite the chill.

"What did you want to talk to me about?" I say, once my meal has arrived.

I expect he'll say "Nothing." Instead, he silently attacks his burger, ripping off a chunk and seeming to swallow it whole before taking another bite.

I wait.

"Ioana wants me to look after you," he says. "Put your interests first. Seemed easy enough. I'm working with a lawyer who is trying to free your brother from a wrongful charge. That's in your best interests."

"Okay."

"But what if it's not?" He swipes a fry through ketchup and crams it into his mouth.

My gut tenses. "You think Oliver shot Martine?"

"No, no. That part's clear."

"But some other part is not."

Another bite of his burger. "I shouldn't have taken the job with Dinah."

I soften my voice. "I'm very glad you did."

"But I failed to see the possibility that it could conflict with keeping you safe. I promised Ioana I'd do that, and now . . ." A grunt and another bite.

"Can you talk to Ioana? Get her take on whatever this problem is?"

"Shift the ethical dilemma to her shoulders?"

"Ah. Yeah, that doesn't work." I sit back and sip my beer. "Let me guess. You found out something that you think I should know, but you can't tell me because you work for Dinah, and she hasn't approved it."

"Not exactly. But yeah, something's bugging me, and I think you should know, but if I'm working for Dinah, I shouldn't go down this road. She knows nothing about it, so I'm not directly violating a client's privacy, but I know it's a violation . . ." He crams in another fry. "I'm babbling."

"It's too late now to tell me to forget it. I'll be imagining the worst."

He takes a gulp of his beer. Then he sets the glass down with a clack. "I don't believe Oliver shot Martine. I don't believe he killed Laura. It's just . . ."

"Something's bugging you."

He glances around, as if hoping for a sudden grease fire in the kitchen.

"Dinah will call you tomorrow with something the cops found," he says. "I'd already uncovered it, and she was trying to figure out what to do with it when the cops beat her to the punch. It's Saturday. The media won't have it for a day or two."

"What did you find?" I ask, my voice tight.

"Martine had a couple of private music students age out recently. She wanted to replace them. She liked the extra income. Your brother had discouraged that, saying she was doing too much already."

My hands tighten around my glass. "Echoes of what the tipster said about Laura. That Oliver was interfering with her business. Oliver admitted he was concerned that Laura was taking on too much and blowing deadlines, but it could be seen as classic controlling behavior. A partner is resentful of other claims on your time but phrases it to make him sound like a thoughtful guy who's only concerned about your well-being."

"Yeah. The tipster said Laura claimed she was losing friends and business because of missed messages. Martine wasn't able to replace her students—no one seriously answered her postings—and she was worried there was a reason. Like a bad review or something. She recently discovered it was actually . . ."

"Missing messages," I whisper.

He nods. "Potential clients were emailing her, as requested, and she was only getting the worst of them—creepy older guys, and parents chewing down her fees."

"Okay." *Breathe, just breathe.*

"I found out she'd been hacked. Someone was deleting all legitimate interest. The police have discovered the same thing."

"You think Oliver was deleting those messages, and he'd done the same with Laura, interfering with her friendships and business."

"With Laura, we have a friend who says Laura claimed to be missing messages. This friend thought Laura was making up excuses for her bad behavior. Those were texts, which are much harder to interfere with. With Martine, someone was accessing her email from a device she doesn't own and a location with a very well-hidden IP address. Also, when I say she was 'hacked' I should be more precise. They figured out the password."

"Or had access to it," I whisper.

"Which doesn't mean it's Oliver. Martine didn't stumble on the missing emails by accident. Someone contacted her anonymously. You want my theory?"

I nod mutely.

"Laura was blaming the missed meetings and such on texts gone astray," he says. "People do that all the time. Oh, I didn't get your message. Oh, didn't *you* get *my* message?"

Like him emailing me asking for help, and me supposedly pretending not to get the email. That stings, but he's right. It's easy to blame technology because it *does* happen.

He continues, "The tipster was a friend who knew Laura was blaming missed texts and suspected it was an excuse. This tipster then accesses Martine's email—there are many ways to get login information. She finds business emails to delete and then calls in the tip."

That makes sense. I just . . .

I run a podcast about things like this. Control issues that are easily explained away.

Does that make me more attuned to the possibility my brother really did delete those messages? Or does it just make me suspicious and paranoid, doubting even when the explanation is clear to a professional private eye like Castillo.

When you're a hammer, everything looks like a nail.

When you've devoted your life to spotting predators, every dog looks like a wolf.

Castillo doesn't wait for my response. "Anyway, Dinah will tell you about it tomorrow, and she wants you to put it into your podcast to jump ahead of the press. Including the part about it being an anonymous tip, like the original call to the police."

"Which means this isn't the ethically awkward thing you needed to tell me."

"I don't need to *tell* you something. I need to ask . . ." He looks at his burger-free plate and then at my mountain of wings.

"Would you like some of my wings, Dean?"

"What? No."

"I'll trade you wings for fries."

"You want fries? Sure."

I use my fork to take a few fries and then pile wings onto his plate. If it's not a remotely even trade, he doesn't comment, just digs in.

"Forgot to eat dinner," he says. "Didn't realize it until I got my burger."

"Oh, I know what that's like. Get wrapped up in work, and then eat something and suddenly realize you're starving."

He nods and downs two wings before saying, "After I found Martine's account had been accessed, I started thinking about your emails disappearing."

I stop with the beer glass halfway to my lips. I put it back down. "The email you sent about your cousin."

"Two emails."

"Okay, yes, two, but it happens, right? Emails go astray."

He's quiet for so long that I start to fidget.

"Dean?"

"It does happen, but in reliable ways. It can go into the spam folder, but you said you checked that. Someone can mistype the address. I didn't do that. Or it can bounce back to the sender, which also didn't happen." He meets my gaze. "Do you have a lot of emails disappear, Amy?"

"No."

"Never?"

My cheeks heat. "I can't say *never*, but when it happens, I know the sender is lying. Like when I meet a guy who takes my number or email, and then when I bump into him again, he claims he texted or emailed or whatever. Standard social white lies."

"Assholes," he says. "Yeah, okay, people do that shit, but how often would someone say they emailed you and you never got it?"

I think hard. I never really considered that. Like I said, the ones that stick in my head are the ones where a guy blew me off and then felt obligated to pretend he tried making contact. Otherwise, it's things like being a teaching assistant and having undergrads swear they sent in assignments . . . but they're unable to show me the sent email. Or someone thinking they'd emailed me, but weren't sure, so they resent.

Is that suspicious? Oh, I'd love to say that those guys were all *desperate* to connect with me, and their emails and texts did vanish, but my ego isn't that bulletproof. And it's not as if we're talking dozens of times. Two, maybe three? No more than is average for single young women who meet guys at bars while out with friends. The guys sobered up and changed their minds.

"Maybe one every few months?" I say. "I understand where you're going, Dean. If Oliver deleted Laura's messages and Martine's emails, he could also be tampering with mine. But what possible reason would there be? No one's going to delete emails asking me to speak to your cousin's wife after his murder."

"Yeah, I know." He takes another fry from his plate. "That's the problem. There's no reason for it, and I don't think Oliver was tampering with the others, either."

"Your emails went astray. I know you don't believe that but—"

"They were read."

"What?"

He pulls meat from another wing. "As a PI, it's in my best interests to use an app that returns read receipts. I want to know when someone's read my email so they can't pull that bullshit. *Oh, I never got your invoice. Oh, sure, I said I'd answer your questions, but I never got them.* Tech-savvy people know how to turn off the read receipts because, yeah, it's invasive. Yours aren't turned off."

"It's like texts, right? Read receipts can show when they've been delivered or read."

"Yeah. Those emails were delivered and read. That's why I was so sure you'd seen them. That's why I was pissed."

"You knew they went to the right address, and you knew they were read. If I didn't read them"—I hold his gaze—"which I swear I did not, then someone with access to my account did and deleted them."

"Yeah."

"But again, why?"

He scratches his beard stubble. "I don't know. I've looked for other possibilities. Last week, when we discussed it, you seemed serious about not getting them, so I tried to think up an alternate explanation. I couldn't. Then Martine's missing emails came up, and it got me thinking about yours. The problem, like you said, is motive. The only one I can come up with was someone wanting you to look like a hypocrite. Oliver wouldn't do that. Someone else, though? Can you think of anyone? An ex-boyfriend, maybe?"

"Between the podcast and my thesis, I haven't had time to date in . . . a while. My last actual relationship ended two years ago and on decent terms."

"So do you want me to drop this?"

"No. I'm kind of freaked out, to be honest. Especially if Oliver is being targeted by someone who can crack passwords. What else could I have missed?"

"Do you want me to check your account?"

"Please."

He meets my gaze. "Even if it turned out to be Oliver?"

I lock eyes with him. "Especially if it turned out to be Oliver."

As Castillo expected, Dinah calls me the next day to talk about the unauthorized email access—Martine's, not mine. I haven't heard back from Castillo on that, and I refuse to bug him, however much it's bothering me. It's the weekend, after all. He deserves a break.

I keep thinking maybe this will vindicate me and prove I didn't get Castillo's emails . . . and then I realize I'm hoping someone has hacked my account and been deleting emails. I'm not even sure how I'd deal with that. Castillo sent his six months ago. That'd mean months of missed emails. And what if the hacker did more than delete them? What if they were replying as me?

I can't think about that. I need to focus on the rest. After I got the call from Dinah, I recorded the podcast I'd scripted once I got back from the evening out with Castillo. I've already established that I'm no longer following my weekly posting routine. I will post at least once a week, more often as I have updates. This is an update.

Raven thought that following Oliver's case would be an easy solution to my problem. I just need to be impartial. How tough could it be?

How tough? I spent three hours writing and rewriting a fifteen-minute episode. I can't just present the facts. That would take three minutes, and my listeners expect more. They expect *me*, Amy Gibson. They expect my opinions, personal thoughts and musings.

In this case, I also need to raise the possibility that the anonymous tipster is the one doing the email tampering . . . while in no way sounding as if I'm saying Oliver *couldn't* have done it. I walk that tightrope, and then I do what I must—all apologies to my brother. I talk about how things like deleting messages are straight from the predator handbook, control and gaslighting in one.

The podcast is up by midmorning. Then I'm in a holding pattern again. I don't hear from Castillo. I don't hear from Dinah.

I do spend a couple of hours in a meeting with Raven. I lost a third sponsor when I went public as Oliver's sister, but two bigger potential sponsors are ready to sign on as my subscriber numbers shoot skyward.

I feel guilty about that. No, I feel like *shit* about that. My only consolation is that Dinah is pleased with my podcasts and that Oliver listened to the episodes and had no objections. That makes me feel a little less like the ghoul profiting from her brother's misfortune.

It's otherwise a quiet day. Excruciatingly quiet. Time ticks past, and when it's finally late enough to go to bed, I practically dive in, just wanting the day to be over. Instead, I lie there, staring at the wall, until I break down and take a sleeping pill.

When my phone rings, I'm so deeply asleep that I think I'm dreaming of my alarm going off. It seems to take an impossibly long time for me to comprehend that my cell phone is ringing, and then longer still to realize I need to answer it.

Without thinking to check caller ID, I hit Talk and groan, "Hello?"

"Amy? It's Dinah."

That has me scrambling up. "Sorry, I was asleep."

A strained chuckle. "I'd hope so, at two in the morning. Take a moment. I need to speak to you."

Those words are a bucket of ice water. Oliver's lawyer is calling at 2 a.m. and needs to speak to me.

"What happened? Is Oliver—"

"He's fine. Let me say that first."

"Okay, but—"

"There was an incident. An attack. At the jail."

My breath stops, and I can't breathe. I manage to say, "Oliver was *attacked*?"

"Yes, but he's all right. He was taken to the hospital. They're assessing him now and deciding whether surgery might be required."

"Surgery?" My voice squeaks as I remember Martine, shot and rushed to surgery.

"I wanted you to know before you heard it anywhere else. I will keep you updated—"

"Which hospital?" I slap on the bedroom light. "I'm heading out."

"There's nothing you can do, Amy."

"I can be there. In the waiting room or wherever you are." I pause, bra in hand. "I can, right?"

"You can, although I have to warn you that you won't be able to see him. He's under guard."

"That's fine. Just tell me where he is."

FOURTEEN

I hurry out to the parking lot. I'm moving on autopilot as my brain bounces between worry and self-recrimination. Is Oliver really okay? What if Dinah just said that so I wouldn't panic? What exactly happened? I have no idea because I didn't damn well ask.

Dinah said he'd been attacked, and that could mean anything. Why didn't I ask? Why didn't I call her right back? Why didn't I text? I should do that now. No, I'm heading there, and I can't bother her with questions that will only beget more questions.

I'm jogging to my car when a shadow moves. A figure, over by the line of evergreens separating the parking lot from the neighborhood beyond. It startles me at first. While the building has underground parking, after what happened to my mother, I prefer the outdoor lot, with a busy road running past. Well, busy during the day. It's silent now, as it had been the night Castillo met me out front.

Seeing the figure startles me, as if I've forgotten I'm outdoors at night. But then I relax. It's a parking lot. Someone has parked and is just coming home after an evening out.

Except it's not eleven o'clock. It's after two.

I'm alone in an outdoor parking lot at two in the morning.

No, it's worse. I'm *not* alone.

Part of me shoves the thought aside in annoyance. *Really, Amy? People work shifts. People go to bars. People, as you may recall from your distant past, go on dates that last into the wee hours of the morning.*

Don't be so silly, Amy. It's a well-lit outdoor parking lot.

Then there's the other part. The part that gets angry with myself for getting angry with myself.

Are you dismissing a legitimate concern? Of all people, you know what can happen in parking lots. Don't pull that shit.

The correct path is route number three. Don't let myself get distracted by either of those reactions, and focus. Act as I would if I were walking past a yard and a dog started barking ferociously—be alert and aware.

That would be easier if the person had walked past those trees and continued on toward the apartment building. They haven't. They've disappeared into the shadows, and there they remain.

Shit.

Am I sure I saw someone?

Yes.

Really sure?

Yes, damn it. Stop that. Don't second-guess. I am absolutely certain that a human-sized figure stepped into those shadows.

Someone checking out the cars, looking for an easy break-in. But in this part of the city, that's rare. I'm sure there *are* addicts— they just haven't reached the stage where they need to be checking out cars for spare change. The neighborhood isn't connected to any areas that see that significant foot traffic, and it's a long bus ride from there to here, with the buses having stopped hours ago.

That doesn't mean it isn't someone looking for easy money. A teenager or young adult who lives here with their family and has an addiction to feed.

Be alert. Be aware. Don't make an obvious target.

I don't have my purse or laptop bag. I grabbed my keys and my phone, which is also my wallet. It is almost certain that whoever I saw is just waiting for me to leave. They aren't yet ready to mug someone for twenty bucks, and I'll give them no encouragement to start. Walk with my chin up, gaze moving across the lot. Alert and aware.

My brain catalogs and assesses details as I go. My car isn't directly under one of the many lights, but it's close enough to one that I won't be surprised by anyone leaping from the shadows. There's no car on the driver's side of mine, which is even better—before I get there, I can see the entire left side, and there's nobody there.

When I reach the car, I already have my key fob in hand, and I'm glad I accepted Oliver's hand-me-down car a few years ago. He'd been concerned about mine, which was, well, what I could afford: a ten-year-old base model. He convinced me to take his old Audi because it had all the modern safety features, including a key fob that lets me unlock the door as I'm reaching for it, with my gaze still up and alert. In one smooth move, I'm inside with the doors locked. Then, heart stuttering, I can't remember whether I heard the car doors unlock. I *had* locked them the last time I drove the car, right?

My gaze lifts ever so slowly to the rearview mirror. The back seat is empty. Exhaling, I twist to be absolutely certain.

You're fine, Amy. You startled someone casing cars. When you come back, remember to park under a light and double-check that the doors are locked.

I start the car and hit Reverse. Oliver jokes that I'm a bit of a stunt driver. He's far more cautious, which is why that ding in his current car pained him so much—God forbid someone think *he'd* been careless.

Mom taught me to drive, just as she taught me how to change oil and replace tires. Having a car like this, with all the cameras and sensors, sometimes feels like cheating. I reverse fast and then hit the gas and turn sharp, heading for the exit at the back of the lot. I like that one better—it avoids a stoplight that'll take forever to change at this time of night.

When I make that sharp turn, the row of evergreens bursts into light in my halogen headlamps. They're so bright that I'm constantly having people flash their high beams at me. And they're bright enough to light up the shadows around those evergreens ... where whoever had been stalking the parking lot retreated to hide.

I spot the person's back. They're on the move, and all I can see is a dark-hooded jacket on a figure, maybe my height or a little shorter. A boy? A woman? Then, as if in a split-second delayed reaction to that burst of light, they glance over their shoulder and—

I hit the brakes. My heart stops. I swear it just stops.

It is a single second. A flash of a woman's face, turned away fast even as my brain is processing.

I sit there, stunned and breathless.

It isn't possible.

Isn't it?

Oh, hell yes, it's possible.

I slam the car into Park, throw open the door and get out. I'm striding forward when I realize I have just done a very reckless thing.

I realize it . . . and I don't stop. I need to be sure of what I saw, and the fury over the possibility keeps me striding forward, and it takes a moment to realize no one is there. She's gone, footfalls slapping over the ground beyond the evergreens. I break into a run. There's a path through the trees where people have pushed through to make a shortcut from the neighborhood behind to the main road. I run through it just in time to see her getting into a car.

Oh, no, you don't get away that easily.

I race back to my own car. It's still running, and I'm grateful for the distraction that kept me from shutting it off. I put it into Drive and roar from the parking lot just as her car speeds from where she'd pulled over.

I hit the gas, which would work much better if she didn't do the same. It'd also work better if I dared drive as fast as she does through this residential neighborhood. Yes, it's two in the morning, but I still see a cat crossing the road and someone driving the other way—pets and people I could hurt—and I cannot go full out, pedal to the floor. She has no such compunction, of course, and I rage at that as I tear after her, not daring to do what I know I must: get in front of her and cut her off.

Get closer, a calm voice whispers at my ear. *If you lose her, you need to have something for Castillo.*

That's what finally settles that frothing rage. I imagine myself admitting to Castillo that I'd had this woman in my sights and I lost her. He'll give me shit for pursuing her, but I damn well better be able to give him a make and model and license plate number.

I take deep breaths. Then I hit my high beams and get as close to her car as I dare.

Toyota Corolla. White. Older model. No obvious rust or damage. License plate ... ?

Now I'm cursing again. A few years back, Ontario switched to a plate with laminate blue lettering that's known to peel off, leaving white letters and numbers against a white background. She's made sure hers is as faded as possible. Unlike removing or obscuring the plate, this won't get her pulled over. I turn off the high beams and manage to make out a 3 and an *O* ... or maybe an 8 and a *D*.

I need to cut her off. Yes, I'm well aware that I'm doing a very dangerous and very reckless thing. I imagine Castillo throwing up his hands and giving up on me, every iota of credit I've gained lost.

But what are my alternatives? Call and ask him to take over a car chase?

I know this is probably a bad idea, but I have her in my sights and I am not letting go. I need to get out of this neighborhood, and once I do, we're on open country roads for two kilometers.

Just get her there. Let her think she's winning and—

She zooms around a corner, and I let out a crow of victory. She's leaving the neighborhood. She had to, eventually, but she's tired of this game already, and she's on a straightaway for the traffic light. The same light I'd been trying to avoid because it's on a sensor at night and takes forever to trip.

Is she going to make a right turn at the light? That would take her into the countryside.

Please, make a right. Please, please, please. Otherwise, she'll have to run a red, but it's not as if there's any actual traffic to worry about.

I gun it. She does the same, so I ease back a little. No need to alarm her now. Whichever way she goes, I'll have a minimum of two kilometers to catch up before she hits civilization again.

Looks as if she's going straight through the red. Fine, I—

A truck is coming along the crossroad. A white cube van, taking its time, seeing that the Walk light is still on, meaning the light won't change anytime soon. No need to rush . . . Putting it on a collision course with the car I'm chasing.

Look right, I want to shout. *Look and see cars roaring your way and either hit the gas or the brakes.*

The cube van continues along, the driver oblivious.

I'm running on pure adrenaline. I calculate the trajectory. She has to stop. If she doesn't, that van is going to hit her.

She does not stop. She flies through the intersection, the cube van driver seeing her at the last moment and hitting the brakes, spinning their vehicle right in front of me, as my target continues on, unscathed.

I brake hard. The driver—a middle-aged guy—looks up from his shock, lifting a fist . . . only to see me and stop.

Apparently, I don't quite look like the young male stunt driver he expected.

I wave apologetically and drive carefully around the back of his vehicle so he doesn't get a better look at me or my car.

Soon I'm on the through road and hitting the gas again, but there's no sign of a car ahead of me, not even the distant glow of red rear lights.

I've lost her.

I'm so distracted by what just happened that I'm inside the hospital, wondering where to go, before I remember that Dinah wanted me to call when I arrived so she could walk me up to the waiting room. Even then, I don't call right away. I stand off to the side in the Emergency ward, holding my phone.

Am I going to tell her what just happened?

She needs to know. But right now, there's nothing she can do about it, and everyone's focus needs to be on my brother. Get past that, and then I'll figure out how to handle this.

I call Dinah, and she comes down to escort me to where we can wait for Oliver.

"He's in surgery," she says as we head along an eerily empty hall. Somewhere in the distance, gurney wheels squeak.

"What happened?"

"He was attacked."

I bite back frustration at the short answer. "By his cellmate?"

She hits the elevator button. "We don't know."

"How? It was the middle of the night. No one else could have done it."

The elevator arrives, and we get on.

"It happened earlier this evening. They were having a movie night. There was a commotion, a bit of a shoving match. Oliver was getting out of the way when he went down. The guards cleared up the fracas and found him on the floor. He'd been stabbed."

"What?"

"Someone stabbed him with a homemade knife."

"A shiv?" Even as I say that, my cheeks heat, feeling silly. It's the right word . . . just not one I ever expected to use in real life.

My brother was shivved in a prison riot.

I want to laugh hysterically and scream at the same time.

"Amy?" Dinah lays her hand on my folded arms, and I look up to see the elevator doors are open and two nurses are waiting to step on.

I murmur an apology to them as I hurry off the elevator, letting Dinah steer me into a corner.

"Take a moment," she says.

I move away. "I'm fine. So Oliver was caught up in a disturbance at the prison and stabbed."

"That's what it looks like."

There's another question there, but I hold it back in favor of the more critical one. "Is he okay? Is he going to *be* okay? How serious is the wound?"

"It wasn't a deep cut, thankfully, but it did do some damage. The surgery is to stop internal bleeding."

"Okay."

"Surgery always comes with risks, but this wasn't a case of rushing him into surgery in hopes of saving his life."

I shiver, and she makes a face, her hand gripping my arm.

"That sounded more dire than I intended," she says.

"I know what you mean," I say. "They're operating now to avoid bigger problems later, rather than performing an emergency lifesaving procedure."

"Yes."

I look down the hall, and she takes that as a sign that I'm ready to continue on. We return to the hall, and she leads me to a tiny waiting room. I glance around. Small, perfectly square room. Four chairs, all of them empty save for Dinah's jacket on one. There's a wall TV, but it's turned off.

As I take a seat, a nurse pops her head in, and Dinah goes over to speak to her. I'm hoping it's news, but the way the nurse's head swivels my way tells me she was just wondering about the newcomer. When she leaves, Dinah settles into a chair next to me.

I say, "Are we sure it was an accident?"

She glances over, saying nothing.

"The stabbing," I say. "Was it definitely an accident? Was Oliver just in the wrong place at the wrong time?"

Her gaze finally rests on me. She's going to make me finish. Force me to say what I'm thinking, even if I'm trying not to squirm at how paranoid it sounds.

"Is it possible someone targeted Oliver?" I say. "That they took advantage of the fight to stab him? Or that the whole fight was started as a diversion for stabbing him?"

"Yes."

"Yes to . . . ?"

"All of that."

FIFTEEN

Oliver is in the recovery room. The doctor said the surgery went well. The bleeding has stopped. He'll be in the hospital for a couple of days before he's free to go.

Free to go back to jail.

"Oh, he isn't returning to jail," Dinah says. "Not for one minute longer than necessary, and not at all if I have anything to say about it. He'll request bail now."

"He said that?"

"No, but if he still refuses, then he's finding himself a new lawyer. I don't think he was accidentally caught in a prison squabble last night. He was targeted. With Martine heading to Toronto, there's no reason he needs to stay in jail."

"Agreed." I pick up a cardboard cup of coffee, see the cream congealed on top and set it back down. "Don't forget we were warned about this."

She frowns. "Warned?"

"Dean told you about my online interaction with the woman who showed up at my show, right?"

"Yes, but . . ."

"She said Oliver would seek bail in twenty-four hours. She used it to imply he wasn't as committed to the course as he pretended."

Dinah curses under her breath.

"Yep," I say. "Awfully coincidental. She made it seem like a warning *about* Oliver, but in retrospect . . ."

"It was a threat. One we'd only see once he was stabbed twenty-four hours later."

"He was staying in jail because he thought that would be safest for everyone else."

"And whoever is doing this showed it isn't safe for *him.*"

"Or they want him to think it isn't safe, so he gets bail, and then he's out, where they can frame him for something else." I make a face. "I really have seen too many movies, right?"

She doesn't answer for a moment. Her gaze has gone distant. Then she snaps back to herself and shakes her head. "No, not at all. I think that's a possibility we need to consider. Strongly consider."

There's something else.

The words are on my lips when Dinah's phone rings. A hand flap my way tells me that she needs to take this. As she goes to leave the room, I try to mouth that I need to speak to her, rather urgently, but she doesn't look back.

If it was that urgent, Amy, why haven't you told her yet?

Because . . .

Because I'm in the hospital, after my brother has been stabbed, and what happened earlier feels unreal. It feels impossible. I keep imagining telling Dinah and seeing her look of disbelief.

No, seeing her look of *concern.*

She'll think I'm mistaken. I'd just been woken by the news that my brother was in the hospital. I'd seen someone skulking around the lot, mistaken her for another in the dark and scared the shit out of a stranger by chasing her through the neighborhood. The fact that I actually still insist on who I saw proves that I . . .

Well, I'm not in the best place, mentally, am I?

No, I trust Dinah. She will question my story as if I were a witness on the stand, and then she will draw her own conclusions.

I'll tell her as soon as she comes back. I must—with each hour that passes, it'll seem odder that I didn't mention it, and more likely that I didn't mention it because I doubt what I saw . . . which I do not.

I wait for about fifteen minutes before I step into the hall, looking for Dinah. There's no sign of her.

I glance both ways as I listen for the sound of her talking on her phone, but because it's no longer the middle of the night, there are voices everywhere. I follow one that sounds vaguely like Dinah to find a volunteer stopped with her breakfast cart, talking to a nurse.

The smell of the food hits, and I never thought I'd say this about hospital food, but it sets my stomach growling. I check my watch. After eight? Okay, that explains it. I walk up and down the hall, listening for Dinah.

A nurse stops me with, "Can I help you?"

"I'm just waiting for my brother to get out of recovery," I say. "But I was with someone else, and I was just looking for her." I describe Dinah, and the nurse says she saw her talking on her phone while walking.

"Can you tell me where I could grab breakfast for us?" I ask.

The nurse directs me to the dining hall on the third floor. Getting there seems simple enough, and it would be in a regular rectangular-shaped building. This one has wings going off in all directions, and somewhere along the way, I make a wrong turn, because when I get off the elevator on the third floor, I don't even see the cafeteria listed on the directional arrows.

When I inhale, though, I smell coffee. I head in that direction, imagining a cartoon version of myself, drooling and following the tendrils of caffeinated brew. In the cartoon world, that works well. In the real one, I'm not a bloodhound. I lose the smell and have to admit I probably just caught a whiff of someone passing with a coffee in hand.

I'm in a busy corridor, looking for anyone who might direct me. Then the smell comes again . . . and I catch sight of people carrying cups from both Tim Hortons and Starbucks. Two more steps, and I stop short, my chin jerking up as I see one of those people with her morning joe.

It's a woman in her midthirties. Willowy build. Long dark-blond hair pulled up into a messy bun. Perfectly cut features that have men and women doing a double take, even with the dark circles under her eyes. Dressed in a long shirt and yoga pants, she's moving slowly, still recovering from her injury, but otherwise, the hospital band around her wrist is the only sign she's a patient.

"Martine," I say.

She jerks back so fast that milky coffee puddles on the top of her cup.

"Oh," she says, and her gaze darts around, as if I'm Castillo-sized and blocking her exit.

I move to the side so she doesn't feel trapped, but she only stands there, the pulse in her neck quickening.

"I shouldn't be speaking to you," she says.

"I just—"

"I can't talk about it, Amy. I'm sorry. I know how much you care about . . ." She inhales. "Please don't. Okay?"

"I—"

"You love your brother. I get that. I really do because I . . ." She swallows. "I'm sorry this is happening to you, and if he had nothing to do with it, then I'm sorry it's happening to him, but I can't fix this, Amy. It's in the hands of the court. I only told them what I saw."

"I know, and I wasn't going to mention Oliver. I wanted to know how you're doing."

She pulls back. "Oh."

"What happened to you—however it came about—is . . ." I shake my head. "I'm so, so sorry. I hope you're okay. That's all I wanted to say." I pause. "Are you leaving today?"

She nods, fingering her cup as if eager to be gone.

"Good luck," I say. "Oh, and because I wouldn't want you to get a nasty surprise, I should let you know I'm not here by accident. Oliver was admitted last night." I lift my hands. "Don't worry. You won't see him. He's under guard. But he was attacked in the jail. Stabbed by another inmate. He's fine. He's just recovering from surgery."

"Oh!" Her eyes round.

"Anyway, I'll let you go," I say. "I just wanted you to know this was only a random encounter. I literally bumped into you in my pursuit of coffee. I'm glad you're doing okay, Martine. I really am."

I start to walk away.

"Amy?"

I turn.

"I could . . ." She glances back in the direction of the cafeteria. "I'd like to know what happened to Oliver, if you have a moment."

"Sure. I need to get upstairs soon—I want to be there when Oliver wakes up—but I can fill you in while I'm caffeinating."

I get coffee—one for me and one for Dinah—and I'm hoping Martine and I can sit down, but it's clear she doesn't want to settle in. She murmurs that she'd like to walk, and I have to give her that. I tell her about the prison fight, and how Oliver's surgery went well.

"I'm so sorry," she says quietly, cupping her coffee in both hands as she walks. "That's . . . I'm just sorry."

I nod. There's not much else I can do. If I point out that it's part of prison life, then I'm reminding her who put him there, and she doesn't deserve that.

"I only told the police what I saw," she says. "They keep trying to get me to remember some detail that proves it was Oliver, and I can't. I don't know if they want me to make one up . . ." Her shoulders pull in as she shivers. "I won't do that."

"Thank you."

"I'd been so sure it was him. Who else would be in his car?" She pauses and looks at me. "Now it feels silly. He drives to my house, waits for me to come out, and he's wearing a mask to shoot me? I'd obviously recognize the car. Why wear a mask?" She inhales. "I shouldn't say that. I can't be certain it wasn't Oliver."

"It's fine. That's between us," I say reassuringly. "The facts are there, and they'll prove what happened. I trust in that."

I stop and take a deep breath. Can I do this? A few minutes ago, I'd been pleased with myself for lowering her guard and winning a chance to question her. Now I need to push past the urge to drop it, to leave her in peace.

I won't push hard. But I do need to know.

"Can I ask you one thing, though? Between us? I've heard you had emails vanish recently, and it . . . it worries me. I want to think Oliver would never do that, but the police and the prosecution seem to think he would, and . . . I'm confused."

She gives a short, humorless laugh. "Then that makes two of us. Why would Oliver interfere with my job? There's no point. It's not as if I'm constantly working or canceling with him because of it, and even if it was, he'd talk to me about it. He certainly wouldn't delete emails."

"Were there . . . any signs? Of controlling behavior?"

"No." She takes a few more steps. "I know what that feels like. From past relationships." Based on what Oliver has told me, she's talking about her ex-husband. "I saw nothing of that with Oliver. If I had, I'd have run the other way. He's always been sweet and considerate."

I nod.

She glances over, her gaze softening. "I'm sorry you're going through this, having to question your brother. I know you two are close. I envied that, and . . . I wanted to respect your boundaries, Amy, but I always thought I'd love to have a coffee with you sometime, just the two of us. Get to know you. Overcome whatever concerns you had."

I frown. "Concerns?"

"I know I wasn't what you wanted for Oliver."

My frown grows as I shake my head. "But you were. I told Oliver how much I liked you. How good I thought you were for him."

"Oh, okay."

She seems confused, but before I can pursue it, she murmurs, "I should get back upstairs. It was nice talking to you, Amy. I hope Oliver is fine."

"Thank you."

"Did I just see you talking to Martine Dupont?"

The voice rumbles right behind me, making me jump so fast I nearly spill Dinah's coffee. Castillo appears and plucks the cup from my hand.

"Thanks," he says and takes a slurp of it.

"That—"

"—was for Dinah? Good thing we both like caramel lattes. It was hers, right?" He points at the half-finished drink in my hand. "Unless you're so tired you were doubling up?"

Before I can respond, he says, "Tell me you didn't corner Martine and try convincing her to withdraw charges."

I give him a hard look. "I wouldn't do that. Also, being the daughter of a lawyer, I know Martine can't withdraw them."

"Okay, yeah," he concedes. "So what did you talk to her about?"

I tell him.

He gives a grunt that almost sounds like "Nice." Then he says, "What'd you get?"

I shrug. "Not much. She doesn't think it was Oliver who shot her, but that's between us. She didn't mean to admit it."

"She's already retracted her positive ID to the police, so nothing new there."

"As for the emails, she can't imagine why Oliver would delete them. She also can't think of anything else he did that seems controlling. I get the sense her husband was, and so she knows the signs. She didn't see them with Oliver."

The next grunt sounds like "Good."

"That's it," I say. "But before we go to see Dinah, there's something I need to talk to you about." I glance around. "I was going to tell Dinah, but she had a call and . . . I should probably run it by you first."

"I'm flattered."

"Don't be. Whether it's you or Dinah, you're going to think I'm full of shit. I'm used to that from you. It won't sting."

"Now I'm definitely flattered. Good to see I'm toughening you up."

I check his expression to see whether he's joking. I can't tell.

"I need to talk to you, too," he says, "about your email account."

I stiffen. "Was it hacked?"

"Come sit down, and I'll explain."

We sit in a quiet corner of the café, and Castillo quickly scans the room. There are just two people near us, both working on laptops. Satisfied that we have enough privacy, he relaxes, his knees splayed, coffee held between them as he leans forward.

"Let's get this out of the way," he says. "Your email seems to have been accessed, but I don't think it was Oliver. If it was, I'd expect he had your password. That's unlikely."

"Because I change it every few months, and it's a randomized sequence of letters and numbers."

"Which also means it's unlikely to be leaked in a data breach, and your provider hasn't had one in years. Now, Oliver could get your current password if you logged in on his device and didn't log out."

"I've never used his devices."

"Okay. Someone can also get it in a phishing attack or by getting you to download malware. You seem security conscious enough to avoid that."

"I'm paranoid-level careful about that. From the cases I study, I know it's a way to get someone's info."

"That leaves hacking your WiFi through a security flaw in your router and stealing your login information, which is high-tech hacking and clearly not the guy who can barely operate his security system. I do see evidence of emails being deleted—fully deleted, or as much as they can be. Someone is going in and deleting select ones before you see them."

I'm silent for long enough that he says, "Amy?"

Just because Oliver isn't tech savvy doesn't mean he couldn't hire someone who is.

I squeeze my eyes shut. Now I really am being paranoid. Why would Oliver pay an expert to hack my email and delete messages from someone asking for help in the very area I specialize in?

I hate this. I'm the person who might know my brother best, and there is nothing in him that makes me suspicious, but here I am, letting that whisper of doubt snake in.

When you're a hammer, everything looks like a nail.

"Amy?"

I snap out of it. "What kinds of emails were deleted?"

Castillo rubs his chin. "Hard to say, because there's not enough left, and I can only dig back a few months. I didn't find anything that seemed to be the ones I sent or the ones sent by guys you met."

I try for a smile. "Damn. Here I was hoping they've all been spamming me, desperate to connect, having missed their chance with me."

"Their loss."

That is a very nice thing to say, even nicer because he says it so casually. But I must acknowledge it's not the first nice or considerate thing he's done. He came to my apartment in the middle of the night to tell me Martine had been shot and Oliver arrested. He was against featuring Oliver in the podcast, not because it could affect the case, but because it could put a target on me. He took me out for beer and wings, and he might have said it's because he needed to talk to me, but I'm sure he'd seen me gazing longingly at the restaurant.

Dean Castillo can be an asshole, but mostly he's just blunt and prickly, and if he says anything truly asshole-worthy, I call him on it.

I return to the subject at hand. "Should I stop using that email then?"

"If you have another account—a school one or whatever—I'd suggest using that for now."

"Okay."

I sip my coffee and try not to dwell on the fact that there are people out there who think I ignored their emails.

"One more thing," he says. "The person you were talking to online said you'd met her before, presumably through Laura. That might help narrow down who it could be. I'll need a list of friends and family of hers that you met."

"Actually, let's put a pin in that. I might . . . I might have solved that mystery."

He quirks one brow.

"Before we get to that, there was someone in my parking lot last night. When I was heading here."

His cheek twitches. "Someone near your car?"

"No," I say. "Which is why I didn't think much of it, beyond making sure I stayed aware. I figured it was someone casing the lot, looking for an open vehicle with twenty bucks tucked in the visor."

"Yeah."

"So, I got in my car, staying aware, checking the back seat, even if I did feel like I was overreacting."

"Don't."

I offer a small twist of a smile. "I don't always practice what I preach. Checking, yes. Not still feeling as if I'm overreacting? That one's tougher. Anyway, this person was over by a boundary line of evergreens. They'd slipped into the shadows, presumably waiting until I was gone, and I was going to let them. I needed to get to the hospital for Oliver. So I backed up, and I turned toward the rear exit, which they apparently didn't expect. I also turned sharper than they might have expected."

"Yeah, I've heard about your driving."

I raise my brows. "I have a perfect record. Not so much as a ticket."

"Ever been pulled over?"

"Er, yes."

"The cop took one look at the young and attractive white woman and decided to let you go with a warning?"

My cheeks heat. "Point taken."

"But *your* point is that you startled this guy, right?"

"Woman."

That has him jerking upright, gaze locking with mine. "The one from your show?"

"No." I take a deep breath. "It was Laura."

SIXTEEN

Castillo scuttles me out of the café. This is not a conversation for an even slightly public place. I should have known that—I was just eager to tell him before he took off like Dinah and left me kicking myself for not saying it sooner. Because I know I won't be able to see Oliver anyway, we both text Dinah and let her know we're leaving.

Castillo walks me to my car and then hops in the passenger seat and directs me to where he's parked. From there, I'm supposed to follow his pickup to his office—don't take my own route, don't leave his rearview mirror view. Follow him and then wait in my car until he can walk me up to his office.

We don't speak another word until we're in the office with the door shut. He waves me to a chair and pulls his over, and it's only then that I realize he hasn't said the words I expected: *Are you sure it was Laura?*

"I know what happened the day she supposedly drowned," he says without preamble. "Right up until the moment she dove in. Then I know what happened later with the investigation. Those are the parts that matter to Dinah, so they're what matters to me. But what happened after she went in?" He shakes his head. "I only know that while her body wasn't found, no one questioned that she was dead."

"Because it was Lake Superior."

When anyone expresses confusion over why Laura was declared dead so quickly, I need to explain what that means. This isn't some little lake in the Muskoka region, ringed by cottages, crossable by canoe in thirty minutes. Lake Superior is the biggest and the deepest of the Great Lakes. There are oil tankers lying on her bed, taken down in her storms, rotting there, complete with unrecovered crew members.

Castillo knows this, and so when I say it's Lake Superior, he only nods.

I continue, "Where she went in was miles from shore. There was one island she could have reached, but it's a rock barely big enough for a picnic. They still searched it, of course. No sign of her there, and it would have been a very long swim underwater from the boat."

"Because no one saw her come up for air."

"Right." I settle into my chair. "According to Oliver, she jumped in and surfaced, and then swam a bit, joking with him, as the witnesses heard. Then she swam farther from the boat before ducking to swim underwater."

"Putting some distance between her and the boat."

"Yes. She was about twenty meters off the starboard side when she dove under. Oliver waited for her to come up . . . and kept waiting. After a few minutes, he started to worry and then panic. There were the guys who'd seen her dive in, so he shouted to them for help. At the time, he says he was worried about overreacting but decided that was better than *under*reacting."

"Good call."

"Less than five minutes after Laura disappeared, he was shouting for help. Then he jumped in himself, with a lifebuoy. He's not much of a swimmer. He paddled around with the ring, looking for her, but that water . . ."

"Pitch black. Can't see your hand in some parts."

I nod. "This was one of those parts. The other boat came. A couple of the guys jumped in to help, and the one still on the boat radioed in a distress call. There was a huge search."

"You were part of it. I remember Ioana saying that. You drove ten hours to help."

The way he words it sounds as if I did something heroic, but I didn't. My brother's wife had drowned. He'd come to me when I needed him, and I was damned well going to do the same.

"There was no sign of her," I say. "Eventually, she was declared dead. It didn't take the usual seven years."

"Because she disappeared 'in circumstances of peril,'" Castillo says.

"It isn't as if she walked away and vanished. She disappeared in a situation where there wasn't any other possibility. Which means . . ." I look up at him. "I saw her last night. I know that's going to be hard for anyone to accept after she was ruled dead for very good reasons. I have no idea how she survived an accident like that."

"She couldn't," he says simply.

I tense. "I saw her, Dean. I understand that you need to question that. So drill me. Please. I can tell you exactly what I saw—*who* I saw. Laura Harding was in my apartment building parking lot, and maybe that doesn't make sense, but she was. I saw her, and she ran. She drove off. I pursued until I lost her. That wasn't some random woman who resembled Laura and happened to be looking for a twenty-dollar bill in an unlocked car."

Five seconds tick past. Then he says, "You done?"

I scowl at him.

He continues, "When I said, 'She couldn't,' I meant that she couldn't have survived an 'accident' like that. What kind of accident could it even be? There was nothing to bump her head on or hold her under temporarily. It was presumed she suffered some kind of medical emergency underwater, but if she did, then she would have drowned. Not drowning means there *was* no accident."

It takes a moment for me to understand what he means. "You think she staged her own death?"

"You got another explanation?"

When I don't answer, he says, "Option one would be that Oliver helped her disappear. That they set this up together."

My head jerks up. "What? No. I can't—*No.*"

"Two reasons he might do that. First, insurance scam. They wanted to divorce and decided she'd fake her death, and he'd give her the insurance money instead of a settlement."

I stare at him.

He lifts one shoulder in a shrug. "I know someone who worked a case like that. But here, it wouldn't make sense because the life insurance policy was one Laura bought years ago when she was single, and it paid out ten grand, which is one thing that kept the cops from looking too hard at Oliver. The other situation would be if Laura was in business trouble, and he helped her fake her death to escape it. But there was never any sign of that, and he's smart enough to know that if she drowned while boating with him, he'd be a suspect."

I don't answer. There's nothing to say to that beyond sputtering that I was with Oliver after Laura disappeared—I saw his panic and grief, and that was not faked.

Castillo continues, "There was a prenup, right? That was another reason the police didn't look too closely at Oliver. It wasn't a case where his wife threatened to leave and take half his money, so he killed her. It was an ironclad prenup that said they had to be married at least a decade before she got anything."

I'd known there was a prenup—which did factor against the possibility Oliver killed her. But I didn't know the details. The stipulation makes sense, though. However much Oliver loved Laura, he had to be sure she wasn't marrying him for his money and planning to divorce after a couple of years.

"So here's what I see," Castillo says. "Laura's a strong swimmer. There's an island nearby. She swims toward it and then goes underwater the rest of the way, maybe surfacing just enough to breathe. Either she rests there, or she's planned this so well she's stashed equipment there to get her to shore. Does she have any scuba experience?"

I nod slowly as it comes together. "Her family was into scuba diving. She'd taught it as a teenager. She wasn't doing much while with Oliver—and it wasn't his thing—but she definitely knew how. There was also a report of someone who said they saw her out on the lake the day before, alone, before Oliver arrived at the rental cottage. As far as I know, the police didn't pursue it because it was a moot point."

"Nothing wrong with her taking a boat ride by herself. Unless she's staging her own death by leaving things on a tiny island she can swim to. From what I remember of the file, Laura was the one who chose the route that day."

"She was piloting the boat."

"Was that unusual?"

I shrug. "Not really. Oliver is easygoing and Laura . . ."

"Laura was not. *Is* not."

"She had very definite opinions about what she wanted, and it was the one thing I admired her for. If she wanted to pilot the boat, Oliver would step back. If she wanted him to do it, he'd step up."

Castillo leans forward. "You said it was the one thing you admired her for. Not one *of* the things." He looks at me. "You didn't like Laura."

I instinctively flinch. "I . . ."

"We aren't speaking ill of the dead here, Gibson. We're getting a handle on a woman who seems to have faked her death."

I nod and then steel myself for the confession. "At first, I liked Laura a lot. She was strong-willed and independent, and I thought she made a good match for Oliver. For a CEO, he can be a bit too laid-back. A bit too accommodating."

"Then your opinion changed?"

"It . . ." I shift in the chair. "It soon became clear she didn't feel the same about me She was never outwardly rude. It was the way Oliver very obviously ran interference that tipped me off."

"Example." It's not a question. It's a demand. More data required.

"I was living in the guesthouse. Before Oliver married, I'd make dinner a few times a week, and we'd eat together. After Laura came, I knew that would change, so I suggested we just share Sunday dinners. Soon he was making excuses—bad ones—and when I point-blank asked if Laura would prefer to skip the dinners, he stammered denials. Stuff like that."

I pull my legs under me. "Last week, you asked whether moving out was my idea or Oliver's. I said I moved out so Laura could use the cottage for her office, that I'd decided it was time for me to go."

"It wasn't you deciding. It was Laura."

"Again, Oliver tried to run interference. I overheard something about her wanting the cottage, and I asked him. He denied it, but I could tell he'd been put in a very awkward position. I wanted to move out that day. But that would have seemed like I was stomping off in a snit. So I was out as soon as I leased an apartment."

"You *were* angry, though."

I shake my head. "I was embarrassed. The way she handled it made me feel as if I was too dense to realize I'd overstayed my welcome. Or like I was overly dependent on Oliver, a burden to him, which is the last thing I ever wanted. I was embarrassed and humiliated. When they got engaged, I offered to move out. She's the one who talked me out of it. And then . . ."

"Then she decided she wanted the cottage for an office and made you feel like you were leeching off your brother."

"Leeching and also defending my spot in Oliver's life. Like by staying in the cottage, I was interfering with their marriage."

I clench my hands, clasped on my lap. "I felt awful. Immature and oblivious."

"Nah, it was her problem. I dated someone like that a few years back. She'd insist it was fine if I had to work late, had to slip off in the middle of the night, couldn't afford to take her to the places her last boyfriend took her. But then she'd turn around and complain about it later. I figured out that when she was saying all that stuff was okay, I was supposed to somehow realize it wasn't." He waves a hand at himself. "Have you met me? If you say you're okay with beer and wings, I'm going to presume you're okay with beer and wings."

"As you should."

"When she pulled that shit, I got out. But someone who is a little less"—he shrugs—"*me* would have thought they'd missed cues and screwed up. You didn't. It was Laura's problem."

"Eventually, I came to realize that. It was tough. This was the woman Oliver planned to spend his life with. I'd hoped we could be friends. Not besties, but friendly, you know? Maybe grab lunch now and then, just the two of us. When I reached out, though, she made me feel like I was a needy kid, hoping for a big sister." I pull my shoulders in. "It was really awkward, and after she died, the guilt came back. Had I misjudged her? Had I not tried hard enough?"

I make a face and roll my shoulders. "Enough of that. This isn't Amy-therapy-time. The point is that Laura's death shook me. It was tragic for her, and it was awful for Oliver. But, no, I didn't like her."

"Meaning she could have been the woman you were messaging with the other night?"

"The one who accused me of being a stuck-up little bitch? Implying I was glad that Laura was dead? That I was too close to my brother and there was something creepy there?" I nod. "Parts one and two were the Laura I knew. Not that she ever said those things to me directly, but I got the message loud and clear. That last part?" I shudder.

"That was goading you. Taking a close sibling relationship and making it seem inappropriate, which is going to freak anyone out. Low-hanging fruit."

"Which would also be Laura. She was petty, and she could be nasty to anyone who crossed her." I stand. "May I grab a glass of water?"

He leans back. "I'm not interrogating you, Amy. Tell me you need a break."

"I just need water. This is . . . a lot." I walk to the minifridge and take out the filtered-water jug. "I know I saw Laura last night, but I haven't processed what it means."

"Any chance she was the troll at your event?"

I shake my head as I pour the water. "Too big of a stretch physically. I'm presuming that was a friend."

Castillo is quiet. I ask whether he wants water, but he only waves his hand in what I assume means no.

"I've been digging harder since that woman got in touch with you the other day," he says. "The obvious answer has always been that it's a friend of Laura's. I'd gotten access to her accounts through Oliver." He looks up. "Did you get the impression Laura had a lot of friends?"

I shrug. "I got the impression she had a lot of people she could go to lunch with. Acquaintances. Then a few close friends, mostly from her college days. I know there was tension there—that was the thing about her skipping lunch dates without warning and whatnot."

"Yeah, she had a lot of acquaintances, like you said. That was mostly networking. Then there were three college friends. One lived in Calgary. The other two were local. All three said she drifted after the marriage. By the time she died, she was estranged from the two local ones. She ignored messages. She missed dates. That sort of thing. One of them is now living in the States. The other is not the woman you saw. She's Black."

"Okay," I say.

"The ones living in Calgary and the States could have come back to do this for her, but neither matches the description, and I confirmed they were in their home cities the night of your event. While it's possible Laura has made a new friend, it's just as likely . . ."

He trails off and scoots his chair back to grab his laptop. He pops it open, and his fingers fly over the keyboard.

"I was running my image search last night." He spins the laptop around to face me. On the screen are three photos of white women in their forties, all roughly resembling the troll—the same long face and pointed chin.

"That's her," I say, with some surprise. "The one on the left. She's the one who came to my event. She would have been wearing a wig, and she was dressed a lot differently—more middle-aged camouflage—but that's definitely her. Where did you find her?"

"I tinkered with the still shot from the library security footage until I could run a reverse image search, which I localized to

Southern Ontario. These three popped up. The one you picked is from the website of a business in Waterloo that rents actors."

"Rents . . . actors?"

"Hire someone to serenade your girlfriend on her birthday. Or set up a gag to punk a friend. Whatever you might need an actor to do, and from the comments, people have a lot of uses for them, from a plus-one at a wedding to playing a body at a murder-mystery party."

"Or showing up at a podcaster's live show and accusing her brother of murdering his wife?"

"Yeah, that one's definitely not listed on the website. But if this is the woman . . ."

"It is. Absolutely."

His fingers fly over the keys again before he closes the laptop. "Working theory then. Laura faked her death. Do you have any idea why?"

"No. If she wanted out of the marriage, she could have gotten a divorce. It must have been something else, unconnected to Oliver, but the police never turned up anything she'd need to escape, so I don't know."

"So she fakes her death, is gone for three years, and then something brings her back."

"With the goal of putting my brother in prison. Framing him for killing his girlfriend, which means she actually needs to kill—or at least shoot—Martine." I pull back, arms tucking into my sleeves as I wrap my arms around myself. "That's . . ."

"Cold?"

"More than I can wrap my head around, to be honest. But we already knew someone had shot Martine and framed Oliver.

It's just harder to go from it being an anonymous psycho to a person I knew."

"The security system dates back before her death. If Oliver's never updated it, he may not have changed the codes, either."

"He hasn't—I know it, and it's the same. Laura was the tech-savvy one. If the system is accessible online, she could have done that."

"Yeah, it is. That's part of the reason Dinah couldn't use it as proof someone hacked in. Oliver could have remotely accessed it himself, cloaking his device so it looked like unauthorized access."

"But why was she in my parking lot last night?"

"I don't know, but I think we need to check your car."

SEVENTEEN

Castillo finds a tracking device inside my car fender. He doesn't remove it. He just takes photographs. Then he heads back inside without a word.

I follow him. "Am I supposed to leave that on my car?"

He still says nothing. When we reach the office, I have to grab the door before it shuts behind him. He walks in, plants himself in his desk chair and turns to stare straight forward, doing nothing.

"If that's a hint for me to leave, Dean, you need to be more direct. Also, you need to take that thing off my car because, weirdly, I don't feel like being tracked by my murderous sister-in-law."

He turns to look at me, and his face is empty until he blinks, as if my words ran on a delay.

"You're not going anywhere," he says. "If you need something from home, I'll drive you and walk you up to your apartment."

"Okay . . . So . . ." I cast a pointed look around. "I just hang out here while you work."

"I'm thinking."

"I got that."

"I think better when no one's plaguing me with questions."

"*Plaguing* you?" I sink into a chair. "You are a *delight*, Dean."

"So I've been told."

He leans back in his seat. I have been dismissed. I could get grumbly about that, but I'm figuring Dean Castillo out. There's a decent, even thoughtful, guy under that exterior. But the exterior isn't a facade, either. He genuinely gives a shit about people he's deemed worth giving a shit about . . . and he's genuinely fine with you knowing when he *doesn't* give a shit about you.

I seem to be landing on the "gives a shit" side, and it might not even be because Ioana would want it. If he's deep in thought, it's about the case and also about how to keep me safe, and since he's the expert in that, I appreciate it. So I will keep silent.

The problem with keeping silent is that it lets me fall into my thoughts and worries. I can't wrap my head around the idea that Laura could be alive. No matter what I thought of her, I would have been happy to hear she survived. But why did she fake her death? And why is she coming after Oliver? And—maybe most of all—why would she go after Oliver by shooting an innocent woman?

I'm scared for Oliver and for Martine. And I'm angry, too, because my mother is dead and not coming back and *this* woman did come back from the dead and used her resurrection to try to kill another woman and frame her husband.

I know my mother has nothing to do with this, but in my head, the two cases tangle. Mom was legitimately murdered by a partner, and Laura tried to frame my brother for doing the exact same thing, and that is heinous to me on a level I can't quite explain.

I glance around, needing a distraction. I take a legal pad from the supply stack, along with a pen, and I start making notes.

"You done?" Castillo says after I've filled the first page.

"Hmm?"

"Whatever you're writing out?"

"My shopping list. I'm trying to decide between French yogurt and Norwegian. I'm partial to the French. It comes in the cutest little glass jars." I set down the pen. "I'm working through the case, trying to get everything straight in my mind. If Laura is behind this, what does that mean? How does it impact what I thought I knew—about her and about what's going on?"

He grunts, and I'll delude myself into thinking he's impressed by my logic. That's so much better than breaking down into a babbling mess.

Laura is alive.

Laura may have shot Martine.

Laura is framing my brother for attempted murder.

Laura put a tracker on my car.

Does that mean Laura is going to frame me for something?

Try to kill me? Ahh! Someone save me!

I'm making light, but if the first few statements are correct—back from the dead, Laura shot Martine and is framing Oliver—then the rest is an actual possibility.

"What are you going to tell Dinah?" I say.

"That's what I've been working out. We have a valid suspect."

"Yes."

"Problem one is convincing people that Laura is still alive. They won't believe you. You're his little sister, and you have a podcast. Maybe you're doing it for publicity. Maybe your imagination has run away with you."

"Yes."

When he meets my gaze, I say, "Do you expect me to deny it? I know exactly how unreliable a witness I seem. I'm a PhD candidate with a successful podcast. That *should* buy me some credibility. It doesn't, because that's not what people see."

"Good. Remember that. It sucks, but remember it. Now, I'm more reliable, as witnesses go. Private investigator. Solid record. Military background. Even this"—he waves at his damaged cheek—"buys me credibility. People take me seriously. I'm not sure why. But they do."

I snort, but his look says he wasn't being sardonic. Two minutes in Castillo's company, and it's obvious why he commands respect. He's a big guy whose facial expressions run the gamut from serious to deadly serious. He looks like the last person who'd jump to conclusions or tell wild stories. That's for women like me.

"The problem is that I'm the one who saw her, not you," I say. "Are you saying you need to see her before we can pursue this lead?"

He shakes his head. "No, but I do need to pursue it before I tell Dinah. With Oliver being stabbed, there's a lot going on, and she'll have work for me. If I tell her I'm chasing a very promising lead, but it's not ready to share, she'll let me prioritize it."

"But if you say that lead is 'Laura back from the dead,' it'll seem so unlikely that she'll want you moving on."

"Yes. For the sake of establishing a record, I'd like you to tell me what you saw again, but on video this time, so it's time-stamped. Meanwhile, I'll tell Dinah I have that promising lead, and she'll decide what I should pursue. Reasonable?"

"Reasonable."

Castillo has texted Dinah. While he waits for a response, I give my testimony, covering my ass and making sure no one can claim I sat on this information. I told Castillo, and he made the executive call to investigate first.

Dinah gets back to Castillo and confirms she doesn't have anything urgent for him. The police are investigating the stabbing, and Oliver has, reluctantly, agreed to apply for bail, so that's where her own focus will be today.

"What's the next step?" I say. "You're leaving that tracker on my car for a reason. I'm guessing you want me to drive around and see whether Laura bites."

"This isn't a movie, Gibson. I'm not throwing you out as bait for a killer. Chances are, she wouldn't bite anyway. My guess is that she only wants to know where you are and what you're doing. That's why I didn't take it off. I'd rather have parked the car at your apartment—I don't want her wondering what you're doing *here*—but it's a little late for that."

"Should we take the car to my apartment? Leave it there?"

"Maybe. I don't know yet. I'm still thinking."

"So I should shut up again?"

"Not yet."

Despite saying that, he rolls back in his chair and stretches his legs to stare at the ceiling again. I rip the page from my legal pad and barely get the pen onto the page before he says, "Good. Take notes. I've always wanted a secretary."

I peer at him. "You do know there are other names for the position now."

He waves at the pad. "Since you have the equipment at hand, you can take notes. Ready?"

I lift the pen.

He dictates. It's basically a list of what we—sorry, *he*—needs to investigate. There's the tracking device and what he wants done with it long and short term.

Then there's the actor who played the troll. She's a potential link to Laura. Next is Laura herself. Can Castillo lure her? Not using me as bait, but otherwise. But she knows I saw her, which adds a new wrinkle.

I don't complain about the admin work. Partly, I'm interested, but also I'm not inclined to return to my apartment, under the circumstances.

When he finishes, he takes the pad and pen and starts scribbling. It really does look like scribbling—a few notes, but mostly arrows and lines and strikeouts and question marks. Then he slaps the pad onto his desk.

"The actor," he says. "We'll start there."

"We?" When his eyes darken, I lift my hands. "That isn't a complaint, Dean. I'm just confirming that I understand correctly, because if I infer and I'm wrong, I'll get a lecture on how you're the PI and I'm the client."

"I don't lecture. I just say 'I'm the PI, you're the client.' But yeah, unless you've got someone you can hang out with and I drop you off there, I'm stuck on bodyguard duty."

"Well, at least you didn't say *babysitting* duty."

"I was being nice. You had a long night." He hauls himself from the chair. "I've got a home and work address for this lady. We're paying her a visit."

EIGHTEEN

We decide to drop off my car first. That isn't a simple matter of just leaving it in the lot. There is a process, because it's currently being tracked by my not-dead murderous sister-in-law. First, Castillo needs to follow me, while hanging back both to see whether Laura is on-site and, if she is, to avoid her noticing him.

I park . . . and then, according to very clear instructions, I must sit in the car and fuss with my makeup. Apparently, Castillo has only the vaguest idea of "things women do," and reapplying makeup before going *into your empty apartment* is one of them.

I do something far more normal instead—I check messages on my phone and answer one. By then, Castillo is in place at the building's back door, pretending to be tinkering with something under the hood—which is apparently the male equivalent of "putting on makeup" stalling tactics.

Once Castillo is in place, I head inside the building. He texts that it's clear, and I come out the back door and hop into his truck. Yes, it is a *process*.

Now, nearly two hours after we left the office, we're in the parking lot of a telecom business in Waterloo. While Grand Forks isn't known for any particular industry, in Waterloo, it's tech. There are three cities—Waterloo, Kitchener and Cambridge— that merge together, and tech is their thing. Birthplace of the original smartphone: the BlackBerry.

This isn't a company I've ever heard of, but there are dozens like it. On the city outskirts, tucked into an industrial area, the building—according to Castillo—has about a hundred work- ers, including one Janet May, human resources rep by day and actor-for-hire by night.

On the drive, we discussed a plan of action. Okay, we argued about it. I had an idea, and Castillo hated it. In the end, I won, because my plan is more likely to work, and he has to admit it. That doesn't keep him from grumbling right up until I'm too far away to hear him. Nor does it keep him from firing off texts with instructions and warnings. But I get my way, and that's what matters.

I walk in the front door. Castillo isn't with me, which was the part he hated most, but having him looming at my side guar- anteed failure. Also, establishing him, in any way, as someone associated with me isn't wise, which is why we went through all that performance theater in my apartment parking lot.

As I enter the telecom building, I check my reflection in the glass. It's not quite what I wanted. I'm still wearing the jeans and pullover I grabbed when I ran out last night. At least it's not sweats. This is a tech company, so I'm hoping casual will cut it.

I proceed to the front desk. I don't have a choice—there's a secured door behind it.

"Hello," I say to the young man behind the desk. "Kristen Hale, for Janet May, please."

"You have an appointment, Ms. Hale." It's a polite statement requesting confirmation, rather than a question.

"One thirty." I check my watch. "I'm five minutes early."

He nods, and I step back from the desk to look at a poster—a stylized schematic of whatever device they produce.

"Ms. Hale?"

I glance over to see him on the phone. "Hmm?"

"Ms. May doesn't have you on her schedule. May I ask what this is regarding?"

"Oh. Umm." I move closer to the desk and lower my voice, though there's no one else around. "I'm . . . not sure I should say. It's regarding her, um, side gig."

"Side—?"

He doesn't get a chance to finish. Janet must say something on the other end of the line, because he nods and disconnects. "Ms. May will be right out."

"Thank you."

I walk back to the poster and continue studying it, my back to the door Janet will come through. It whooshes open, but I still don't turn until I hear that door shut and she says, "Ms. Hale?"

I turn, and the look on her face . . . ? Call me petty, but I revel in that look. The first flash of confusion—*Do I know you?*

Then the recognition. Then the panic, a glance over her shoulder, as if she's ready to retreat, but the door is already shut, and we have a witness.

"Ms. May," I say, walking over with my hand out. "Thank you for seeing me."

I get a deliciously deadly look for that, but she keeps her face turned from the desk clerk.

"I think we need to talk," I say. "Would you like to step outside? Or is your office available?"

Silence as her mind whirs, a rat in a maze looking for an escape route and then realizing there isn't one.

She pivots on her heel. "My office, please, Ms. Hale."

I follow her inside. As I do, I get a better look at her. There'd been no doubt from the website photo that she was my mystery woman. She's an actor, though, which means the woman leading me down the hall doesn't look like the one in the photo, who doesn't look like my troll from that night. Three roles. Three costumes.

That night, she'd been playing middle-aged podcast fangirl. A little dumpy, mostly invisible, her makeup ill-applied, as if it'd been a long time since she'd worn any. The website photo showed someone who knew exactly how to apply makeup . . . and style her hair and select an outfit that said "quirky and fun." This version is the corporate HR rep, in a skirt and jacket and heels, minimalist makeup and no-nonsense hairstyle.

I follow her on a route that seems to circle the building twice. I catch glimpses of cubicles and the murmur of voices and the click of keys, but May sticks to halls of closed doors. When she finally opens one, it's a "quiet room" for making business calls or holding one-on-one meetings.

May flips the sign to In Use and shuts the door behind us. Then she crosses the tiny room, parks herself in front of a chair, turns to me and waits. Her arms twitch, as if she's physically restraining herself from crossing them. She's HR. She knows what a defensive posture looks like. She won't fall into that trap. Nor is she falling into the one of verbally defending herself. She just waits.

"Someone hired you to interrupt my event," I say.

"Yes."

Her gaze bores into mine. Tension sparks off her, but she's holding it tight. She wants me on the offensive, coming at her hard, losing my cool, maybe breaking down in tears.

But I don't speak, which makes her seem to struggle against the urge to shift her weight. Finally, she says, "It was a job. A legal job."

I nod. There are so many things I could say to that. Legal, yes. But ethical? Castillo's research showed that Janet May's son has done a couple of years for possession with intent to sell. How would she feel if someone hired me to storm into her workplace, accusing her of running a family drug-dealing business?

That'd be okay, right? Just doing my job. Gotta make a living somehow. If it's an issue, take it up with the person who hired me.

I say none of that. I just nod, and I keep nodding until she does shift her weight in discomfort. Then her arms cross before she forces them back down.

"I'm going to need to ask you a few questions," I say.

Her lips quirk in a humorless smile. "You're the police now?"

"No, but we can call them if you'd like."

She tenses. "I didn't do anything illegal—"

"Are you aware that my brother is in jail for attempting to kill his girlfriend?"

Her expression says no. Yes, it's a big case in Grand Forks, and it would certainly be in the news here, but the news isn't what it was twenty years ago, as I've learned from the cases on my podcast.

There'd been a time when you couldn't have avoided hearing about a big regional case. Now, people get their news from so many sources that they could easily miss local stories.

May finds her footing quickly, her face shuttering as she shrugs. "I guess he did murder his wife then, didn't he?"

Again, I will not rise to the bait. No sarcasm or outrage about her taking a job that she seems to have presumed was slanderous trolling, if she wasn't convinced Oliver did it.

"The court will decide that," I say calmly. "Though I doubt the case will get that far."

A derisive snort. She's relaxing now. She has my number—I'm the silly little sister who'll go down in flames defending her killer brother.

"The night of my event," I say, "Oliver was indeed being questioned by the police, just as you said. He was brought in based on the anonymous tip you delivered to the police."

"I didn't—"

"My brother's attorney has conducted voice analysis on the clip. That's one downside to being in the part-time acting biz—there are many examples of your voice online. We know it was you."

I'm lying here. I'm not even sure the tip was May—it's an educated guess, presuming Laura wouldn't dare use her own voice in case the recording was played for Oliver.

May's face spasms, confirming our suspicion. Then it hardens. "I was given a script. That's all."

"A script you were told to deliver from a pay phone."

Her lips tighten even more. "Yes."

"You called the police, pretending to be giving a tip, based solely on a script. You pretended to have firsthand knowledge of the veracity of what you were reading, yet for all you knew, it was a work of fiction. There's a name for that, Janet, and it comes with two to five years in prison."

I'm exaggerating, but her expression says she sees the truth of what I'm saying. She lied to the police. That's illegal.

Again, she finds that hard expression. "Maybe, but if it's true, is anyone going to care how the police got the tip now that he tried to kill his girlfriend?"

"Someone hired you to phone in a false tip. They also hired you to make a public accusation at my event. Then, the next night, someone hacked my brother's alarm system and stole his car. That car was used to lure his girlfriend from her home, whereupon someone in that car—someone wearing a mask—shot her two times."

I meet May's gaze. "Someone is framing my brother for murder. There is evidence—now being investigated—that it's the same person who bought your ticket for my event."

She blinks. "What?"

"Whoever hired you is the prime suspect in an attempted murder. My brother's lawyer will be turning that evidence over to the police. So you have two choices. You can talk to me, and Oliver's lawyer will give you time to prepare for when and where the police show up on your doorstep. Or you can kick me out, and she'll call the police, and they'll be here before you can get to your car."

In her place, I'd have questioned my story, but from what I've seen so far, Janet May will buy it. She didn't expect the woman she trolled to confront her at work. She didn't know that the guy she trolled had been arrested for attempted murder. She didn't think through the ramifications of delivering a false tip. Now all that has hit her at once, and the last thing she's capable of doing is stepping back and analyzing my story. It makes sense on the surface, and she's too flustered to dive deeper.

"I want to contact the police myself," she says.

"Okay."

She leans toward me as if I hadn't just agreed. "I'll go to the station after work. I'll tell them that I just saw the news about your brother and realized I had information."

"Okay."

"If I tell you what I know, you'll give me that much time?"

"Oliver's lawyer won't notify the police until first thing tomorrow morning."

"Fine." She backs up against the desk and crosses her arms over her chest. "It was all legal."

"I never said it wasn't."

"I was contacted directly, not through the agency, but I still paid the agency their cut. You can check."

"That really isn't our concern."

"Well, I did." She sounds satisfied, probably thanking her lucky stars she was ethical in that one regard—otherwise, her agency might now learn she freelanced and cut her loose.

She takes out her phone. "I'll tell you what I know, but the client paid cash. Actual cash, delivered, payment in full the day of the event." She turns around the phone. "Here's the correspondence."

It's text messages. I screenshot the thread with my phone.

"I tried calling the number afterward," Janet says. "I wanted to let her know what happened. It was out of service." She points at the end of the thread. "My last text—after the event—wasn't delivered."

The thread starts with someone—presumably Laura—reaching out and saying she got Janet May's number and is looking for an actor to play a role. That role involves going to a local event and accusing the speaker of something. There's a bit of back and forth, Janet asking questions, seeming wary, only to relax when it turns out she won't be accusing *me*—she'll be talking about my brother.

According to the texts, Oliver Harding got away with murder. His sister runs a podcast that's supposed to draw attention to domestic violence, and her own brother is guilty of the worst kind. People need to know.

I can be angry about what Janet May did. I can be furious and outraged. I'm not sure, though, given these texts, that I can blame her. Even if she'd looked up Laura's death online, it'd be easy to decide there'd been a miscarriage of justice. Men *do* get away with femicide. Can I blame May if she'd convinced herself that she was doing a good thing?

It also doesn't hurt that she was paid double her rate. That would make me suspicious, but again, I choose not to judge.

May agreed to the job, and the sender arranged to send the money, the ticket and details before 5 p.m. on show day.

"The ticket came prebought," Janet says. "She'd even printed it out rather than give me a virtual version."

So the person who'd posted on my forum wasn't May. I'd already figured it was Laura, given our online interaction two days ago.

"Can I see what she sent you?" I ask.

"It was a script. I'd screenshot it, but I've deleted it."

This proved that May knew the whole thing was shady. Still, not judging. It won't get me where I need to be.

"I didn't follow the script exactly," May says. "It's better to put things in my own words. It sounds more natural."

"Okay."

"All the relevant data was there, though."

"And after that?"

She shrugs. "Like I said, I tried telling the client that I'd finished—by text and by phone—and couldn't get through. I figured if they were concerned, they'd get in touch. Otherwise, the job was done, so I gave my agency their cut and moved on."

"Did she ask for anything other than what I saw?"

"Nope."

"Nothing extra? No online postings? No follow-up?"

She shakes her head. "Attend the event. Stand up and say my piece. Then leave whenever I want. That was it."

NINETEEN

I'm in the truck with Castillo. He's reading May's text-thread photos on my phone.

"That's it?" he says.

"Yep, like I said, this was their only point of contact."

"What about the envelope? The one she sent the cash in?"

"I asked about that. She shredded the envelope with the script, deleted the script photos from her phone and even removed them from her trash. I asked how the script and payment had been delivered. She said they were in a Canada Post express envelope—one of those prepaid ones—but there was no return address, and it didn't seem to have passed through the postal system."

"Laura bought it and delivered it herself."

"Seems so. Janet May lives in a single-family dwelling.

Alone—she divorced last year and got the house. No security system. No nearby cameras that she knows of."

"I'll check on that," he says. "You get an address?"

I text it to him. "I know you're going to need to tell Dinah, and I also know I shouldn't have promised she wouldn't contact the police until morning."

"Nah, that's fine. Better for Janet to come forward on her own, especially if it meant you got all that without Dinah having to get it through the prosecutor."

"So what next?"

"Lunch," he says. "Then I need to talk to Dinah. In person."

"About Laura?"

"I'm not sure yet."

Earlier, when Castillo said he was going to talk to Janet May, I'd expected to be left on the sidelines. Now, when he says he needs to speak to Dinah, I expect to be part of that conversation . . . and instead, I find myself sidelined.

After lunch, Castillo takes me home. That's not his first choice—or his second—but I argue that it's the safest place for me. He checks my car and then escorts me in and sweeps the apartment. There's no sign that anyone has been near the car or in my apartment. He only departs after imparting all appropriate warnings. Stay inside. Leave the security system on and the door locked. Don't answer anyone who buzzes—he'd text before he came over himself. Repeat, stay inside. Don't order food. Don't open the door for any reason.

I have neither need nor inclination to go out. I just had a late lunch, and half of it is in a takeout container. Castillo even went through a drive-through to get me a coffee and pastry so I could have an afternoon caffeine-and-sugar break. He's promised to contact me this evening, and if it seems as if he expects me to stay inside tomorrow, too, I'll have a chat with him about house arrest, but we aren't at that point yet.

For now, I'm looking forward to a few hours of seeing and speaking to no one.

I settle in at my desk and flip through my email. That only takes a few minutes. I have a half dozen nasty-grams from strangers that get filed—I know better than to delete them. I also have people asking for interviews. Two are legit enough that I forward them to Raven. The rest is just school stuff and spam.

I'm finishing my inbox cleanse when Raven texts.

> RAVEN:
> Your brother got stabbed last
> night??? Please tell me you
> didn't mention that because
> you're madly working on the
> podcast episode

Shit! I've been so wrapped up with the Laura revelation that I forgot about the stabbing. Not the stabbing itself, obviously, but the ramifications for Oliver's case and the podcast.

> ME:
> I'm on it!

> RAVEN:
> When can I expect to see it?
> The news already broke

ME:

I was in the hospital all night
waiting for him to get out of
surgery, and then I had to do
something urgent enough that
I couldn't beg off to record a
episode

RAVEN:

Urgent as in podcast-worthy?

ME:

Yep . . . when I can reveal it

RAVEN:

Fine, you're forgiven—if you
can get the scoop. Now give
me the stabbing

ME:

Nah, you haven't pissed me off
enough for that. Not yet

RAVEN:

Oh, I'm sure there are days you
wish you could. You have an
hour. Then I want the stabbing
episode up and a text telling
me it's there

I'm supposed to run scripts by Dinah. Technically, that was
an offer made by me rather than a requirement imposed by her.

I know with everything going on she won't have time to vet it. So I make an executive decision. There's nothing controversial in the script. I have enough inside information that I don't need to beef up the episode with extra chatter.

I give Dinah's version of the events leading to and following the stabbing. I say that I received a call and drove to wait while Oliver was in surgery. I don't want someone saying they saw me at the hospital, implying that I'm covering up the fact that, in spite of everything happening, Oliver and I are still close.

Do I suggest the stabbing was not accidental? Here, I'd like to think that I was a little bit clever. I laid out the facts, knowing that would be enough. Listeners will question just how accidental it was. There isn't any need for me to connect the dots for them, and if I had, it would have screamed bias. It would also have set people arguing against any case I built.

Just the facts, ma'am.

Record the episode. Promise additional information when such is available. Post. Notify Raven.

After that, I decide I've earned my brownie. I eat it as I haunt my website forum looking for responses to the new episode. I'm nervous posting without either Dinah or Castillo's thumbs-up, and I want to be the first to know whether I've made a mistake or worded something in a way that's open to misinterpretation.

I watch the counter climb as listeners tune in. It's no coincidence that they're so quick on the ball—since I started covering Oliver's case, we've added an alert to our usual subscriber newsletter. Those who sign up are automatically notified when I post a new episode.

There's some chatter on the board. I'm not in incognito mode, but no one reaches out. They rarely do. They presume it's a member of my staff, as VAW Survivor3 did the other night.

I stay out of the actual threads, instead using the cheat of refreshing my screen on the main page so that I can read a preview of all the most recent posts without going in and revealing that I'm reading them.

There's nothing concerning happening. Just people discussing the latest episode. They're already debating whether Oliver could have been targeted in the stabbing.

```
He's accused of trying to kill his girlfriend.
It's like being a serial killer or a pedophile.
Someone's going to decide to play judge and jury.
```

```
Are you sure that'd be it? Seems to me he's been
framed. Maybe whoever is doing that realized they
don't have a strong enough case against him.
```

```
And what? Hired someone on the inside to kill him?
```

```
No, she has a point. Someone really has it out for
this guy.
```

Yep, his not-so-dead wife, apparently.

I still can't quite wrap my head around that. Part of me screams that the police need to know. Oliver needs to know. *Now.* The wife that Oliver is being investigated for killing is not dead and may have shot Martine and framed him. Why am I sitting on this?

Because the only evidence to support my wild claim is my own eyewitness report of seeing her ... at night ... in a dark parking lot . . . right after getting the news my brother had been stabbed, when I'd been understandably shaken.

We're giving Janet May until tomorrow to come forward. I'm giving Castillo the same time frame to make a decision about telling Dinah, and if he doesn't—or I disagree with his choice—I'm moving forward myself.

I'm about to sign off the forum when someone pings me. The first thing I do is check the user profile.

VanChick84. Location: Vancouver, BC. Occupation: physiotherapist.

VanChick84 joined the forum a month ago, and there's an established pattern of activity. Not a ton, but enough to show she isn't another VAWSurvivor3, creating a fake profile and only asking about tickets to my event.

VanChick84: Hey

I reply with a wave emoticon.

VanChick84: I know you probably aren't really Amy, but that's okay

AmyGibson: Actually, I am

VanChick84: Well, like I said, it's okay if you aren't. I'd just like to get a message to her, please

AmyGibson: Sure, what's up?

```
VanChick84: I need to talk to her
```

```
AmyGibson: You are
```

```
VanChick84: I mean in person. ASAP. I know she
lives in Grand Forks
```

```
AmyGibson: Okay
```

```
VanChick84: I'm there now
```

The hairs on my neck prickle.

```
AmyGibson: Okay
```

```
VanChick84: I know that's going to sound weird,
but I had to come. I can't say this in an email or
a text or even a phone call
```

```
VanChick84: There are things Amy doesn't know
about her brother. Things she needs to know.
Secrets I've kept since Greta died
```

Greta.
Oliver's college girlfriend who died by suicide.
VanChick84 doesn't wait for a response.

```
VanChick84: I was her friend. Her best friend. I
also . . . I did something awful, and that's why
```

I never came forward about Oliver, and I'm not
sure I can even now. But I need to talk to Amy

AmyGibson: This is Amy. Really

VanChick84: Okay. I've been following your podcast
since before all this started. You seemed like
someone I could talk to. Unburden myself on. I've
been lurking, trying to work up the courage to
reach out

VanChick84: Then all this happened, and I knew I
had to speak to you

VanChick84: I hoped that if I flew across the
country, you'd know I'm serious

VanChick84: Now I can see it just looks creepy and
suspicious

AmyGibson: If you're going to tell me that Oliver
killed Greta, he wasn't even in the same country
when she died

VanChick84: I know. I was . . . I was there. I
mean, I'm the one who found her. She definitely did
it. But there's more to the story

My fingers are flying over the keyboard. I'd bookmarked
the only reference I could find online to Greta's suicide. It was

a site that had once been run by UBC students trying to call attention to suicides among their classmates. The site had removed actual cases years ago, but I was able to find the reference using the digital archives.

According to the archived post, Greta had died in her college dorm and been found by a friend. That information wasn't exactly a secret, but nor was it publicly available.

```
AmyGibson: Oliver was stabbed in jail last night.
I'm supposed to stay home until they know what
happened
```

```
VanChick84: Maybe I can come over?
```

I almost laugh at that. Uh, no, weirdly, I'm not letting you come into my apartment when I'm here, because someone tried to kill my brother and I might be in danger myself.

```
AmyGibson: I'm not seeing anyone right now
```

```
VanChick84: I guess that makes sense
```

```
VanChick84: And it probably sounded creepy that I
asked
```

```
VanChick84: I'm doing this all wrong
```

```
VanChick84: I'm sorry I bothered you. I shouldn't
have come
```

AmyGibson: Wait. If you have something, I'd like
to know what it is

Silence. It goes on long enough that I think she's disconnected.

VanChick84: Can we meet in a public place?

VanChick84: This is just really hard for me. I kept
quiet for so many years, and it's been tearing me
up, but I'm still . . . I'm still afraid

AmyGibson: Of Oliver?

VanChick84: No. Maybe I should be, but this is
more personal and more selfish

VanChick84: I'll meet you anyplace you want

AmyGibson: Let me see what I can do. I'll give you
my number. Call me tomorrow morning

VanChick84: I fly out tonight. Again, I'm sorry. It
really was a quick trip. I lied to my husband. He
thinks I just spent the night in Whistler at a
work conference. I need to get back tonight

AmyGibson: What time is your flight?

VanChick84: 7:10 out of Grand Forks, with a
connection at 9:45 to Vancouver

I quickly check the flights. Those are correct—it's the last flight from Toronto to Vancouver.

VanChick84: We can meet anyplace you feel safe.
Please. I've lived with this for eighteen years,
and if I don't come clean now, I'm going to change
my mind

VanChick84: Your brother isn't who you think he is.
I know you won't want to hear that. Maybe he can
get help. Either way, though, you seem like someone
who'd want to know the truth

AmyGibson: I am. Hold on while I think

I pop off a message to Castillo, explaining as succinctly as I can. Then, as it sits in Delivered status, I mentally zoom through my options.

I don't want to meet at the coffee shop down the road. It's too close to home. Of course, the advantage to that one is that I could walk. I definitely shouldn't drive my car with that tracker on it. The best option would be to grab a rideshare and meet her at a bakery I frequent near the university. It's quiet this time of year, when only summer students like me are still around. It's also easily accessible—the car can drop me off and pick me up right out front on a major road.

It's safe. That's the important thing.

What would be even safer, though? Getting a ride from Castillo.

I call him, but it goes to voice mail.

"Hey, it's Amy. Can you check your texts, please? It's urgent."

VanChick84: Are you still there?

AmyGibson: I am. Just thinking

I check my watch. It's already four thirty. She's going to need to be at the airport by six. That doesn't give me time to delay.

I'd be meeting this woman at a very public coffee shop, during the late afternoon. As risks go, it's bare minimum.

So why am I hesitating? Because Castillo told me to stay here, and I don't want to look careless by traipsing off to meet a stranger. If someone thinks I'm not terribly bright, I'm going to prove them wrong, even if it means awkwardly wedging "PhD student" into a conversation. If they think I'm a spoiled rich girl, I'll be quick to accept "financially stable girl" while trying to clarify that my "trust fund" is actually an inheritance, and not exactly millions of dollars at that.

If a guy like Castillo—hardworking, capable, stable—thinks I'm a bit of a twit, then I'll do backflips to prove him wrong.

Even if it means losing this lead? One I can pursue safely?

I look down at my phone.

Damn it, Dean.

If he can't return my urgent messages, then screw him. I'm sorry, but I am *not* irresponsible. I'm not silly or careless.

AmyGibson: Can you meet me for coffee in the university district in 20 minutes?

VanChick84: Any chance of finding a place closer to the airport?

AmyGibson: I'll make sure you're on your way in plenty of time. It's a short drive, and it's a small airport, no lineups

VanChick84: That should be fine. I'm checked in, and I only have carry-on. As long as I'm there by 6:30, I'll be good

TWENTY

As soon as I've sent VanChick the address, I call a ride-share. I take every step with caution. Check the building hall. Stay aware of my surroundings. When an elevator arrives with someone on it, I pretend I forgot something and wait for an empty one. Then I stay in the apartment lobby until my car arrives.

Once in the car, I text all the details to Castillo. Copy and paste them into an email and send that, too. Then I phone Dinah.

"Hey," I say when she answers. "I'm not calling to pester for updates on Oliver, though I'll obviously take them if there are any."

"He's awake, and there aren't any complications. He still can't have visitors, but I'm hoping they'll let him video chat with you later."

I smile. "Good. I'd like that."

"I've convinced him to seek bail. It did take some convincing. Your brother is a very stubborn man, Amy."

"I know," I sigh. "Will he be in the hospital for a while, then?"

"The doctors want to observe him for a couple of days. I've also convinced him not to rush and—if he can bring himself to do it—not undersell the pain he's in. I'd like to get bail sorted before he needs to return to prison."

"Good call. Thank you." I glance out the window, watching passing traffic. "Before I let you go, my actual reason for phoning is that I'm looking for Dean. I need to discuss something with him, and he's not answering messages."

"I saw him about an hour ago. Then I had to take a call, and when I finished, he was gone. He had a laundry list of things he was investigating. If he checks in, I'll tell him you're looking for him."

"Thanks."

Her voice lowers. "Is it about Laura, Amy?"

I go still, hand tightening on the phone.

She continues, "He told me that you thought you saw her."

Thought. I don't miss that word.

I bite back the urge to say that I did see Laura, beyond any doubt.

"Yes," I say evenly. "She put a tracker on my car."

"Dean showed me photos of that. Someone did put that tracker on your car."

Someone.

She's being kind here, in deference to a longstanding relationship. Otherwise, she'd be carving up my story with razor-sharp blades.

Silence stretches. She's waiting for me to push. To insist it was Laura. To get defensive and demand action.

"I trust you'll do whatever you think is right with that information," I say, my tone cool.

"Amy . . ." she says, a sigh in her voice.

"I won't say anything on the podcast yet," I say in the same tone. "I trust that you'll make the right decisions here, based on what you know about me. I have no doubt who I saw, but I understand you have more important leads to pursue." *Okay, that's a low blow.*

"Amy . . ."

"If you speak to Dean, please tell him I left messages."

"Let's meet later," Dinah says. "I'd like to hear the story in your own words."

"Dean has that on video. Please let me know if there's any update with Oliver, either his condition or his bail. Thank you."

I end the call just as the driver stops in front of the coffee shop.

As expected, the shop is quiet. That is to say, it's not jam-packed with studying students, as it would be during the term. It's still about a third full, a few tables occupied by summer students and laptops, the remainder by regular people happy to be able to actually get a seat.

I scan the occupants. The only people sitting alone are on laptops. I take a closer look at them, as discreetly as I can.

Of the people older than me, only one is a woman, and she's a senior citizen. I order a decaf cappuccino—two coffees in one afternoon would keep me awake all night. Then, while I wait for it, I snag a table at the back and sit facing the door.

We were supposed to meet at 4:50. At five, I'm alone in that corner, sipping as slowly as I can. I keep checking my phone, each time needing to remind myself that I didn't give her any contact information.

At 5:10, I open the forum on my browser to see whether VanChick tried to contact me there. Then I leave it open as I scan the coffee shop. I feel a bit like Castillo, casing out a dangerous alley.

Speaking of Castillo, have I heard back from him? I check my phone. No, I have not. But that doesn't matter. The point is that I can't see any way this is a trap. Well, not unless VanChick is another actor hired by Laura, and she strides in and starts shouting accusations at me. I can't see Laura pulling that stunt twice, and even if she does, I'm prepared.

I'm wishing I'd brought my own laptop. Earlier, I'd been thinking that I didn't mind being locked up in my apartment, but now that I'm here, seeing others working, it would have been a change of scenery. The dangerous part was getting from point A to point B. It doesn't matter if I linger, as long as I'm gone before sundown—and the coffee shop closes well before that.

I'm debating whether to give up when a car pulls up with the rideshare logo in the window. Perfect.

Before I can step from the table, a woman scrambles out of the car, clearly flustered and saying something to the driver while checking her watch. With a wave to the driver, she sprints through the door before stopping herself.

She has a dark ponytail, a yoga enthusiast's body and YouTube-tutorial-perfect makeup that makes her look my age, but on close inspection, she's probably in her late thirties. She's rolling a carry-on bag behind her. She sees me and hurries over.

"Amy?" When I nod, she sighs in relief. "I'm so sorry. I had two—*two*—drivers ghost me. I was just asking that one to come back and pick me up in a half hour, or I might not get a car." She pauses, as if there is something she forgot. Then she thrusts out her hand. "Beth."

I don't ask whether that's her real name. I just shake her hand.

"Coffee . . ." She looks around, still flustered, her hands shaking.

"I'll grab it. Sit and relax."

"Oh, my God, thank you. I was already nervous, and this . . ." She flutters her hands.

Beth tells me what she wants to drink, and I head up to the counter while she settles in with her luggage. When I glance over, she's taking deep, practiced breaths.

I place her order, return to the table and slide in. "They'll bring it by."

"Thank you," she says again. Her voice shakes. "Though at this stage, maybe I should have asked for a nice, calming tea. I do not need more caffeine, though at least it'll make me talk faster."

I smile. "It's fine. We have time. I'll set my alarm so we're sure you aren't late."

"Thank you." She makes a face. "I know I keep saying that, but really, thank you for all this, meeting me and being so nice. I must have sounded like such a flake, telling you I flew across the country to talk to you. I've never done anything like that. If my husband found out . . ."

She trails off, gaze on her hands. I glance down to see pink polish failing to cover bitten fingernails.

"I suppose I shouldn't say things like that to someone like you," she murmurs.

"Hmm?"

Her gaze stays on her hands. "Admitting I'm afraid of my husband to a woman who runs a podcast warning about abusive partners." Her gaze shoots up to mine. "He's not. Abusive, I mean. I just don't like to upset him. You aren't married, right?"

"I'm not."

"Well, when you are, it's good to keep things running smoothly. Danny and I got married right after college. He's a really good father. A good provider, too."

She doesn't say he's a good husband, but I try not to read anything into that. I'm here to listen to what she has to say about Oliver. That's it.

She continues, "If I say that I'm worried about him finding out I came here, it's only—"

She stops as the server delivers her coffee. She waits until the guy is gone and then lowers her voice. "It's only that he'd be concerned. I can be a bit scattered." A wan smile. "Shocking, huh? Anyway, Danny worries about me, and if he knew I'd come across the country on my own, he'd freak out. Also, what I'm going to tell you—"

Her phone rings with some nineties dance tune. As people look over, her eyes widen, and she quickly turns it to vibrate. Then she squeaks an "Oh no." Her gaze lifts to mine. "It's Danny. I have to answer this."

She might have said he isn't abusive, but that look in her eyes tells me everything I need to know.

"Go ahead," I say gently. "We have time."

She answers. I busy myself on my own phone, so I'm not listening to her conversation. He must be asking how she's doing, and she overdoes it, babbling about the conference. He doesn't seem to pick up on her nerves, and instead seems to be telling her about some class-related issue that a teacher called for.

Beth keeps shooting apologetic glances my way. She makes little "hurry up" motions but says nothing to him, only keeping her answers brief, as if not to prolong the conversation. He's clearly feeling chatty, though, and she doesn't seem willing to cut him off, undoubtedly afraid it'll seem suspicious.

From my end, it sounds like a very normal conversation for such a situation, one spouse at home while the other is away. That doesn't mean it isn't a controlling relationship . . . or a toxic one. This is where people go wrong, like thinking a pleasant-seeming guy would never murder a woman who gently ended their relationship. They might have concerns about a husband's behavior, but then they see him acting normal and tell themselves they're wrong.

As the conversation stretches, Beth's panic begins to tinge those looks my way, and my "it's okay" smile gets increasingly strained. It doesn't help that I'm starting to feel the effects of being up since two in the morning. I really shouldn't have opted for decaf.

I struggle to keep my smile on . . . while both not yawning and not checking the time. Finally, I motion that I'm going to use the bathroom. In there, I splash cold water on my face and blink. Just another hour, and then I can go home and nap. And with any luck, I'll actually hear what Beth came to say before she leaves.

When I get back to the table, Beth is still on the phone, but she says, "Oh! I'm late for the next session! Can I call you later?"

He must agree, because she signs off and starts babbling apologies.

"It's fine," I say, with a smile that I hope sells the sentiment. "Is everything okay at home?"

"It is. He just wanted to talk." She inhales. "Okay, now let's get on with this before I run out of time."

My smile that time is definitely genuine. *Yes, please, let's do that.*

"I'm going to start with a confession," she says. "It's also an explanation. The reason I haven't come forward. The reason I still can't come forward." Another inhale as her gaze darts around, making sure no one can overhear.

"I . . . I had a thing with your brother. An . . ." She glances away, looking abashed. "I'd say an affair, but that sounds a lot more formal than . . ." Another glance away.

"You hooked up with Oliver."

"Yes." She twists the paper napkin in her hands. "I know this is weird to talk about when he's your brother, and I don't know what he's like now, but back then . . ."

I brace myself, something I've been doing ever since she contacted me online. She said it's about Greta's death, something about Oliver, something bad. That's why I so desperately wanted this to be a setup. Otherwise . . .

Dinah has warned me that I will hear things. People will speak out against Oliver.

Oh, sure, he seemed nice, but you didn't know the real Oliver Harding.

I worked for him, and he behaved inappropriately.

I went out with him in high school, and he was an asshole.

In light of accusations, people rethink their interactions with the accused. That's good if they've always felt something was "off" and no one listened to them. It's not so good if they're twisting memories to fit a new narrative.

Castillo says there's been remarkably little of that with Oliver. Oh, there isn't a tsunami of support, and I don't expect that. Even his own sister won't use her podcast to defend him. We have all seen far too many cases where people defended the accused . . . only to realize they were horribly wrong. But we aren't seeing any narrative reworking, and Dinah's pleased by that.

So now, when Beth says those words, *I don't know what he's like now, but back then* . . . I brace as she trails off.

"This is awkward," she says, shifting. "So apologies in advance, Amy, if it's uncomfortable. But your brother? He was—is— very good-looking, in case you don't realize that, being his sister. He was also a genuinely nice guy. Smart and sweet and hot . . . and my roomie's boyfriend."

"Okay . . ." *Not what I expected.*

"The other thing . . ." She twists her wedding band. "I met Danny in high school. We've been together ever since."

I pause, as I realize why she's telling me this. "You were with your husband when you hooked up with Oliver."

She nods. "That's why I can't come forward. Bad enough I was sleeping with my roomie's guy, but I cheated on the boy-friend who's now my husband."

I nod, not knowing what to say.

"I don't want to make excuses," she says, glancing away. "My boyfriend was hundreds of kilometers away. I was lonely. Oliver was having trouble with Greta, trying to help with her depression and getting frustrated when he couldn't. We talked, a lot, and one night . . ." She shrugs and looks away. "He felt terrible afterward. Worse than I did."

"So it was just the one time."

Her shoulders hunch in. "I wish I could say that, but I . . ." She takes a deep breath, as if steeling herself, before meeting my eyes. "I fell for your brother, Amy. Hard. He was having such a tough time, and I . . . made myself available."

So she used the situation to keep sleeping with Oliver, preying on his vulnerability.

I'm good at keeping my expression neutral—I've interviewed people for the podcast who make my stomach churn, those who refused to believe a victim or still supported a killer— and I need to call on all that practice to keep my revulsion from showing.

"You said there was something to do with Greta's death and Oliver," I say.

She nods. "It wasn't his fault. I'm just afraid this . . . thing will come out. When Greta died—"

My alarm goes off, startling us both.

"Oh!" Beth says, her eyes rounding in panic. She checks her watch. "I can stay five more minutes—"

Her phone beeps. She picks it up, and the panic in her face intensifies. She shoots a look at the front window . . . where the rideshare car that dropped her off idles.

"Oh God," she says. "I forgot I'd prearranged pickup. Maybe she can just wait there . . ." She trails off as she sees the problem. The rideshare car is pulled over on a busy road, blocking the right lane during rush hour.

"Can you come with me?" she blurts. "I'm covering the fare through my app. The car can drop me off at the airport and then take you home. We'll talk on the way."

I nod and rise, and the floor seems to sway, the exhaustion sweeping over me.

Beth scrambles to grab my arm. "You okay?"

"Long night. Really shouldn't have gotten decaf."

I shake myself, and we head to the little car. Beth fumbles with the trunk, and a pickup driver trapped behind the car lays on his horn.

"I've got it," I say.

I get the trunk open while she climbs into the back seat. I struggle to put the suitcase in. It's not heavy—I'm just too tired to quite manage the spatial-awareness puzzle of getting it into the trunk.

The truck blares its horn again, still trapped by nonstop traffic in the left lane. I get the suitcase in and the trunk closed, and then I slide into the back seat.

The driver—a woman with frizzy hair and sunglasses—gives me a lightning-fast nod before pulling from the curb and joining traffic.

"Are you sure you're okay?" Beth asks me. "You really don't look good."

I don't feel good, either. I think back to what I ate earlier. The restaurant lunch? The snack Castillo bought?

"Amy?" Beth says.

"I'm fine." I manage the best smile I can. "Now, you were saying something about Oliver?"

"Right! Sorry. I'm a little flustered."

"It's okay."

She nods and lowers her voice so the driver can't overhear. "I think Greta found out the night she died."

"Found out . . . ? Oh, that you and Oliver were hooking up."

My brain *really* isn't firing on all cylinders. *Is it hot in here?* I reach for the window, but the driver has the child lock on. Before I can ask for it to be released, Beth continues.

"Yes, about me and Oliver. I . . . I'm worried that's what pushed her over the edge. I'm afraid she accused him of hooking up with me, and they argued, and she took her life. That doesn't mean he's to blame, but maybe, if he didn't say the right things, if he tried to defend himself?"

I shake my head. "The police investigated after Greta's suicide. Oliver was quick to cooperate. There was no sign they'd been in contact that day. The police checked both phones . . ."

My words slur, and I blink hard.

"Amy?"

"Just . . . it's been a long day."

"Oh my God, that's right! Oliver was stabbed. I saw it in the news. I meant to ask how he's doing, and I completely forgot."

"He's . . ." More slurring. "He's okay."

"That's good. I still care about him. I mean, how could I not, right? He's rich and hot."

I blink at her.

She continues, "Oh! And single now, right? After that thing with his girlfriend? He must be single. Do you think I could see him? Or you could just give him my number, let him know I still think about him." Her eyebrows waggle.

"Wh . . . *what?*"

"Where exactly was he stabbed?" More brow-waggling. "Not any place important, I hope."

What the hell is going on here?

My mind feels as if it's slogging through molasses. There's a dim awareness that something is very, very—*get out of the car now!*—wrong, but I feel as if I'm watching this in a movie, internally shouting at a clueless character while my butt stays firmly planted in the seat.

Wrong. So wrong. Need to get out.

I reach for the door handle, but my fingers only claw in the general vicinity, unable to grasp.

Hands grab me. I twist, panic rising far too slowly. I flail, my hands still all but useless, barely obeying. One manages to snag Beth's hair as I try to push her back.

Beth pushes me away . . . and her hair stays in my fingers, a wig pulling half-free. She yanks it from my hand and then calmly pats it back into place.

My brain screams for me to fight, shout, anything. There's a driver right there, in the front seat, and I can't even make my mouth move enough to call for help, managing only a garbled sound that's swallowed by the traffic.

Beth looks over at me, her expression distressed. "I'm so sorry. I didn't have a choice. They were threatening me, and I . . ." She sniffles. "I had to do it, or they'd have gone after my children. I'm so sorry."

Then she rolls her eyes, and the false sniffles disappear. "Yeah, no. Not at all sorry. And screw the kids. Well, if I had any, I'd say screw them. They can fend for themselves, right?"

My mouth works, the world blinking, as if someone is flicking a light switch.

"This is about money," she says, almost cheerfully. "Let's just hope Oliver wants to see his little sister again, huh?"

I blink, struggling to focus. I'm sliding down in my seat. I manage to turn forward, to see the driver, my mouth opening again, trying to tell her something is wrong.

The driver pulls off her sunglasses and meets my gaze in the rearview mirror. The eyes that look back at me are so familiar my brain stutters to a complete halt.

"Night night, Amy," Laura says, and everything goes dark.

TWENTY-ONE

I wake three times before I accept that I've been kidnapped. The first two times, I startle up in a panic, only to decide I'm dreaming at home in my bed. I don't try to sit up or turn on a light or do anything to confirm this conviction. Blame the drugs swirling in my system. I wake, and the drugs pull me back under, my brain so groggy that "dreamed I was kidnapped" seems the only explanation.

Hell, even once I'm awake enough to realize otherwise, "dreamed I was kidnapped" feels like the only answer.

Kidnapped? Really? My sister-in-law kidnapped me? Things like that don't happen in real life. It's like . . . Well, it's like my sister-in-law faking her death. Or my brother being framed for attempted murder.

Or my mom being taken from a parking garage at eight a.m. and murdered by a guy she'd briefly dated.

It feels unreal. All of it does. But I know what happened to my mother is true, and I am equally certain that Oliver is being framed and that Laura is alive so . . . Is this *so* unbelievable?

It feels unreal because it's happening to me. Why would Laura kidnap *me*?

I remember what Beth said about money. Is that what this is? A kidnapping for cash?

And who the hell is Beth? Not Greta's former roommate. She's the right age, but they must have known I couldn't access much information surrounding Greta's death.

I'd given Beth two opportunities to drug my coffee. First, when I offered to order her drink because she'd been so obviously flustered. Second, when I used the bathroom to give her privacy on a call. I'd been a decent person, and she'd taken advantage of it.

Yeah, not much point in being indignant over that. The important part is that I've been kidnapped.

I noticed right away that I'm not bound and gagged. I'm just in a dark room on what feels like a cot.

I'd been knocked out while we were driving through the heart of Grand Forks. Are we still there? In a house? An apartment? An abandoned building? I have no idea . . . because I was unconscious when we arrived.

If I thought I was in the city, I'd scream. But Laura is smart. If I'm not gagged, that means no one will hear me, and I'll only alert her that I'm awake.

I take a moment to listen, hoping for some distant sound that will give me a sense of my surroundings, but it's quiet. I inhale and smell mildew. No clues there then.

I rise slowly from the bed. Then I stand. My knees wobble— I'm still groggy—and I pause to let the light-headedness of standing pass.

Once I've gotten my balance, I feel my way around in the pitch dark until I touch a wall above the head of my cot. There's another wall to my right, with the cot pushed up against it.

Hands to the wall, I follow it only a meter before reaching a corner. I continue feeling along that until there's what feels like a doorframe. My fingers lower to a doorknob. I very carefully turn the knob, bracing against a squeak—

"Hello, Amy," Laura's voice says right outside my door.

I stop.

A humorless chuckle. "I can see the knob turning. I know you're up and around."

I still don't answer. I'm hoping she'll come in. That would give me a chance to do something, anything. Attack her. Push her aside and flee.

But again, she's smart, and I'd like to think I am, too. If I'm not bound, she isn't going to open that door.

She sighs. "You never were the brightest bulb, were you?"

I bite my tongue. She's trying to get a rise from me, just like online when she hinted about me being "too close" to Oliver.

"I shouldn't be surprised you ignored the message I left at your car," she says. "I had hoped for better, but alas . . ." The door shifts, as if she's leaning against it. "I know you never liked me much, Amy."

"I liked you fine, Laura. You're the one who didn't like me."

There's silence. Then, "Is that what he said? Of course it is. Oh, Oliver, you are so predictable. Let me guess. He didn't say it outright. He just hinted and insinuated while acting as if he was trying to keep you from knowing."

I want to ignore her, chalk this up to more needling, but in my mind, I hear Martine.

I wanted to respect your boundaries, Amy, but I always thought I'd love to have a coffee with you sometime, just the two of us. Get to know you. Overcome whatever concerns you had.

I know I wasn't what you wanted for Oliver.

I shake that off. It'd been obvious that Laura didn't like me, and if Oliver tried to keep me from knowing, that was what any decent person would do.

"Aren't you going to ask me why I did it?" she says after a few moments of silence.

"Why you did what? Faked your own death? Shot Martine? Framed Oliver? Or kidnapped me? It's a long list, Laura, and I'm not sure where to start."

Another of those humorless laughs. "Seems Beth was right— you're a little quicker these days. She's the one who came up with that silly story about Oliver hooking up with Greta's roomie. I didn't think we needed to be so subtle. She'd been doing her homework, checking into you, and she thought subtlety was required. Good call, too. You're more paranoid than I expected. Still, you *did* get into a car with a stranger."

I grind my teeth. In one breath, she's calling me paranoid— not careful or cautious but paranoid—while in the next, she's implying I did something foolish. I didn't. I got into a car with the proper rideshare logo, in broad daylight, during rush hour.

"Amy?" she prods.

"Why did you try to kill Martine?"

"Jealousy. She's sleeping with my husband." A pause. "Is that what you expect me to say?"

"No, because you left Oliver. You don't give a shit who he's with these days. You shot her to frame Oliver. So I guess it's not so much a question as the fact that I can't comprehend murdering an innocent stranger to hurt someone else."

"Why not? Men kill their children to hurt their wives. Women kill their children to hurt their husbands. Comparatively speaking, killing a stranger is far less monstrous, don't you think?"

I snort an answer.

"You should be nicer to me, Amy. You forget where you are. But you were always like this. The kind of girl who strolls through life, grabbing with both hands, heedless of others. Or *is* that the real you? You don't seem like someone who'd care about their brother's girlfriend getting shot more than they'd care about being kidnapped themselves. Hmm. Maybe we aren't what we seem. Maybe we just appear that way to those whose perception is controlled by others."

Before I can answer, Laura says, "I didn't kill Martine. I injured her. I knew what I was doing. Someday, she's going to look back and realize that I actually saved her. I don't expect a thank-you card, but she'll understand."

"That you saved her from my brother?"

"Believe that . . . or don't believe it, Amy. I don't know you, despite having been your sister-in-law for two years. I still can't tell whether you're a victim or a co-conspirator."

"Victim of *Oliver*?"

"Ah, *co-conspirator* then." She cuts off my protest. "Yes, my vote is for *victim*. You seem far too earnest to run a podcast about predators while sheltering one. He's using you, like he uses everyone."

"Then explain," I say, my voice lowering. "Explain what happened to you so I understand."

"So you can defend him, you mean."

"No, I—"

She cuts me short. "I'm not justifying myself to you, Amy. I don't actually give a shit whether you believe me or not."

"Are you saying you faked your own death to escape Oliver?"

"I'm not playing this game."

I move closer to the door. "It's not a game. I want to understand. You faked your death, but now you're back for justice?"

"Still not playing."

Yeah, she's not playing—because she's the one *running* the game.

Let's say Laura faked her death to escape Oliver. Forget whether or not I can see him driving anyone to that. Say it happened, and that's a fact. She flees and then, three years later, realizes she's left a predator at large.

That happens. Women come forward years after they escaped, and then get "Why didn't you say something sooner?" Well, because their priority—understandably—was getting to safety. Once they feel safe, they may think of others in their abuser's life, and they go back to accuse him.

That makes sense. Laura flees Oliver's abuse and then returns to ensure other women don't suffer at his hands. And to do that, she . . . shoots the woman she suspects he's now abusing? Shoots her and then gives up on justice—while he's still awaiting trial—and instead kidnaps his sister for money?

None of that makes sense.

Laura faked her own death for reasons unknown. Was she in trouble? Did she have some greater plan—a miraculous return, complete with book deal? Had Oliver done something—cheated on her, maybe—and this was her revenge?

What matters is that she's back, and she has some vendetta against Oliver, and she's decided she'll settle for cash. Maybe that was the goal all along.

"What do you want from me, Laura?" I ask, not really expecting an answer.

"Nothing," she says. "I just came to explain what's going on so you don't scream yourself hoarse and ruin your pretty hands banging at the door."

I scowl. "Have I done any of that? I presume if I'm not gagged and bound, screaming and pounding wouldn't do any good."

"Smart girl. Maybe you'll get that PhD after all. We're outside the city, Amy. No one will hear you shouting, though you're welcome to try. Best thing you can do is sit tight and wait for Oliver to pay up. Oh, and there is a light in there. I'll let you have the challenge of finding it—give you something to do. Turn it on, and you'll find reading material, a toilet, food and water."

"You do know Oliver's in the hospital, right? He can't bring you any money."

"He's getting bail, just as I said he would. In a day or two, he'll be out. Then you'd better hope he pays up."

TWENTY-TWO

I don't panic. Maybe that's the lingering drugs deadening my reaction. Or maybe it's just common sense. Laura isn't threatening to kill me. She hasn't tortured me. I won't think of what's to come if Oliver doesn't pay, because I know he will. He'll pay, and she'll let me out, and then she'll run again. I'll tell the police, and they'll know who was framing Oliver, and he'll be free. At great cost, but at least it's only a monetary one.

I find the light. It's a switch by the bed that illuminates a bare bulb in a socket. From that, I can see my surroundings. I'm in a windowless room, maybe eight feet long by five feet wide, like a pantry or walk-in closet. The walls are builder-beige with obvious marks where someone has hastily repaired before painting, and the floor is what looks like remnant carpet, poorly installed. A slapdash job on a house put up for sale or rental.

The "no windows" part means none of that helps right now. It's just data I can give the police later to find it for any clues.

I tug up the carpet in one corner. Under it is . . . another carpet. Yep, definitely a half-assed job. I note the color of both carpets and leave that corner pulled up. I can imagine Castillo rolling his eyes at that.

Yeah, Gibson, the cops aren't searching every damn country house recently for sale or rent, looking for that one where you pulled up the carpet.

I don't care. It makes me feel as if I've done something.

As for the rest of the room, the only furniture is my cot, which has a pillow and blanket. Oh, and a portable toilet. On the toilet seat is a stack of magazines, bottled water, energy bars, apples and bananas. I'm allergic to bananas, and I can't imagine Laura forgot that, not after the time she brought over "zucchini bread" she'd bought at a market and my EpiPen saved my life. Oliver had been livid. Laura claimed it'd been labeled Zucchini, so it was hardly her fault.

The bananas are a raised middle finger. So are the magazines, which are all library discards of *Cosmopolitan*. At least they have fiction excerpts.

Laura has taken my watch—because it's a smartwatch, with other functions—so I have no idea what time it is. Did I sleep through the night? Is it *still* night? Late the next day? Who knows?

I do spend some time trying to figure out an escape. Even if I know it's pointless, my sense of pride won't let me be the victim who sits there reading *Cosmo* when there's actually an escape route. There isn't. One door. Solid and locked, and when I so much as push on it, someone outside tells me not to bother.

Was that Laura's voice? Beth's? Is Beth her accomplice? Or just someone she hired?

I attempt to talk to Laura again. She doesn't bite. I attempt to hear that other voice again, to see whether it's Beth or someone else. There's no response, even when I rattle and bang on the door.

I make mental notes of what I see and hear. Yeah, that's 99 percent pointless when I can only see this tiny room and can only hear the house creaking and occasional footsteps or a toilet flush.

Eventually, I break down and drink some water and eat a bar. Both are wrapped, which means they're safe, right? Nope. Within twenty minutes, I feel the now familiar symptoms of sedation. I struggle to stay awake. I don't know why. It's just that sleeping feels like giving up and accepting my situation. Just like last time, though, the drugs work.

I wake once. There's someone in the room with me. I'm still groggy, and the light has been turned out, so all I know is that I sense someone there. Then I hear breathing.

"Laura?" I croak.

A pressure on my bare arm. I yank, but someone's holding it. The pressure becomes a poke. A needle.

I let out a yelp as cold fills my veins. Then I struggle, but hands hold me down, almost calmly, as if I am a struggling child. Within moments, I'm asleep again.

"Put down the knife and raise your hands!" a voice barks.

I try to open my eyes, but my lids feel like lead.

The voice comes again, even sharper. A male voice.

A cop.

Rescue.

I inwardly exhale in relief. I still can't open my eyes, but that voice is like an angel's song. They've found me. Laura is under arrest.

"Let go of the knife!" the voice snaps.

There's a hard prod at my shoulder, a rough poke. I struggle again with waking and manage to open my eyes a crack. Harsh light blinds me.

"Amy Gibson! Put down the knife!"

Amy Gibson?

Me?

I pry my eyes open, and I expect to see a police officer bending over my cot. Instead, I'm staring at pant legs.

I'm on the floor? Did I fall off the cot?

I tense my muscles to try rising, and I make it up onto one elbow.

"Stop!" the voice booms, hurting my head. "Do not move until you have put down that knife."

"Knife?" I croak.

There's a movement, something just above my visual range. I lift my head and find myself looking into a gun. I fall onto my back as my hands fly up.

"Drop it now!"

Even as he says it, something falls from my hand. Something I'm only vaguely aware that my fingers have been wrapped around. Then I see my hands, raised in front of me. Red. My hands are red. I move one, and it's sticky and wet.

Blood. My hands are covered in blood.

There is a knife on the floor in front of me, and my hands are covered in blood.

"Lift your hands higher," the man snaps.

I do. Then the scene comes into focus. Two police officers. A man and a woman. Both have their guns trained on me. I'm lying on an unfamiliar floor. There's an open door behind the female officer, and beyond it, green fields under an early morning sun.

"Laura," I croak. "You need to find Laura. She kidnapped me."

"Keep your hands where we can see them."

I do, and the female officer comes over with cuffs. I blink, but I don't move. I'm too numb and drugged and shocked to move.

"I don't understand," I say.

"Stand up," the female officer says.

"I . . . I'm not sure I can. I've been drugged. I'm sorry. I don't understand what's happening."

"I need you to try standing," she says, not unkindly. "If you can't, we'll help you, but I'd like you to try. No sudden moves. Okay, Amy?"

I nod. "May I use my hands?"

"You can."

Even if I weren't drugged, it wouldn't be easy, rising with my hands bound, but I manage it. I stand, teetering and struggling to focus. I glance over my shoulder, being careful to leave my hands where they can see them.

Then I see something on the floor behind me. Blood. A pool of blood. My gaze lowers to a pile of what looks like wet clothing—

No, my gaze lowers to a *body*. A body covered in blood-soaked clothing, head thrown back, dead eyes open in outrage and shock.

"Laura," I whisper, and my knees give way.

TWENTY-THREE

The sight of Laura's body evaporates any remaining shell shock from the drugs. I've been found with Laura's stabbed corpse, a knife in my grip, my hands covered in blood.

I look over at Laura again, her sightless eyes staring at me.

Dead. Laura is dead.

Except in my mind, she's been dead for years, and to now have her dead again? My mind can't quite compute that, as if this is another trick.

It's not a trick. Her empty eyes tell me that.

She's dead, and I don't know how to feel about that because she'd been the monster who shot Martine and framed Oliver.

And kidnapped me. That seems inconsequential now, or maybe that's just me, shoving my own trauma aside.

Laura is dead, and I was found holding the knife, and *holy shit, I was found holding the knife that killed Laura.*

The officers don't want to hear my explanations. They can't do anything with them, and I know that. What are they going to say?

Huh, okay, that makes sense—you can go.

Deciding whether I did this or not isn't their job. I've been found at a murder scene holding the presumed murder weapon. These cuffs are staying on, and I am going to the station and probably to jail.

So why do I tell them what happened? Because the fact that I explain *does* matter. Or, more accurately, if I *didn't* try to explain, that would be a strike against me.

These officers can attest that I immediately started protesting with the same story that I will continue to tell because it is the truth.

Also, if I'm that cool and calculated, maybe I am still in shock.

No, while I *am* in shock, I don't calmly relay my story. I'm freaked out, panicking, struggling to keep from going wild. Laura is dead. I was found by her body. I was holding the bloodied knife.

The officers manage to get me outside, as I struggle not to fight them. A pickup roars down a long dirt road, dust enveloping it until it reaches the house. Then a door flies open, and Castillo comes running, and again, my knees buckle, this time in relief.

"What's going on here?" he says, bearing down on us. "Why is she in cuffs?"

"Sir, please step back—"

"I didn't do it," I blurt. "Laura's dead, and I didn't do it. She kidnapped me."

Castillo's face sets, hard and grim. "I know."

"Now she's dead. Stabbed. I was found holding the knife, but I was unconscious. She drugged my food. I woke up with these officers standing over me."

"Sir, please—" the officer repeats.

"I'm three meters away," Castillo says. "I'm a private investigator, and Ms. Gibson is my client."

"That's fine, but—"

"Amy? Dinah is in court getting Oliver's bail. I can't get through to her, but I've left messages. I'll meet you at the station."

"Sir . . ." the officer says.

Castillo lifts his hands. "Still staying where I am. I'm not interfering or trying to stop you."

The officers put me into a car.

"They'll have summoned backup," Castillo calls over to me. "They'll need to stay until it arrives before they can leave. I'll wait here with you."

"Sir . . ." the officer warns.

"Show me where I can wait that doesn't threaten your scene, but I *am* waiting. Like I said, she's my client, and she's just been framed for murder. I'm not going anywhere."

The only way I can process the rest of the day is to imagine scripting it for my podcast. I'd never admit that to anyone for fear of sounding exactly like what I've been accused of being—an attention hog who'll mine any personal crisis for subscribers.

I will never actually record that episode. The police don't deserve it. They are doing what they must, under the circumstances, just as they did when Martine accused Oliver of shooting her, but that doesn't make it any easier. I am terrified and trying not to freak out, knowing if I freak out, they can use that against me, but also knowing if I'm too calm, that also acts against me, and how the hell am I supposed to be?

Innocent. Act like I feel, frightened and confused. I'm in a police station, being questioned by people who think I stabbed my sister-in-law to death.

And that's not even the worst part. This is what would be hard to explain in a podcast. Being questioned is actually easy, because at least it feels like progress. That only takes a couple of hours, split over several sessions, and Dinah is there with me. The rest is waiting. Endless waiting, alone and terrified and barely able to process what happened, what *is* happening.

Laura is dead, stabbed to death, and I've been framed for her murder. Not just accused of it, but released from the room where she'd been holding me captive and staged to look as if I'd murdered her.

I remember someone in my room, the prick in my arm and the cold coursing through my veins. I'd woken just long enough to register someone there, in the darkness.

Was it Laura, making sure I stayed asleep with a stronger sedative?

Or was it her killer, having known I was there and planned it enough to bring a sedative injection?

The point, for Dinah, is that I was clearly drugged. She insisted on a toxicology screening. The results of that are still pending.

She also had photos taken of the site where I claim to have been injected—and there's a pinprick wound to support that.

I didn't kill Laura and then randomly fall asleep over her dead body. I was clearly drugged, and even the police recognize that, though in their version, I fought back *despite* being drugged. They are also allowing for the possibility that I killed Laura in a drug-induced psychotic state.

Is *that* possible? Laura injected me with something that reacted wrong, and instead of knocking me out, it put me into a psychotic state? I overpowered her and killed her and don't remember it?

I won't say that's *im*possible. I can't. I can only tell my story. My food was drugged, and I drifted off, but then someone injected me, and that's the last thing I remember.

The theory Dinah gives the police is that the food-drugging was meant to put me to sleep during my captivity, so I'd be as little trouble as possible. The injection was with something stronger, to ensure I didn't wake up while being moved and positioned beside Laura's dead body.

That'd be my interpretation, too, but I let Dinah do all the explaining. If I theorize about what happened, then it sounds as if I'm fabricating a narrative or, worse, that I already had one and fashioned the crime to fit it.

The police seem to accept that I *was* kidnapped. There's the room where I was kept, complete with everything I remember about it, down to that spot where I pulled up the carpet. Also, Dinah and Castillo had reported me missing, possibly taken against my will. My messages to Castillo got that ball rolling.

It turns out that Castillo hadn't gotten my messages because he'd been asleep. After multiple long nights of work, he'd set his alarm for a twenty-minute catnap. Only it hadn't gone off. He'd slept for two hours, with his phone intentionally silenced for twenty minutes of peace.

When he woke, he got my messages and called. Getting no response, he contacted Dinah. They went to my apartment and found no sign that I'd returned after meeting with Greta's old roommate.

From there, Castillo went to the coffee shop, and one of the staff recognized my photo and said I'd been with another woman, and we'd gotten into the back seat of a rideshare together. A security camera in the area had picked up the rideshare car idling in front of the coffee shop. The license plate was stolen. The car wasn't registered with the rideshare company, who'd had no drop-offs or pickups at that coffee shop that day except mine.

At that point, Dinah reported me missing.

How did they get all that done so quickly? They didn't. I'd been missing for thirty-six hours. I got into that car at 5:40 on Monday afternoon, and the police found me over Laura's body after receiving an anonymous tip at 5 a.m. Wednesday morning.

The Crown attorney wants me to confess to killing Laura in self-defense. I escaped the room, semi-drugged, got hold of a knife and stabbed her to escape. That's a valid defense, according to them.

Yeah . . . As someone who's spent her academic and professional career studying domestic abuse, I know that self-defense is never a simple "get out of jail free" card. It's also not what happened.

I tell my story. I tell it again and again, and I do not waver because it's the truth.

Between interviews, I am alone in a cell, and I don't know how to cope with that. In the last couple of weeks, I've treasured those rare moments when I literally cannot be doing anything. Those moments when I can ignore the poke in my head that says, if I'm so much as standing in a cashier line, I should be answering emails or reading a journal article or doing something productive because I do not have time to just stare into space.

Now I have hours of that, without my phone, without a book, without anything, and my brain feels like an animal trapped in a cage. I am alone with my thoughts and fears and panic at a time when all I want is distraction. I find it by mentally writing those damn podcast scripts that I'll never record.

The police can hold me for up to twenty-four hours without laying charges. They hold me for twelve, and then they announce that I'm free to go, and no charges will be laid at this time, pending further investigation, do not leave the city and so on.

All I hear is the first part.

I am free to go.

I step out of the holding-cell block, blinking and disoriented. Then I see a face. Oliver's face.

There's a moment where I think we're just passing in the halls, a grotesque coincidence, two siblings framed for murder seeing each other at the police station. Then I notice how he's dressed—in a button-up shirt and loafers, shaved, his hair perfect—and I remember he got bail this morning. The evidence of that ordeal is still etched on his face, drawn and haggard. Then he sees me and lights up, breaking into a jog that has my guard raising her hand in warning.

When Oliver reaches me, the guard murmurs, "You can go now," and I fall into his arms. He holds me tight, and I breathe in the smell of his shaving lotion, so familiar it makes my eyes tear.

"You're safe," he says. "It's all over."

Is it? I'm still under suspicion. Compared to Oliver's situation, though—out on bail with trial pending—my ordeal at least *might* be over.

"I'm sorry for what happened to you," he whispers as he hugs me. "For the charges, yes, but for everything else. You were kidnapped, and then you had to deal with this."

My knees quake, and the tears squeeze out. I've been trying so hard not to feel sorry for myself. A woman is *dead*. But Oliver is right. I was kidnapped, and instead of being whisked to a hospital, surrounded by friendly faces, I was put in jail, with only a brief visit by a doctor whose stony expression suggested I deserved all my scrapes and bruises.

I cling to Oliver until I become acutely aware that we're in a public place, with people slipping and dodging around us. Then I wipe my eyes and straighten.

"We need to get your things," Oliver says. His mouth quirks in a dry smile. "I know the drill."

"Can I . . . Can I step outside?" I say. "Please. I won't go down the stairs."

He hesitates. Then he sees my desperation. "Okay, just . . ."

"Stay on the steps," I finish.

He leans in to squeeze my shoulder and kiss my cheek. Then he strides toward the desk while I make my way outside.

I step through those doors, and my knees threaten to buckle completely. I won't say it's the blast of fresh air, because we're in downtown Grand Forks and the air stinks of exhaust and cereal from a nearby factory. It's freedom, though. I am outside. The only thing holding me back is that promise to Oliver, as much as I long to break it and run down the stairs and just keep running until I collapse in giddy exhaustion.

I went from captivity to jail, and that hadn't fully hit me until I stepped out those doors. As hard as I'd tried to be positive in that farmhouse bedroom, I'd known there was a chance I might never leave it. As hard as I'd tried to be positive in that holding cell, I'd known there was a chance I might only leave it to be transferred to a jail cell.

All the terror of not knowing sweeps over me, and I need to grip the railing to keep from running, if only to reassure myself that I *can* run, that none of the uniformed officers climbing the steps will grab me and drag me back inside.

I'm inhaling deep breaths when I spot someone moving fast on the sidewalk. Seeing me, he breaks into a jog, until he's climbing the stairs two at a time.

"Dean," I say.

As I open my arms, I realize what I'm doing, and I start to pull back, but he accepts the invitation and hugs me, and I fall against his chest.

"I'm sorry," he says. "I'm so sorry, Amy."

I pull back and look up at him.

"I didn't get your calls," he says. "If I hadn't decided to take a fucking nap—"

"Don't," I say firmly. "You were exhausted, and you fell asleep. I'm the one who broke curfew to go meet a stranger."

He shakes his head. "I logged into your site and saw your conversation with her. You were right to go. If I hadn't been able to drive you, I'd have told you to meet her anyway. It seemed safe even to me."

"Then no one is to blame except Laura, right?"

When he hesitates, I say, "Dean . . ."

"I shouldn't have shut off my phone. That was careless and—"

"No one is to blame except Laura," I say firmly. "If you insist on taking part of it yourself, then I have to take part of it, too, and I don't think I deserve that."

He catches my smile and gives a gruff quarter laugh. "Yeah, okay. Fair."

Someone jostles us, just a homeless person wobbling up the stairs, but it makes Castillo steer me into the corner and then turn to shield me. My gaze drops to a bag in his hand.

"Uh, right," he says. "So, Dinah texted that you were being released soon, and I wasn't sure anyone was able to meet you, so I came, and I wanted to get you something . . ."

He shoves the bag at me, as if it contains contraband you absolutely shouldn't be exchanging on the steps of a police station. I open it to find a small potted flowering plant.

"Ooh," I say as I hold it up. "Pretty."

He makes a face and then pushes his hands into his pockets. "I suck at gifts. I actually stopped at the bakery first because I know you like brownies, but then I remembered you were in a coffee shop when you were . . . you know."

"Ah. Thank you. I *do* need plants in my apartment."

He makes another face. "I didn't know what else to get. They don't make cards for this."

"Cards for 'Sorry you were kidnapped and accused of murder'?"

"More like 'Sorry I didn't get your messages, which led to you being kidnapped and accused of murder.'"

I lift a finger.

"Yeah, yeah, I'll stop." He looks around. "Can we go some-where and talk? You must be starving. What's your favorite spot?"

"Are you offering me wings and beer again, Dean?"

"Nah, we're going all out this time. Tacos and margaritas."

"Actually, if you're serious, I would totally go for that. How about—?"

"Amy?"

I glance to see Oliver barreling our way. He grabs my arm and nearly yanks me off my feet getting between me and Castillo.

"Hey!" I say. Then I realize the problem—I'm on the police station steps, and all he saw was me in the corner, seemingly blocked by a big guy.

Castillo puts out a hand. "You must be Oliver. Dean Castillo. We haven't officially—"

"I don't care who you are. Step back. Now."

"Oliver!" I say. "This is Dinah's private investigator. *My* inves-tigator, the one I recommended to her. He's been working on your case."

"Oh." Oliver's gaze takes in Castillo from ball cap to work boots, and I tense, sensing his disapproval, but then he relaxes. "Right. Of course. I should have recognized the name." Oliver thrusts out a hand and shakes Castillo's. "Thank you. If there's ever anything I can do for you, just let me know."

I'm about to remind Oliver that Castillo is *still* working on his case—both our cases now—but then I realize that would be reminding Oliver that he's still facing trial.

"Actually, you can buy our dinner," I say, a little too brightly. "Dean promised me tacos, and I am totally taking him up on that. Tacos, loaded nachos and a pitcher of margaritas."

Oliver blinks, as if surprised, and looks between us.

"To catch up on the case," I say. "Dean and I need to talk about what happened and where we're at."

Oliver turns, slowly, to Castillo. "My sister just endured kidnapping and prison. She's not in any shape to be grilled—"

"Whoa!" I say. "No, no, no. Dean offered to feed me because I'm starving. I'm the one saying we should talk about the case."

"I think you need a break from that," Oliver says. "Food, yes. Absolutely. But if Dean will take a rain check, I really think you need takeout and quiet time. A hot shower. Clean clothing." He touches my arm and lowers his voice. "You've had an ordeal, Amy. I know you want to bounce back, but please, take a moment to recuperate."

"Your brother's right." Castillo's voice is an apologetic mumble, so uncharacteristic it annoys me. It annoys me because I want him to be Dean Castillo, brusque and blunt, telling Oliver to step off and let me make up my own mind. I'm a grown woman. If I want tacos and margaritas and shop talk, that's my call.

Castillo isn't doing that because he thinks Oliver's right, and maybe he is—maybe I *am* in shock and too eager to prove my resiliency, but damn it . . .

Damn it, I want tacos? No, I want Castillo's particular brand of companionship. I want to sit on a patio, kick back and drink and talk. I don't want to be coddled.

Except, looking at Castillo's face, I'm not sure he could give me that right now, either. He feels guilty, and I hate that, but maybe Oliver has a point. I do need a shower. I do need clean clothing.

Give me the evening to recuperate, and then I can reconvene with Castillo and talk business.

"Fine," I mutter, a little ungraciously.

Oliver murmurs something to Castillo and passes over his card.

"I'll call you," I say to Castillo as we start to leave.

"I need to get you a phone first," Oliver says.

"What?"

"Your phone wasn't found at the scene. But I've ordered one, and it'll be ready in a few hours. Gives you just enough time to relax before you hop back into the saddle."

He gives me a smile, but I can't return it. I mutter another "Fine," and we head to the parking lot, Castillo walking in the other direction.

TWENTY-FOUR

When we're in the car, I put the plant on my lap, and Oliver seems to see it for the first time.

"An apology from the Grand Forks PD?" he says.

I snort and shake my head.

He goes still. Then he drums his fingers on the steering wheel. "Is that from Dean Castillo?"

I shrug. "He feels bad about not getting my texts. Which he shouldn't. He'd been up working all night. He was entitled to a nap. Just bad timing."

"Hmm."

Oliver backs the car out, and it's only then that I notice it's not his car. Because that would be impounded for evidence. I open my mouth to ask about that, when he says, "How well do you know him, Amy? I had the impression it was his boss who worked for you."

"His *partner*, yes, but she's on a case in Toronto."

The silence stretches as he navigates through the downtown core. The tension has me hoping he's just going to drop this, because I have an uncomfortable sense I won't like where he's—

"I understand he feels guilty," Oliver says slowly. "But bringing you flowers?"

"It's a potted plant."

"And taking you out for drinks?"

"Dinner. Because I just spent two days being held captive, and I wanted to go out."

His fingers resume drumming the steering wheel.

"If you have something to ask me," I say, "then ask."

"He just seems . . . interested in you beyond a professional capacity."

"Are you asking whether I'm seeing him?"

"What? No. He's not . . . No. He isn't your type. He's not on your . . . You know."

I sit there, silently seething, knowing exactly what Oliver is implying. I saw the way he looked at Castillo, dismissing him in a glance.

"I just want you to be careful, Ames. You're a very pretty girl—"

"I'm twenty-eight. Not a girl."

"That came out wrong."

"It came out patronizing. There's a difference."

He takes a deep breath and then blurts, "You were kidnapped, Ames. Taken captive by Laura and at least one accomplice, and the person you reached out to was this Dean guy, who conveniently didn't get your messages."

"You think Dean—?" I don't even finish that, just shake my head. "No, Oliver. Dean was not in cahoots with Laura, and if you insist on continuing in that direction, you can drop me off at the next corner."

"I'm asking how well you know him. How well Dinah knows him. He's . . . rough. I know that sounds horribly elitist, but he got those scars somewhere."

"In a *war* zone, Oliver. He was an American soldier. That's shrapnel scarring."

"Are you sure?"

"Jesus, seriously?" I wave at the red light ahead. "Drop me off there. Please."

Oliver sighs. "I'm handling this wrong."

"You keep saying that . . . and then you dig the hole deeper."

He stops at the light and looks at me. "You were kidnapped. By someone I brought into your life. Then you were framed for killing her. Am I overreacting about Dean Castillo? Yes, I am. But at this point, I want dossiers on all your neighbors and your classmates and everyone who comes within fifteen meters of you. I'm *freaking out*. It will pass. Just . . . let me get my footing, okay? And yes, if I'm out of line, say so."

"You're out of line."

"Noted. Dean Castillo is no longer a topic of conversation."

"Thank you."

"Now, where were you going for tacos?"

I hesitate, still feeling surly, but he gives me a pleading look. "Amy . . ."

I sigh and tell him.

———

We pick up dinner. Oliver also insists on getting margarita fixings at the liquor store. Then we head out of the city.

"I rented a house," he says when I ask. "There's been media camped outside at my place since I was released this morning, and there's been suspicious activity at your apartment, too. Dinah and I discussed it, and we agreed she should rent us a house under her name. It's temporary."

"Okay."

"Also . . ." He hits buttons on the dash. When Dinah answers, he says, "It's Oliver. Can you please confirm that you rented a place for us and where it's located?"

"It's a new house on Dingle Road, just south of the city limits. Two stories. Four bedrooms." Dinah pauses. "Is Amy giving you a look?"

He chuckles. "She is."

"Amy?" Dinah says. "This is how we're proceeding from here on, at Oliver's insistence, which I agree with. Someone out there wishes you harm. We aren't taking any chances."

"Including the chance that my brother is secretly kidnapping me?"

"*No* chances," Oliver says. "I don't know what Laura said to you. I'm afraid to ask. I want you to be one hundred percent confident that I am who you've always thought I was, no matter what Laura said."

"We are going to need to talk about what she said," Dinah says. "Whoever killed her, presumably her accomplice, is still out there. We didn't go through that in the police questioning—no need to put a bigger target on Oliver—but we have to be on top of this."

"Honestly?" I say. "She didn't say anything specific about Oliver. I actually tried to get her to do that, and she refused. It was all vague accusations."

Dinah pauses, and it takes me a moment to realize why.

"I'm not saying that to protect Oliver," I say. "I understand attorney-client privilege, and I agree that if Laura told her accomplice about specific grievances or abuses, then you both need to know what they were. But she didn't tell *me* anything specific."

"Because she didn't have anything to tell," Oliver grumbles under his breath. Then he sighs. "That sounded defensive."

"No, it sounded like a man who has been framed," Dinah says.

"Do we know why she faked her death?" I say. "I asked, and she wouldn't answer."

When silence falls, Dinah says gently, "Oliver? We've discussed this. That's going to be everyone's question, and if you don't answer, it looks like you were the reason. That she was so scared of you she faked her death."

"Money," he says, finally, as if it's a dirty word. "We were having marital problems. She offered to let me buy my way out of the marriage for a million bucks. I refused because I wanted to work on the relationship. After she died, I discovered money missing from accounts that I didn't think she had access to. Over half a million. I presumed she was siphoning it off, preparing to leave and take the million whether I gave it to her or not. Then she died."

"I can verify all that," Dinah says. "Oliver came to me when he found the missing money. It was after the police declined to charge him in her death. He wanted to know what to do about it. I said he could tell the police she'd taken it and then try to recover it from wherever she stashed it. But if he did, it gave the police cause to reopen the investigation."

"It gave him a motive to drown her," I say. "He found out she'd been siphoning money to get around the prenup, so he killed her."

"Yes. I would now presume she took as much as she dared and then faked her death. Three years later, she decided to come back for more."

"Money," I whisper. "She did it all for money."

I struggle to comprehend that, but even as I do, I'm ashamed of myself for the struggle. I don't get it because money isn't important to me. It's not important to me because I've always had enough.

Laura must have married Oliver thinking, if things went south, she could get around the prenup. When she couldn't, she took what she could. She must have thought it would be enough. It wasn't. It never would have been, as long as Oliver was alive and willing to shell out more.

The house is a mini-mansion in a new semirural subdivision. When we pull into the drive, Oliver slows and looks around.

"This is . . . isolated," he says.

"Not what you expected?"

He shakes his head. "The rental agent said it was in a quiet neighborhood, but I expected other houses."

There are houses on either side . . . They just aren't finished construction yet. Even when they are, they'll be a hundred meters away.

"Is this okay?" Oliver says. "Please feel free to say it's not. After what you went through, maybe you'd be happier in the city."

"No, this is fine."

"Are you sure?"

I nod. "I could use the peace and quiet."

I've had my tacos and my drink and . . . how awful is it if I say that I spent the whole time wishing I was on a patio with Castillo instead? I love Oliver, I really do. I love catching up with him over lunch or hanging out at his place for an evening, watching a movie. But for eight years, he's been my big brother, with all that entails. He's an older sibling, not a friend.

Of course, two weeks ago, I'd have done everything in my power to *avoid* going out for dinner with Castillo, certain it would be awkward and intolerable. I won't say we're *friends*, but there's a different vibe now. Once we chiseled away the mutual preconceptions, I could relax, knowing that I'm *not* what he expected. And he's not what I expected, either.

With Oliver, I'm always a little not quite myself. I want him to be proud of me. I want to fit into his world. I might come from an upper-middle-class home, but it wasn't the same as Oliver's. When Mom came home from work, she kicked off her heels and pulled on sweatpants, and we binged reality shows with pizza.

I could have gone with Castillo to that restaurant, wearing no makeup, my hair in desperate need of a wash, my clothing rumpled, and not only would he not have cared, but I wouldn't have given a shit, either. I'd been through an ordeal, and I deserved a break.

Oliver and I eat dinner in the living room while watching a movie on the wall-sized TV. Then I declare it's time for my shower.

"Anytime you want to talk, I'm here," Oliver says as he turns off the movie. "Or if you don't want to talk, that's fine, too."

"Maybe later. I'm just feeling . . ." I shrug.

He comes over and puts an arm around me. "It's okay. I'm still getting my footing myself. Part of me wants to jump into work like nothing happened, and part of me wants to go to bed and stay there for three days."

"Exactly."

"Which means I won't judge any choices you make right now, Ames. As long as you're safe, you can do whatever you like. You're safe here."

I nod and look out the front window.

"There's a security system," he says, as if that's what I was thinking. "I changed the code as soon as we arrived. If there's anything . . . Wait. Your phone. I should have gotten the pickup notice by now."

He takes out his cell and frowns at the apparent lack of messages.

"It's fine," I say.

"No, it's not. Let me see what's going on."

I planned on taking a shower, but then I walk into my room and see an ensuite bathroom and clawfoot tub. Luxury-brand bath bombs sit atop a tray, and that seals the deal. I start the water and plunk one in. When the tub is full, I turn off the taps to hear the distant sound of an angry voice. I open the bathroom door. Oliver's voice wafts up from downstairs.

"I was promised the phone would be ready today. In fact, I chose this particular model *because* you could have it ready today."

"It's fine," I say when he comes to the bottom of the stairs to tell me.

"No, it's not," he repeats. "I've called another store. I can pick up one tonight. Are you okay being here while I do that?"

I hesitate. Am I okay being alone at night? To get a phone I don't urgently need?

"Tomorrow is fine," I say.

"Are you sure?"

"I am."

TWENTY-FIVE

It really is a good thing I don't have my phone, because if I did, I'd be on it, feeling the need to answer messages. Instead, I crawl into bed after the bath, and the next thing I know, I'm waking to a gentle knock on the door.

"Ames?" Oliver stage-whispers.

I pull the sheet over me and croak, "Come in."

As he does, I check the bedside clock. Nearly ten.

"Ugh," I say. "I only meant to shut my eyes. Sorry. I should probably just make an early night of it."

He hesitates, one foot in the room. Then I notice the room isn't bright because I left a light on. Sunshine streams through open blinds.

"Shit," I say. "Is it ten in the *morning*?"

He winces at the profanity but covers his reaction with a smile. "You were tired. I'm glad you slept well. I wouldn't have bothered you, but I didn't want you waking up to an empty house."

I rub my face. "You're going out?"

"Stopping in at work for a meeting I couldn't cancel. I'll also be picking up your phone. I should be back by noon with lunch. There's a basket of croissants and fruit, with juice in the fridge. The coffee machine is set up and ready to go."

"Okay, thanks."

"I know you might want to step out for a walk, and while I'd rather you didn't . . ."

"I'm an adult and can make my own choices? Even if they already led to me getting kidnapped?"

He gives a rueful smile. "I wouldn't have mentioned that. But yes, you are an adult. The security system will be on, but I left the code."

"Thanks."

"Have a good morning, and try not to do too much."

Try not to do too much. Yeah . . . By eleven thirty, I'm looking for things *to* do.

I had a leisurely breakfast, and normally, I'd do that while skimming the news or reading an online magazine, but I need a device for that. The only print magazines around are the pretentious kind Mom called "aspirational," in a tone that clearly said she didn't understand why anyone would aspire to that lifestyle.

There's a whole library of books, and that seemed promising, until I discovered that most of them seem to have been bought by the crate at an estate sale, the kind of leather-bound shelf fillers purchased to construct the appearance of a well-read library. There are no classics, no long-lost works of fascinating literature or history, just old books. So many old books.

I settle for watching TV, but after twenty minutes, I've had enough. I'm poking around the house when a rap comes at a back window. I nearly trip over my feet getting to it. Oh, sure, about halfway there, I think, *Um, why is there a rap at a back window . . . on a house surrounded by fields?* At this point, if it's another kidnapping, at least escaping it will give me something to do.

When I see who it is, I grin and heave open the window. Only once I get it open do I remember the security system, but no alarms go off. It must be the kind that only covers the doors. Good thing Oliver didn't realize that.

The house is raised, meaning even on the main floor, I'm looking down at the person standing in the empty flower beds.

"Hey, stranger," I say. "You wouldn't be trying to break in, would you?"

"And announce my presence by knocking?" Castillo says.

"You're a decent thief, giving the occupants fair warning." I start to back up. "Come around front—"

"Can't. That's why I'm at the back window like some damn creeper. I'm not supposed to be here. Not supposed to even know where you are. And there's a camera at the front and back doors so . . ."

"Ooh, secret rendezvous."

"Yeah." He shoves his hands into his pockets. "It's a little creepy, so feel free to tell me to get lost."

"What? No. I will *pay* you to talk to me right now, Dean. I am dying of cabin fever. Oliver took off for a work meeting, and I am learning just how much of a device-obsessed millennial I really am . . . at least when the owners of this house have terrible taste in reading material and I'm not supposed to go outside. When I was a kid, other girls would get grounded— stay home, no devices—and I always wondered what that was like. Now I know. It sucks." I pause. "I'm blathering, aren't I?"

A ghost of a smile. "You're bored. Full confession—I knew Oliver wasn't here. I also knew that if you weren't answering my texts, you didn't have a phone yet." He lifts something.

My eyes widen. "Oh my God, is that the tablet from your office? Please tell me you're letting me borrow it."

"Rent it. Hundred bucks an hour." He catches my eye. "Kidding."

"Hey, right now, I'd pay it."

"Yeah, but I didn't think it through. How am I supposed to drop it off without Oliver knowing I've been here?"

"I'll hide it."

"Your brother is already investigating me, Amy."

"What?"

He lifts his hands. "Not like that. He's ordered a background check, and I don't blame him. Hell, I make a living doing stuff like that. Mine's clean, but I am also very aware that he thinks I might actually be creeping on you."

"No, he—"

"I got the hint, Gibson. It's okay. My point is just that I don't want to give him any reason to think I'm a bad actor, and showing up here is *not* the way to do it. I just . . ." He shrugs. "I didn't like the idea of you being locked up in the country without any way of reaching out. Even if you're with your brother, he should have thought . . ." Another shrug.

"That this feels a little like luxury kidnapping? He means well, but yes, this isn't exactly how I want to recover. But if you're telling me that you aren't leaving that tablet, after you showed it to me . . ."

He sighs. "No, I'll leave it."

"How about you give me the tablet for twenty minutes? I'll access my email and answer messages, and then you can take it."

"I also brought you a phone." He takes a cell phone from his back pocket. "It's a basic burner from a bunch we keep at the office." He pauses and makes a face. "Am I being weird? Over-thinking it?"

"No, you're being sweet."

"Shit. That's worse. Can we stick with *weird*?" He runs a hand through his hair. "I *am* overthinking it. I'm feeling guilty about not getting your messages, and now I'm"—he waves around him—"standing in a garden, hiding from security cameras, to make sure you don't feel . . ."

"Like a princess trapped in a tower?" I grin at him. "I'd let down my hair for you to climb up, but it's not quite long enough. Let me come out the back door. Oliver knows I might step outside, and that's all the camera will show. I'll hide the phone and tablet, and I promise I'll keep them hidden from my tower guard."

I word it lightly, joking, but even as I do, I realize how it sounds.

No, not how it *sounds*. How it is.

I'm going to pretend I'm just stepping outside—alone—for a moment, while Castillo stays out of camera reach, and then I'll sneak the phone and tablet inside.

It's your brother, Amy, not your kidnapper.

I know, but he's worried and—

And what? You're an adult. Let him know someone brought you a tablet and phone. Tell him to back off.

Castillo doesn't want to cause trouble.

Yes, this makes me uncomfortable, but I'll work it out later. I hurry to the back and nearly throw the door open when I see the blinking security light.

Damn it.

I run back to the window. "I need to turn off the system. Oliver left the code. Just hold on."

Then, minutes later, I'm back at the window. "I can't find the code."

He frowns up at me. "It's not where he left it?"

"He didn't say where he left it, meaning it's in an obvious place. Or he thought he told me. I've checked the fridge door, the kitchen table, the end table under the security panel. Nothing. But the windows obviously aren't armed, so I'm coming out this way."

I expect Castillo to argue. Climb out a window? Don't be silly. Just let him pass me the tablet and phone. When I glance at him, though, his expression is troubled.

He's thinking what I'm trying very hard not to think. That this all feels like too much. An isolated house with cameras. No phone. Missing security codes.

But Dinah knows where I am. She approved this house, and I trust her the way I don't trust anyone else.

Not even Oliver?

I trust Dinah. That's what matters.

"Dean?"

He shakes off whatever's bothering him. "Okay. I'll help you down."

I remove the window screen. Then I pull over a chair and climb out. As promised, he catches my legs and lowers me to the ground. Not once does he grumble or even joke, and that has my stomach twitching.

Every time I've questioned anything Oliver has done, I've rested easy in the knowledge that no one else sees a problem. Now Castillo seems unsettled.

I take the phone and tablet, then we walk to a picnic table around the side, out of camera reach. I take a seat on the bench, but Castillo stays on his feet and prowls the edge of a strip of woods, as if wolves lurk on the other side.

The phone doesn't have data access. I can use it to make calls, so I'll feel less isolated, as he said. I appreciate that, especially when he's preprogrammed in his number, Dinah's and a few others. In an hour or so, none of this will matter—I'll have a replacement phone—but I do appreciate the gesture.

I tuck the phone aside and power on the tablet. The browser pops up right away. I flip to the WiFi. It spins, telling me it's searching for a connection. When it doesn't find one, I sigh.

"Too far from the house for WiFi," I say. "And I didn't look for *that* code."

"Just hotspot with my phone. Probably safer."

He takes out his phone, hits a few buttons, and "DC's phone" appears as a hotspot option. I connect.

I'm launching my webmail when I stop, my head jerking up.

"Hear something?" he says, pivoting toward the front of the house.

"No, I just realized . . . My cell phone. Do you think Laura's killer took it?"

"It's possible. It's also possible that it's at the farmhouse somewhere—we just can't access the scene to check. When you went missing, I asked a contact to ping your phone. Last known location was up by the university. After that, it was shut off."

"But if the killer took it . . . They have access to my stuff, right? They just need to unlock the phone and they can read all my messages and *send* messages. As *me*."

"It's an iPhone, right? Facial recognition and passcode?"

I nod.

"Then unlocking it is damn near impossible," he says. "My niece somehow locked my sister's a few years back, and it was bricked. Full factory reset only, which means the data was gone."

I exhale.

"Chances are, it really is in that farmhouse," he says. "But the police are aware that it's been missing since you were taken. You don't need to worry about the killer using it to frame you. Or sending nasty emails to your professors."

I manage a smile. "Really more concerned about being framed for murder these days."

He moves closer. "If it's any consolation, it was a half-assed job. They did a decent one of framing Oliver, but even that's falling apart. This was just . . ." His hands ball at his sides. "It was a dick move." He makes a face. "That came out wrong. You were kidnapped and arrested for murder. That's more than a 'dick move.'"

"You mean they weren't seriously trying to frame me. I was just a convenient distraction tool . . . who went from captivity to prison for it."

"Yeah."

He resumes patrol as I access my webmail. I flip through and . . . It is a little disheartening to see that there are no urgent "OMG, where are you, Amy?!" messages. Not from friends. Not from my advisor. I've been so busy lately that if I go days without contacting anyone, it's just par for the course.

That's not entirely true. One person knew I was gone. There are three messages from Castillo, increasing in urgency. Raven also noticed I'd gone quiet. She reached out twice, asking whether everything was okay because she hadn't heard from me since Monday.

I look up at Castillo. "My producer doesn't seem to know what happened to me. And part of her job is monitoring Google alerts on my name."

"Yeah, it stayed out of the news."

"My kidnapping? Or my arrest?"

He comes over and leans against the picnic table. "The police weren't convinced it was a kidnapping until you were found. Then they agreed not to release it to the press. You can thank your brother for that. Whatever strings he can pull, he didn't use them when *he* was arrested. But he did use them for you. From what I understood, there was an agreement not to publicize your arrest unless you were formally charged, and if you weren't, then details of the kidnapping were to be withheld because they could impact your brother's trial. They'll likely come out soon, but first, the Crown wants to decide how they're handling the Laura situation."

"Oh."

"That's good, right? You don't want it in the news, I presume."

"Definitely not. I just . . ." So what do I say to Raven? Is it a secret I need to keep? Also, something about it . . .

"Amy?"

I shake my head. "It's fine. I'll tell my producer that I'll talk to her soon. Those are the only messages I need to answer until I can access my texts and voice mail."

"You can get your voice mail using my phone if you remember your password."

"I do, actually. I was changing my plan recently and had to look it up." I accept his phone and call my own number. When I get voice mail, I log in and play the messages. The volume is jacked up, and Castillo walks farther away to give me privacy.

The first two are from him. I fast-forward through. Next is one from Raven. Then a spam call. Castillo again. Raven again. Another spam call.

"Hello, Ms. Gibson," says an accented voice I recognize even before my landlord gives his name. "I am so sorry to bother you. I know you are going through a great deal at the moment, but your rent payment . . ." He coughs. "It was returned for insufficient funds. If you are having difficulties, please speak to me, and we will work it out. Again, I am sorry for bothering you at this time."

I glance up to see Castillo pivoting my way. He quickly looks toward the road.

"I know you heard that," I say. "It must be a mistake. My rent is paid out of my trust fund. I don't have full access to it until I'm thirty, but it can be used for living expenses."

He nods, and I realize I've said more than I needed to, but he only asks, carefully, "Any chance it could be empty?"

I shake my head. "It's not millions but . . . My mom did okay."

"It's probably a glitch."

"I guess so . . ."

"If you're worried, call the bank," he says. "See what's going on."

I do that. He walks farther away now, and I lower my voice for the conversation with the bank. When I finish, I take a moment to absorb what I've been told. Then I rise and walk over to him.

"Dean?"

He turns. "Hmm?"

"My rent isn't coming out of my trust fund."

He frowns. "You have it coming out of another account?"

"No. My only other account is a checking one for daily use. It rarely has enough in it to *pay* for a month's rent. That's not where the money comes from, though. I asked them to check, just in case."

"So where is it coming from?" He pauses. "Wait. Is Oliver paying your rent?"

"No, of course not." My tone sounds defensive, and I take it down a notch. "My brother doesn't pay for anything. He certainly tries, but I have the trust fund for rent and tuition, and I can cover daily expenses with what I make as a TA during the school year, plus a trickle of income from the podcast."

"Are you sure?"

"Am I sure I can cover my own expenses?" I bristle. "I know what you think of me, Dean—"

"Yeah, I *did* think your brother paid your bills, but only because he's rich and you're still a student. If you say you're paying them, I believe you. I'm only asking whether it's possible he found a way to pay your rent, because that would explain the problem."

"Bail, you mean? He emptied his accounts to pay bail?"

"No, but as a bail condition, he only has access to a personal account. Anything else he can withdraw money from has been restricted."

"So he doesn't empty his accounts and flee the country."

"Something like that."

I open my mouth to say that's not the answer. I am definitely paying my own rent.

I am, aren't I? When was the last time I checked a statement from my trust fund? Never. I don't even get them because it's a reminder of why I have that money—my mother was murdered.

I call the bank back and ask for the last ten transactions on the account.

They're all interest payments . . . even though I paid tuition a month ago. Well, no, I sent an email to the lawyer in charge of the trust fund, who authorizes the transfer for tuition. But that money never came out.

Nothing is coming out of my trust fund.

"I need to transfer nine hundred dollars to my personal account," I tell the bank clerk.

"I'm afraid that isn't possible. It's limited to authorized transactions only."

"No, I'm allowed to withdraw up to a thousand dollars a month for living expenses."

"I don't see that here, Ms. Gibson."

"Check again. While I've never used that exception, it's how the fund is set up."

"I'm sorry, Ms. Gibson, but that doesn't seem to be how this account is structured. You'll need to contact the administrator or the trustee."

I frown. "There is no trustee. Just the administrator."

Silence.

"*Is* there a trustee registered to this account?" I ask.

Silence.

"Who is the trustee on this account?"

"I'm afraid I can't divulge—"

"Is it my brother? Oliver Harding?"

"I would suggest you contact the administrator, Ms. Gibson. There's nothing more I can do for you here."

I end the call. Then I look over at Castillo, still standing there, his expression unreadable.

"I need to talk to the fund administrator," I say. "But Oliver is going to be back any moment."

He says nothing, just waits.

"I know I shouldn't ask ..." I begin.

"Go ahead."

"Will you take me back to town?"

"Come on."

TWENTY-SIX

Once we're away from the house, I message Oliver on the tablet.

ME:
Couldn't find the security code
and started getting antsy. I'm
locked in a house, unable to
leave it or reach out to anyone.
That isn't safe, Oliver

I want to leave it there, the rebuke hanging, demanding an explanation.

No, I want to add another line, ask what the hell he was thinking and actually demand an explanation. Instead, I type:

ME:

After being kidnapped, I
couldn't stay there like that.
I left, and I'm walking to town.
I'm fine.

He texts back immediately, but I don't read it. I'm too pissed
off. I'm also in the middle of using Castillo's phone to call the
lawyer who administers my trust fund.

I explain the situation.

"Yes, Oliver is the trustee," he says. "That's how you wanted it."

Some people would automatically deny it, but I'm the type
who does the opposite—even when my gut says I did not agree
to this, I rack my brain, just in case.

I would not forget something this important.

"When did you and I discuss this?" I ask, as calmly as I can.

The lawyer hesitates, as if he's doing the same thing—pausing
to be certain of his memory.

"Oliver discussed it with you, and you signed the papers. In
front of a witness."

"In front of you?" I say. "After we discussed it?"

Now the lawyer's tone takes on an edge of defensiveness.
"You signed these papers, Amy. I can pull them up right now
and send your signature, along with that of the notary who
witnessed it and took your ID. It's all very legal."

It clicks then, as he mentions the notary. After Mom's death,
I didn't want any part of the trust. It felt like blood money. I'd
wanted to donate it. Oliver had talked me down off that ledge,
and he was right—my mother would be thrilled if I tithed to

charity, but that money was for me. I'd finally agreed to sign the papers.

Did I read them first?

No. After a page, my brain swam, and I just signed in front of the notary. A stranger I can't even remember.

The lawyer continues, "This doesn't mean Oliver has access to your trust, Amy. I wouldn't have allowed that."

"He just controls my access to it."

"He *manages* your access. It's what you wanted. You were young, and you understood the importance of safeguarding your mother's gift to you."

"I was told I could access a thousand dollars a month for expenses. I tried to take some out today and couldn't."

"You'd need to discuss that with your brother. I can assure you, though, that he hasn't so much as taken a management fee, which he would be entitled to. I can send you the annual reports."

"I've just gotten the last few months of transactions. There's nothing but interest. My rent is supposed to be paid directly from it."

"I . . . would take that up with your brother."

"And my tuition?" I press. "What happened last month when I sent you a request for a withdrawal?"

"I would also take that up with your brother."

My temper flares. "No, I am taking it up with you, as *my* lawyer, who administers *my* trust."

"I can give you the information you want, Amy, if you insist, but I believe it should come from your brother."

"Because he's paying my tuition and my rent," I snap. "*Secretly* paying them."

"You're obviously upset, but Oliver isn't stealing from you. Quite the opposite. He's covering your expenses so you don't need to dip into your trust fund."

"My brother's accounts are frozen, which is how I found out because my rent wasn't paid. I need you to switch payments to my trust fund and—"

"I can't do that without your brother's consent."

I loosen my grip on the phone before I clench so hard I break it. "Then you need to ensure I can withdraw my thousand dollars a month. If you tell me you cannot do that, either, I will be placing more calls to obtain second opinions on the legality of what you've done. *I'm* your client, not Oliver. I requested tuition funds from *my* trust. I requested that my rent also be paid from that trust. You seem to forget that my mother was a lawyer. I have all the contacts I need to investigate this and replace you. Now, make the changes I requested and send a confirmation message to my email."

I end the call. Then I sit there, breathing deeply.

I turn to Castillo. "I presume you heard that."

"Yeah."

"And?" I say finally.

"If I'm understanding it correctly, you thought your tuition and rent were coming out of your trust. Instead, Oliver is paying them."

"I should be happy about that, right?"

He selects his next words with care. "I'm going to guess he offered to pay them, and you said no."

"Right."

"You were clear that you wanted to pay."

"Right."

He sneaks a look my way. "Then it's a shitty thing to do. He might have thought he was doing a good deed, but it's shitty because it makes you feel indebted to him when you didn't want that."

I exhale and lean against the headrest. "Thank you."

"If that lawyer is saying you should be grateful, he's in cover-his-ass mode. You made your wishes clear, and he ignored them. That's an ethical issue. My guess is that the lawyer thought he was doing you a favor. Your brother wants to pay? What a nice gesture. But the truth is . . ."

When he trails off, I say quietly, "I want to say it feels like financial control, but Oliver's not taking my money. He's protecting it."

Castillo doesn't answer, and I shift in my seat. "Now I'm the one overthinking, aren't I?"

"No, I'm just not sure how much I should say." He glances over. "Your brother thinks I'm creeping on you. You're a pretty girl with a trust fund." He makes a face. "A pretty *woman*. See? I can't even get that right."

"The point is that if Oliver thinks he's protecting me from you, he's out of line. He's also out of line having you investigated. You're being gracious saying you understand."

Castillo shrugs. "In his place, I'd do the same. Still, that doesn't mean I'm not a little annoyed, and I'm concerned that my opinion might be tainted by that."

He turns onto the highway back to the city. "You're upset now, but he's still your brother. It's like when a friend complains to me about his girlfriend, and personally, I think she's trouble, but if I say that, and they get back together . . ."

I laugh under my breath. "Been there, done that. Don't trash-talk the ex until you're sure they're *staying* an ex. But in this case . . ."

I glance over at Castillo and lower my voice. "I think we're talking something more serious than a troublesome girlfriend. Oliver has been accused of controlling behavior with Laura and Martine, and there's some evidence for that, though it's also easy to explain away. I'd like to talk this through, if that's okay. I'm not going to come back later and make you regret giving me your opinion."

"I know. I'm just . . ." He changes lanes and uses the adjustment for a moment's silence. "I'm very aware I'm on thin ice here. Oliver doesn't trust me . . . and I just swooped in and snatched you."

"No, you gave me a ride when I asked for one. Being an adult, I'm free to leave my brother's 'protection' at any time."

He exhales. "See? I'm digging this pit as fast as I can. You're right, of course. You are also right to say this feels like financial control. Yeah, he's giving you money, but he's still controlling yours. Putting you at a disadvantage through obligation. Whether he realizes it or not is another thing. However, I'm more concerned about the fact he got himself appointed trustee. How did that happen?"

"That's my fault. I hated anything to do with the trust fund, and when he gave me papers to sign, I skimmed a page or two and signed. He *did* tell me to read them."

Silence.

I rub my temple. "He told me to read them while knowing I wouldn't. Being the sole trustee puts him in control. There's also the fact that I'm supposed to be able to withdraw, and I can't. All of this could be a misunderstanding. He's paying for my tuition and rent. He's not taking management fees from my fund. I might have misunderstood about the trustee thing. The lack of access could be an administrative glitch."

"Yes."

"Or my brother could be controlling my money."

"Yes."

I stare out the window. Then I look over at him. "Are there reporters staking out my apartment?"

"What?"

"Oliver suggested the media was staking out my apartment building, which is why we couldn't go there. But he also made sure the story of my kidnapping and arrest didn't leak. He could have meant they were there because he'd been released on bail." I think back. "Also, he worded it as having heard there was suspicious activity at my apartment, meaning if there isn't, he was just misinformed."

"Yeah."

"He definitely didn't shoot Martine. Laura admitted to that. He didn't drown Laura, because she was still alive. She'd clearly staged her death because she'd set up the proper equipment to escape. He didn't stab her yesterday, either, because he was in the hospital under guard."

"Yeah."

"So my brother *isn't* a killer. But was Laura telling the truth about him controlling and gaslighting her?" I look to the window again. "Is he doing it to me? Or am I being paranoid, doubting the one person who's had my back since my mom died?"

"Can't answer that, Gibson. I can only ask you another question."

"What's that?" I say as I look back at him.

He meets my gaze. "Do you want to find out?"

The answer should be easy. So damn easy. Then why does it stick in my throat and make my heart hammer?

"No," I say. "I don't *want* to find out. But I need to. Can you help me with that?"

"I can."

We reach the city, and Castillo pulls over in a gas station lot.

"I need to call Dinah," he says. "And then Ioana."

For a moment, I think he means he wants their advice. Then I understand and curse under my breath.

"I've just put you in a very bad position," I say. "Professionally."

"If it's a bad spot, I put myself there when I snuck out to where Oliver was . . ."

"Holding me captive?"

"I was trying to think of a less judgmental way to put it."

I shake my head. "You can go back to being judgmental, Dean. At least in this. Whether he was protecting me or not, it was, at best, misguided. But I shouldn't have asked you to take me—"

He lifts a hand. "Can we agree that we're both adults and stop doing that? You made your choice, which was to leave your brother's protective custody, and I made mine, which was to help you. The longer I wait before contacting Dinah and Ioana, the worse this will be."

"Of course." I turn toward the door. "I'll go for a walk while you do that."

"Rather you didn't. Won't stop you, obviously, but if you're only leaving to give me privacy, I don't need it."

"Okay."

TWENTY-SEVEN

While I suspected that Oliver would eventually realize someone picked me up—and that someone might have been Castillo—my messaged lie about walking away helped Castillo here. Dinah hasn't heard anything from Oliver about my disappearance, which means Castillo is voluntarily admitting it to her. A point in his favor. Not that he seems to need it.

Castillo has Dinah on speakerphone, and she knows I'm there. When he finishes the story, she only sighs, deep enough that it hisses over the connection.

"Amy?" she says. "Your brother is very sweet, but he's also becoming a pain in my ass."

"Not just yours," I mutter.

"I agreed with not taking you home last night. I wasn't sure a house in the country was necessary, but it wasn't unreasonable. He should have realized that leaving you there would be triggering after what you went through. And if you don't like me using the word *triggering*, too bad. That's what it was. You endured a double trauma, and the fact you're holding up so well only means you're going to crash later."

"Thanks . . ."

"I'd do the same. Soldier on by sheer willpower, cushioned by shock, until it hits. Which isn't going to happen while you're still being traumatized, however unintentionally. Oliver was wrong to desert you there. You were right to leave. Dean was also right to check on you. Is there anything else I should know?"

I glance at Castillo.

"Amy?" Dinah says.

"There's something else," I say, "but I shouldn't discuss it with Oliver's lawyer."

There's a long pause. Then she says, her voice lower, "If there's anything of concern, Amy, I don't have to *be* Oliver's lawyer."

"I'll get back to you on that."

Another hiss of breath, this one less a sigh than frustration. "I don't like the sound of that. If you are in any danger—"

"I'm fine," I say. "I would tell you if I wasn't."

Castillo cuts in. "On that point, I need to resign as your investigator in this case, Dinah."

A pause. "Please tell me it's because you're helping Amy look into her concerns, and not that you're quitting over your own concerns."

"Helping Amy," he says. "But it'd be a conflict of interest to keep working for you on Oliver's case."

"God*damn* it. You think he's done something, don't you?"

"I'm sorry," I say. "There are just some troubling signs, and as someone who runs a podcast about red flags, I can't ignore them, even if they're really more of a washed-out pink."

"Fine. For now. But if those flags hit red, I want a call. Immediately. As for you quitting, Dean, that actually makes my life easier."

"I figured it might," Castillo says.

"Wait." I look from Castillo to the phone. "Why . . . ?" Neither answers, but then it hits me. "Did Oliver ask for Dean to be removed?"

"Not in so many words," Dinah says, "but the conversation was heading that way. He has concerns."

"Yeah," Castillo says. "He's investigating me. I got a professional courtesy call from another firm."

Dinah curses under her breath.

"I've got nothing to hide," Castillo says. "Except two wives, five kids and that man I shot in Reno, just to watch him die."

"Funny guy," Dinah says. "Okay then. If you have recommendations for other investigators, let me know, but at this point, I don't think we'll need them. The Crown wants to talk to me about Oliver, and I get the feeling it'll be a very good talk."

"Dropping the charges?" I say, perking up.

"Thanks to you and Dean, I believe so."

I glance at Castillo, who only shrugs.

Dinah continues, "Your testimony to the police—about Laura confessing—was apparently convincing. It wouldn't have done more than raise reasonable doubt, but Dean tracked down a neighbor of Oliver's who has a security camera monitoring their driveway. On the night Laura stole Oliver's car, it picked up someone walking past. She was wearing a hoodie, but apparently, something caught her attention at the right moment, and she glanced over. We're getting analysis to sharpen the image, but it looks enough like Laura that I suspect the Crown isn't going to proceed with the charges against Oliver."

I exhale a long, shuddering breath of relief. Then I thank Dinah and promise to keep her updated.

Castillo calls Ioana next. He's tense—anything he does can affect the agency. But she fully supports his choices and reminds him that it doesn't matter if my brother gets pissy. Oliver isn't his client. Dinah is, and Dinah has been thrilled with his work and equally fine with his choices.

After that, I tell Ioana my concerns about Oliver.

"I hate to say this, Amy," she says when I finish. "But after hearing that, there's little doubt that Laura was, at least partly, telling the truth about your brother."

My hands tighten on my thighs. "Okay."

"What he did with her credit card *is* financial control. What he's doing with your rent and tuition is also financial control. Same as making himself trustee. Whether he's benefiting directly or not, he's placing himself in a position of control over your finances."

Pain stabs through me. "I know."

"He also shouldn't have whisked you out of the city into physical and cyber isolation after what you went through."

"I know."

"However, all that adds up to . . . Well, apologies to you, Dean, but it's a very garden-variety sort of control that men often exert over women."

"Not arguing," Castillo says. "My grandmother never had a credit card. When I was growing up, my dad paid all the bills and gave my mom an allowance for household expenses. That was just how they did things then. My sisters are a different story, but yeah, old habits die harder than they should sometimes."

"Exactly. Oliver thought he was right to cancel Laura's joint card because she wouldn't stop spending. He thinks he's right to control your trust fund, Amy, because he's not dipping into it—he's safeguarding it for you. He's wrong. But that's what you two need to work out."

"Do I confront him now?" I say. "There are things I want to look into first. I'd like to talk to Martine, if I can."

"Do that. Don't confront him. Just be firm that you need some time away, and if possible, get Dinah to back you up. That should help."

Castillo doesn't think I should return to my apartment, and I agree. We've picked up a burner phone from Castillo's office and I've texted Oliver to say, as nicely but firmly as possible, that what he did unsettled me, and I need time away, but I don't trust that he won't show up at my apartment.

The safest option is to go to Castillo's place, which is super awkward. In the end, I admit that I just hate putting him on the spot. He says not to worry—he'll add accommodations to my bill. I think he's kidding, but I don't actually care if he isn't.

He drives to the east-central part of the city and pulls into the parking lot behind a three-story walkup.

"You can say it," he says.

"Say what?"

He waves at the building. "I live in a shithole."

"I wasn't even thinking that, but if you did, it'd be understandable. You have two wives and five kids to support, while hiding from that murder you committed in Reno."

"Yeah, yeah." He pulls into a spot. "Before you actually *do* worry why a guy with a decent job lives here, there's no sordid explanation. No drugs or gambling. Not even an ex-wife and a kid. I just . . ." He shrugs. "After that house in the country got sold out from under me, I decided I was tired of renting. Too much uncertainty. I'm living in a shithole because it's cheap, and a guy like me isn't worried about living in a rough neighborhood. I can save for a downpayment on a house."

"Okay."

"And that was more than you needed to know. I just didn't want you worrying that I'm an addict or an alcoholic."

I hop out of the pickup, calling back, "I wasn't."

"Good. Don't worry about being here, either. If I need to leave, you're coming with me. Now let's get inside and get to work."

The building might be a "shithole," but Castillo's apartment is freshly painted and immaculately clean with better furniture than mine.

"It's nice," I say as I walk into the living room.

He grunts, and I realize that might have sounded condescending. I open my mouth to fix it, but my gut says I'm safest just keeping it shut. Castillo heads past me into the kitchen.

"You hungry?"

No, but he's already taking stuff from the fridge, so I say, "Sure."

"I can fix some sandwiches. Or if you didn't get enough Tex-Mex last night, I made enchiladas I can reheat."

"Enchiladas would be great."

I'm still standing in the living room, as if stuck there. I'm moving toward a leather armchair when a photo on the wall catches my eye. It's a black-and-white shot of a woman swinging a toddler up into the sky, the little boy giggling. I presume it's art, but when I step closer, something in the woman's profile reminds me of Castillo.

"One of my sisters," he says when he sees me looking. "And one of my nephews."

I walk around the room, taking in what I now realize are all family photos. An older couple. Children. A bride and groom. They're all gorgeously shot, and I'm about to ask who's the photographer in his family when I see one in the back hall. It's two men and a woman in army fatigues, sitting on the ground, obviously exhausted, faces streaked with dirt, but laughing as they share a cigarette.

"You took these," I say.

"Yeah."

"They're gorgeous."

He shrugs and flips over the enchiladas he's reheating in a pan.

I'm about to say more when my phone buzzes. I glance down and then away again.

"Oliver?" Castillo asks.

I nod.

"He keeps texting?"

I nod again.

"You could ask him to stop."

That's the obvious solution. But what if I ask, and he ignores me?

I'm already trying very hard not to doom spiral. Oliver is the only family I have left. My father lives less than an hour away, and I haven't seen him in years. When I got my master's, I downed two shots and called to invite him to the ceremony. I got his voice mail. Left a message. The next day, a lovely gold watch appeared with a note in a looping feminine hand.

"Congratulations on your master's degree! So proud of you!"

Yeah, not only was it written by his PA, but she'd penned the sentiment as well, because it absolutely didn't come from him. I resisted the urge to toss the watch in the trash, sold it and donated the proceeds to the local women's shelter.

My father has a daughter. She's fifteen. I'm just some distant relative, like the child of an old friend. I cannot express how much that hurts, but I've learned to accept it. In accepting it, I do the only thing I can—I look to Oliver as my family.

What if my brother is exactly what Laura accused him of being? A controlling, gaslighting manipulator? What if he's been controlling me? Gaslighting me? Manipulating me?

What if I ask him to stop texting, and he doesn't?

I take a deep breath and look at my phone.

OLIVER:

Please let me know you're okay, Amy. If you need time away, that's fine. Just tell me you're safe.

ME:

I'm safe.

OLIVER:

Are you sure? Are you with
someone?

ME:

I'm fine. I've talked to Dinah.

OLIVER:

Okay. That's good.

ME:

Can I ask you not to text again
today? I really need a break.

OLIVER:

Okay. I'm sorry.

I stare at the screen, waiting for more. When it doesn't come, I pocket the phone as Castillo sets plates on the table.

"Do you still want to reach out to Martine?" he asks.

I nod.

"I can do it if you'd like," he says, "but I'd say the request comes from you. I think that's important."

"I'll do it."

"Do you want to discuss what you'll say?"

"Please."

TWENTY-EIGHT

I send a message to Martine. I explain that it's me, and I tell her what we both ordered at the hospital coffee shop—as proof that it's me. I tell her things have happened, and she's going to hear them soon, and could I speak to her? I have questions about Oliver. I'm willing to communicate in whatever method she thinks best.

It takes an hour for a response to come. Then it's a simple "I'll think about it."

I want to push, to tell her about Laura. Castillo convinces me to let it drop, and he's right. What if the situation were reversed, and I suddenly got a message supposedly from Martine, claiming she'd been kidnapped by Oliver's dead wife and framed for her murder . . . when I could find nothing of the sort in the news?

Castillo spends the afternoon and evening online, with digging, digging and more digging. Sometimes I'm there, answering questions about Oliver to help his research. Most times, though, I'm sitting and thinking. There are things I could do, but they're all busywork, and I can't bring myself to do them. My brother lied to me. He's in control of my trust fund. He imprisoned me in a house in the country "for my own good."

Did he really write down the security code? Was he really having such a hard time getting my phone replaced? Did he really explain what was in those papers I signed? Is it really a mistake that I can't access my trust fund?

And what if he's done nothing wrong? What if I'm the paranoid brat mistrusting her own brother, who has been nothing but kind and generous and supportive?

What kind of sister goes from "My brother is the best!" to "OMG, my brother might be controlling my life!" within hours?

The kind of sister blinkered by her own trauma and passions. A sister whose mother was murdered by a man in her life. A sister who has devoted her academic and professional career to spotting predatory and controlling men.

When you're a hammer, everything looks like a nail.

I tell myself I'm doing the right thing. I'm doing what I would advise any woman in my position to do. Don't ignore your concerns. Investigate.

And what does Castillo find, after hours of that digging?

Not a damn thing.

Which is good, right?

It would be, if Castillo declared all was well and Oliver was in the clear. But he can't do that until my own questions have been answered. I need to know what happened with my trust fund. I signed those papers. I don't doubt that I did. I can't prove that Oliver didn't tell me what was in them, even if I'm certain he did not.

I need to find out why I lost access. There must be a paper trail for that, one that proves it was a mistake ... or proves Oliver ordered the change and lied to me.

Castillo tries to give me his bedroom for the night, but that just makes an awkward situation even more awkward. I insist on the couch, and we make an early night of it. Tomorrow, I'll go to the bank and find out who ordered the stop on my trust fund withdrawals, and I'll get my rent payments transferred to it. And with any luck, I'll hear back from Martine.

I'm dreaming that I'm back in that room where Laura held me captive. Except it's not Laura. It's Oliver. He's outside the door, and I can hear him there, and I'm crying and begging him to let me leave, but he keeps saying this is for my own good. I can't look after myself. I couldn't handle my mother's death, and he needed to rescue me. Now I put myself in Laura's sights, and he needed to rescue me again.

I obviously need protection. A man's protection. His protection.

That's when I stop crying and start raging at him. Meeting Beth was a reasonable decision to do what seemed like a reasonable and safe thing. I am not a child. I don't need his protection.

"Are you sure?" a voice says outside the door, and this time, it's not Oliver.

"Laura?"

"Are you sure you don't need your brother, Amy? I think you do. I think you're one of those girls who are happy to have a big strong man to look after her. You can't seem to find one of your own, can you?"

"I don't—"

"Poor little Amy. Can't keep a man except her brother. Why do you think that is, Amy?"

I want to ignore her, but it's a dream, which means I fall for her taunting, even when I'd know better in my waking life.

"I'm busy," I say. "I just haven't found the right guy."

"Is that the answer? Or does Oliver drive them away? No one's good enough for his little sister. I remember Milo. Such a nice boy. Whatever happened to him?"

I grit my teeth. "He dumped me. You know that."

"Are you sure? I seem to recall . . . Oh, never mind. But now there's Dean Castillo. Oliver *really* doesn't like Dean. Says he's chasing you for your money, but you know what the real problem is. You're getting a little too comfy with Mr. Private Investigator, and Dean Castillo isn't the sort of man Oliver can buy off like he did to Milo."

"Oliver didn't buy off—"

"Why do I waste my breath? You aren't interested in listening. You like where you are, safe under your brother's wing. Otherwise, you wouldn't have ignored the message I left, would you?"

"What mess—?"

I bolt upright so fast that I tumble off the sofa. A door slaps open. Footsteps run in, and I can make out the dim figure of Castillo in the dark.

"My car," I say as I scramble up. "I forgot about my car."

Castillo turns on a lamp with one hand as he rubs his face with the other. He's dressed only in sweatpants. Scarring dapples his left shoulder, spraying onto his chest. There's another scar over his abdomen, thick and ragged, and the sight of it makes me forget what I was saying.

"You were dreaming," he says. "You're okay. We left your car in your parking lot, remember? Because of the tracker."

I shake my head as I snap back to myself. "That's not it. I remembered something Laura said about my car when she held me captive. She said I'd ignored the message in my car. She was saying a lot of things, and I was groggy and not paying much attention. I completely forgot about it."

"A message? In your car?" He pauses. Then he says, "Shit. The tracker wasn't the only thing she left that night." He turns toward the door and then back to me. "You want to go now?"

"Please."

We reach my car fifteen minutes later. It's still parked behind my apartment building, exactly where I left it.

"Wait here," Castillo says, and he's out of the truck before I can argue.

I watch as he circles my car, giving it a wide berth. I slide out of the pickup, and at the sound, he glances over sharply, but I motion that I'll stay where I am. He nods and circles again.

Because this could be a trap. I wouldn't have thought of that, even given what Laura did to me. After a second pass, Castillo approaches. He bends to where the tracking device is—in the wheel well—and he shines his flashlight in and cranes his neck. Looking to see whether there's a message taped in there. Then he straightens and waves me over.

"Check any place you can think of," he says.

We do that and find nothing.

"Are the keys upstairs?" he asks.

I shake my head. "The fob is on my keychain, which is in my purse."

"Lost along with your phone."

"But I can get into the car. There's a key safe. I locked myself out once, and that was once too often."

I walk to the gas tank flap and open it. The key safe is tucked inside, out of sight.

"Could Laura get the message into a locked car, though?" I ask. "I guess maybe if it's just a sheet of paper it could slide in somewhere?"

"Window is most likely. Push it past the rubber."

I open the driver's door and check the back seat. I'm pulling it forward when Castillo shines his cell phone light on something across the floor. A piece of white peeking from the passenger side.

I hurry around and open that door, and an envelope falls out.

TWENTY-NINE

We're back in Castillo's apartment. I haven't opened the envelope. I just sat with it on my lap as we drove back in silence. Now I'm on Castillo's sofa with that envelope still on my lap. He hands me a beer poured into a glass, and I take two long draws while he folds himself onto the chair across from me.

He sips his beer and says nothing. Just gives me the time I need, and after one more draw on my beer, I set the drink aside and pick up the envelope.

On the outside, there's a little drawing that looks like a playing card. Next to that, it says "Open Me."

"Alice in Wonderland," I murmur.

Castillo grunts. "That something Laura liked?"

I shrug. "Not that I know of, but I get the sense I didn't know her at all."

At his snort, I say, "Understatement of the year?"

"From what I dug up, I'm not sure how well anyone knew her," he says. "Some people gushed about how nice she was . . . and some said you shouldn't speak ill of the dead, so they had nothing to say. My guess? She was nice when it got her something. Otherwise?" He shrugs.

"Otherwise, she wasn't above faking her own death, shooting an innocent woman and kidnapping her sister-in-law to get a payout from her former husband."

He puts his feet up on the coffee table. "Yeah, but considering how it turned out, she's not exactly a master criminal. She got greedy. If she'd waited another day, Oliver would have been out of prison, and she could have made her ransom demand."

"Instead, she jumped the gun and did something that made her partner-in-crime—the fake Beth—nervous. They fought, Fake-Beth killed her and framed me. Or that's the theory."

"Now I just need to find Fake-Beth. I made a bit of progress on that last night, after you went to sleep. I think . . ." He trails off and waves a hand. "And you're letting me distract you from opening that envelope."

I want to ask him what he found. A lead on Fake-Beth? Does he know who she is? Where to find her? But he's right that I'm letting him distract me, and until Fake-Beth is caught, I'll only have more questions.

More questions . . .

I look down at the envelope with that cutesy drawing. Ironically cutesy, I think.

Who were you, Laura? Who were you really? I hate you for what you did to Martine. I hate you for what you did to Oliver. I suppose I should hate you for what you did to me, but that crime seems insignificant compared to the others.

Insignificant? She kidnapped you. Held you for ransom.

It is not insignificant, but whenever I approach my feelings on that, I shrink back. I want it to be insignificant. A minor trauma. I am terrified, though, that it's a seed nestling down and starting to sprout black tendrils that will drag me into a dark pit.

Castillo shifts on his chair, and I get the message. Open the envelope, Gibson.

It's not sealed. The flap is just tucked in. When I tug it out, the edge slices my finger. I pull back as blood wells along a thin cut.

"Appropriate," I murmur.

Castillo hands me a tissue. Apparently, I'm not getting a bandage until I read the message. Fair enough.

I tug out a single sheet of paper. When I open it, expecting to see a note, I frown. It's a photocopied lab report.

I skim the report. It's a DNA comparison of two subjects. There's a lot I don't understand in those codes and numbers, but one part is highlighted. Highlighted in pink, no less.

Subjects unrelated.

My gaze trips up to the only handwriting on the report. It's so neatly written in black ink that I initially mistook it for part of the official report. It's not. Where the report had said "Subject A" and "Subject B," Laura struck through that and wrote beside it. One word beside each.

~~*Subject A*~~ *You*

~~*Subject B*~~ *Oliver*

I stare at the report. Then I pass it over to Castillo. He skims over it. Stops. Backs up and rereads.

"More games," he says.

"Why?"

"Because she's a manipulative shit-disturber."

I shake my head. "Agree in principle, but what would be the point of telling me I'm not related to Oliver?"

"Driving a wedge between you two." He shifts, leaning back to get comfortable on the chair again. "I don't much like the crap Oliver's pulled with your trust. No, strike that. It is, beyond any doubt, inexcusably paternalistic bullshit. But this?" He waves the report. "Just a manipulator playing head games from beyond the grave."

"Except she wanted me to read that *before* she kidnapped me. She thought I had read it. Read and dismissed it. Playing head games would be insinuating I wasn't related to Oliver, like when she insinuated we're unnaturally close. This looks like she suspected we weren't related and then went to the trouble of collecting samples and getting a DNA test. Only she didn't take it to Oliver. She took it to me."

Castillo says nothing. Not agreeing but not dismissing me outright, either.

I continue, "A game would be to introduce a worm of doubt that might have me questioning. I wouldn't get it tested myself. That'd be paranoid. I'd dismiss her nonsense . . . while letting that worm wriggle in. She didn't do that. She *gave* me the test results."

"Writing your name on it doesn't mean it's actually you."

"I know that, but now I'll want to prove her wrong, so I'll pursue it, and it's a question easily answered. This isn't whispering lies in my ears. It's a direct challenge. Don't believe her? Check for myself." I point at the report. "Does that look legit?"

"In the sense that it's an actual report from actual DNA tests, yes."

"Then I think Laura's game wasn't suggesting I'm not related to Oliver. It's *telling* me that I'm not. Shit-disturbing in a much more significant way."

He fingers the paper quietly for a moment. Then his gaze lifts to mine. "You believe it?"

"I . . ." I fall back against the sofa. "I don't know. If this is true, then Oliver and I don't share a father. While it could mean his father isn't James Harding, I don't think that's the answer."

"*Your* father isn't James Harding."

I pull my legs up, arms wrapping around my knees. "He never paid child support. Never paid alimony. My parents split before I was born. He's never been part of my life. My mom tried to cushion that—all kinds of excuses—but basically, I just decided it was because he was an asshole."

"And he *is* a verified asshole, which made that easier to accept."

I glance up, and Castillo shrugs.

"I did my research," he says. "No one thinks James Harding is a decent guy. The scuttlebutt is that he's estranged from Oliver because Oliver outperformed him after he handed over the business. Professional jealousy. But that wouldn't explain why his younger son went to England for university two years ago and hasn't even come home to visit."

"I didn't know that. But yes, according to Oliver, James isn't Father of the Year. Oliver says I was lucky to escape when I did. I figured it was the new-wife situation. James remarried as soon as the ink was dry on the divorce papers. He never had a chance to get to know me, and Mom didn't want to force him to pay or visit me, so off he went to form family number three. But now . . . maybe there's another explanation. Like he knew I wasn't his biological child."

I rearrange my legs under me. "But if Mom fooled around and got pregnant with me, why let on James Harding is my father? Like you said, he's a verified asshole. I can see him walking out and demanding a divorce. But pretending he's my dad?"

When Castillo says nothing, I glance over.

He looks at me. "I wasn't going to say this because he's your father, but Dinah had me digging pretty deep into the family stuff, thinking James might be the reason for Oliver being framed, even possibly the one doing the framing, to get the company back. I discovered James had been paying wife number three's rent and credit card bill for over a year before you were born."

"She was his mistress."

"You don't seem surprised."

I finish off the beer. "I figured that ever since I realized how fast he remarried." I tuck my feet in, more comfortable now. "That makes more sense. I couldn't imagine Mom fooling around if he'd been faithful himself."

"He didn't just mess around. He had a full-time mistress installed. Your mom found out and probably had a fling. A one-night stand or whatever. Maybe your mom admitted to James that you weren't his, and he let himself officially be your dad in return for an easy—and cheap—divorce."

"Or maybe he doesn't know and just thought he got lucky with Mom letting him go, as you say, cheap." I lean to take back the report. "Either way, I will get tested so I know the truth. The problem is Oliver."

"He thinks you're his biological sister."

I nod. "And now he's going to find out that the woman he's been treating like a little sister is a stranger."

"No, he's just going to find out that the woman he thinks is his biological relative isn't. You're still his sister. If he deserves it."

"If he's not intentionally controlling my trust fund. And possibly more."

"There are no signs of more, Gibson. I've been digging. I got nothing."

I remember my dream, Laura saying Oliver had been scaring away guys. I remember the guys who swore they emailed. I remember Milo, who'd ghosted me with vague excuses, and Laura saying Oliver paid him off.

Except that was a dream. Laura never actually said that. And I certainly can't suggest to Castillo that I think Oliver deleted messages for potential dates, or I sound like that silly girl who's certain no guy would ever lie about contacting her.

Then I remember the one thing I can mention. "If Laura was in my parking lot putting that note in my car, then who put the tracking device on it?"

He lifts a finger. "Just because Laura put a note in your car doesn't eliminate the possibility she also attached the tracker. Didn't you say it was Oliver's old car? If he wanted to track you, he could have found a much less conspicuous place to put it. My guess is that Laura put it there so you'd *think* Oliver was tracking you. Sure, you saw her by your car, but that was just for the message. If you discovered the tracker, she'd blame Oliver. More signs of controlling behavior."

"Maybe," I murmur.

"Like I said, I'm seriously pissed off with him, and he has a lot to answer for, but all we have against him for sure are instances where he's been financially controlling. Everything else might be traced back to Laura."

"She comes back from the dead needing money and goes after Oliver for it. Frames him for shooting Martine. Drops anonymous tips that he gaslit her—when the only thing proven is the credit card. Does the same with Martine. When that doesn't go as planned, she kidnaps me for ransom."

"Which definitely doesn't go as planned."

We lapse into silence. After a few minutes, he says, "If that DNA test is right, I'm sorry. That's a shitty way to find out."

I nod, unable to speak.

"Oliver is still your brother," Castillo says. "Same as James would have been your father if he'd played the role. That's what matters. Not DNA."

I nod again. Then I shake it off and say, "What did you learn about Fake-Beth?"

Instead of answering, he heads to the kitchen and takes another beer from the fridge. When he hands it to me, I take it. Then I notice he's only brought one, and his first has barely been touched. I hesitate, and he follows my gaze.

"I'm a lightweight," he says, "and I want to be on guard tonight. Also, I'm not the one who just discovered her father may not be her father."

I open the beer. He sits and then clears his throat. "On that subject—drinking, not parents—since your brother is already investigating me, there's something I should mention before he does. I don't drink much because I used to drink too much.

There's a DUI that'll pop up in his search. Six, seven years back. After that, my sisters gave me an ultimatum, and they're scary enough that I agreed."

"I'm sorry Oliver's investigating you."

"Like I said, it's fine."

"It's *not* fine," I say, meeting his gaze. "He's investigating you, and he had you removed from the case before he even got back the results."

Castillo rubs his mouth. "I'm more worried about you right now. Let's answer those questions first."

Except didn't he just suggest he's *not* concerned about Oliver? He keeps giving my brother the benefit of the doubt, even after I've stopped.

For me.

I realize that now. Castillo has his doubts, and he's hiding them until he has proof, rather than admit he thinks my brother might be up to more than financially controlling me. He's keeping me close and suggesting I not speak to Oliver right now. Making sure Oliver can't get to me until Castillo has the answers he needs.

The answers I need.

Castillo continues, "Oliver is going to tell you what he finds in that background check, and I'd rather it came from me. Here's the condensed Dean Castillo bio, with the warning that it's clichéd as hell. We'll skip childhood. It was a normal middle-class American Latinx boyhood. Just a kid from a good family, doing normal kid things. Senior year rolls around, and I'm planning on college for criminology, with the end goal of becoming a cop. Had a girlfriend, and I applied to the same college as her, got my future all planned out including 2.5 kids.

The week I got my college acceptance, she dumped me. I took it hard and joined the army."

He glances over. "Did I mention the clichéd part?"

"I don't actually know anyone who joined the army after his girlfriend broke up with him."

"Well, now you do. It was a mistake. Becoming a cop would also have been a mistake. I'm not a paramilitary kind of guy. I muddled through in the army, putting in my time until I'd earned a free education. One month from the end, I was coasting. Over in Iraq, but not seeing any action, just helping with civilian stuff. Bunch of us were out grabbing coffee. As boring and mundane as you can get." His one foot taps the floor, and his voice goes gruff. "Suicide bomber. One survivor—the guy who'd stopped to tie his fucking bootlace."

"You."

His nod is abrupt. "Never can keep them tied. My mom says that's why—because someday, it was going to save my life. It did. Still messed me up pretty bad. Hence the drinking. I survived the bomb, and I should have been thanking God for sparing me. I wasn't. *Because* I survived."

"Survivor's guilt."

"Three guys dead. Two had kids. One was getting married in a month. So why me? Why the guy who had nothing to go home to? It messed me up good. After the DUI, I got back on my feet. Came to live with one of my sisters in Ottawa. Started working as an investigator there. Did a job with Ioana, and she lured me down here. Best move I ever made." He sits back. "That's it. Nothing really for Oliver to dig up besides the DUI. Rest is just"—he shrugs—"life."

"I'm still furious with him for digging."

A twist of a smile. "I'm just sorry he won't find anything more interesting."

"Well, I think it's interesting."

"You need to get out more, Gibson." He settles back. "Drink your beer. As for Fake-Beth, I might have a lead from the car Laura drove. It was rented by a woman roughly matching Fake-Beth's description. It's a shady rental place, and I suspect the license she used was fake, but I'm not sure the credit card is. I'm trying to decide whether to push them on that or hand it over to the police. I'll ask Dinah in the morning. Meanwhile, in searching for her, I think I might have found the real Beth."

I stop mid-draw on my beer and lower it. "Greta's actual roommate?"

"Whose first name is actually Beth, and whose social media profile suggests Laura did her homework. Which wasn't easy."

I nod. "She's a hard woman to find. Or at least, her connection to Greta isn't easy to find. I went searching after Fake-Beth got in touch. Doing my homework. Making sure I wasn't being tricked. Which turned out so well for me."

"Took me days to find the real Beth. Greta's death wasn't exactly front-page news, and Beth is only mentioned as 'the roommate.' No name, and she says nothing more than that she found Greta's body."

I lean back, fingering the bottle. "When my mom died, everyone wanted a comment. Dinah helped me with that, but it was overwhelming. I wanted to say something, to honor my mom and lash out at the guy who killed her, but it was all so raw. Beth must have gone with 'No comment.' Having been about the same age when Mom died, I find it hard to believe she'd have refused comment on her own. Someone counseled her. Probably her parents."

"Maybe, but if so, she's sticking to it. I've reached out three ways, and I got myself blocked."

I straighten. "Really?"

"Yep, fifteen years later, and she's still not talking."

"Can I give it a try?"

"I was going to ask if you would."

THIRTY

I send two messages to the real Beth, Greta's former room-mate. Both come from my social media, not my email, at Castillo's request. At least with the social media, my identity is clear. I am who I say I am: the younger sister of Oliver Harding who runs a successful podcast on victimization.

After that, the plan is to go back to sleep, but it's already five, and there's no way I'm getting any more rest. When I notice the light is still on in Castillo's room, I slip over and say softly, at the door, "I'm still up if you are."

A moment later, he opens the door, still tugging on his T-shirt.

"You don't have to come out," I say. "Even if you're up, that doesn't mean you want company."

"If the company comes with coffee, I'll take it. I didn't want to wake you."

"You aren't. I'm anxiously awaiting return calls from Beth *and* Martine, while hoping I don't get one from Oliver."

"He's been quiet since you asked for that?"

I nod.

"Good."

Castillo pads into the kitchen and pops a pod into the coffee maker. When one cup is done, he passes it to me and starts another. "You want to talk to Oliver today? Maybe set up a meeting?"

"A negotiation?"

"Yeah. I'd offer to be there, but that'll just make things worse. Someone should be there, though. Just in case. Do you want to ask Dinah? I know you were concerned about telling her the financial stuff while she's still Oliver's lawyer."

"I'll think about it. You're right that I could use a third party here. I'm thinking—"

My phone buzzes. I'd downloaded my social media apps and turned on the notifications, and when I look over, that's what I have.

"A DM from Beth," I say as I quickly open the app. "It's the middle of the night there. I didn't expect an answer for hours."

I tap on the message screen, and my heart sinks. I show it to Castillo.

BETH:
I can't talk to you.

Castillo swears. I start tapping in a response when she sends another.

BETH:

Literally, I cannot talk to you.

I'm frowning at the phone when another message comes. This one is a snapshot of some kind of form. I squint at my phone. Then I enlarge it, which barely makes it legible. I scale and twist it until I can see the top line.

"It's an NDA," I whisper. "She signed a nondisclosure agreement."

"With who?"

I recenter the document until I can see the names.

"My—Oliver's father."

"Shit."

Another message comes in.

BETH:

He offered to pay my tuition if I didn't talk about Oliver and Greta. I thought that meant talking about Oliver in relation to her suicide, and that was fine, because Oliver wasn't even there

BETH:

If his daddy was going to pay my tuition to keep his son's name out of the papers, whatever. Let him pay. I didn't have anything to say anyway. Then I did, and it wasn't even about

the suicide, but I checked what
I signed, and it means I can't
talk about Oliver at all

"Ironclad nondisclosure," Castillo says, reading over my shoulder. "It stops you from saying *anything* about a specific person. At her age, she wouldn't have realized that."

ME:
I understand

BETH:
Well, I don't. I didn't look closely
enough. Just took his word for it
and signed on the dotted line

Like I did with Oliver and my trust fund papers.

BETH:
So I can't talk about him. I'm
sorry

ME:
It's okay

BETH:
It's not. I know what's going on
over there. I've been following
your podcast since I saw the
news. You seem like someone

I could talk to, and I really wish
I could

ME:

I understand. Really

BETH:

It's not me you need to talk to,
though. It's Greta. And I realized that's what I can do. Let
you hear from Greta

Behind me, Castillo grunts, and when I glance over, his nar-
rowed eyes say he's thinking the same thing I am. Is Beth going
to set me up with a medium to talk to Greta's ghost?

BETH:

Here you go. There's more, but
I've spent the last hour copying
the most important bits

She starts firing more attachments at me. Before I can even
open one, she sends another message.

BETH:

Greta's diary. I found it when I
was cleaning out our dorm
room. I kept it. I didn't think
she'd want her parents to have
it. A few years later, I went back
and read it

BETH:

Before you get worried, your
brother didn't kill Greta. He
was in Seattle, as reported.
What he did do . . .

BETH:

I'll let you read it in her words.
It took me a while to really
understand what was going on,
but I think, from what I've
heard on your podcast, that
you'll read between the lines
better than I did

BETH:

I'm sorry. I know this isn't what
you'll want, and if you want to
delete these messages, I get it

ME:

I won't. Whatever it is, I need to
hear it. Thank you

Selected Entries from the Diary of Greta Haas

October 6

*Beth finally dragged me out to a party last night. I met a guy, and
we did something I never do with guys at parties. I couldn't help
myself! He was cute and funny, and before I knew it, I was throwing
caution to the wind and . . . talking to him. Yes. I spent the entire*

party talking to a boy. Shocking, right? Now let's see if he actually calls me.

October 7

He called! Oliver and I are going out for dinner next weekend. Fancy, huh? First, I need to study for midterms, because if my parents find out I went on a date during exams, they'll kill me. Best thing about university? What they don't know won't kill them.

October 27

I failed my Business Analysis midterm. My parents are going to be so pissed. If they knew I was dating Oliver, they'd blame him, but he actually helped me study. I should never have let them talk me into taking business. I hate it so much. Of course, if I didn't take business, they wouldn't have paid, so there's that . . .

November 20

Just got off the phone with my parents, and I'm freaking out. I hate this program. I hate it so much. I won a fucking provincial award for art, but oh no, you can't make a living at that, Greta. You need a real job. Fuck them. At least Oliver understands. He knows I can't drop out, but he's helped me pick different courses for next term, ones he's sure better suit me.

December 7

I just found out my high school friends are having a Christmas party and I wasn't invited. It's girls only, and they thought I wouldn't come without Oliver. They're just mad because I'm in university and I have a boyfriend and I've been too busy to keep up. Screw them. That's what Oliver says. We'll go out with Beth and Danny, someplace nice, Oliver's treat.

January 3

New year! New term! I'm going to do so much better. I took Oliver's advice and quit seeing my therapist. He's right. I'm not getting anything from her that I can't get from talking to him. I'll tell my parents I'm still seeing her and just keep the money. God knows, I might need it if I don't do better this term. But I will! Just watch me.

March 22

I'm supposed to go home for Easter, and I can't sleep. My parents are going to kill me. I failed half my first-term courses, and now I'm still failing. I'm not any better at this area of business, and Oliver's disappointed in me. He never says that, but I can see it. I've failed everyone. I can't do anything right. I'm going to do what Oliver suggested, though, and tell my parents I'm too busy to come home for Easter. They'll understand. Then I can spend it with Oliver instead.

April 15

Oliver dumped me today.

I shouldn't say it like that. Dumping sounds like he was mean or cruel. He wasn't. He was as sweet as always.

I'm too much for him. Too needy. Too broken. He'd never say that, of course. He says he doesn't want to tie me down over the summer term, but when I said I've never felt tied down, he didn't change his mind. I'm the one tying him down. Weighing him down. I see that, and he has been so amazing, and I fucked up. I fucked everything up, and I can't face my parents, and I don't know what I'll do without Oliver.

No, that's a lie.
I know what I'll do.

I've read the diary entries. Read them. Digested them. Read them again. Then I slap the phone down and stand.

"I need to go for a walk," I say.

Castillo looks up from the copies I sent him. He pauses, and I brace for him to point out that it's 6 a.m. and I'm not supposed to be wandering outside in case Laura's accomplice is still around.

"Okay," he says as he gets to his feet.

I shake my head. "Alone. Please."

"Yeah, I get that. I'll stay ten paces behind. But I wouldn't want you walking around at this hour, in this neighborhood, whatever the circumstances."

I head for the door, where I put on my shoes and pull on my sweater. He says nothing, only follows me out. I walk fast. Not trying to lose him. Trying to lose myself. To outrun what I just read.

I keep going until I spot a tiny playground. It's empty, given the hour, and I veer into it. I walk straight to the dilapidated equipment and stand there, breathing as if I ran the whole way. Then I sit on a swing. When I look up, Castillo's on the edge of the playground, glancing around as if wondering where he can hide himself to give me my privacy.

I wave to the swing beside me.

He walks over. "I won't fit in that."

I start to stand, but he waves me down.

"Fine, I'll try," he says. "If it collapses, don't say you weren't warned."

It doesn't collapse. It might be ancient equipment, but if it's held up this long, it's not giving way under the weight of one guy, even if he's not exactly child-sized.

Castillo settles onto the swing as I flex my knees, swinging ever so slightly.

"My brother drove Greta to suicide," I say.

He makes a noise that has me looking over, jaw setting.

"What?" I say, sharper than I intend. "Are you going to tell me he didn't?"

He pushes back a bit, matching my motion. "Nah, I was just going to say what you were already thinking, so there's no point saying it."

"That I'm overreacting."

When he speaks, his words are careful and slow. "No, that there are many factors that go into someone making that choice, and Oliver was one of them for Greta. A significant one, but not the only one."

A significant one.

My heart drops.

What did I want Castillo to say? That I was completely over-reacting, and Oliver played only the smallest of roles in Greta's choice?

I know better.

Oliver controlled and restricted Greta's life under the guise of helping.

Had he thought he was really helping? Maybe. But he infantilized her. He took control in everything and made her completely reliant on him. He was her lover, her best friend, her tutor, her financial advisor, her therapist.

And then he dumped her.

Grief and self-hatred had poured from that final entry. Poor Oliver, who'd tried so hard to help her, and she'd failed. She'd been too much for him. The love of her life, lost because even he couldn't put her back together.

That is truly the worst of it. That she never saw his role in what happened. That she died thinking it was her fault, that she hadn't been enough.

"I've felt like that," I blurt.

Castillo stiffens so fast that I'm confused until I realize what we'd been discussing.

"Not like killing myself," I say quickly. "At least, not seriously. After Mom died, it got bad. Dark. I know it's clichéd to say you've fallen into a pit, but that's exactly what it was like. Everything was dark, and I knew I had to climb out, but I just wanted to curl up in the darkness. Not die. Just not . . . be for a little while."

"Yeah."

I glance over. He meets my gaze, almost tentatively.

"After the bomb," he says. "The bomb, the hospital, the surgery . . . My sisters say I fell into a pit. I didn't. I jumped in."

He goes quiet and then shakes his head. "This isn't about me. Sorry. Go on."

"No, you go on. I'd . . . I'd like to hear it."

He glances over, as if to be sure I'm serious. Then he says, "I jumped into that pit and drank until I couldn't think anymore. Couldn't feel anymore. My family worried I might do something. I wouldn't have. I just needed time to 'not be' for a while, like you said. I thought I'd pull myself out when I was ready. I didn't. I had to be dragged out, kicking and screaming."

"Your family did that for you."

"Yeah."

"Oliver did it for me. There have been times I've felt like Greta did. Like I wasn't worthy of his attention. I was the screwup little sister he had to keep rescuing."

Castillo frowns. "Screwup? You're getting your doctorate. You have your own podcast—and people actually listen to it."

My lips twitch. "Yes, the listening-to-it part is important. When I step back and examine my life, I'm doing great. But sometimes, I feel like Oliver is still propping me up, and it's not fair to him. He came to help me once, and he got stuck with me."

"I don't get that impression *at all*." Castillo pauses. "Is it possible he's the one making you feel that way, like he did to Greta?"

"I . . . I don't know. I can't specifically point to anything he's done."

"Maybe just a general sense that you need him? The guy took over your trust fund. Whatever he intended, that move says you needed his help, when I don't get the feeling you did."

I say nothing.

"There's something I've been digging into," he says. "I'd like to keep doing that. Even more now. Are you ready to head back?"

"I am."

Martine messages me at nine o'clock on the dot.

MARTINE:

Yes

ME:

?

MARTINE:

Yes, I'll talk to you

ME:

Thank you. Can I call?

MARTINE:

No. I have conditions. We meet
in person. You don't bring your
cell phone because I don't
want any record of our conversation. You come alone. If
that's not good enough, we
don't meet

I show the messages to Castillo.
"Okay?" I say.
"Not really."
"But we can handle it?"
"Yeah."

ME:

That works. Just tell me when
and where.

THIRTY-ONE

Martine wants to meet in a park. The city has lots of them—it's the one thing it's known for. She's picked one of the less popular ones. It's less popular because it has little to recommend it besides lots and lots of trees, with walking trails. There's no playground. No dog park. The trail doesn't allow cycling, and it doesn't link up with any other neighborhood trails. It's not even along the river that gives Grand Forks its name. Once upon a time, this park was known primarily for drug deals, but that's long since been cleaned up, and what remains is . . . not much, unless you live nearby and really want a forest path for dog walking.

Martine asked me to come alone. That doesn't mean I've left Castillo at the apartment. He's close enough that if anything goes wrong, I won't have far to run before he sees me.

Do I expect anything to go wrong?

I don't dare even answer that question.

Martine has given me a spot to meet, and I'm pleased with it. While it's far along the forest path, it's near a strip mall, and that's where Castillo waits. Less than thirty meters will separate us.

I pass a couple of dog walkers as I head in. It's windy and cold for May, and both are sticking to the small trail, doing the shortest possible circuit with their doggie bags in hand. I still survey them, noting details, even eyeing the woman wearing a windbreaker that could cover a weapon, before chastising myself for being jumpy.

I keep walking until I've found the spot Martine mentioned, at a large rock just off the path.

She's not there yet. I'm early, having wanted a moment or two to scope out the area. I'm standing near the path when a sound has me spinning. A figure steps from the trees, and I fall back, my gaze whipping in the direction of that strip mall where Castillo waits.

"It's me," the shadowed figure says, hands rising.

"Oliver?" I say.

He stays where he is, keeping that distance between us as his shoulders slump. "I'm sorry, Ames. I shouldn't have done this."

"No shit."

He flinches at the profanity. "I know it was wrong, but . . . after you reached out to Martine, she got in touch. She was worried about you. We've spoken since I got out. She knows I didn't shoot her, and I've explained about Laura, and she understands. I don't dare say we're getting back together yet, but I'm still hopeful. The fact she reached out when you contacted her . . . I think that shows where she stands."

I don't speak. I can't. I'm too furious.

"I tried to do what you asked and give you space," he continues. "But then ... Remember how I have an investigator checking out Dean Castillo? I worried that maybe you were staying with him, and I told myself that was ridiculous, but I asked him to have a look, and he confirmed it."

I still say nothing.

Oliver takes a tentative step toward me. "Dean Castillo, Amy? Really? You thought I was a threat, so you called *Dean Castillo*? Let him talk you into staying at his *apartment*?"

"You thought I was smarter than that. Is that your next line?"

"I would never say it." His voice drips with reproach. "I know how smart you are, but I also know that Dean Castillo is a pathological liar. He told you he got those scars in the army, right? Suicide bomber? That's the story he likes. He didn't get them in the army. They dishonorably discharged him for improper behavior with a local girl. A local *teenage* girl. The scars are from an accident. He got drunk and rolled his truck." He reaches for his phone. "I can show you the evidence here."

He passes over his phone with a police report on it. I skim through it and pass it back.

"You don't believe it," he says. "Did he tell you why he joined the army? I've gotten that story, too. Something about his high school girlfriend dumping him. Last month, your podcast profiled a guy who stalked a girl all through high school and no one did anything. He considered her his girlfriend."

I clamp my jaw shut against a response, even as my blood boils.

He continues, "In Castillo's case, he *did* date the girl. For a few weeks in his junior year. She broke it off. He chased her for two years. Scared off any guy who came close. Even got into the same college. Finally, on prom night, he broke into her bedroom, and the police actually got involved. Not involved enough to charge him . . . just enough to give him an option: join the army."

"Okay."

"You aren't believing any of this. You're taking his word—the word of a near stranger—over an investigator's report. Dean Castillo is manipulating you, Amy."

"Why?"

He throws up his hands. "Look in the mirror. You're a very pretty young woman, and he's . . . Well, he's not exactly on your level, is he? In any way. High school grad. Living in the worst part of town. Only has a job because Ioana Balan felt sorry for him. He sees a pretty and vulnerable girl with a trust fund. He's used what's happening to weasel into your life, and now you'll never get rid of him."

Oliver meets my eyes. "He's exactly what you warn women about, Amy, and you don't see it because you teach them that predators don't look like predators. He *does*, and so you've bent over backward to give him the benefit of the doubt."

"Okay."

Oliver rocks back. "Damn it, Amy. What do I need to do to convince you? You're picking a stranger over your own brother."

"You don't need to look out for me, Oliver. You're not actually my brother."

I wait and watch his gaze. He goes dead still. Then he rubs a hand over his mouth.

"Who told you?" he says, his voice soft.

"So it's true?"

He pushes back his hair and sighs. "This is not how I wanted you to find out. Was it Laura? Of course it was. She hinted at it once. Said how you and I look nothing alike and made a really distasteful joke about . . ." His face screws up. "I won't repeat it. I didn't tell her the truth, but I should have known she wouldn't drop it."

"You knew."

He shifts his weight. "My father told me when you moved into the guesthouse. He thought I was doing too much for you, and so he dropped that bomb."

"What'd he say?"

"That your mom fooled around, so he left. Not true, by the way. My stepmother told me the truth. She'd been having an affair with my father, and your mom caught them. My stepmother thinks your mom had a fling after that. When your mom got pregnant, she was upfront that the baby wasn't my father's. They negotiated a settlement."

"She took nothing except his name on my birth certificate."

"According to my stepmother, that was actually his idea. Otherwise, everyone would know your mom cheated on him, and his ego couldn't take that. She had to give you his name and pretend you were his kid and never ask him for a penny in alimony or child support. In return, he wouldn't ruin her."

"Your stepmom told you that?"

His mouth twists in an ironic smile. "Being still married to him means she knows exactly what an asshole he is. I think she's afraid to leave. I've offered to help, but . . ." He shrugs. "The point is that I know we aren't biologically related, and I don't care. I spent most of my life thinking of you as my little sister, so that's what you are."

I wrap my arms around my chest. "I know about Greta."

He frowns. "What about Greta?"

I tell him what I gleaned from the diary. With each word, his face pales. When I'm done, he looks as if he's going to be sick. He steps back and braces against a tree.

"Okay," he says.

"You deny it? She was lying?"

He slowly shakes his head. Then he turns to me. "Have you ever done something you thought was okay at the time, and then you look back and realize it wasn't, but you tell yourself maybe you're overreacting?"

I don't answer.

"What Greta says I did?" he says. "I did it. All of it. I thought I was helping. I thought—" His shoulders hunch in. "I was an insufferable ass. I think that's why I was attracted to Greta, God help me. She needed me."

"You could save her."

He winces. "Yes, and I know how awful that is. She wasn't a project. She was a person. But I saw how Dad treated his wives, and I was determined to be a good partner. And when I couldn't? I did something worse than anything my dad has ever done."

"You broke up with her."

"I *abandoned* her. Ran off to Seattle to party with my friends. Came home to find out . . ." His voice chokes, and when he speaks, it's barely a whisper. "I was responsible. I kept waiting for someone to say it, and no one ever did. I can only guess she didn't tell anyone."

"The NDA helped with that."

His chin jerks up. "What?"

"Your dad had her roommate sign an NDA preventing her from saying anything about you. He paid for her schooling to protect you."

"He what?"

I don't answer. He stands there, assimilating. Then his face hardens. "That bastard."

"He protected you."

"I didn't need protecting."

"And neither do I. I don't need you controlling my trust fund, Oliver. And I sure as hell don't need you controlling my social life."

"Your . . . ?" His face screws up. "What?"

Castillo had initially dismissed Oliver as my email hacker. Last night, he found something that proved he'd been too hasty. The outside access did come from Oliver's devices. He must have hired someone to get into mine, and Castillo dug up enough to determine exactly what Oliver had been deleting.

"You've been tampering with my email and probably my cell phone, which you insisted on paying for. Just like you did with Laura, and probably Greta and Martine. Deleting messages you didn't want me to see. Messages from friends you deem unworthy. Guys you deem unworthy. Even an acquaintance reaching out, asking for help for his cousin after her husband was murdered."

"*What?*"

"Did you think you were helping?" I lock gazes with him. "Protecting me from toxic friends and unworthy guys? From acquaintances asking favors?"

"You give too much of yourself, Amy. You need to focus on your career. You aren't a therapy service. Let your podcast do that—it makes you the money you deserve. Your time is valuable."

"So you admit to tampering with my messages."

"No, I'm just saying—"

"Martine never called you about me. You still have access to her texts, and you saw mine to her. I suspected that all along, and if you think I'm alone?" I shake my head. "I'm not that careless. I came because I needed to be sure. And I needed to talk to you."

I look him in the eye. "You weren't attacked in jail. You injured *yourself.* Laura told me to expect you'd get out on bail soon. She knew that because you'd received her demand. You knew she was alive, and you needed out of jail to deal with her. The problem was that you overdid the injury—or whoever you paid overdid it—and you ended up in the hospital longer than expected."

"I never received any demand from Laura, Amy. I was injured in a prison fight. Wrong place, wrong time. Who told you I faked it? Castillo? He's a liar. What part of that don't you understand yet?"

"Did you kill Laura?"

He blinks. "What? From the *hospital?*"

"Dean got word this morning—"

"Dean. Of course. *Dean.* The lying—"

"A camera picked you up leaving the hospital that night. You could have killed Laura."

"So why haven't I been arrested? This doesn't make any sense, Amy."

"The police need to confirm it was you on that tape. They're interrogating your guard now. Either you tricked him or paid him off. Laura got a message to you saying that she had me. She demanded a ransom. You snuck out and dealt with her yourself."

A pause, seconds ticking past. Then he swallows and looks away. "Fine. Yes. She got a message to me in the hospital, and I knew I had to act fast. She's unstable, as you learned. I already knew it. I should have made sure everyone knew it, but then she—she seemed to be dead, and I was under investigation, and I could hardly tell the truth about her then, could I? I got the ransom from home—I always have money in the safe. Then I met and paid her. She promised to release you. After that . . ."

He looks away again. Then he turns to me, his voice soft. "You were drugged, Amy. Drugged and understandably panicked. You didn't know what you were doing."

Rage slithers in. I've been holding it back so well, but now it finds a crack, and I start to shake. "You're saying I murdered—"

"You defended yourself. You didn't understand she was setting you free. You were drugged and scared and confused." He moves closer to me. "I won't ever tell anyone, Amy. I promise."

A chill runs through me.

I look into his eyes, searching for a monster. I have devoted my podcast to teaching women not to expect monsters. There is no wolf in sheep's clothing. No Mr. Hyde behind Dr. Jekyll. There are just people who convince themselves that what they are doing is okay. They need to control, to manipulate, to possess, and you— their target—are standing in the way of that, and why the hell don't you just stop fighting and give them what they want?

I still want to see the monster, and when I do not, something in me crumples with grief. I look into the eyes of this man who considers himself my big brother, and I hear him threaten me in that same soft tone he always uses, full of love and compassion and the conviction that he is doing the right thing.

Protecting *me*? No, he's protecting himself.

"You don't need to keep 'my' secret," I say, willing my voice to be steady. "Go ahead. Tell the police your theory, and I'll tell them mine. Let them investigate."

"I'd never put you through—"

"I didn't kill Laura, and you *know* it."

"If you don't remember what you did, that's understandable. The drugs and the shock and the trauma—"

"Stop!" I snap, getting in his face. "Tell the police your theory, or I will. I have nothing to hide, and if you think you're holding that threat over my head—"

"I'd never—"

"You'll subtly blackmail me with it . . . while making me so worried about being investigated that I won't tell them the rest. I won't tell them that you injured yourself in jail. I won't tell them how you took control of my trust fund and my social life. I won't tell them about Greta and the pattern of control and manipulation and gaslighting. I'll be too scared to say anything. It's not you keeping *my* secrets, Oliver. It's me keeping *yours*."

"You need to calm down, Amy."

"Fuck you."

There's not one iota of shock at my profanity. Instead, his face goes hard. "Don't you speak to me like that. I'm your—"

"Nothing. You're my *nothing*. You're just a guy who wormed his way into my life."

"I saved you. Don't you forget that. You're as bad as Greta. Ungrateful little—" He bites off the next word. "I took care of you, all of you. Greta. Martine. You."

"And Laura."

His eyes blaze. "Laura was a mistake. She acted so sweet and helpless . . . until she had me hooked."

I smirk. "You mean she played the game better than you. What happened? Did you threaten her, and she decided to cut her losses and run?"

"I've never threatened a woman in my life. She expected after a year or so of putting up with her, I'd happily pay her to leave, in spite of the prenup. When I refused, she stole money and faked her death. Dragged me into it as a final parting middle finger. I said you were as bad as Greta? No. You're another Laura. Dragging me down into the hot mess of your wretched little life."

"Then wash your hands of me. I'm not your sister anyway."

I turn and start to walk away. Oliver grabs my shoulder, whipping me around. I lash out blindly, at first, but then manage a real punch to his throat that has him staggering back, releasing me.

Then I run.

I race to the path and into the woods beyond.

Just thirty meters.

That's what Castillo said. He's only thirty meters away. Run to him. Shout for him. He's close, and he'll hear me. He knew I was almost certainly meeting Oliver instead of Martine, and so we were prepared.

Oliver comes after me. He doesn't shout. He doesn't call. He just runs, and so do I. When I stumble, his fingers graze my arm, but I wrench away and keep going. There, ahead, is Castillo's truck.

I wave my arms. He'll see me. He'll get out.

When the driver's door doesn't fly open, I blame the woods. Castillo can't see me because I'm still in the forest, still in the shadows of this overcast day. I charge out and—

The truck is empty.

THIRTY-TWO

I stop dead.

"Huh," Oliver says, panting from behind me. "Isn't that Dean Castillo's truck? Wherever could he be?"

I spin on Oliver. "What did you do to him?"

"Bought him off, of course. You thought you were so clever, having Castillo play backup. But however pretty the damsel in distress, a man's got bills to pay."

"Bull*shit*."

"You don't think—"

"His truck is there, Oliver. What'd he do, walk away and leave it behind?"

"Hmm, fair point. Well, I suspect he got himself into a bit of trouble, parking so close to a residential neighborhood with binoculars in his truck. He does have them, I presume, being a private investigator. I think someone called the police, reported seeing him using them to spy on little girls. Police take that kind of thing very seriously, it seems. I'd have thought they'd have just made him move on, but apparently, he looked shady enough to be taken in."

"You—"

Oliver grabs me. I don't see it coming. I still do not see the monster, however hard I look, and when he grabs me, I'm not ready for it. He yanks me off my feet, and before I can fight back, I'm in the forest again, pinned to a tree, his hand at my throat. When I kick, his hand presses into my windpipe.

"I'm not going to hurt you, Amy."

I kick, and he presses so hard I'm choking and gasping.

"Liar," I rasp.

"If I've ever lied, it's for your own good. All I've ever tried to do was help. You need to calm down. You're hysterical."

I start to kick him again, but he pins my legs with his knee.

"I'm right about Castillo," he says. "You'll see that if you just stop this nonsense. I don't care if you killed Laura. I understand. I will never turn you in."

I speak, each word coming with effort against his hand, pressing into my throat. "And in return, I won't turn you in. Is that the deal?"

"I did nothing wrong, but I can't afford the professional embarrassment. Neither of us can. You have a career, a future to think about. I'm protecting that for you."

"You're protecting *yourself*. That's what matters. You."

"No, Amy, what matters—"

I kick with my other leg. He slams his hip into me, pushing me into the tree, his hand tightening on my throat until I can't breathe. I start to gasp, but he just keeps pressing.

"I'm not going to hurt you, Amy."

I choke out, "Is that what you said to Laura before you stabbed her?"

His hand clenches my neck so hard and fast that I start to wheeze, wildly thrashing and fighting. He just keeps pressing, his face impassive.

"I don't want to hurt you, Amy. Stop making me—"

I slam my fist into his throat, the same spot I'd hit earlier. He coughs, and he doesn't release me, but the tension eases enough for me to wrench away. I spin to run. He catches the back of my jacket, and I throw it off, sliding free as I run for the strip-mall parking lot. *Just get there. I only have to—*

I see the entire lot now. There's only one vehicle in it. Castillo's. Where the hell are the cars? Weren't there other cars . . . ?

My brain cycles back to scouting the area. The lot had been empty, the stores all equally empty. That made it a good place for Castillo to park. No one would bother him, and he'd hear me if I shouted.

Unless my brother made sure he wasn't there.

It doesn't matter. There's a residential neighborhood right across the road.

Across the road . . . and behind an eight-foot solid fence.

I run. I just run. There has to be someone around. It's a quiet area, but it's daytime and surely someone will see.

Like my mother. Broad daylight, people coming into the parking garage for work and no one—

Oliver grabs me. When I try to twist, his foot flies out and kicks my shin. Pain slams through me. I stumble. He yanks me off my feet. I manage to scramble to my knees. He grabs my ponytail, whipping my head back. His hands go around my throat.

Car tires squeal.

I lift my head. They'll spot us. Please—

Long grass. That's all I see. I'm in a ditch, and Oliver is pushing me down, and no one can see me. I fight with everything I have. I get on my knees again, my head coming above the grass just as a car screeches to a halt.

A police car.

It's a *police* car.

The back door opens . . . and Castillo flies out, running for me. Another police car comes around the corner, and an officer climbs from the first car. They shout something, but I don't hear it. I only hear the pound of Castillo's boots as I stagger to my feet and he runs toward me.

EPILOGUE

I'm recording the podcast I've been putting off for the past week. I couldn't talk about what happened in that park, so I immersed myself in the other parts of the story. I told listeners about the kidnapping and Laura's death. The rest, though? I didn't comment on that, and I turned off social media so I wouldn't see people clamoring for the rest of the story.

Now I've given the tale its ending. How Oliver was arrested for assaulting me. How the officer guarding him at the hospital admitted to accepting a bribe to let him out of the hospital for an hour. How Oliver was then charged with Laura's death when forensic evidence put him at the scene of the crime. It's a manslaughter charge, not murder, and he has confessed to it and is in plea bargaining negotiations now with his new lawyer. Dinah has dropped him.

According to Oliver, he met with Laura and claimed he didn't have the money—his accounts being frozen—but offered ten grand from his safe. She refused ... and he'd followed her back to the farmhouse, where they'd fought and she'd fallen and hit her head.

The autopsy had already concluded that she'd died from striking her head on the stone fireplace, the stab wounds occurring postmortem. He's not admitting to the stabbing, because it would admit he set up his own sister. It's also, I think, a bit of revenge—let people think that I attacked Laura after Oliver freed me. Maybe even let them think she might not have been dead when I stabbed her. But I didn't, and there's no evidence I did. The Crown just doesn't feel like adding "indignity to a dead body" to Oliver's charges when they already have their manslaughter confession.

As for Fake-Beth, the police caught up with her, and she eventually gave her side of the story. She'd met Laura last year and claimed she only agreed to help kidnap me because Laura said that Oliver and I had tried to kill her in that boat. According to her, she began to suspect Laura had darker motives and left shortly after I'd been kidnapped. It's true that she left—there's proof she got on a plane while I was in captivity—but eventually, the real story came out. She'd collaborated with Laura purely for the money, as she'd said in the car, and then left after Laura gave her a downpayment on her fee.

I recite the facts of the case for the podcast. They're as dry and dull as I can make them, as if ... Well, I'd say that I relay them as if they happened to a stranger, except that I hope I treat strangers with more compassion than I do myself here. I get through it, and then I know it needs more, as much as I would love to leave it at that.

I stop the recording. Take a deep breath. Adjust my headset. And then I press Record again and begin.

"When I talk to survivors of partner abuse, they sometimes speak about grief. They say it feels as if they lost the loved one who abused them, and I've always struggled to understand that. I get it now. I grieve for the brother I knew. I would love to say my version of Oliver didn't exist, but that's not true. There is always good, and that's what we grieve for. Grieve at our loss and rage against our loved one for not being so utterly vile that we can write them off entirely.

"Oliver was my big brother for eight years. He did pull me out of the pit after my mother's murder. I'll let the armchair psychologists speculate on why he did that. On whether he ever truly cared about me or whether I was just another dependent to make him feel important. I know that I loved him. I know I will miss having him in my life. And I know I'm going to need a lot of therapy." I let myself give a strained chuckle at that.

"I didn't see the monster. I'm not sure there *is* a monster. Oliver did what he thought was right and fair. For the past two weeks, I've been grappling with whether to shut down my podcast. I feel like an impostor. I talk about predators, and I missed the one front and center in my life. But that's *why* I'm not stopping. Because if I can miss it, anyone can, and that was my purpose here, talking to survivors and digging into the cases, and that let me keep pushing for answers with Oliver when I really just wanted to tell myself I was overreacting. If I can do that for someone else, great. And even if I can't, these are stories that need to be told, and so I'm going to keep telling them."

I take another breath, not bothering to stop the recording. "This is Amy Gibson, signing off for a while as I take a break. But I'll be back, and I hope you'll still be here when I am. Thank you."

I stop the recording. Then I sit there, head bowed as I breathe before I straighten and send a text.

ME:
Done.

MARTINE:
And . . . ?

ME:
I think it's okay? Mostly, I'm
just glad to be done it

MARTINE:
Want me to have a listen?

ME:
Only if you're okay with it

MARTINE:
I am. Pass it over. I'll let you
know if it's shit

I've gotten to know Martine better in the past week than I had in the six months she dated Oliver. She reached out after his arrest, and we discovered—to the shock of neither of us— that the reason we'd always circled at arm's length was that Oliver hadn't wanted us getting closer.

He'd done the same thing he did with me and Laura—dropped insinuations and hints that suggested the other person didn't quite take to us. With Martine and I both being the quiet sort, it was easy to do. Just don't encourage contact. Leave the impression that Martine liked me well enough but as Oliver's little sister and nothing more. The truth is we have a lot in common besides our shared experiences at Oliver's hands.

I send her the raw recording. Then I rise from the desk and look across the room. Castillo sits there, patiently waiting.

Yes, Oliver had lied about Castillo. I'd known that, but Castillo still insisted we get the actual report from Oliver's investigator, which proved it. The history Castillo told me was the truth. The rest was just lies my brother wove as fast as he could, confident I'd believe his version. Because he was my big brother, just trying to protect me, and why would he lie?

I walk toward Castillo.

"Recording complete," I say. "As you may have noticed."

Castillo puts down the book he'd been pretending to read. "You did good, Gibson."

I make a face. "I did adequately. Now I just need to be sure I post it."

"I can't help with that. I'm no good at being pushy and obnoxious, as you know."

I smile. "I'll take all the pushing you have. And thank you for being here while I recorded that. I appreciated it."

He grunts something I don't catch. Then he pushes to his feet and checks his watch. "Seems a reasonable hour for tacos and margaritas, if you're feeling up to cashing that rain check."

"An evening out with a friend?"

He grunts and shrugs. "Whatever you want."

"Is there something else on offer?"

A mumble I don't catch.

"What's that?" I say, walking over. "Is there an option for *more* than an evening between friends?"

He shakes his head. "If you want to ask me out, Gibson, do it. All this beating around the bush isn't my thing. I'll probably say no, but go for it."

I smile and step in front of him. "Would you like to go out for tacos and margaritas with me, Dean Castillo?"

"As your date?"

"Sure, as my date."

"That means you're paying, right?"

I loop my arm through his. "It absolutely means I'm paying. Now let's go."

A Catholic Scientist Harmonizes
Science and Faith

Also by Dr. Gerard M. Verschuuren
from Sophia Institute Press:

Forty Anti-Catholic Lies
A Mythbusting Apologist
Sets the Record Straight

In the Beginning
A Catholic Scientist Explains
How God Made Earth Our Home

A Catholic Scientist Proves God Exists

How Science Points to God

A Catholic Scientist Champions the Shroud of Turin

Dr. Gerard M. Verschuuren

A Catholic Scientist Harmonizes Science and Faith

SOPHIA INSTITUTE PRESS
Manchester, New Hampshire

Scripture passages are taken from the *Revised Standard Version of the Bible: Catholic Edition*, copyright © 1965, 1966 the Division of Christian Education of the National Council of the Churches of Christ in the United States of America. Used by permission. All rights reserved.

Sophia Institute Press
Box 5284, Manchester, NH 03108
1-800-888-9344
www.SophiaInstitute.com

Sophia Institute Press is a registered trademark of Sophia Institute.

paperback ISBN 978-1-64413-284-5

ebook ISBN 978-1-64413-285-2

Library of Congress Control Number: 2022931366

First printing

To
Fr. Robert Spitzer, S.J., Ph.D.,
a staunch defender of the harmony
between science and religion

Contents

A Catholic Scientist Harmonizes
Science and Faith

1

Can Science and Faith Live in Harmony?

The idea that science and faith can live together is an issue of vital importance for people of faith. Yet, more and more people nowadays claim science and faith cannot really live together. They caricature religious believers as "schizophrenics." On weekdays, they are critical, want proofs, look for arguments, and believe something only if there is no further doubt. Then, on Sundays, they turn a switch, set their understanding to zero and their gaze on infinity; they have no need for proofs, they open their mouths and swallow revealed truths and absurd dogmas.

The contrast painted in this parody is clear: religious believers live a "schizophrenic" life. It is the life of science and reason on weekdays and the life of religion and faith on Sundays. Of course, it is a travesty, but a very widely held one nowadays, heavily promoted by media and academia. Let's see why it is a false contrast.

a. A False Contrast

The contrast the above parody creates is false. On the one hand, we cannot be asked to accept in faith what we cannot understand, can we? God gave us brains and now expects us to use them to understand even the mysteries of faith, to the extent such understanding is possible. So, faith must have something to do with reason.

A Catholic Scientist Harmonizes Science and Faith

On the other hand, we cannot be asked to put all faith aside either, can we? Reason itself depends on faith to begin with: faith in our senses, faith in our intellect, faith in our memories, and faith in what others have discovered. Besides, there is more to life than reason. Faith can cover issues that science and rationality are inherently incapable of addressing, but that doesn't make them unreasonable or unreal. Seen this way, faith provides answers to questions that would otherwise be unanswerable. So, reason must have something to do with faith.

This means that "weekdays" and "Sundays" cannot be disconnected from each other, as the caricature suggests. They should be in close harmony—the harmony of faith and reason, or science and religion. The Boston College philosopher Peter Kreeft uses the following analogy: "Walking to the beach is like reason and swimming is like faith. You have to go to the place where you can swim before you can swim. And you have to go to the place where you can believe before you can believe."[1] In other words, reason takes us to the water so we can swim in faith. But when we are swimming, occasionally we need to go back to the beach of reason to get our footing back. That is the "back-and-forth" of faith and reason—or of faith and science, if you will.

As a matter of fact, there is no conflict between faith and science. The idea of a conflict is a myth. Professor Kreeft uses another analogy to portray the perceived conflict between science and faith. It's the analogy of that Western in which one cowboy says to the other: "This town ain't big enough for both you and me. One of us has to leave." Many think of science and religion in a similar way: there is not enough space for both science and religion in this

---

[1] Peter Kreeft, *Yes or No: Straight Answers to Tough Questions about Christianity* (San Francisco: Ignatius Press, 1991), 23.

world — one of them has to leave. If one of the two makes progress while the other does not, then the one that gains must do so at the cost of the other. But is that really true?

The truth is that science and religion can coexist; they have coexisted; they coexist now; and they will continue to coexist in the future. Neither one has to leave; the world is big enough for both science and faith. They have the same goal of explaining *reality* — either the material part of reality or the immaterial part of reality. Science and faith are the two windows, or the two ways, that let humans look at the world they live in. Yet, there is only one world, and it is the same world these two windows try to reveal. Closing off either window would make us partially blind.

On September 12, 2006, Pope Benedict XVI delivered an address at the University of Regensburg in Germany. He gave a magisterial description of the relationship between faith and reason when he stressed that they complement each other: reason purifies faith of superstition and fanaticism, and faith broadens the horizons of reason to address the most fundamental questions of life.[2]

How can we defend this solid claim that seems to go against what many people nowadays tend to believe? Why is there no conflict here? Interestingly enough, the belief that there is a conflict between the two is in itself a *belief* that needs to be based also either on science or on faith. Is that possible? To find out we need to analyze what this belief is based on. In order to begin this analysis, we will argue that human beings have not only a religious nature but also an intellectual nature. Let's see where that takes us.

---

[2] The lecture was entitled "Faith, Reason and the University — Memories and Reflections."

b. Our Intellectual Nature

The case for reason and reasoning is easy to make. There is not one person who does not reason. In everyone's life, there are numerous moments when we do some sort of reasoning. To go to the store, for instance, we decide to go in the morning because we have an appointment somewhere else in the afternoon. It may not be a sophisticated kind of reasoning, but it is based on the "reasonable" assumption that we cannot be at two different places at once. Sometimes, we reason in a much fancier way: often when we are exposed to someone's sneezing, we develop cold-like symptoms, so reason tells us we should shun sneezers and perhaps take medication. Or think of this one: individuals left to themselves cannot realize all the good things they might otherwise obtain; therefore, they realize they must live and work with others. This last example was the way of reasoning used by a famous philosopher, Aristotle.

As a matter of fact, each time we engage in a discussion or dispute, we use reasoning to defend our position or to explain why we disagree with the position of others. Each time we look for any kind of explanation, we are in search of some form of reasoning. Reasoning is part of our intellectual nature. Aristotle, for instance, once came up with the following line of reasoning: since a lunar eclipse is caused by the interposition of the Earth, the form of this line will be caused by the form of the Earth's surface, which is apparently spherical—and not flat.[3] Thanks to reasoning, Aristotle was far ahead of his time without any fancy scientific research. This is just another simple example of what reasoning can do for us.

Another example of reasoning is claiming that nothing can make itself exist. We intuitively know that you cannot be your own father or mother. But a more explicit kind of reasoning can make

---

[3] Aristotle, *On the Heavens*, bk. 2, chap. 14.

this idea practically undisputable. It goes like this: For something to create itself, or produce itself, it would have to exist before it came into existence—which is impossible by mere logic or reasoning. So, nothing can just pop itself into existence; it must have a cause, because it does not and cannot have the power to make itself exist—it cannot be the cause of itself. Nothing comes from nothing, as the saying goes.

Most of us use reason many times a day. But some, like mathematicians and philosophers, have made reasoning and using reason their profession. They don't use a laboratory—their desk is their laboratory. But even scientists in their labs need to go back to their desks to think about their experiments and their results, checking the validity of their arguments. There could be no science without the use of reason. More on that later.

Because human beings seem to have a "natural" tendency to reason, it makes sense then that we categorize one another as members of the species *Homo sapiens*—where *sapiens* stands for "wise" or "intelligent." More specifically, St. Thomas Aquinas calls a human being *animal rationale*, a term that more accurately defines us as animals that use reason (*ratio*). Rationality is our hallmark. Our capacity for reasoning sets us apart from the rest of the animal world. Pope John Paul II, in one of his encyclicals, went even as far as saying, "the human being is by nature a philosopher."[4]

Rationality is our capacity to make rational judgments and decisions (which does not mean, of course, we always think rationally!). In fact, it is rationality that gives us access to the world of truths and untruths—a world beyond our control. Rationality is our capacity for abstract thinking and having reasons for our

---

[4] John Paul II, Encyclical Letter on the Relationship Between Faith and Reason *Fides et Ratio* (September 14, 1998), no. 64.

thoughts, thus giving us access to the "unseen" world of thoughts, laws, and truths. We peer further back in time, and further forward into the future, than any other animal. No other species would ever think to ponder the age of the Universe or fancy how the world will end. Weighing evidence and coming to a conclusion are rational activities par excellence. Reasoning leads us from one idea to a related idea; it is a matter of pondering realities beyond those that we experience through our physical senses, thus allowing us to transcend the current situation through the mental power of reasoning. It is our gateway to truth.

Philosophical giants such as Aristotle and St. Thomas Aquinas would put it this way: all we know about the world comes through our physical senses, but that's not the end of the story. It is then processed by the immaterial intellect that extracts from sensory experiences that which is *intelligible*. Well, it is the rationality of our intellect that makes the world intelligible and understandable; it gives us the power to discover truths about this world and to comprehend the Universe through reasoning. It is the mind's rationality that gives us access to the laws of nature and the structure of this Universe, for instance. Without rationality, we would not even know there are laws of nature. However, laws of nature are not just mental creations; they must be anchored in reality and truth. Reason is needed to discover them, otherwise they would elude us.

The power of reasoning is uniquely human. Rationality does not exist in the rest of the animal world—in spite of contrary claims made by some scientists who believe that rationality came to us through genes developed in the course of evolution. So, from now on, I will use the word *animal* only for nonhuman animals, for there seems to be a deep divide between the two.

Animals may be intelligent to a certain degree, but they certainly are not rational, reasoning beings. True, pets sometimes outsmart their owners when they play a whole repertoire of tricks on their owners' emotions. But that is a matter of intelligence at best, not intellect. When a dog avoids another dog by which it was bitten earlier, it does so because of a material cause—a bite—which makes the dog do so. It is more like a conditioned reflex, that is, a result of conditioning, not reasoning.

More generally, it could be said that, although animals do have the capacity to sense and remember things, they lack understanding in the sense of asking questions, formulating concepts, framing propositions, and drawing conclusions. They show no signs of abstract reasoning or having reasons for their "thoughts" (if they have any). For instance, they do not think in terms of true and false; they do not think in terms of cause-and-effect with "if-then" statements and "if-and-only-if" statements. Instead, animals are "driven" by motives, drives, instincts, emotions, stimuli, and training—not by reasoning. Animals live in a world of direct and immediate experiences because they do not have an intellect endowed with the human faculty of rationality, regardless of their intelligence. Animals drink because they are thirsty; that is not a mental reason but a material cause. Human beings, on the other hand, can drink because they have various kinds of reasons for doing so other than quenching their thirst.

Before we go on, it is important to make a distinction between intelligence and intellect. Rationality is a matter of intellect rather than intelligence. Whereas intelligence can be graded on an IQ scale, intellect cannot. One can be intelligent to various degrees (or even intellectual to various degrees), but one cannot have intellect to various degrees. Since intelligence works only with perception of sense data, animals may show various forms of intelligence in their behavior, since intelligence is a brain feature and as such an important tool in survival. For instance, we find spatial intelligence in pigeons and bats, social intelligence in wolves and monkeys, formal intelligence in apes and dolphins, and practical intelligence in rats and ravens, to name just a few. Intelligence is a matter of processing sense data, which is something even a robot can do by "cleverly" processing sounds, images, stimuli, signals, and the like.

Intellect is vastly different from intelligence. Like intelligence, intellect also uses sense data, but unlike intelligence, it changes perception into cognition. It does so by using mental concepts, which make sensory experiences intelligible for the human mind. The concept of gravity, for instance, helps us understand what happens around us when objects fall to the ground or when planets orbit the Sun. The intellect has the capacity to create concepts through which we are able to understand and know the world we live in. So, this raises the question as to what a *concept* is.

A concept is the result of abstraction from what we have experienced through the senses. For instance, we have seen several round objects, and then we abstract from this the concept of *circle*. This concept is highly abstract. It is very unlikely that we ever encounter a perfect circle in this world, which means we do not really "see" or perceive a circle. Besides, the concept of circle does not include any specific size, whereas all circular objects around us do. True, we can visualize a circle without imagining any specific size, but concepts have a universality that perceptions and images can never have. Therefore, the concept *circle* can be used for any specific circular object regardless of its size and its imperfections.

No wonder, then, that concepts play a crucial role in how we know the world. Thanks to concepts, we can see similarities that are not immediately evident through the senses and not directly tied to what we perceive. Everyone can see things falling, but to perceive gravity one needs the concept of gravity in order to see what no one had been able to see before Isaac Newton. The concept of gravity allows us to "see," for example, the similarity between the motion of the moon and the fall of an apple.

To take another example, biologists were not able to see the similarity in building blocks between animals and plants until the concept of *cell* had been developed. Neither could they see the similarity between leprosy and tuberculosis until the concept of *bacteria* had become available. Through concepts like these we see similarities that would have eluded us if we didn't have those concepts. We do not really or directly perceive gravity, bacteria, cells, genes, circles, and the like, yet these concepts make the world more understandable and intelligible to us. Again, that's not a matter of intelligence but of intellect.

Some may object to all of this that we are making too much of concepts. Although they don't have intellect, animals are still able to do the same thing with their intelligence, aren't they? True, animals do see similarities by mere perception; that's how they can identify, recognize, and categorize food, predators, and mates. They may even be able to recognize a circle when presented with a circular object, which could be considered a simple form of abstraction. However, their seeming act of abstraction is closely tied to a perceptual act. Here is why.

Dogs, for instance, can only learn to recognize a circle when presented with a specific circular object. We could call this *perceptual abstraction*, because it is closely tied to actual perception. Humans, on the other hand, can also see similarities through concepts, even apart from any perceived object. Only human beings can think about a circle or about circularity in general, apart from any specific perceived object. That's what we do in geometry, for example. We could call this *conceptual abstraction* to distinguish it from *perceptual abstraction.*[5] We are even able to conceive of a circle with three or four dimensions.

Conceptual perception and abstraction are unique to human beings. Concepts are our powerful tools to see similarities even when they are not directly visible. Although animals are able to see similarities, too, that doesn't mean they use concepts, though some people think that they do. Their reasoning goes like this: concepts classify things; animals classify things; therefore, animals use concepts. But this is a false argument, the conclusion of which does not logically follow from its two premises. It's like saying that humans are mortal; animals are mortal; therefore, animals are humans.

Concepts may even refer to something invisible. A more telling case in point is the concept of *tomorrow.* There is nothing to point at to explain this concept—other than a calendar, but that requires the concept of calendar as well. Animals don't have the concept of tomorrow. That's why they don't know they will die someday. For animals there is no "tomorrow," for that requires having the concept of *tomorrow.* That's the reason why animals cannot think about the possibility that someday there may not be a "tomorrow" in their lives. Deprived of concepts like these, non-human animals must work exclusively with what is directly observable. This may remind us of Ludwig Wittgenstein's remark: "We say a dog is afraid his master will beat him; but not, he is afraid his master will beat him tomorrow."[6] Why not? Because a concept like *tomorrow* is part

---

[5] This distinction comes from Mortimer J. Adler, "Is Intellect Immaterial?," chap. 4 in *Intellect: Mind over Matter* (New York: Macmillan, 1990).

[6] Ludwig Wittgenstein, *Preliminary Studies for the "Philosophical Investigations": Generally Known as the Blue and Brown Books* (New York: Harper, 1958), 166.

of *conceptual* abstraction, rather than perceptual abstraction. For animals there is no "tomorrow," because that requires conceptual abstraction.

Despite all of this, when looking at things, we often tend to do so either in an anthropomorphic way or in a dehumanizing way. In the field of biology, for instance, the anthropomorphic approach makes animals look like humans-in-the-making, and the dehumanizing approach makes humans look like glorified animals. Something similar can be seen in the field of artificial intelligence: the anthropomorphic approach makes computers look like machines outfitted with a human mind, and the dehumanizing approach makes the human mind look like a computer. In either way, we are actually, and often intentionally, ignoring or neglecting the specific differences between both sides of the equation—which makes either approach rather deceiving.

However, the warped perception of anthropomorphism cannot obliterate the fact that there is an enormous disparity between animals and humans. G. K. Chesterton said it well: "The more we really look at man as an animal, the less he will look like one."[7] Unlike animals, humans are conscious of time: they can study the past, recognize the present, and anticipate the future; they even desire to transcend time, thinking about living forever. Only humans wonder, "What caused or will cause what and why?" Only human beings have inquisitive minds, asking questions such as "Where do we come from?" and "Why are we here?" Only humans have the capacity to be scholars and scientists; they can even study animals, whereas animals can only watch humans, never study them. Animals may at best look inquisitive but never are they inquisitive. Humans are inquisitive, even if they don't look it.

[7] G. K. Chesterton, *The Everlasting Man*, pt. 1, chap. 1.

A Catholic Scientist Harmonizes Science and Faith

Human beings are always in search of some kind of worldview or explanation of life—which certainly goes far beyond their need for food and sex. In short, human beings are questioning, reasoning beings: they are driven by rationality, which gives them the capacity of making rational decisions—without any guarantee, of course, that those decisions are always rational. In short, humans could not live without reason. They have an intellectual nature. From early childhood on, they never seem to tire of constantly asking the famous question "Why?" Without why-questions there would not even be any science.

c. Our Religious Nature

Not only are we rational by nature, we are also religious by nature. We are "born believers," so to speak. We believe in something above and beyond us. Human beings have a built-in tendency to look beyond their own limits. Even when I say about myself, "I am only human," I am comparing myself, not with something "below" me (such as a cat, a dog, or an ape), but with something or someone "above" me and transcending me. Only the finite human mind is capable of catching a glimpse of the Infinite. *Infinity* is a concept in the same way *tomorrow* is one. Even children are able to see that the alphabet ends with z, but numbers keep going and going. This capacity of conceiving of infinity is sometimes called self-transcendence—referring to the transcendence of something or someone more than our own selves. And belief in the transcendent is at the heart of all religions.

Religious questions about "meaning" are clearly transcendent questions. They presume that life has a meaning beyond itself. Whenever we act, we take a risk on how this act is going to work out. We put ourselves in a larger setting that makes our doings purposeful and meaningful, although we cannot oversee the total setting by observation and reason alone. Because of our limitations, we act in faith by believing in "tomorrow," hoping for a good outcome and trusting that it makes sense to do what we decided to do. In knowing about our limits, we are able to look beyond those limits.

No one can live without some form of basic faith and trust. This means all of us were born with some kind of faith. Without any trust in our own doings and in the future ahead of us, we would be completely "paralyzed" in life. Instead, we are all "believers"—believers in "tomorrow" and in a wider setting or framework that surrounds and transcends us. In essence, each religion gives an answer to the ultimate questions of life. Religious believers have faith in something or someone larger than themselves. What individual religions add to this basic faith and trust is that they offer their believers a more specific "outline" or "framework" of this wider setting. Other than religion, there is no area of human interest that is concerned with the ultimate meaning and purpose of life.

Religious faith carries us above and beyond our limited capacities by making us aware of the "framework" in which we live. This framework is like the framework surrounding a spider's web—without such a framework, there could be no web. Likewise, religious faith is about the "web" of our lives, and this framework is commonly referred to as God. God is the framework in which "we live and move and have our being," as the apostle Paul put it (Acts 17:28).

However, it must be acknowledged first that the meaning and purpose of life can be found in a wide variety of items—ranging from money to property, from clothes to cars, from clubs to gangs, from games to gambling, from alcohol to sex, from politics to technology, from magic to witchcraft, from horoscopes to spiritism. Each one of these can become the one and only purpose of someone's life. However, if we consider religion to be related to the ultimate quest for ultimate meaning, most of these other kinds of faith and trust would not qualify as religious; at the most, they would qualify as superstitious—a form of secondhand religiosity. They don't give an ultimate meaning to life, a "firm ground" to stand on, a safe framework to live in. They are merely idols or surrogates that just deceive us with fake or proximate answers to ultimate questions. This is a deception that leads to a religious-like adoration for other gods than God—the gods of the stars (astrology), the god of earthly possessions (Mammon), the goddess of nature (Mother Nature), the idols of sex and food.

However, to be completely oriented on money or sex, to devote one's whole being to the pursuit of beauty or pleasure—in short, to devote oneself unconditionally to anything less than God—is surrendering oneself to idols we create ourselves. That's what it means to *idolize* something. These so-called gods are so human and so little divine, so shallow, and so little transcendent, that faith in them does not qualify as religious faith. It is, at best, a make-believe faith. On the contrary, the real religious faith is about the framework "in which we live and move and have our being."

The Jewish and Christian traditions explicitly state that there are many gods—many idols—but there is only one real God. The Bible could not have said it more clearly: "You shall have no other gods before me" (Exod. 20:3). So, when we don't worship the real God, we must be worshipping idols instead, for we are *by nature* worshippers. What this leads to is also well described by Chesterton: "For when we cease to worship God, we do not worship nothing, we worship anything."[8]

---

[8] Quoted in Richard Keyes, "The Idol Factory," chap. 1 in *No God but God: Breaking with the Idols of Our Age*, ed. Os Guiness and John Seel (Chicago: Moody Press, 1992), 32.

Not surprisingly then, faith and religion also set us apart from the animal world. We can be called *Homo sapiens*, but also *Homo religiosus*, because we have something like a "religious nature." Only humans have this transcendent dimension. Only humans have this belief in a transcendent framework—a Transcendent Being. This belief is one way of coping with our knowledge that we are limited, that the future is uncertain, that death is inevitable, and that someday there will be no tomorrow. Religion diminishes the hurt of death's certainty and the pain of losing a loved one with the prospect of reuniting in another life—not as a form of wishful thinking but as a pillar of religious faith, not as a product of genes but as a given embraced by the human mind. Humanity has always known this, intuitively, from its very beginning. In early primeval history, we find already evidence of elaborate burials. Such burials with grave goods indicate a belief in an afterlife, for the goods are there because they are considered useful to the deceased in their future lives.

It is because of man's universal drive for self-transcendence that we can find evidence of this even in the earliest archaeological data, such as art and burial rituals. The observation that religion seems universal made some biologists claim it "must" therefore be encoded in our genome. Blaise Pascal—the mathematician, physicist, and philosopher—had a better explanation. He used to speak of a hole in each one of us, an "infinite abyss [that] can only be filled only with an infinite and immutable object, that is to say, only by God Himself."[9]

---

[9] Blaise Pascal, *Pensées*, 7.425, quoted from "Pascal's Pensées," Project Gutenberg, Project Gutenberg Literary Archive Foundation, April 27, 2006, https://www.gutenberg.org/files/18269/18269-h/18269-h.htm, 425.

It is highly unlikely that the "hole" Pascal speaks about is programmed in our genes—and the same holds for religion. Our universal drive for self-transcendence does not seem to come from our genes. Of course, I cannot transcend myself on my own, but because I myself was made in the image of God, I perceive more than myself whenever I perceive myself completely. As St. Bonaventure put it, "We cannot rise above ourselves unless a higher power lifts us up."[10]

It is man's drive for self-transcendence that explains why belief in God as a transcendent being is so universal in human history. The rising number of atheists in modern society seems to belie this, but we need to acknowledge that even among the greatest philosophers there is hardly any controversy about the existence of some absolute or infinite Being. As the late philosopher Fr. Joseph Bochenski, O.P., put it a few decades ago,

> The fact that there is such a being is the common conviction of Plato, Aristotle, Plotinus, St. Thomas, Descartes, Spinoza, Leibniz, Kant, Hegel, Whitehead—and even of dialectical materialists, the official present and past party philosophers of communism, if these smaller minds are, in any way, comparable with the greater ones. Although all these philosophers vehemently deny the existence of the Judeo-Christian God, they claim at the same time that the world is infinite, eternal, boundless, absolute.[11]

---

[10] Bonaventure, *The Soul's Journey into God*, in *The Soul's Journey into God, The Tree of Life, The Life of St. Francis*, trans. Ewert Cousins (Mahwah, NJ: Paulist Press, 1978), 59.

[11] Joseph Bochenksi, *The Road to Understanding: More than Dreamt of in Your Philosophy* (North Andover, MA: Genesis Publishing Company, 1996), 116.

2

What Is Science?

In modern society, science is not only heralded by scientists but also by most non-scientists. It is based on one of the most impressive track records in human history. It is a success story that keeps persistently adding new achievements to the list, with no end in sight. Therefore, it should not come as a surprise that science has given us reason, not only for high hopes, but also for extravagant claims.

That assessment may be true, but it is not quite clear what precisely it is that makes science *science*. Not only has the way science is done changed in the course of history,[12] but also is there quite some misunderstanding as to what science is nowadays. Many laypeople, and even some scientists, have outlandish ideas about science. The late Fordham University philosopher Francis Canavan, S.J., makes a sobering remark in this context: "Science is what scientists say it is. And who decides who are scientists? Scientists do. They set the standards by which persons are recognized as doing properly scientific work, as distinguished from dilettantism, quackery, and magic."[13]

---

[12] The term *scientist*, for instance, was only coined in 1833 by the English philosopher and historian of science William Whewell.

[13] Francis Canavan, *Fun Is Not Enough* (St. Louis, MO: EnRoute Books and Media, 2018), 187.

A Catholic Scientist Harmonizes Science and Faith

To begin with, when speaking of science, people often have very different things in mind. Most agree that physics and chemistry are "real" sciences. But what about psychoanalysis, to just mention one case of disagreement? Or take economics. It is very hard to find two economists who agree with each other on any economic issue. Even certain parts of the life sciences, such as evolutionary theory, are questioned by some as to whether they deserve to be called science. Then there are some sciences that are hardly experimental—with astronomy on one side and paleontology at the other end. But that doesn't seem to make them less of a science.

Apparently, there is a great deal of disagreement as to what science stands for. Some say it is a systematic enterprise that builds and organizes knowledge in the form of testable explanations and predictions—but that makes for a very pliable rule. What all sciences do seem to have in common, though, is that they are about material things and issues that can be dissected, measured, counted, and quantified. In general, all sciences are empirical, but not necessarily experimental. They strive for empirical evidence—evidence acquired by means of the senses, particularly by observation and often also by experimentation. The evidence they look for may be found either "in the field" or "in the lab." Let's leave it at that for now.

a. A Caricature of Science

A simplistic view of science has it that "real" knowledge—that is, scientific knowledge in the minds of many—is only possible as a result of continued measuring and counting. An inscription on the facade of the Social Science Research Building at the University of Chicago reads, "If you cannot measure, your knowledge is meager and unsatisfactory."

no such thing as "seeing in a neutral way" or "observing
it expectation." Even the idea of similar observations only
sense if we know ahead of time what the assumed similar-
based on. This means that all observations are somehow
ory-laden."[14] How could a "meaningless" observation ever be
ant to testing a scientific theory? The best way to search is to
an idea of what you are looking for—it may be the wrong
, but it's very hard, if not impossible, to just search "blindly."
Seen this way, scientific research may be described as a "dia-
gue" between scientists and nature—that is, a dialogue between
ssible observations (hypotheses) and *actual* observations (facts).
Ultimately, all hypotheses must be under the control of *reality*.
Let's make clear from the outset that a hypothesis is basically only
an "invention," which is very different from a "discovery." To find
out whether the invention qualifies as a discovery, we need *test*
implications derived from this hypothesis—so as to make sure the
hypothesis is more than an invention but is in fact a discovery
about reality. There is that pivotal role of reason and reasoning
again. The ultimate purpose of our reasoning is not to change the
world but to understand it. Obviously, if there is no real world to
understand, there is no science.

Science stands or falls by deriving test implications from its
hypotheses, which are basically predictions that can be tested either in the field (empirical testing) or in the lab (experimental
testing). They are of the type "If hypothesis X is true, then . . ." or
"If hypothesis X is not true, then . . ." Simply put, the outcome
of each test implication can go one of two ways: the test decides

---

[14] This term was introduced by N. R. Hanson, *Perception and Discovery:
An Introduction to Scientific Inquiry*, ed. Matthew D. Lund (New
York: Freeman, Cooper, 1969).

How do we get to such allegedly secure scientific knowledge?
The answer seems quite straightforward: by using our senses and
making observations and measurements. In this view, scientists
collect "observations" by using their senses for observation and
their hands for experimentation. Once they have repeated the same
observation multiple times and have gathered a series of singular
observation statements, they can generalize them into a more
general statement, or even a law—for instance, of the type, "All
metals expand when heated," or "All solids dissolved in a liquid
raise the liquid's boiling point," or "All radioactive elements decay
at a fixed rate," or "All acids turn litmus paper red," or "All plants
and animals are composed of cells," or "All organisms require a
source of energy." According to the simplistic view of science, the
keyword of scientific statements and laws should be the word *all*.

What the scientists did in the previous cases is make the step
from "some" to "many" observations, and ultimately to "all" similar
observations—that is, from a *finite* number of cases to an *infinite*
number of cases. This is a decisive step from a series of singular
observation statements to declaring a general law that applies to all
similar cases. However, this view of science is basically a caricature:
it portrays science as an accumulation of singular, empirical observations linking two or more variables together—for example, the
link between acids and litmus, or between the length of iron rods
and temperature. Finding a link between two or more variables is
often considered to be the main goal of scientists, at least to begin
with. But is it really?

The problem here is that we don't want to end up with merely
anecdotal or circumstantial evidence based on only a collection
of haphazard observations. That's the main reason why scientists
sometimes aim for a long series of repeated, identical observations.
For instance, if dipping blue litmus paper in acid is repeatedly and

frequently accompanied by the observation of the paper's turning red, we may conclude that dipping blue litmus paper in acid is the *cause* of its turning red. This is a conclusion about *all* similar cases based on *some*, or preferably *many*, similar cases. However, that's a conclusion hard to corroborate in a definitive way, as we will never be able to check *all* cases.

Another problem of this simplistic view is that scientists are supposed to base their conclusions on similar cases. But what does *similar* mean? The idea of these scientists is that they think they can build science from the bottom up starting with simple similar observations. In their view, it's only through observation statements that science is supposed to grow, according to the simplistic view. Science is presumably built on the foundation of "barren similar observations." However, that would only be possible if we knew what it is that makes observations *similar*.

The following example may clarify the underlying problem in a simplified way. Imagine you want to find out whether the headache someone developed is caused by gin on the rocks, or by whiskey on the rocks, or perhaps by rum on the rocks. In the caricature view of science, scientists should extensively experiment with these three drinks, to come to the surprising conclusion that the headache is caused by ice cubes, because that is what all these drinks have in common and makes them similar.

This conclusion seems quite reasonable, until you come to know of the more-embracing concept of alcohol—being a generic term for gin, whiskey, and rum combined. Only thanks to the concept of alcohol can one detect a *relevant* similarity in these cases. Similarity stands or falls with the concept that unifies the observations. This explains also why no one saw the similarity between falling apples and orbiting planets before Isaac Newton had made the connection—and it took him a while too in order

to come up with the unifying concept o
cases similar.

Concepts tell us what is *relevant* in sc
all observations are equally relevant. Rele
litmus color has to do with acids (rather tha
what the expansion of iron has to do with ten
with atmospheric pressure)—to mention jus
words, there are relevant factors and there ar
How do scientists determine which factors are i
are irrelevant?

Unfortunately, observations do not come wit
marked relevant or irrelevant. So, what is to cou
factor for causing water to boil, for example? Does va
sure matter? Yes, it does. Does the purity of water i
does. Does the method of heating make a difference? N
Does the time of the day make a difference? No, it d
we could add an unlimited number of additional factor
or what determines which ones are relevant and which

One thing is clear: what is relevant in scientific resear
to be identified before any methods can be used. Since we
take all factors or all circumstances into account, we must
hypothesis stating that the factors and circumstances we do co
are the only relevant ones. Every scientific investigation begins
an assumption—usually called a hypothesis—which determi
which factors are considered relevant. Again, a hypothesis is need
before we can even speak of observation statements. Consideration
like these force us to take on a more realistic view of science.

b. A More Realistic View of Science

As we saw in the previous section, mere observation is not a very productive starting point for scientific research. As a matter of fact,

either for or against the hypothesis. In other words, the hypothesis either makes true predictions or false predictions about reality. These predictions either confirm or refute the hypothesis under investigation.

Seen this way, scientific research is like a dialogue between the possible and the actual, between fiction and reality, between invention and discovery. If the test implications come true, we receive *confirmation*; but if a test implication is not confirmed, we speak of *falsification*. Research is like a game of questioning and answering, of searching and testing, of trial and error, by falling over and picking oneself up again. It is like a dialogue between subject and object: the subject (the scientist) asks a question couched in a hypothesis, and the object (nature) gives an answer phrased in terms of test results. It is a process that could be likened to the investigation of a detective. Seen this way, research may look like a simple process. But a few remarks need to be made about this seemingly simple process.

First, most research begins with a hypothesis—rather than with observation statements. But we need to be aware of what this entails. In science, discoveries typically start as inventions—usually called hypotheses. But it is important to realize that not all inventions lead to discoveries. To use an analogy, the person who invented Atlantis did not discover Atlantis; it remains a legendary island (at least until further notice!). The same is true in science: most inventions do not make it to the stage of discoveries. The invention of Vulcan, for instance—a planet supposed to orbit between the Sun and Mercury—never made it to a discovery and was eventually thrown out as a false invention.

Nonetheless, some scientists think they have made a discovery when all they have in mind is an invention, a hypothesis. However, a hypothesis is only an invention in the scientist's mind until it has been shown to be also a discovery about reality. The late Nobel laureate and physiologist Peter Medawar once said, "Science will dry up only if scientists lose or fail to exercise the power or incentive to imagine what the truth might be."[15] But he also gave a wise advice to scientists everywhere: "The intensity of the conviction that a hypothesis is true has no bearing on whether it is true or not."[16] Because of this, science has an important rule for hypotheses if they are to be of any use: they must have observational consequences for them to qualify as scientific.

In other words, scientific hypotheses are basically happy guesses or bold conjectures, which are not derived or discovered from observation statements, but they are invented first by some scientist *before* they lead to observations. Obviously, they are not wild guesses—that's why a complete novice will hardly make any scientific discovery. Yet guesses guide us as to where and what to search. Even in simple cases such as, "Iron expands with heating," we have a hidden hypothesis stating that a certain variable, the length of the iron rod, is dependent on another variable, temperature. Next, we derive from this hypothesis predictions that can then be tested in the field or in the lab as to whether they are inventions that do lead to discoveries. Research typically begins with asking the right questions—by means of new concepts, models, hypotheses, and theories. But they need to be tested further in the field or in the lab.

Second, to explain certain scientific puzzles, several hypotheses may qualify simultaneously as an explanation of the same observation, for the simple reason that different hypotheses can explain

---

[15] P. B. Medawar, *Advice to a Young Scientist* (New York: Basic Books, 1979), 91.

[16] Medawar, *Advice to a Young Scientist*, 39.

the same observation. Think of a few observation points marked in a graphic and try to draw a curve through these points. You will find out there are many, even infinitely many, possibilities (hypotheses), unless you have a certain preference in mind—say, for the smoothest curves only. Similarly, when a certain disease is found to be contagious, that can be explained by various causes, such as bacteria, viruses, fungi, or what have you.

An example of multiple potential explanations can be found also in the early stages of astronomy, where at least three theoretical frameworks were able to explain the observations seen in the skies at night: the geocentric model of Ptolemy with the Earth in the center, the heliocentric model of Copernicus with the Sun in the center, and the model of Tycho Brahe who had the Moon and the Sun revolving around the Earth, but the other planets (Mercury, Venus, Mars, Jupiter, and Saturn) revolving around the Sun; so he had the Sun with those planets together revolve around the Earth.

All three models were in essence equally able to explain and predict phenomena in the sky. Interestingly enough, the model of Ptolemy and the model of Copernicus were in fact mathematically identical for all observations available at the time. Besides, Tycho's system, too, fit all the prevailing data (although soon, Galileo's discovery of the phases of Venus revealed that the Sun, the Earth, and Venus were sometimes configured in ways not possible in the Ptolemaic system). Eventually, Tycho's system would only fall out of favor on theoretical grounds, almost a century later, when Newton's theory of gravity made it inconceivable for the solar system to orbit the small mass of the Earth.

Third, the fact of the matter is that trained scientists "see" much more in their observations than laypeople—they see "things" that other people might easily miss. As the philosopher of science Norwood Hanson puts it, "There is more to seeing than meets the eye."[17] The same holds for the other senses: when a chemist, for instance, smells sulfur dioxide, a layperson smells only rotten eggs. Although they have the same sense data, chemists know about gases, and they know more about gases than laypeople, so chemists can learn more from their sense data. That's why laypeople often look but do not see or listen but do not hear.

Fourth, if observation statements were indeed the foundation of science, then science can only talk about what we can observe (color, temperature, weight, movement, and so on) but never about their causes, which are often not directly observable—causes such as electricity or gravity. For instance, it's not possible to determine which battery is empty and which one is full by merely weighing the two.

On the other hand, the history of science shows us that research does not just keep adding more and more new observation statements to its previous collection. Often, earlier scientific insights are being overturned. At times, theories that have served for a while can suddenly be abandoned. Occasionally, observation statements that seem to refute what was accepted before are set aside. In other words, the idea of a steadily growing fund of observation statements in science is hard to corroborate.

Fifth, scientific research is most of the time a minefield of hidden variables, which forces scientists to control their variables carefully before making observation statements. Apparently, scientists don't just hunt for more and more observations, under various settings, but they limit themselves to a strictly *controlled* setting. They usually do so by removing the process or object under investigation from its natural context, typically done in a lab. Expressed more technically, during the experiment, interfering variables must be

[17] Hanson, *Perception and Discovery*, title of chap. 4.

ruled out or kept under control. Therefore, scientists often limit themselves to a simple setting.

To put this in an image, an experiment typically takes place in the test-tube-like shelter of a laboratory, removed from the complexity of nature. In a test tube (*in vitro*), for instance, a biological experiment is easier to keep under control than inside the body (*in vivo*). And something similar holds for the other sciences. Physics, for instance, often deals with "closed systems," which are basically systems in a metaphorical test-tube. Reducing complex phenomena to a manageable model related to an analyzable problem is a successful way of doing research. This means there is always a so-called *ceteris paribus* clause involved to the effect of "everything else being constant." The consequence of this clause is that other, possibly interfering variables must be kept under control or are assumed to be constant. Even such a "*ceteris paribus*" clause is only understandable and possible under the assumption that not everything is equally relevant. No observation statement can start this process on its own.

Sixth, observations are not solely determined by what observers see on the retina of their eyes. What scientists see through microscopes or telescopes, for instance, is very different from what laypeople discern—yet they may have the same images projected on their retinas. It's the same story for what x-ray pictures reveal, which explains why medically trained professionals see things differently (and usually much better) than beginners. Even if we assume that observations are the same for everyone—which they are not, except for images on their retina—we still need to acknowledge that observation statements involve theories of various degrees of sophistication, which makes them theory-laden. In short, all observation statements must be made in the language of some theory, however vague or primitive. That's where concepts come in again.

Seventh, the assumption that observations are similar and look alike in certain respects—for example, being magnetic, being acidic, being cellular, being infectious, being toxic, and so on—seems to ignore the fact that this similarity is not visible until we know already what it is that similar cases have in common and what makes them similar—which requires the proper concepts. In other words, we need to identify first what is relevant to our problem, because similarity cannot be established until it has been identified in a word, or actually in a concept.

Scientists cannot mechanically infer from a few cases to all similar cases until their similarity has been conceptualized first. Since things can be "alike" in numerous ways, we need a unifying concept of similarity first before we can classify and categorize things as similar. Before we can notice a carnivore, for instance, we need the notion of a carnivore to begin with. Without the concept of carnivore, we cannot see carnivores.

Apparently, the meaning of concepts is not acquired through observation. When observers see several red things, they are supposed to discern that their common element is redness. However, a set of red things does not select itself. The criterion which includes certain observational experiences in the set of red things presupposes the very concept, redness, which it is meant to explain. In other words, pointing at a set of red things does not automatically generate the concept of redness. The truth of the matter is that observations do not create their own observation statements. We can only observe red things by using the concept of redness.

What can we conclude from all of this? Science is a tentative enterprise, leading to acceptance, revision, or rejection of a hypothesis or theory, or even of an entire paradigm or research program. What is accepted today may be modified or even discarded tomorrow. Because the cycle of searching and possibly finding is a never-ending, cyclical process, science never ends. Do not confuse this cycle, the so-called *empirical cycle*, with a vicious circle; it is more of a spiral than a circle—hopefully a cycle spiraling upwards and not downwards.

c. Science Needs Reasoning

Some might still maintain that science is only based on and determined by observation and experimentation, not reasoning. True, science is just not possible without observations and usually experiments, but we also pointed out these are quite useless, or even impossible, without reasoning. Science needs reasoning and thinking both before and after observations and experiments come into play.

In other words, scientists must think before and after making observations and doing experiments. Just opening one's eyes doesn't lead science anywhere. Observations and experiments can only do their job thanks to reasoning. As the late Fr. Canavan puts it, "Science depends on minds that can judge what is a fact, which facts constitute evidence, and when the evidence leads to a firm conclusion."[18]

Interestingly enough the problem we have here was already expressed by the ancient philosopher Plato, although in a slightly different context, when he said: "How would you search for what is unknown to you?"[19] Plato noticed a seeming paradox here: we are in search of something unknown; otherwise we would not need to search anymore. Yet it must be "known" at the same time. Otherwise we would not know what to search for, or would not even know if we had found, or not, what we were searching for. That's where thinking and reasoning must come in.

[18] Canavan, *Fun Is Not Enough*, 187.
[19] Plato, *Meno*, 80d.

By the way, Plato's description of the above problem is in itself an impressive case of thinking and reasoning.

The idea that iron expands when the temperature rises is not just based on a series of observations of iron rods expanding with increasing temperature. That's a caricature of science, as we found out, and it misinterprets how scientists really operate. Yes, they do and must use their senses and perform experiments, but not without using lots of reasoning. Let me clarify this with a few simple but telling stories taken from the history of science.

Case #1: Harvey—Blood Circulation

Let's start with the simple case of how William Harvey discovered the existence of a closed blood circulation. He did so at a time when there was much confusion about the bloodstream. Strange conceptions had been around for centuries.

Galen of Pergamum (ca. AD 150), a Greek physician, surgeon, and philosopher in the Roman Empire, thought that the expanding and contracting movements of the heart cause the blood to move up and down the blood vessels, as it is with the tides—some kind of two-way traffic in the blood vessels. However, in order to allow blood to move from the veins to the arteries, Galen had to postulate pores in the septum of the heart. That was obviously not an observation but a hypothesis or an assumption on his part.

Andrea Cesalpino (1509–1603), an Italian physician, was one of the first scientists to acknowledge the problems inherent in Galen's system. He tried to deal with the valves in the veins—which the anatomist Hieronymus Fabricius (1537–1619) had called "little mouths"—by suggesting that they regulate how much blood is going to seep from the arteries back into the veins. Without knowing it, he was preparing the way for Harvey's closed circulatory system.

Michael Servetus (1511-1553), a Spanish physician, tackled another problem. He wondered how blood can flow from the right to the left side of the heart through pores that were never observed. It seemed more acceptable to him that blood should flow from one part of the heart to the other by way of the lungs—and thus he introduced a one-way traffic between heart and lungs. Ironically, in postulating a partially closed system, he replaced the unseen pores in the heart with unseen tiny vessels in the lungs. Again, what he claimed was not an observation but a hypothesis.

It was William Harvey (1578-1657) who deserves the prize for finally reshuffling the pieces of the puzzle into one new system. An idea was born! Harvey's new idea was not really a discovery but more of an invention—it was more based on reasoning than on observation. In fact, he never actually saw the connecting blood capillaries needed for a closed circulation. We do not know what exactly gave him his revolutionary idea. Was it Aristotle's idea of perfect circular motion, or perhaps the thought of an outlet needed for a pumped inflow, borrowed from the developing technology of pumps? We do not really know.

Whatever it was that guided him, Harvey hypothesized two one-way circulations controlled by a heart pump—one between heart and lungs, another one between heart and the rest of the body. Apparently, the capillaries did not show the closed circulation of blood, but it was the other way around: the very theory of a closed blood circulation allowed him to deal with many anomalies of the older views. It allowed him to solve several anomalies: no unseen pores anymore, no tides anymore, no accumulation of pumped inflow anymore, and no useless valves anymore!

At the same time, however, Harvey had introduced his own, new problems. How can arterial blood become venous blood, and where exactly does this happen? As Galen had created pores in the septum, Harvey needed a different kind of connection to obtain a closed system. Only eventually would this theory make the vessels visible when better microscopes would become available, but that was only later. What we can learn from this is that Harvey's new theory certainly was not based on the observation of capillaries.

His contemporaries were very aware of Harvey's new problem. An external referee in the British Medical Research Council at the time had to write a comment on a grant application submitted by Harvey. The referee's report says:

> He claims never to have observed pores or holes in the heart.... By contrast, I have never seen any evidence for the existence of blood vessels providing a link between arteries and veins in the periphery of the body, as is stipulated by the scheme of Dr. H[arvey]; such vessels would have to be of an extremely fine calibre to escape the eye and would pose an insurmountable mechanical resistance to the flow of blood.[20]

That was indeed a real problem for Harvey's hypothesis.

Although Harvey never saw the connecting blood capillaries needed for a closed circulation system, he held on to his new idea, despite contradicting evidence. Only time would tell that his bold conjecture was indeed correct.

Case #2: Galileo – Orbits

For centuries, the orbits of planets had been explained by Ptolemy's geocentric theory, which has all planets orbit around the Earth. Based

---

[20] Wolf Seufert, "Forum: The Ancient Art of Peer Review—Wolf Seufert Has Been Digging into the Archives," New Scientist, January 4, 1992, https://www.newscientist.com/article/mg13318024-900-forum-the-ancient-art-of-peer-review-wolf-seufert-has-been-digging-into-the-archives/.

on this model, sailors had been able to navigate the seas with their ships, and astronomers had been able to predict eclipses. Apparently, that's not what the problem of geocentrism was. But its model had become such a complex system, with its numerous epicycles—circles moving on other circles—that hardly anyone believed it corresponded to the physical reality of the Universe. It worked all right, but it was not believed to be true, which is an entirely different issue.

As a matter of fact, there were serious problems with geocentrism. Here is one of them. When observed from one night to the next, a planet appears to move most of the time from West to East against the background stars. Occasionally, however, the planet's motion appears to reverse direction, for a short time, from East to West. This reversal is known as *retrograde motion*. How had Ptolemy been able to explain this? He hypothesized that planets are attached, not to the concentric spheres themselves, but to circles attached to the concentric spheres. These circles were called *epicycles*, and the concentric spheres to which they were attached were termed the *deferents*. Then, the centers of the epicycles executed uniform circular motion as they went around the deferent at uniform angular velocity, while at the same time the epicycles (to which the planets were attached) executed their own uniform circular motion. That's how the observation of retrograde could be explained! Yes, it could, but at the cost of being a case of very convoluted thinking.

It was time for a change, which came in 1543 when Nicolaus Copernicus (1473–1543) launched his heliocentric theory saying that the Earth travels around the Sun, as do the other planets. Copernicus explained the apparent retrograde motion of the planets as being the result of the relative speeds of the Earth and the planets circling around the Sun when observed from the Earth. Thus, he was able to explain retrograde motion in a way and with a theory different from Ptolemy's. A century later, Galileo Galilei

(1564–1642) would adopt the Copernican model and passionately promote it as a proven theory, which it was not at the time.

Interestingly enough, whereas Ptolemy was able to calibrate his geocentric model by adjusting the size and speed of the epicycles and deferents, Copernicus and Galileo were able to calibrate their heliocentric model by adjusting the size and speed of a planet's orbit. As to whether this makes the heliocentric model more scientific is debatable. Besides, the new model worked with circular orbits—instead of the more accurate elliptical orbits introduced later by Johannes Kepler—so it would still need the so despised epicycles of the Ptolemaic model to correct for its own inaccuracy.

In addition, the heliocentric theory had its own problems and had to face several challenges. The most important issue was an argument that had been made nearly two thousand years earlier by Aristotle himself. If the Earth did orbit the Sun, the philosopher argued, then stellar parallaxes would be observable in the sky. In other words, there would be a shift in position of a star observed from the Earth on one side of the Sun, and then six months later from the other side.

When another astronomer at Galileo's time, Tycho Brahe (1546–1601), tried to detect the test implication of a parallax with his instruments—which were the most sensitive and accurate ones in existence at the time—he failed. Therefore, he concluded the heliocentric theory had to be wrong. So he came up with an alternative theory, which had the Moon and the Sun revolve around the Earth, but had the other planets (Mercury, Venus, Mars, Jupiter, and Saturn) revolve around the Sun; so he had the Sun with those planets together revolve around the Earth. His model was in fact a combination of geocentrism and heliocentrism.

Another problem for the heliocentric model was the so-called "tower argument." If a stone is dropped from the top of a tower erected on the moving Earth, it will fall toward the center of the Earth. While it is doing so, the tower will be sharing the motion of the Earth, due to the Earth's spinning. By the time the stone reaches the surface of the Earth, the tower will have moved from its original position and therefore, the stone would strike the ground some distance from the foot of the tower. In fact, however, the stone strikes the ground at the base of the tower. That seemed to be a detrimental observation for heliocentrism. So, the Earth cannot be spinning. Right?

No, not quite! Galileo did not accept this seeming counterevidence as falsifying evidence. Instead, he developed the concept of relative motion and the law of inertia. An object held at the top of a tower and sharing with the tower a circular motion around the Earth's center will, after it is dropped, continue in that motion along with that tower and will strike the ground at the foot of the tower. This way, Galileo was able to avoid trouble for his theory by giving a different interpretation to his observations.

Case #3: Semmelweis – Fever

Strange as it may sound, the idea of surgeons washing their hands before doing surgery is only 150 years old. Until then, all hospitals were pools of filth. Surgeons loved to speak of the "good old surgical stink" and took pride in the stains on their unwashed operation gowns as a display of their experience.[21] The man who finally discovered the need for surgeons, and others, to wash their hands to prevent infection was Ignaz Semmelweis (1818–1865).[22]

---

[21] Lindsey Fitzharris, *The Butchering Art: Joseph Lister's Quest to Transform the Grisly World of Victorian Medicine* (New York: Farrar, Straus and Giroux, 2017).

[22] See for more details: Carl G. Hempel, *Philosophy of Natural Science* (Englewood Cliffs, NJ: Prentice Hall, 1966), 3–8.

Semmelweis was a physician at a hospital in Vienna, Austria. The hospital housed two obstetric clinics, the first for teaching medical students, the second for training midwives. Semmelweis soon discovered an odd statistic in the records: maternal mortality rates at the first clinic, where the students were trained, had twice or sometimes three times the rate found in the midwife-staffed second clinic. Those were observations that didn't immediately make sense to him.

To explain the difference between the two clinics, Semmelweis tried eliminating various possibilities, ranging from the mother's position of giving birth to eliminating a frightening walkthrough by a priest when patients were dying. But he could not find any confirming evidence. He excluded "overcrowding" as a cause, since the second clinic was always more crowded, and yet the mortality rate was lower. Other people had assumed the cause to be an epidemic, but Semmelweis found this falsified by the fact that fever hardly occurred in the city of Vienna itself. Sound reasoning was guiding him.

After eliminating various other hypothetical variables, Semmelweis concluded that the only *significant* difference between the two clinics had to be the staff: department 1 was run by medical students, department 2 by midwives. Wasn't that an obvious difference? Not so until Semmelweis hypothesized that an examination by students might be rougher than usual. However, the replacement of some students by midwives had no effect. Early in 1847, by "chance," Semmelweis noticed that a colleague wounded by the lancet of a student while doing an autopsy died with the same symptoms that Semmelweis had observed in the victims of child-bed fever.

This led Semmelweis to note that the doctors and medical students often also performed autopsies, while the midwives did not—in short, he came up with a possible *relevant* difference. It turned out to be a rather simple hypothesis based on reasoning. The medical students took no hygienic steps between working on autopsies and delivering babies, and often used the same instruments for both activities. Therefore, he hypothesized that "particles" from the cadavers were responsible for transmitting the disease. He actually spoke of *cadaveric matter*, which the students' hands supposedly carried from the corpses under investigation to the women under treatment. It may look like a strange concept, but it did throw some light on the problem he was facing.

Based on this concept, Semmelweis reasoned that child-bed fever could be prevented by destroying the cadaveric material adhering to hands. He therefore issued an order requiring all medical students to wash their hands in a solution of chlorinated lime. And promptly, the mortality from childbed fever began to decline. Soon after, Semmelweis broadened his hypothesis. When he had examined a woman with cervical cancer and then moved on to examine twelve other women in the same room, he noticed that eleven of them would die from childbed fever. So, he concluded that the cause of childbed fever was not only "cadaveric matter," but also "putrid matter derived from living organisms," as he described it. Finally, Semmelweis had "seen" what caused child-bed fever. What began as an invention turned out to be a discovery.

Case #4: Pasteur—Germs

Louis Pasteur had already become familiar with microorganisms early on in his career. He had demonstrated that a tiny microorganism in yeast is responsible for the fermentation of sugar into alcohol. He also demonstrated that, when a different microorganism contaminates the wine, lactic acid is produced, making the wine sour. This led Pasteur to the idea that microorganisms causing fermentation could also be the cause of certain diseases. Thanks to this knowledge and to the concept of microorganisms, he was able to attack the idea that life emerges from what had long been called "spontaneous generation," which holds that living creatures can arise from nonliving matter.

He achieved this by using flasks with swan necks drawn out in a flame, so dust particles and germs would get trapped in the lower curve; plus, he used a yeast broth in the flasks heated at high temperatures, assuming this would kill all microorganisms. This design was based on powerful reasoning. After several weeks, Pasteur observed that the broth in the swan-neck flask had not changed at all; but when the swan neck was broken, germs readily entered the flask and made the broth look discolored, clouded by molds and microorganisms.

Pasteur thus showed two things to the supporters of spontaneous generation. First, although the fluid was boiled, he showed that heating could not have destroyed any "active principle," since the fluid still had the ability to support life when the swan neck was broken. Second, he had not barred any "active principle" from the air—as his opponents had suggested—because air was still free to enter and leave through the unobstructed pathway of the flask's neck.

The outcome seemed to be devastating for the theory of spontaneous generation. But the dispute was not settled that easily. The theory of spontaneous generation was still retaining some strong supporters.[23] Between 1861 and 1863, Felix Pouchet carried out the same experiments as Louis Pasteur had done. They both used

---

[23] See, for instance, Harry Collins and Trevor Pinch, *The Golem: What Everyone Should Know about Science* (Cambridge, UK: Cambridge University Press, 1993), 79–90.

flasks with necks drawn out in a flame; they both used a nutrient solution, boiled and sealed. But there were also some minor, perhaps significant differences. For one, Pasteur used a yeast infusion, while Pouchet a hay infusion. The second was that, high in the mountains, the neck of the flasks was broken. To do so, Pasteur used heated pincers, while Pouchet a heated file. Could these differences explain that Pasteur found no rotting in nineteen out of twenty flasks, whereas Pouchet found rotting in eight flasks out of eight?

Observations do not always have the last word in science. What to do with the difference between these observations? What had gone "wrong" here? Pasteur blamed Pouchet for using a file instead of a forceps. Pouchet, on the other hand, could have blamed Pasteur (but he did not) for not having used a hay infusion. Had Pasteur used a hay infusion, he would have been in for quite a surprise, as it became known in 1876 that hay infusions support a spore that is not easily killed by boiling.

The main issue at hand in the dispute between Pasteur and Pouchet was this: What happens when a nutritive medium, which is sterilized by boiling, is exposed to clean air? Pasteur protected his theory by defining all air that gave rise to life in his boiled flasks as contaminated. This was a decision he made. Notice the assumptions he held: germs can be killed by heat, and germs can contaminate air. With the latter assumption, he refused to be swayed by what, on the face of it, was falsifying evidence. Or should we rather say that he was obstinate in the face of counterevidence? It is only afterwards that it was possible to designate his decision as successful.

Case #5: Le Verrier–New Planets

Most astronomers at the time of the French astrophysicist Urbain Le Verrier (1811–1877) loved to work within the framework of

Isaac Newton's research program. After the planet Uranus was discovered in 1781, astronomers were able to predict its orbit by using Isaac Newton's unified laws.

However, when they carefully followed Uranus's motion in its slow eighty-four-year orbit around the Sun, they noticed that something was wrong. Uranus didn't quite move as it should according to Newton's theory. Hence, they refined their measurements and took more careful observations—yet the anomaly did not go away.

Obviously, astronomers of the day didn't think the unexpected observation was the end of Newtonian gravity. Instead, they came up with another hypothesis for the strange motion of Uranus by postulating some large and unseen object that must have affected the planet's orbit. Calculations showed that it would have to be a planet as large as Uranus and even farther away from the Sun. No observation made them think so, but theory did.

It was not until 1846 that Le Verrier predicted with the use of Newton's laws where this hypothetical planet had to be located.[24] Some of his colleagues in Germany had the courage to direct their telescopes to the spot where Le Verrier had told them to look. Lo and behold, within half an hour, they spotted the planet Neptune. Instead of a demise, this observation became a victory of Newtonian physics.

Several years after his discovery of Neptune, Le Verrier went after one more planetary puzzle. It had become clear to him and other astronomers that Mercury was another planet that wasn't moving either as it was supposed to. The point in its orbit where it made its closest approach to the Sun shifted a little more than

---

[24] See for more details: James Lequeux, *Le Verrier—Magnificent and Detestable Astronomer* (New York: Springer, 2013).

Newton's gravity said it should each Mercurial year. Just as with Uranus before, the anomaly didn't go away with more persistent observation. It stubbornly remained, defying what Newton had claimed. Was this another threat to the Newtonian theories?

No, once again, Newtonian gravity was not thrown out. Instead, Le Verrier tried what he had done before: calling in an unseen planet—this time, a tiny rock so close to the Sun that it must have been missed by all other astronomers. He named this planet *Vulcan*. Le Verrier and others feverously searched for Vulcan, aiming powerful telescopes at solar eclipses in an attempt to catch a glimpse of the unseen rock during the brief minutes while the Sun was totally blocked by the Earth's moon.

No one was ever able to spot Vulcan. The astronomy community finally gave up the search, concluding that Vulcan simply wasn't there—another invention that did not make it to a discovery. But even so, Newton's theory of gravitation wasn't discarded. For years, the mystery of Mercury's orbit remained unsolved, without any serious suggestion that Newton's theory was wrong, until finally, in 1915, Albert Einstein used his bold and daring theory of general relativity to show that he could succeed where Le Verrier had failed.

So Newtonian gravity was ultimately thrown out, but not just because of observations that had threatened it. It wasn't until a viable alternative theory had arrived, in the form of Einstein's general relativity theory, that the scientific community could accept the notion that Newton might have missed a few things.

Conclusion

The findings we mentioned in the previous cases were not so much based on observation but on reasoning and thinking. Harvey did not *see* capillaries, Galileo did not *see* stellar parallaxes, Semmelweis did not *see* germs, Pasteur did not *see* bacteria, Le Verrier did not *see* planet Neptune. All of these became visible only after they had been captured in hypotheses.

What should we conclude from these and many, many other similar cases? Observation does not generate new theories. It's rather the other way around: new theories make new observations possible. There is no such thing as seeing-in-a-neutral-way, or observing-without-expectation, so we found out. All observation is somehow based on hypotheses and theories—on thinking and reasoning, that is. These hypotheses and theories help us see what we could not see without them. How could a "meaningless" observation ever be relevant to testing a scientific theory? The best way to search is to have an idea of what you are looking for—the idea may be wrong, but it's very hard, if not impossible, to just search "blindly." All of this requires reasoning before observations and conclusions are even possible.

d. What Is the Logic behind Science?

To make our reasoning more reliable, it should be guided and inspected by the laws of logic. Hence, the question is this: What is the logic behind the reasoning used by scientists, and how safe is this kind of logic?

We discovered already that scientists can use different ways of reasoning. One of them, popular in the general conception of science, is reasoning from a single observation statement to a general observation statement. It takes us from a statement about a *single* observation to a general statement about *all* similar observations. That is a way of reasoning which seems to have worked very well in science repeatedly.

However, we do not have here a logically safe kind of reasoning. It's called an inductive argument based on the logic of induction.

Why is *induction* not a logically safe kind of reasoning? The simple answer is this: there is no safe way of reasoning from some cases to all cases. To base one's claim on a few cases could be called "anecdotal" or "circumstantial" evidence. Even if there are many cases, the step from *many* to *all* cannot be warranted by any rule of logic. There is always the possibility that exceptions are waiting around the corner. The claim that all swans are white is in jeopardy once we come across a black swan. The best we can say is that adding more and more cases only leads to more and more *confirmation*, but never to complete proof or *verification*.

That's why induction is basically a never-ending process. Albert Einstein couldn't have said it better: "No amount of experimentation can ever prove me right."[25] Yet, many scientists still swear by induction. They often claim that induction is a good way of reasoning because it has worked so well in science during the course of history, but that claim in itself is based on a form of induction. One cannot use induction to justify induction. So, we need a better way of reasoning in science—that is, a better argument for the validity of scientific knowledge.

Perhaps *deduction* is a better candidate. Earlier we talked about hypotheses and test implications. Test implications are derived from hypotheses. If the hypothesis is true, then the test implications must be *true*. Well, if the test implications are *not* true, then the hypothesis must be *false* (falsification). On the other hand, if the test implications are found to be true, then the hypothesis *may* be true, but not necessarily so (confirmation). If we conclude that the

[25] This is a paraphrase from his "Induction and Deduction in Physics," document 28 in *Collected Papers of Albert Einstein*, vol. 7, *The Berlin Years: Writings, 1918–1921*, (Princeton, NJ: Princeton University Press, 2002).

hypothesis must be true, then we are using an inductive argument again, which is never logically safe. What is logically safe, though, is arguing that the hypothesis is wrong if the test implications turn out to be false. That's why Albert Einstein added a pivotal statement: "No amount of experimentation can ever prove me right; a single experiment can prove me wrong."[26]

The first part of Einstein's statement refers to *confirmation*; the second part to *falsification*. The former conclusion is inconclusive, but the latter is conclusive and logically valid. From this we could derive an important rule for scientific research: for a hypothesis to be of any use and to qualify as scientific, the hypothesis must have observational consequences and test implications—without those, hypotheses are useless. This is the idea behind the so-called *hypothetico-deductive method* in science. If the test implications of a hypothesis turn out to be true, we receive more and more confirmation.

However, no matter how many different confirming test results we have, there is no guarantee the hypothesis is indeed true (just think of false positives and false negatives). Yet, if more and more test results turn out positive, then the hypothesis is on its way to becoming more and more convincing. That is why Bertrand Russell said of science, "Its method is one which is logically incapable of arriving at a complete and final demonstration."[27] In science there is just no place for "knowing for sure." Scientists are entitled to claim that a hypothesis is extremely likely after they have received many confirming test results, implications, and predictions—which is in essence a form of induction again, rather than deduction.

[26] See Einstein, "Induction and Deduction in Physics."
[27] Bertrand Russell, *Religion and Science* (New York: Oxford University Press, 1997), 14.

But there is also another side to the hypothetico-deductive method in science, which potentially gives science more hope of reaching certainty. If a test implication turns out to be *false*, we speak of falsification. That's the part Einstein referred to when he said that a single experiment can prove that the hypothesis is *wrong*. That seems to be good news for scientists! Although they cannot prove, they can disprove—which is still a meager outcome, though.

No wonder, this idea has made many scientists favor falsification over confirmation, making them demand that a good scientific hypothesis must be falsifiable. One of the legendary champions of this idea is the physicist and philosopher of science Karl Popper. He said, "Every 'good' scientific theory ... forbids certain things to happen."[28] In other words, we may not be able to prove anything in science, but at least we can disprove, so the claim goes. Hence, scientists should always be ready to take "no" for an answer when falsifying evidence points that way.

Here is a famous example from science history. Einstein's general theory of relativity was a bold conjecture in 1915 because at the time background knowledge included the assumption that light travels in straight lines. It was Einstein's new hypothesis that gravity makes the path of light bend. If it can be demonstrated that a ray of light passing close to the Sun is deflected in a curved path, then it is not true that light necessarily travels in straight lines. Einstein took the risk that his hypothesis could be falsified, although in fact it was not. What to do, however, if it would have been falsified? Would that have been the end of his theory of relativity?

Not necessarily so, for there are some hidden problems with falsification. When Einstein said, "a single experiment can prove

---

[28] Karl Popper, *Conjectures and Refutations: The Growth of Scientific Knowledge* (London: Routledge and Keagan Paul, 1963), 36, 33–39.

me wrong," he was certainly right if the emphasis is on the word "can" —but not automatically so. It is always possible to reject falsification for the simple reason that falsification is based on counterevidence—that is, on an *observation* that contradicts what the hypothesis or theory had predicted. But as we found out earlier, there are no "clean" or "pure" observations—they are most of the time "theory-laden."

So ultimately, even falsifying evidence depends on verification—on claiming that the counterevidence is indeed true. But if final verification is beyond our reach, so must falsification be. Therefore, it is always possible to reject the counterevidence as spurious. The main point of this argument is that counterevidence doesn't automatically qualify as falsifying evidence. It is always possible to question the validity of any counterevidence, since evidence is based on an observation statement that only qualifies as decisive evidence when it is beyond any doubt—which it never is.

An added problem of falsification is that it is very unusual in science to put a single theory to the test. Almost every hypothesis or theory in science is tied to many other theories and conditions, which means that the hypothesis is only applicable under the conditions and presuppositions as laid down in the theory under investigation. Apart from these boundary conditions, the hypothesis is a castle in the air.

Add to this that in most sciences, observation relies heavily on sophisticated instruments, which makes the impact of theories even more influential. Most falsifying observations owe their existence to a certain kind of measuring equipment and some theoretical background—and either one of these may need some adjustment. Only the experimenter knows the many little things that may go wrong in the experiment (as in the case of Louis Pasteur). Think of testing DNA samples. If the outcome is contrary to what we had hypothesized, it's always possible to say that the sample was not pure but contaminated.

In other words, falsification does not make a falsifiable hypothesis or theory automatically falsified on the first hit. We may have thought we had a new motto for science—saying, "Although science cannot prove, it can disprove" —but now we have to add that science cannot always even "disprove" in a rigorous way. When nature says no to our tests, it is not exactly clear what exactly it says no to.

After these sobering remarks, we must come to the following conclusion. It is hard, if not impossible, to find final certainty in science. Scientists may desperately want certitude, but there is no logically valid way to reach certainty in science. Even the hypothetico-deductive method cannot achieve this goal, as countercvidence is never conclusive.

An added problem is that there may be more than one hypothesis for any set of observations. This means a repeatedly confirmed hypothesis may not be the final truth. Newton's laws, for instance, were confirmed repeatedly, but they had to yield ultimately to what Einstein had come up with. Something similar can be said about the quantum revolution caused in physics by Max Planck. Science is a work in progress, because certainty remains hard to find in science. Fr. Robert Spitzer, S.J., put it in the form of a truism, "Science cannot know what it has not yet discovered, because it has not yet discovered it."[29]

But at least one more caveat should be kept in mind here. Scientific reasoning occurs when logical, mathematical, and empirical elements are combined. But that does not mean that all reasoning is

---

[29] Quoted by Karlo Broussard, "Does Science Make God Irrelevant?," *Strange Notions*, Brandon Vogt, https://strangenotions.com/does-science-make-god-irrelevant/.

of this nature. Scientific reasoning is in fact a truncated version of reasoning, leaving no space for elements outside the mathematical and empirical domain. In short, there is more to reasoning than scientific reasoning. That's where religious faith has a chance to come in and might even be crucial. Let's find out.

3

What Is Faith?

It may sound like a simple question, but what is it that causes faith
to be "faith" in the religious sense? The Protestant theologian Paul
Tillich was right when he said that faith is the most misunderstood
word in our vocabulary.[30] So before we can go any further, we
should weed out some misconceptions about religious faith.

a. A Caricature of Faith

As a matter of fact, there is quite some confusion as to what
faith stands for. Sometimes, the word *faith* is used to talk about
a person's perspective on ultimate questions. At other times, the
word *faith* means a bunch of feelings or convictions that one has
about things—that is, one's deepest "values." At other times, the
word *faith* is practically synonymous with one's "philosophy of
life." Or *faith* can be used to talk about any ultimate cause that
one really believes in and advocates. Or *faith* is practically the
same as some vague kind of spirituality, as promoted in the New
Age movement.

And then there are even those who use the word *faith* for
anything that cannot be true. Mark Twain once defined *faith*

[30] Paul Tillich, *Dynamics of Faith* (New York: HarperCollins, 1957), ix.

this way: "Faith is believing what you know ain't so."[31] The biologist Richard Dawkins expresses a similar opinion when he says, "[Faith] is a state of mind that leads people to believe something—it doesn't matter what—in the total absence of supporting evidence. If there were good supporting evidence then faith would be superfluous, for the evidence would compel us to believe it anyway."[32]

It should not come as a surprise that many atheists, particularly those who work in scientific fields, have put the last kind of faith against the certainty science is supposed to deliver, if you ignore what we said in the previous section. They consider all religious faith irrational, void of empirical evidence and rational arguments. The list of these atheists seems to keep growing by the day. Many of them are scientists who use their scientific authority to make their anti-religious case by turning out pages of anti-faith propaganda.

The neuroscientist Sam Harris, for instance, says: "The faith of religion is belief on insufficient evidence."[33] The astronomer Carl Sagan likewise claims, "You can't convince a believer of anything; for their belief is not based on evidence. It's based on a deep seated need to believe."[34] The biologist E. O. Wilson agrees: "Blind faith, no matter how passionately expressed, will not suffice. Science for its part will test relentlessly every assumption about the human

---

[31] Mark Twain, *Following the Equator: A Journey around the World* (Hartford, CT: The American Publishing Company, 1897), 132.

[32] Richard Dawkins, *The Selfish Gene* (New York: Oxford University Press, 1989), 330.

[33] Sam Harris, "The End of Faith" (lecture, University Synagogue, Irvine, CA, January 18, 2005).

[34] Carl Sagan, *Contact* (New York: Pocket Books, 1985), 91.

condition."[35] Or we have Dawkins again: "Faith is belief in spite of, even perhaps because of, the lack of evidence."[36]

The common message of these atheists is quite clear: religious faith is just blind faith without any empirical evidence or rational backing. We find this idea already with the classic German philosopher Friedrich Nietzsche: "'Faith' means not *wanting* to know what is true."[37] Then Thomas Huxley added: "Skepticism is the highest of duties; blind faith the one unpardonable sin."[38] Benjamin Franklin, himself an inventor and scientist, had already stated, "The way to see by *faith*, is to shut the Eye of *Reason*."[39] Later on, George Bernard Shaw would say something similar: "It is not disbelief that is dangerous to our society; it is belief." And then he goes on, "There's no point of having faith if you have evidence."

Mark Twain put this view in a nutshell: "A man is accepted into a church for what he believes and he is turned out for what he knows."

It's a long litany that could go on and on. In all these statements, faith is equated with "blind faith," based on a leap into the dark. It has presumably no evidence or logic behind it. It is blind

[35] Edward O. Wilson, *Consilience: The Unity of Knowledge* (New York: Knopf, 1998), 6.

[36] Richard Dawkins, "The More You Understand Evolution, the More You Move towards Atheism" (lecture, Edinburgh International Science Festival, Edinburgh, UK, April 15, 1992).

[37] Friedrich Nietzsche, *The Anti-Christ*, 1888, in *Twilight of the Idols and The Anti-Christ*, trans. R. J. Hollingdale (New York: Penguin Books, 1990), sec. 52.

[38] Thomas Huxley, "On the Advisablenesss of Improving Natural Knowledge," 1866, chap. 2 in *Selected Essays and Addresses*, ed. Philo Melvyn Buck, Jr. (New York: Macmillan, 1910), 49.

[39] Benjamin Franklin, *Poor Richard's Almanack*, (1758; New York: Skyhorse, 2007), 94.

to any evidence and blind to any reasonable arguments. In short, it is seen as baseless, irrational, and incredible. It's quite obvious that these advocates persistently put religious faith in opposition to truth, knowledge, facts, and science. Religious faith is always blind faith, in their view. No wonder, religious faith is at the losing end—leaving mere darkness behind.

However, what these people promote here is a misguided view of religious faith, which is a view we find, unfortunately, more and more popularized in media and academia, zealously advocated in many writings of contemporary scientists and atheists. Why is it a flawed view of religious faith? Here is why.

b. A Better View of Faith

Because *faith* is used in such a vague, general, and often confusing way by many people, it has become difficult to defend or explain faith in God. So, we may have a difficult task ahead of us. First, we need to explain what we mean by "faith in God." (From now on, when I use the word *faith*, it typically refers to religious faith or faith in God.)

So, the question for us is this: What do religious believers mean when they speak of faith in God? What is the "object" of their faith? Religious believers are usually very well able to explain to others what it is they believe in. We referred already to what many believers call the *Transcendent*. But that might still be a rather nebulous concept. Perhaps a better answer was given by St. Thomas Aquinas. Although he was Catholic to the core, his approach has a much wider implementation, regardless of any specific religion.

St. Thomas clearly understood that God must be radically different from everything we see around us, including each one of us. His terminology may seem foreign at first, but it has withstood the test of many centuries. His reasoning goes along the following lines, in a paraphrased way. His starting point is that we *receive* our existence: in other words, we could as well *not* have existed. Put in in more technical terms: we are *contingent* beings and could very well *not* have been here. But because we do exist, we can ask for the *cause* of our existence. Of course, we can refer to our parents, to our grandparents, and so on. But do they really explain my existence? Yes, in a sense, they do. But ultimately, they do not. Why not?

Let's stay with the example of children and their line of ancestors. Children do need ancestors, but even an impressive line of ancestors cannot explain everything about parents and their children. The reason is that there is at least one vital question left: What is it that enables parents to *generate* children at all? This calls for a cause, too. Moreover, a sequence of events in time may even be able to go infinitely forward through the future and backward through the past, but the problem would still be that we are dealing here with *time*, which in itself must have a cause as well. Where does time itself come from, then? To use an analogy: a long, or even endless, list of ancestors would be like a series of IOUs, but that series does not create real currency, no matter how long the series is. The fact remains that the entire chain of these causes is just floating in the air, and keeps doing so until we find a "foundation" for it to rest upon, or a "beam" for it to hang from—a cause operating from *outside* of the chain.

Consequently, the explanation for all of this would not take us to another cause in a sequence of *secondary causes*, as St. Thomas calls these causes in a sequence of causes. Instead, it leads us to a cause at a higher level, so to speak. That's what Thomas means when he speaks of the *First Cause*. It is a Cause that exists eternally and explains the sequence of secondary causes—a Transcendent Cause outside and above the sequence of secondary causes. This, of course, is God. God alone is the act of existing itself. Or to put it another way, God's essence—what God is—*is* His existence. God alone is, and must be, existence by nature. The First Cause is, in essence, Pure Existence. All other beings require a cause of their existence.

From this follows that God is a necessary and eternal being who did not come into existence but always has been. In contrast, all other creatures are not God precisely because their act of existing has been received from God who alone is self-existing. Put differently, the First Cause has the power to produce its effects without being caused by something else. It has *inherent* causal power, whereas the secondary causes have only *derived* causal power. Consequently, each creature exists because God, who is existence itself, holds all creatures in existence at every time and place. If God did cease to hold each creature in existence, for instance, they would simply disappear, entirely ceasing to exist.

In other words, there is no cause in this Universe that can do any causing unless it first *exists*. However, it cannot make itself exist. For something to cause itself to exist, it would have to exist before it came into existence—which is logically and philosophically impossible. Things that exist cannot explain their own existence. They are not self-explanatory or self-sufficient. This explains how children do come from their parents *and* God at the same time. In other words, the need for causes must come to an end: there must be a Cause that is not itself in need of a cause and has not come into existence—that is, a First Cause with inherent causal power. The First Cause, God, reigns from "outside" the Universe, thus providing some sort of "point of suspension" for the chain of secondary causes itself.

There is much more to this, of course, but the point I am making here is that this line of reasoning is obvious to anyone who values the power of reason. It comes with our intellectual nature.

We know, through the power of reason, that we cannot cause our own existence. So, religious faith—belief in God and faith in God—is not just a subjective, personal, illogical, or irrational notion. It is in fact logically and rationally justified, making it an undeniable fact. One doesn't have to be a Catholic to understand the argument based on the First Cause, as it is a proof accessible to anyone who honors the power of reason.

But (you might ask) doesn't this approach make faith fully dependent on us instead of God? It may look that way, but it's not quite true. Perhaps St. Paul gives us a different way of looking at it. He uses the example of plants and their growth when he says, "Neither he who plants nor he who waters is anything, but only God who gives the growth" (1 Cor. 3:7). Something similar can be said about faith. Logic and reason provide soil and water to the faith, but it is God who provides the growth of the faith.

Then there are also people who object to all of the above by pointing out that we are merely dealing here with the God of philosophers. In a sense that is true. However, let me make clear first, to avoid any misunderstanding, that the God of our Catholic Faith is indeed the "God of Abraham, the God of Isaac, and the God of Jacob" (Exod. 3:15)—rather than the God of philosophers. No doubt, this God is obviously *more* than the "God of philosophers and scholars" —to paraphrase what Blaise Pascal said in his *Memorial*.[40] That is certainly true, but at the same time it must be stated that the God of the Bible is not *less* than the God we identify with the First Cause. True, the Bible tells us much more about God than we could discover on our own through mere reasoning, but in order to think and talk about this God, we need to know first

---

[40] This text is taken from what is called the *Memorial*, a piece of parchment which was sewn into the lining of Pascal's coat.

that God does exist, and even must exist, otherwise anything else we know and say about God is of no consequence.

One could at least say that the First Cause provides a "point of suspension" for the chain of all other causes, and of all other religious beliefs. It is like the framework around a spider's web. Without that framework, the web could not exist. Without a First Cause, there could not be a chain of secondary causes. God as the ground of our being is the "framework" supporting the "web" of our lives, or as said earlier, God is the framework in which "we live and move and have our being," in the words of St. Paul (Acts 17:28). It is God, the First Cause, who brings secondary causes into existence and allows them to be causes of their own.

To avoid another misunderstanding, we need to stress this point. When St. Thomas describes God as the First Cause, he does not only mean that God is first in the sense of being before the second cause in time, nor in the sense of coming before the second cause in a sequence of causes. Rather, He is first in the sense of being the *source* of all secondary causes, having absolutely primal and underived causal power—a Power from which all other causes must derive their causal powers.

In other words, God is not a deity like Jupiter or Zeus. He is not merely a being stronger than other beings or superior to all other beings. Instead, God is the very source of all being—the absolute ground of all that exists. God is the First Cause, unlike any other gods who are at best secondary causes. As the Bible puts it, "The Lord is our God, the Lord *alone*" (Deut. 6:4, NRSVCE, my emphasis)—and no other gods. Hence, this faith of God is completely different from belief in any other deities.

So, we must conclude from this that faith—more in particular, belief in God's existence—has a very strong rational and coherent basis. It is a basis that science can firmly rest on in its investigation of secondary causes. In other words, faith in God is not a matter of "blind belief" at all.

c. The Logic behind Faith in God

To make any kind of reasoning more reliable, it should be guided and inspected by the laws of logic. This raises the following question: What is the logic behind the reasoning that religious believers use; and how safe is this kind of logic? This question becomes even more pressing when believers claim they can prove that God exists against non-believers who claim God does not exist.

Can faith be backed by the logic of *induction*? Many religious believers would say it's possible. The most common argument is that there is much evidence in nature that points to God and to God's existence, which can function as a growing number of premises used in the method of induction. The Bible seems to agree with this when it says in one of its Psalms: "The heavens are telling the glory of God; and the firmament proclaims his handiwork" (Ps. 19:1). St. Paul adds: "Ever since the creation of the world [God's] invisible nature, namely, his eternal power and deity, has been clearly perceived in the things that have been made. So [non-believers] are without excuse; for although they knew God they did not honor him as God or give thanks to him" (Rom. 1:20-21).

Many believers would probably agree with all of this. However, as we discussed earlier in the context of science, induction and inductive reasoning do not deliver the certainty we need to *prove* that God exists — they can only serve as "pointers" to God. Consequently, many will maintain that God might *not* exist, because there is always some uncertainty left in the logic of induction.

To gain more certainty, we need deductive reasoning instead. *Deduction* can deliver us the kinds of proofs we find in mathematics. However, even in mathematics, we cannot prove anything from nothing, as at least something is needed, axioms, to start the process. Based on a set of axioms in the premises, we can derive a conclusion with final certainty. Based on such a set of axioms, it can be concluded, for example, that the sum of the three angles of a triangle is 180°. Put differently, the certainty of the conclusion is based on the certainty of the axioms (with different axioms, the sum of the three angles can be larger or smaller than 180°). Once we accept the Euclidean premises, we *must* accept the conclusion that the sum of the three angles of a triangle is 180°. That's quite a trivial way of proving things, though. Yet, it's more certainty than we can ever reach in science.

It's still a far stretch, however, to move from mathematics to religion. How could the certainty we find in mathematics help us when it comes to proving God's existence? Well, the "secret" of proving God's existence is not to be found in mathematics but in logic. It can be found in premises based on so-called *universal* statements. They are probably best understood as something like safe starting points or assumptions or principles. They are not the result of empirical induction (like in science), neither are they the outcome of deductive proof (like in math). Instead, they are said to be self-evident—that means, not in need of any further evidence. Denying their proof would be self-destructive. They provide certainty to the premises, which then extends to the certainty of the conclusion.

To get this right, do not confuse universal statements with the general statements we can find in science—for instance, statements such as "all iron expands with heat." In contrast, a universal principle would be something like "all expanding of iron has a cause." This is a universal principle or statement that is absolutely true, independently of any particular cases. Its truth does not become stronger by testing more and more instances, because its truth does not depend on any confirmation, let alone any inductive reasoning. It is a universal principle that is true independently of any observation.

This makes a huge difference. Whereas a *general* statement such as "all iron expands with heat" requires more and more cases for its confirmation—as it's based on inductive generalization—there are also *universal* principles such as "expanding iron has a cause," which are not of an empirical, inductive nature and are true independently of inductive confirmation. The principle that like causes have like effects is also a universal principle that comes before science can even get started. It's a universal principle or statement that is self-evident, admits no exception, and cannot be denied by anyone in his or her right mind.

In other words, universal statements are not something we see over and over again, but they are principles that *make* us see. They come *before* we can experience anything else, for without them, there just are no experiences. They are true independently of any cases, and they do not get more corroborated with an increasing number of supporting cases. The truth of universal statements can be seen without the assistance of science—they are in fact prior to science, and they can be known based on pure reason. Denying them would undermine all other efforts.

A universal statement is the first premise in the deductive argument of proving God's existence. It says, for instance: all things that have come into existence need a cause that makes them exist. Such things we called earlier *contingent*, which means they could have been different and could easily *not* have existed. It's again a universal principle or statement that is self-evident, admits no exception, and cannot be denied by anyone in his or her right mind. As we said earlier, for something to cause itself to exist, it would have to exist before it came into existence—which is logically and philosophically impossible.

But there is a second premise that is needed to stop a potentially unending search for causes. Calling for more and more causes further and further back or forward in time, or farther and farther down the ladder of explanation, can never finish the job— it actually leads to infinite regress, thus leaving the series of causes ultimately resting on nothing or hanging from nowhere, so to speak. As said earlier, this would be like an infinite series of IOUs, but no real currency. All secondary causes combined don't really explain anything. The entire chain of such causes will just float in the air until we find a foundation for it to rest on, or a beam for it to hang from. In other words, even a chain of causes does not explain its own existence. There must be an explanation that is not in need of any further explanation. Nothing less than an infinite, self-explanatory, necessary Being could possibly terminate such an infinite regress.

Summarized, the complete argument for God's existence has the following deductive structure. Premise 1: contingent beings must have a cause that explains their existence; Premise 2: even a sequence of causes needs a cause that explains this sequence; Conclusion: there must be a First Cause, a Necessary Being, who needs no cause to explain its existence, but is existence itself.

There is at least one more logical method reason has to offer us: the *reductio ad absurdum*. It is a form of argument that establishes a claim by showing that the opposite scenario would lead to absurdity or contradiction. In this sort of argument, we begin by assuming the opposite of the claim we want to prove, and then show that from this claim something absurd follows. This demonstrates that the opposite of the claim we want to argue *for* is false, and so that the claim we want to argue *against* must be true.

A simple example could be this: if the Earth were flat, then we would find people falling off the edge. We haven't, so the idea of a flat Earth is absurd. A more sophisticated and abbreviated example runs like this: if there is only matter in this world, then truth cannot exist—therefore, believing that matter is all there is cannot be true. It leads to absurd or contradictory consequences. This technique of reasoning and argumentation has been used throughout history in various forms of mathematical, philosophical, and religious reasoning.

As a matter of fact, the universal statement we used earlier to prove God's existence, saying that all contingent things need a cause that makes them exist, can be conclusively defended by the logical method of *reductio ad absurdum* in the following way: If things would make themselves exist, then they would have to exist before they came into existence—which is absurd and must therefore be rejected. In this case, claiming that something can make itself exist would amount to circular causation. That would be absurd, and therefore must be rejected. To put it differently, you can't give your own existence to yourself or receive it from yourself. As Michael Augros puts it pithily, "You can't be your own father."[41] That's absurd, period.

d. Why Faith Needs Reasoning

To accept that logic and reasoning can help us to prove that God exists is one thing, but to say that we need them also for the rest of religious faith is a different issue in the minds of many believers. So, after explaining what we mean by "faith in God," we also need to explain what is meant by a "Catholic faith" in God. Can reasoning still play a role there?

Many people seem to have a strong suspicion of logic and reasoning when it comes to what they call their "personal" faith. They often go so far as to think that logic and reasoning take away

---

[41] Michael Augros, *Who Designed the Designer? A Rediscovered Path to God's Existence* (San Francisco: Ignatius Press, 2015), 33.

from faith that which makes it really "faith." They sometimes speak about faith in terms of a "leap of faith." Not only is this seen as a leap into complete trust, but also as a leap into the irrational, devoid of any reasoning. This view is usually called *fideism*. Ironically, defenders of fideism have the same conception of faith that we find with the atheists quoted at the beginning of this section. Both groups seem to agree that all faith is blind faith.

Fideism protects religious faith from any further investigation by giving it a monopoly position that demands total exclusiveness and makes itself immune for any attacks. When questioning these believers about their faith, we may get the answer, "You just have to have faith," sometimes accompanied by a shrug. Their slogan seems to be, "Don't think, just have faith." It looks like a very devout attitude, until one probes a bit further.

The "faith-only" perspective of fideism claims that reason plays little to no role in matters of faith. The Church Father Tertullian put it once, in a wild moment, this way: "What indeed has Athens [the city of philosophers] to do with Jerusalem [the city of believers]? What concord is there between the Academy and the Church?"[42] Somewhere else he says about Christian doctrine, "It is by all means to be believed, because it is absurd."[43] The word "absurd" is probably a poor translation. The word he uses (*ineptum*) could be translated more accurately as "improper."

This view seems to indicate that the only valid way to know anything about God is solely through "blind faith" — even if, or

---

[42] Tertullian, *Prescription against Heretics*, trans. Peter Holmes, in *Ante-Nicene Fathers*, vol. 3, ed. Alexander Roberts, James Donaldson, and A. Cleveland Coxe (Buffalo, NY: Christian Literature, 1885), 7.

[43] Tertullian, *On the Flesh of Christ*, trans. Peter Holmes, in *Ante-Nicene Fathers*, vol. 3, 5.

especially when, it is irrational. It's a faith-only position. Faith-only Christians include Tertullian (ca. 160–ca. 230), Søren Kierkegaard (1813–1855), Karl Barth (1886–1968), and to a slightly lesser degree, Blaise Pascal (1623–1662). The Protestant theologian Barth took St. Anselm's motto, "I believe that I may understand," to mean that we must not wish to understand first so as to believe next, but rather the other way around: believe first!

Fideism fosters the extreme conviction that one must not even look for reasons in making the act of faith. This erroneous view was wonderfully expressed by the misguided father of a student at a Catholic college, when he was told that his daughter was learning that theology was "faith seeking understanding." Then the man exclaimed: "But faith doesn't have to seek understanding—that's why they call it faith!" Such people reason (so to speak) that if God's existence were a matter of proof, it would no longer be a matter of faith and, therefore, it cannot be a matter of proof either. This is fideism *optima forma!*

Another well-known fideist is Martin Luther. Although Luther did not place faith explicitly counter to reason, he did put it in opposition to any human efforts, with reasoning being one of them. He once said, "Reason is the greatest enemy that faith has."[44] Interestingly enough, entirely on his own, Luther had added an extra word, *alone* (*allein* in German), to St. Paul's Letter to the Romans 3:28 in his Bible translation: "For we hold that a man is justified by faith [alone] apart from works of law."

Luther's fideism extended even to his own ministry. When challenged about his addition of *alone* to Paul's epistle, Luther responded: "If your Papist annoys you with the word [*alone*], tell

---

[44] Martin Luther, *Table Talk*, trans. and ed. William Hazlitt (1569; London: H. G. Bohn, 1857), CCCLIII, 164.

him straightway, Dr. Martin Luther will have it so."[45] Again, that's faith purely on authority and command.

But is this really what the Bible means when it uses the word *faith*? It's very doubtful. The Bible does not seem to promote a belief in what is irrational or in any type of unwarranted "blind faith." The Bible has actually a proverb against blind faith: "The simple believes everything, but the prudent looks where he is going" (Prov. 14:15). St. Paul says about the Christians in Thessalonica, "They received the word with all eagerness, examining the scriptures daily to see if these things were so" (Acts 17:11). Paul also says, "Test everything; hold fast what is good" (1 Thess. 5:21).

Just as scientists must think in order to make observations and do experiments, so also must religious believers think when it comes to their faith. Thinking that there is no reasoning involved when religious faith is concerned makes a caricature of faith. Rejecting reason would undermine the foundation of faith and would deliver an easy victory to the enemies of faith that we mentioned earlier.

On the contrary, religious faith never involves a sacrifice of intellect and reason. God wants us to *understand* all we know about Him and about His Revelation—to understand, that is, by way of reason. St. Augustine famously warned us that it is "dangerous to have an infidel hear a Christian ... talking nonsense."[46] Nonsense is a form of irrationality, which may include blind faith. St. Augustine could not have said it more clearly: "Believers are also thinkers: in believing, they think and in thinking, they believe."[47] Thus he

---

[45] Patrick O'Hare, *The Facts About Luther* (Charlotte, NC: TAN Books, 1987), 201.

[46] Augustine, *The Literal Meaning of Genesis*, bk. 1, chap. 20, my translation.

[47] Augustine, *De Praedestinatione Sanctorum*, 2, 5, quoted in John Paul II, *Fides et Ratio*, no. 79.

introduced his famous formula, at around 400, which expresses the coherent synthesis between faith and reason: "Believe so you may understand" [*crede ut intelligas*].[48] Pope John Paul II stressed this synthesis in his encyclical *Fides et Ratio* by saying, "Against the temptations of fideism, however, it was necessary to stress the unity of truth and thus the positive contribution which rational knowledge can and must make to faith's knowledge."[49]

The same idea can also be found in St. Anselm's two famous phrases made during the eleventh century. His first phrase says, "I believe in order to understand" [*credo ut intellegam*],[50] which underscores the role of faith for better understanding. He underlines that faith is often necessary to better understand the world, ourselves, and our faith. Anselm's second well-known phrase is of equal importance. It speaks of "faith seeking understanding" (*fides quaerens intellectum*),[51] which stresses the role of reason to explain faith. Again, Anselm is right: faith needs reason for us to understand faith better. This also tells us that faith cannot be "unreasonable." Both phrases taken together emphasize the unity of faith and reason.

Given this longstanding tradition, the Catholic Church has a definite stance regarding the relationship between faith and reason, very distinctive from other religions. She does not see them as competitors or contestants, but as equivalent participants in the

---

[48] Augustine, *Tractates on the Gospel of John*, in *Nicene and Post-Nicene Fathers*, vol. 7, trans. John Gibb, ed. Philip Schaff (Buffalo, NY: Christian Literature, 1888), 29:7.

[49] John Paul II, *Fides et Ratio*, no. 53.

[50] Anselm, *Proslogion*, in *Proslogion: With the Replies of Gaunilo and Anselm*, trans. Thomas Williams (Indianapolis, IN: Hackett, 1995), 1, p. 6.

[51] Anselm, *Proslogion*, prologue, p. 2.

search for truth, even when it comes to religion. Reason comes from God as much as faith does. Peter Kreeft describes it well:

> Christianity inherited faith … from the Jews, and reason … from the Greeks, and the central intellectual project of the whole middle ages was a marriage or a synthesis of these two things. They were different, but they were made for each other, like Romeo and Juliet. It was a storybook marriage, but it was a happy one. And perhaps the best way to characterize the modern world is the word "divorce." The two partners have sort of set up houses on their own and produced all sorts of arguments against each other.[52]

To deny the unity of faith and reason leads to a detrimental form of fideism. It is not surprising that fideism can ultimately lead to a form of skepticism—skepticism, that is, about the possibility of real human knowledge, at least so in the area of religious knowledge. It may sound strange at first sight, but fideists come very close to their enemies, the agnostics. What agnostics and fideists have in common is that they both underestimate the power of reason. Agnostics believe they have no way to argue either for or against the existence of God, for they see no rational means of finding out either way. When it comes to God, reason is supposed to be entirely powerless. That's where agnosticism and fideism meet: they both deny that reason can bring us any closer to God.

Yet fideists would probably retort that there must be more to religious faith than a cold, heartless affirmation of God's existence.

---

[52] Peter Kreeft, "Two Cultures: Faith and Reason," Catholic Education Resource Center, accessed January 13, 2022, https://www. catholiceducation.org/en/religion-and-philosophy/philosophy/ two-cultures-faith-amp-reason.html.

In a sense they do have a point: there is more than that in faith, but at the same time, certainly not less. The *Catechism of the Catholic Church* describes Catholic faith as follows: "Faith is first of all a personal adherence of man to God. At the same time, and inseparably, it is a *free assent to the whole truth that God has revealed*."[53] Religious faith is having confidence in something you may not have experienced with your own senses. St. Paul says, "We walk by faith, not by sight" (2 Cor. 5:7).

However, even if religious faith is about the unseen, it is not "blind"; it's not an act of "believing without any reason." Just the opposite is true: religious faith is the act of believing in something unseen for which we do have good reasons. We can reason and argue from what is seen to what is unseen, from what we are familiar with to what we are not familiar with, from secondary causes to a First Cause.

Hence, we cannot reduce faith to pure commitment, without any further knowledge or reasoning. When we say we love God, we need to know first who God is. You cannot love what you do not know, as you want to know the person you love. Knowledge, truth, love, and will are strongly interconnected. Faith and knowledge are not contradictory: what we know about God helps us to have faith in God. Whereas faith without commitment amounts to "disbelief," commitment without knowledge is in fact "blind belief." Neither one is a genuine option for a Catholic faith.

Not surprisingly, the slogan of fideism—"Don't think, just believe"—has given agnostics a powerful weapon: "Don't believe, just think."

---

[53] *Catechism of the Catholic Church*, 2nd ed. (Washington, DC: Libreria Editrice Vaticana–United States Conference of Catholic Bishops, 2000), 150, emphasis in original. Hereafter cited in text as CCC.

Of course, there is much more to religious faith than the belief that God exists. Can logic and reason still play a role beyond that basic belief? The answer is a definite yes. St. Thomas gives us a good summary of what reason does for faith.[54] He says that reason prepares the mind for faith, explains the truths of faith, and defends the truths of faith.

What does he mean by that?

Preparing the Mind for Faith

The first role of reason is *preparing* the mind for faith. In fact, it is by reason that we come to know and understand what faith and belief are. Reason opens the gate to faith and leads us to God, which is the basis of everything else we find in the Scriptures. Reason is the vehicle, which, if driven correctly, takes us to the door of faith. Although reason in and of itself cannot cause faith without God's special grace, the use of reason is normally a part of a person's coming to faith and serves to support faith in innumerable ways. Aquinas speaks here of the "preambles" of faith.

This is basically what the so-called proofs of God's existence do for us. Reason can establish the rational grounds for belief by proving God's existence, His attributes of being all-knowing, all-powerful, all-present, and all-good, His authority or credibility as all-wise and trustworthy, and by proving that God has also revealed Himself in history, especially in the Person of Jesus Christ. St. Augustine made this very clear when he stressed the role of thinking and reasoning:

> For who cannot see that thinking is prior to believing? For no one believes anything unless he has first thought that it

---

[54] Especially in Aquinas, *Super Boethium De Trinitate*, q. 2, art. 3, response.

is to be believed.... [It is] necessary that everything which is believed should be believed after thought has preceded; although even belief is nothing else than to think with assent.... Everybody who believes, thinks—both thinks in believing and believes in thinking.... If faith is not a matter of thought, it is of no account.[55]

Explaining the Truths of Faith

The second role of reason is *explaining* the more detailed truths of faith. St. Anselm called such a crucial intellectual and spiritual activity "faith seeking understanding."[56] Believers should strongly endeavor to use their God-given reason to explore the depths of their faith and to discover its doctrinal truths. The Bible itself encourages the attainment of knowledge, wisdom, and understanding (Job 28:28; Prov. 1:7) and promotes such rational virtues as discernment and testing (Acts 17:11; Col. 2:8; 1 Thess. 5:21). Stretching mental and spiritual muscles to apprehend doctrines such as the triune nature of God and the Incarnation of Jesus Christ moves one from an initial stage of faith to a deeper stage of reflection and a greater sense of God's majesty, and an even deeper and clearer understanding of the divine truths. In the words of Pope John Paul II, "Faith grows deeper and more authentic when it is wedded to thought and does not reject it."[57]

Let's explain the role reason plays here with one example, the doctrine of the Trinity. Understood properly, this doctrine

---

[55] Augustine, *On the Predestination of the Saints*, in *Nicene and Post-Nicene Fathers*, vol. 5, trans. Peter Holmes, Robert Ernest Wallis, and Benjamin B. Warfield, ed. Philip Schaff (Buffalo, NY: Christian Literature, 1887), bk. 1, chap. 5.

[56] Anselm, *Proslogion*, prologue, p. 2.

[57] John Paul II, *Fides et Ratio*, no. 79.

tells us in essence: the Father is not the Son; the Son is not the Father, and the Spirit is neither Father nor Son. They are all "one" precisely by not being each other — one in being, diverse in Person. The classic formula, since Tertullian, has been "one God, three Persons."[58] This also tells us that Jesus is God, but God is not Jesus. Without using sound reasoning, we could easily end up talking nonsense.

But that doesn't mean the doctrine of the Trinity is easy to understand. St. Augustine, for one, is very mindful of those who find difficulty in the Christian faith, as he expresses here:

> Some persons, however, find a difficulty in this faith; when they hear that the Father is God, and the Son God, and the Holy Spirit God, and yet that this Trinity is not three Gods, but one God; and they ask how they are to understand this.... They wish to understand.[59]

To rationally aid our understanding, analogies may be helpful. In mathematical terms, the Trinity does not represent $1+1+1=3$, which would amount to polytheism, but rather $1\times1\times1=1^3=1$, which is in accord with monotheism. Or, with the help of a geometric analogy: the fact that we distinguish three dimensions does not mean that we can separate those three dimensions. In a similar, analogous way, the Trinity is like the three "dimensions" of the same and one reality, God. Or think of a triangle: it has three lines forming three angles, yet it's only one figure. More down to earth, St. Patrick famously explained the doctrine of the Holy Trinity to his flock in Ireland by

---

[58] See Tertullian, *Adversus Praxeam*, 25.

[59] Augustine, *On the Trinity*, trans. Arthur West Haddan, in *Nicene and Post-Nicene Fathers*, vol. 3, ed. Philip Schaff (Buffalo, NY: Christian Literature, 1887), bk. 1, chap. 5.

using the three leaves of the shamrock: each leaf represents one of the three Persons, but yet it is still only one shamrock.

Based on this reasoning, we know better what we can and cannot say about the Trinity. As said earlier, we can say that Jesus is God, but we cannot say God is Jesus—and the same can be said about the Father and the Holy Spirit. In short, there is *one* God, but in three Persons. Reason helps us to understand this better and to avoid untrue or absurd conclusions.

Defending the Truths of Faith

The third role of reason is *defending* the truths of faith. When Christian believers say that the authority of the Christian faith is Scripture, they should also seek to understand the very authority in which they have placed their faith. In other words, they should not just believe, but they should also try to understand what they believe and why they believe that. What Christians believe is not irrational but can be explained to and be defended against non-believers by using something we all have in common—reason, that is. That's why religious truths can be defended, even for non-believers and non-Christians, albeit not always persuasively.

Think of the question we posed earlier: How can we seek to understand and defend the authority in which we have placed our faith? Again, our main guide is reason, which finds its origin in God. If reason cannot *prepare* the mind for faith, there is something wrong; if reason cannot *explain* the truths of faith, there is something wrong; if reason cannot *defend* the truths of faith, there must be something wrong. Let's see from different perspectives what this entails.

First of all, after proving the existence of a First Cause, St. Thomas derives from this in a logical way that the God of reason must be utterly unique, and thus cannot be different from the God of faith—otherwise there would be two gods, which contradicts the notion of a First Cause. Once the utter uniqueness of "a god" has been shown, one can begin to use *God* as a proper name to refer to that one, utterly unique Being, in which the God of reason and the God of faith come together in unison.

So ultimately, the God of reason and the God of faith both refer to the same God—one God, not two. St. Thomas argues that the God of reason, by whom everything else is created, "[contains] within Himself the whole perfection of being."[60] If the God of reason is Infinite Perfection,[61] then God must have infinite powers, specifically, the powers of being all-powerful (*omnipotent*), all-present (*omnipresent*), all-knowing (*omniscient*), and all-good (*omnibenevolent*).

Second, there are indeed certain things about God we cannot know by using reason alone. One of them is that God is *trinitarian* or *triune*—Father, Son, and Holy Spirit—which is *not* a conclusion based on mere reason. This does not mean, of course, that we can say whatever we want about the God of faith. The reason for this caveat is simple: even religious faith is something about which we can reason, argue, and debate. As it was said about St. Paul, "He entered the synagogue and for three months spoke boldly, arguing and pleading about the kingdom of God" (Acts 19:8). That means we should still be able to reason, argue, and debate about the triune God of faith, as we discussed earlier.

Third, there is something about faith that transcends reason. Much of what we know by faith about God has come to us through

---

[60] Thomas Aquinas, *The Summa Theologiae of St. Thomas* Aquinas, trans. Fathers of the English Dominican Province (London: Burns, Oates, and Washbourne, 1920; online ed. Kevin Knight, 2017), https://www.newadvent.org/summa, I, q. 4, art. 2.

[61] Thomas Aquinas, *Summa Theologiae* I, q. 4, art. 1.

God's so-called "special revelation"—that is, through the Bible, Jesus' testimony, and Christian Tradition. When St. Paul was in Athens and saw an altar inscribed "To an Unknown God," he invited the Athenians to take the step from a "God of reason" to a "God of faith." He told them, "What therefore you worship as unknown, this I proclaim to you" (Acts 17:23). It is only through faith and God's special revelation that we know God is triune. Although a truth like this about God cannot be known by reason alone, reason must still come back in to show that our faith is not *against* reason—but this doesn't mean it came to us through reason.

Fourth, what both knowing by faith and knowing by reason have in common is a foundation of facts. What we know about God through reason and what we know about God through faith is not just a matter of personal beliefs or subjective opinions—instead, both kinds of knowledge are about *facts*. Why should we believe something? Because others believe it? Not so! Because it feels good? Not so! The only valid argument is this: because it is *true*. That God exists is a fact or not, it's true or not. That God is almighty is a fact, or it is not. That God is triune is a fact, or it is not. Those are facts, just as we have facts in science. What science and religion have in common is that they are both guided by reasoning—by what is right or wrong—and that they both deal with facts—with what is true or false.

Fifth, the question remains as to how we know that the facts of our faith are true. We cannot just say that the Bible tells us so, for that merely shifts the answer to another question: the question of how we know that the Bible is true. The New Testament speaks of giving witnesses to the truth of Christ's life, death, Resurrection, Ascension, and current presence. The key term here is being a "witness," to the truth. The *Catechism* confirms this, "You have not given yourself faith as you have not given yourself life. The believer has received faith from others and should hand it on to others" (CCC 166).

Believing something on the word of witnesses is something we are all familiar with. All human beings naturally live by faith in other human beings. It is quite impossible for anyone to go through life without some faith in what others have witnessed. We cannot start our lives completely from scratch. Instead, we all accept many things on the word of other people, and we cannot but do so. We must depend to a great extent on others as the source of our knowledge, for we are practically unable to verify even a small part of our knowledge on our own. As Stephen Barr puts it,

> For a person to accept as knowledge only what he had discovered and proved for himself from direct personal experience would put his knowledge at the level of the Stone Age. Taking something on authority, then, is not in itself irrational. On the contrary, it would be irrational never to do so.[62]

Therefore, we must trust in the authority and veracity of those who teach us things, including religious faith. Nearly all our historical beliefs, including our beliefs about where we were born and who our ancestors are, come from hearsay. Even the enterprise of science relies heavily on trusting "eyewitness" reports of others, largely in the case of special experiences and experiments recorded in articles and textbooks. Most of what we know about science and its findings is from "hearsay," based on these expert reports. The same holds for what we know about religion.

---

[62] Stephen M. Barr, *Modern Physics and Ancient Faith* (Notre Dame, IN: University of Notre Dame Press, 2003), 11–12.

But there must be more to it, for this still leaves us with the question as to how we know that these witnesses are reliable. Ultimately and inevitably, we must come back to the test of *reason*. Even witnesses to the Faith need to undergo the test of reason to make sure they don't proclaim contradictions or contradict themselves. Witnesses lose their authority if they tell us things that cannot be true because they go against reason. If witnesses cannot be defended by reason, there is something wrong with their witness.

It is interesting to note that someone like St. Augustine had such high esteem for the role of reason and for its central place in his theological convictions that he began questioning the teachings of Mani, which came to be known collectively as Manichaeanism. Augustine became increasingly exasperated with the Manicheans' lack of logic and irrational nature. The breaking point came when he discovered he was ordered to believe teachings about the heavenly bodies "even where the ideas did not correspond with—even when they contradicted—the rational theories established by mathematics and my own eyes."[63] As the apologist Carl Olson puts it, "And so Augustine left Manichaeanism in search of a reasonable, intellectually cogent faith."[64]

Fortunately, so we found out, it is thanks to reason that we can prove that God exists. What science cannot prove about God and God's existence can be done by a metaphysical proof, because it is deductive in nature and uses a universal, self-evident principle as

---

[63] Augustine, *Confessions*, in *Confessions and Enchiridion*, trans. and ed. Albert C. Outler (London: Westminster Press, 1955), bk. 5, chap. 3.

[64] Carl Olson, "Augustine's Confessions and the Harmony of Faith and Reason," *Catholic Answers*, May 1, 2010, https://www.catholic.com/magazine/print-edition/augustines-confessions-and-the-harmony-of-faith-and-reason.

its starting point, so we found out. This allows us to know with certainty that nothing discovered in science could exist if there were no First Cause. We don't need science, and we can't even use science to prove the existence of a First Cause. Just as reason gives us access to the existence of numbers, so it is reason that gives us access to the existence of God. In fact, when we use our reason to investigate the existence of God, we encounter proofs that are more powerful, by far, than any that science could ever provide.

It seems very appropriate to close this chapter with a prayer of St. Anselm:

> O my soul, have you found what you were looking for? I was seeking God, and I have found that he is above all things, and that than which nothing greater can be thought. I have found him to be life and light, wisdom and goodness, eternal blessedness and the bliss of eternity, existing everywhere and at all times.[65]

---

[65] Anselm, *The Prayers and Meditations of St. Anselm*, trans. Sr. Benedicta Ward, S.L.G. (New York: Penguin, 1979), 255.

4

Why Science Needs Faith

Claiming that science needs faith seems to be a contradiction in terms. When we just look at the impressive track record science has developed during the last four centuries, we might easily get the impression science can practically explain everything and doesn't need any faith. This impression might make us wonder if there would still be any space left for faith and religion. The answer to this question depends, of course, on how we assess science on the one hand, and faith on the other hand. The latter issue we will discuss in the next chapter.

In this chapter, we will focus on how faith can easily be misunderstood in relation to science. Many see faith as the opposite of science, where the scientific method is often seen as the epitome of sound reasoning. In this one-sided view, science is taken as being (entirely) objective, methodical, logical, and verifiable, whereas faith is seen as (only) subjective, personal, illogical, and irrational, even bordering on mania or madness—which makes it impossible for them to ever go together. However, this perceived contrast cannot be true. It is based on a distorted and shallow conception of what science stands for.

A Catholic Scientist Harmonizes Science and Faith

a. Science-Alone Is a Dead End

After we discussed the vital role of scientific reasoning in a previous chapter, we still need to face the fact that science on its own is a dead end. Yet, the science-alone attitude has gained much traction in recent decades. It has in fact become a widespread ideology usually called *scientism*. This ideology is so focused on what science *can* do for us that it is blind to what science *cannot* do for us.

Nevertheless, the tremendous power of scientific reasoning demonstrated daily in the many marvels of modern technology has empowered some scientists to think science can do anything we could ever think or dream of. They consider science a know-all and cure-all, at least potentially so. They passionately air this conviction in their books, in academia, through mass media, and over the internet. The latest slogan is, "Follow the science."

Supporters of scientism claim that science provides the one and only valid way of finding truth. They pretend that all our questions have a scientific answer phrased in terms of particles, quantities, and equations. They maintain that there is no other point of view than the "scientific" worldview. They believe there is no corner of the Universe, no dimension of reality, no feature of human existence beyond science's reach. In other words, they have a dogmatic, unshakable belief in the omnicompetence of science. It is a creed that makes for a quasi-religion, based on a strong "faith" in the power of science. In that sense, scientism may sound very compelling, but reason gives us many reasons why we should challenge what scientism claims. So, what then is wrong with scientism?

A first reason for questioning the viewpoint of scientism is a very simple objection: those who defend scientism seem to be unaware of the fact that scientism itself does not follow its own rule. How could science ever prove all by itself that science is the only way of finding truth? There is no experiment that could do the trick. We cannot test scientism in the laboratory or with a double-blind experiment. Science on its own cannot answer questions that are beyond the reach of its empirical and experimental techniques. Science cannot pull itself up by its own bootstraps—any more than an electric generator is able to run on its own power.

Consequently, the truth of the statement, "No statements are true unless they can be proven scientifically," cannot itself be proven scientifically. It is not a scientific discovery but at best a philosophical or metaphysical viewpoint—and a poor one at that. It declares everything outside science as a despicable form of metaphysics, in defiance of the fact that all those who reject metaphysics are in fact committing their own version of metaphysics. Scientism rejects any religious faith and replaces it with its own "faith." This makes scientism a totalitarian ideology, for it allows no room for anything but itself.

A second reason for rejecting scientism is that a method as successful as the one that science provides does not disqualify any other methods. The claim of scientism that science rules out any methods other than the scientific method is obviously an assumption, not a conclusion. A blood test, for instance, is an excellent method to assess a person's health, but that doesn't eliminate many other helpful and reliable methods, such as x-rays, MRIs, and so on, depending on what we are trying to assess. A blood test on its own cannot be used to prove that a blood test is the best and only method there is.

Yet, that's in essence what scientism tries to do. First it declares science's empirical and experimental techniques as far superior to other methods, and then claims that this disqualifies any other methods. Consider the analogy used by the philosopher Edward Feser: a metal detector is a perfect tool to locate metals, but that does not mean there is nothing more to this world than metals.[66] A metal detector is not a good tool to find plastic cups on the beach, for instance. This tool gives us only a limited form of knowledge. Those who protest that this analogy is no good, on the grounds that metal detectors detect only part of reality, while science detects the whole of it, are simply begging the question again, for whether science really does describe the whole of reality is precisely what is at issue.

A third argument against scientism is that one cannot talk about science the way scientism does without stepping outside science. A statement *about* science can only be made from *outside* science. When scientism declares there is nothing outside the domain of science, it must be making a statement from outside the domain of science, which cannot be tested with tools and methods from inside the domain of science.

Nevertheless, scientism steps outside science to claim that there is nothing outside science and that there is no other point of view—which does not seem to be a very scientific, let alone logical move. Stepping outside science is no longer under the control of science and cannot possibly be justified as being scientific. Claiming differently makes for megalomania, which magically changes science into a know-all and cure-all. St. Paul put it in more general terms, "'Knowledge' puffs up" (1 Cor. 8:1).

A fourth argument against scientism is that it focuses exclusively on what can be scientifically tested, and then rejects anything that cannot be scientifically tested as invalid knowledge. However, *neglecting* what is outside the scope of science may be a wise scientific strategy, but *rejecting* what is outside its scope goes one step farther

---

[66] Edward Feser, *Scholastic Metaphysics: A Contemporary Introduction* (Piscataway, NJ: Transaction, 2014).

and turns inevitably into a baseless, unjustifiable ideology. If I neglect certain dangers in life, I cannot therefore reject the existence of such dangers. One cannot just reject what one neglects. It's important to note that the astonishing successes of science have not been gained by answering every kind of question, but precisely by refusing to do so.

As a matter of fact, science has a rather narrow scope of interest restricted to what can be measured, dissected, counted, and quantified. But therein also lies its limitation. First it limits itself exclusively to what can be measured, dissected, counted, and quantified, and then declares anything else as nonexistent because it cannot be measured, dissected, counted, and quantified. That is a form of circular reasoning. Albert Einstein is often quoted as having said, "Not everything that can be counted counts; not everything that counts can be counted."[67]

A fifth argument against scientism is that scientific knowledge does not even qualify as a superior form of knowledge: it may be more easily testable than other kinds, but it is also very restricted and therefore requires additional forms of knowledge. Even if we were to agree that the scientific method gives us better testable results than many other sources of knowledge, this would still not entitle us to claim that only the scientific method gives us genuine knowledge of reality. As we said earlier, a metal detector is a perfect tool to locate metals, but that does not mean a metal detector is a tool superior to any other tools. There is no way metal detectors can tell us anything about the existence of stones or plants, to name just a few items.

---

[67] It is often said this quote was written on a sign or blackboard in Einstein's office at Princeton University, but that is unsubstantiated. The quote is probably more recent, and came perhaps from William Bruce Cameron.

The reason for this is very simple. An instrument can only detect what it is designed to detect. And that is exactly where scientism misses the point. Instead of letting reality determine which techniques are appropriate for which parts of reality, scientism lets its favorite technique dictate what is considered "real" in life—in denial of the fact that science has purchased success at the cost of limiting its ambition.

To best characterize this narrow viewpoint of scientism, an image used by the late psychologist Abraham Maslow might be helpful: if you only have a hammer, every problem begins to look like a nail.[68] The truth of the matter is that our world is not only made of nails. So, instead of idolizing our "scientific hammer," we should acknowledge that not everything in this world is a "nail." Even if we were to agree that the scientific method gives us better testable results than many other sources of knowledge, this would not entitle us to claim that only the scientific method gives us genuine knowledge of reality.

Admittedly, it is true that if science does not go to its limits, it is a failure, but it is equally true that, as soon as science oversteps its limits, it becomes arrogant, a know-it-all, a gross megalomania. No wonder this has led some to criticize scientism as a form of circular reasoning. The late philosopher Ralph Barton Perry expressed this as follows: "A certain type of method is accredited by its applicability to a certain type of fact; and this type of fact, in turn, is accredited by its lending itself to a certain type of method."[69] That's how we keep circling around in our reasoning.

[68] A. H. Maslow, *The Psychology of Science* (New York: HarperCollins, 1966), 16.
[69] Ralph Barton Perry, *Present Philosophical Tendencies* (1912; New York: Longmans Green, 1925), 81–82.

A sixth argument against scientism is that science is solely about material things, yet it requires immaterial things such as logic, reason, and mathematics. G. K. Chesterton liked to ask those infected with scientism, "Why should not good logic be as misleading as bad logic? They are both movements in the brain of a bewildered ape?"[70] If that were true, good logic or math would be as misleading as bad logic or math. Logic and mathematics are not physical, and therefore not testable by the natural sciences—and yet they cannot be ignored or denied by science. In fact, science heavily relies on logic and mathematics to interpret the data that scientific observation and experimentation provide.

Logic and reason are perfect examples of the kinds of immaterial phenomena that we all know exist, but which naturalistic science cannot measure, analyze, or account for. Yet, these immaterial things are real and indispensable, even though they are beyond scientific observation. Take, for instance, the mathematical concept of *pi* (π). As the particle physicist Stephen Barr points out, it is not some private experience, like a toothache; it is not a material object like a melon; it is more than a sensation or a neurological artifact; it is certainly more than a certain pattern of neurons firing in the brain; it is not even a property of material things, for there are no pi-sided melons.[71] Instead, *pi* is a precise and definite concept with logical and mathematical relationships to other equally precise concepts. And concepts are certainly not material entities.

To reduce concepts to a "creation of neurons" obscures the fact that *neuron* itself is an abstract concept. That would make again for a vicious circle: the very idea that concepts are "nothing but"

---

[70] G. K. Chesterton, *Orthodoxy* (Chicago: Moody Publishers, 2009), 33.
[71] Barr, *Modern Physics and Ancient Faith*, 194.

neurons firing is itself nothing but neurons firing. G. K. Chesterton called this "the suicide of thought."[72] Those who claim that mental concepts are merely products of neurons should realize that talking about neurons cannot be done without the immaterial concept of neuron to begin with.

Ironically, scientism itself is one of those immaterial things it is supposed to reject. First, scientists decide to limit themselves to what is material and can be dissected, counted, measured, and quantified. But then scientism kicks in and says that there is nothing else in this world than that which is material and can be dissected, measured, counted, or quantified. However, this verdict itself is not material and cannot be dissected, counted, measured, or quantified. So, we end up with something like a boomerang that comes back to hit whoever launched it.

A seventh reason for rejecting scientism is that no science, not even physics, is able to declare itself a superior form of knowledge. Some scientists have argued, for example, that physics always has the last word in observation, for the observers themselves are physical. But why not say then that psychology always has the last word, because these observers are interesting psychological objects as well? Neither statement makes sense: observers are neither physical nor psychological, but they can indeed be studied from a physical, biological, psychological, or statistical viewpoint—which is an entirely different matter.

Often scientism results from hyper-specialized training coupled with a lack of exposure to other disciplines and methods. This may cause one to not realize that the findings of science are always partial and fragmentary. There is no science of "all there is." Physicists like to speak of a "Grand Unified Theory" (GUT) in physics—a

---

[72] Chesterton, *Orthodoxy*, title of chap. 3.

theory that unifies the three non-gravitational forces—but that is not the same as a "Grand Unified Theory of *Everything*" (TOE).

Although some physicists and many laypeople tend to use the term GUT as equivalent to TOE, the distinction between these two concepts might prevent much confusion. The term GUT would definitely not represent a theory of *all* there is in this world, but at best a theory of *physical* phenomena, rather than a theory of *everything*. It's at best a theory about everything in physics, so the concept of GUT is only a theory tied to physics. A theory of *everything*, on the other hand, would also have to explain why some people believe that theory and some do not. Limiting oneself exclusively to one particular perspective such as physics is in itself at best a metaphysical decision. However, to quote Shakespeare, "There are more things in heaven and earth, Horatio, than are dreamt of in your philosophy."[73] One cannot give science the metaphysical power it does not possess.

An eighth argument against scientism is of a historical nature. The first legendary pioneers of science in England were very much aware of the fact that there is more to life than science. When the Royal Society of London was founded in 1660, its members explicitly demarcated their area of investigation and realized very clearly that they were going to leave many other domains untouched. In its charter, King Charles II assigned to the fellows of the Society the privilege of enjoying intelligence and knowledge, but with the following important stipulation: "provided in matters of things philosophical, mathematical, and mechanical."[74] ("Philosophical" meant "scientific" back then.)

---

[73] William Shakespeare, *Hamlet*, act 1, scene 5, lines 167–168.

[74] The Royal Society originated on November 28, 1660, when twelve men met to set up "a Colledge for the promoting of

That's how the domains of knowledge were separated; it was this "partition" that led to a division of labor between the sciences and other fields of human interest.

By accepting this separation, science bought its own territory, but certainly at the expense of all-inclusiveness—consequently, the rest of the "estate" was reserved for others to manage. On the one hand, it gave to scientists all that could "methodically" be solved by dissecting, counting, and measuring. On the other hand, these scientists agreed to keep their hands off all other domains (education, legislation, justice, ethics, and certainly religion) because those require a different "expertise."

To sum up this discussion, I would think any of the above arguments, or certainly a combination of them, gives us enough reason to reject the claims of scientism. It is in fact based on a "blind faith" in science—comparable to the way some scientists declare religion a matter of "blind faith." In other words, the science-alone attitude can only take us on a dead-end street. It's ultimately based on "bootstrap" magic!

b. The Role of Faith in Science

Despite all the above objections, scientism is still very much alive, albeit often unspoken or hidden underground. The late Dutch physicist Hendrik Casimir (best known today as the namesake of the Casimir effect in quantum-mechanical attraction) once said,

---

Physico-Mathematicall Experimentall Learning." Robert Hooke's draft of its statutes reads literally: "The Business and Design of the Royal Society is: To improve the knowledge of natural things, and all useful Arts, Manufactures, Mechanik practices, Engyries and Inventions by Experiments—(not meddling with Divinity, Metaphysics, Moralls, Politicks, Grammar, Rhetorik, or Logic)."

"We have made science our God."[75] Indeed, science has become a quasi-religion of which the scientists are the priests.

As a result, science is supposed to explain *everything*, but then in a much better way than God once did. It is in this frame of mind that Stephen Hawking once exclaimed, "Our goal is a complete understanding of the events around us and of our own existence."[76] Notice the overconfident inclusion of "our own existence." Scientism likes to broadcast to everyone around that it's all about science — even our very being.

Well, science may be everywhere nowadays, but science is certainly not all there is. Pope John Paul's encyclical *Fides et Ratio* puts it this way:

> Another threat to be reckoned with is *scientism. This is the philosophical notion which refuses to admit the validity of forms of knowledge other than those of the positive sciences; and it relegates religious, theological, ethical and aesthetic knowledge to the realm of mere fantasy.*[77]

Scientific knowledge is not the only knowledge there is. First of all, it is confined to secondary causes, to things that can be dissected, counted, measured, and quantified. Everything else is beyond its scope, which includes the existence and the role of the First Cause, for that's where we enter the domain of philosophy and religion.

Second, if scientific knowledge were indeed all there is, we would run into serious contradictions. If we reduce everything to material,

---

[75] Quoted in Anthony Van Den Beukel, *The Physicists and God: The New Priests of Religion?* (North Andover, MA: Genesis, 1995), 30.

[76] Stephen Hawking, *A Brief History of Time* (New York: Bantam, 1998), 186.

[77] John Paul II, *Fides et Ratio*, no. 88.

measurable entities such as atoms, molecules, cells, and the like, we are committing ourselves to reductionism, which C.S. Lewis famously called "nothing-buttery."[78] We thus end up with statements like, "Love is nothing but a chemical reaction"; "Thoughts are nothing but patterns of impulses"; "Humans are nothing but glorified animals"; "Humans are nothing but a pack of neurons"; "Humans are nothing but a bundle of instincts," "Sins are nothing but genetic errors."

The problem of the "nothing-buttery" of reductionism is that it is suicidal. If indeed our thoughts are nothing but a pattern of impulses in the brain, or the mere product of genes, then this claim itself is also nothing more than the firing of neurons or the outcome of genes. Claims of "nothing-buttery" just defeat and destroy themselves. They cut off the very branch that the person who makes such claims was sitting on. That's absurd and contradictory.

This thought has been expressed in various ways and by several open-minded thinkers. One of them is the biologist J.B.S. Haldane who once worded it this way: "If my mental processes are determined wholly by the motions of atoms in my brain, I have no reason to suppose that my beliefs are true.... And hence I have no reason for supposing my brain to be composed of atoms."[79] Then he continued, "If materialism is true, it seems to me that we cannot know that it is true. If my opinions are the result of chemical processes going on in my brain, they are determined by chemistry, not the laws of logic."

The philosopher C.S. Lewis brings this argument to a close: "The real sciences cannot be accepted for a moment unless rational

---

[78] C.S. Lewis, "Transposition," in *The Weight of Glory and Other Addresses* (New York: Macmillan, 1980), esp. 71–72.

[79] J.B.S. Haldane, *Possible Worlds* (New York: Routledge, 2017), 209; also in J.B.S. Haldane, *The Inequality of Man* (London: Penguin Books, 1932), 162.

inferences are valid: for every science claims to be a series of inferences from observed facts."[80] In other words, we need more than science to explain everything, thus making logic and religious faith serious candidates to bring us closer to an explanation of everything in life. In the examples mentioned above, the logical method of *reductio ad absurdum* is being used again: if materialism is true, then we cannot know that it is true—which is absurd. That is an argument hard to beat.

Third, science has its own presuppositions or assumptions which are beyond the scope of science. Without them, science would not be possible—yet science itself is unable to study its own assumptions and presuppositions in a scientific way. Nevertheless, they represent the "faith" one must have in the scientific enterprise. In other words, there might be much more "faith" hidden in science than most scientists are willing to acknowledge.

The truth of the matter is that science cannot be done without a series of *assumptions*. Many scientists may not be aware of those assumptions, for they are "hidden" like most of an iceberg is hidden under water. The biologist Ernst Mayr speaks of "silent assumptions that are taken so completely for granted that they are never mentioned."[81] Yet, they play a fundamental role in science. They must be there before science can even get started, for without them science could not get off the ground. They are proto-scientific, in the sense that they must come first before science can follow. So, the next question is this: Which are those assumptions? Let's study them in more detail.

---

[80] C. S. Lewis, *Christian Reflections* (Grand Rapids, MI: Wm. B. Eerdmans, 1967), 89.

[81] Ernst Mayr, *The Growth of Biological Thought* (Cambridge, MA: Harvard University Press, 1982), 834.

A Catholic Scientist Harmonizes Science and Faith

Assumption #1: There Is a Real World outside of Us

This may seem an obvious assumption for scientists, but it has been questioned many times—questioned not only by some quantum physicists but also by skeptical philosophers such as David Hume and Immanuel Kant, who think we can't really know anything about the "real" world behind our observations. Some philosophers have gone as far as claiming that the entire world exists only as a dream in people's minds.

Should scientists take these skeptics seriously? Perhaps not. If there is no real world, then science too becomes a hallucination, existing only as illusions inside individual minds. Therefore, to keep science from crumbling, it needs the assumption of a real world.

Without the assumption of a real world outside of us and independent of us, there is no way anymore to distinguish fact from fiction, realities from illusions, and opinions from truths. If there is no objective truth, we are free to believe whatever we like, including utter nonsense. Once scientists give up on the assumption of a real outside world, and of the truths that come with it, they undermine their own findings, changing science into science-fiction. This would be the end of the empirical cycle with its test implications and its conclusions based on confirmation or falsification. In short, reality does not depend on our thoughts: instead, our thoughts should be controlled by reality.

No wonder, Albert Einstein always protested vehemently against such skepticism when he said, "The belief in an external world independent of the perceiving subject is the basis of all natural science."[82] Nevertheless, there have been some nonconsenting voices in the field of quantum physics. The quantum physicist Niels

[82] Albert Einstein, *Ideas and Opinions* (New York: Crown Publishers, 1954), 266.

Bohr, for instance, seems to be telling us that reality does not exist until we observe or measure it. Einstein famously attacked him on this by saying, "Do you really believe the Moon is there only when you look at it?"[83] But at least Bohr does acknowledge that there is indeed a real world that we can observe, but only when we decide to do so by making physical measurements. Besides, one should ask him how we can measure something that doesn't exist; it must have come into existence at least before we measured it, and not because it was measured.

Why does or should science still hold on to its truth claims? It is the real world that often forces scientists to revise their theories in order to come closer to the truth—that's what confirmation and falsification are about. To use an analogy: Who would ever want to drive across a bridge designed by engineers who believed their calculations are merely based on opinions instead of truths?

Besides, if their claim entails that our beliefs are mere artifacts or illusions, such a claim would act like a boomerang that destroys its own truth claims as well. To *know* is to know things in the real world, not to know mental abstractions in the mind. Those who say that the world of science is merely an illusion produced by our brains should seriously be questioned about their own claim, given the fact that this very claim would also become an illusion.

This raises the question of how we know that what we know about the world is about the real world. The shortest answer is: we don't. We can never prove that we are not all hallucinating, or

---

[83] See for instance: Robyn Arianrhod, "Einstein, Bohr and the origins of entanglement," *Cosmos*, October 5, 2017, https://cosmosmagazine.com/science/physics/einstein-bohr-and-the-origins-of-entanglement/.

simply living in a world of computer simulation. We are dealing here with an assumption that science cannot prove on its own. Some people think the existence of mind-independent objects such as stones can be proven by giving a mighty kick to a stone. But objects perceived by our senses are not the same things as truly existing bodies. Even in a dream, we may have similar experiences, and yet they are mere illusions made up in a dream.

Therefore, it does not follow that an objective external world does exist—for we could in fact all be living in a permanent dream world. How would nearsighted people know that the world is not as blurred as they see it? Certainly not by comparing their own images with the "real" images. Perhaps corrective glasses may help them to see better. But once we acknowledge this, we end up talking again about the existence of an objective, real world, distinct from our minds. That's where the buck stops.

Assumption #2: There is Order in the Universe

Not only is science itself a very orderly enterprise, but it also reveals a very orderly Universe. Interestingly enough, the Greek word *cosmos*—a synonym for the Latin word *universum*—means order. The role of hypotheses, theories, and laws of nature is to capture the very order that would be eluding us if we didn't have science. Thanks to science, we see a striking order in the world around us—for example, planets moving around the Sun in very orderly orbits, with all these orbits lying in almost the same plane, making the solar system look like a giant platter. To put this in a nutshell: every morning we wake up in a very orderly world.

It is this kind of order that science is in search of and keeps exploring. Take, for instance, one of the oldest examples of a law of nature, phrased by Archimedes (ca. 250 BC) as follows: "Any object, wholly or partially immersed in a fluid, is buoyed up by a force equal to the weight of the fluid displaced by the object." It expresses a certain kind of underlying order in the Universe.

Put differently, science reveals something astonishing about this Universe: namely that it's not a chaotic entity. Einstein was right when he wrote in a letter of March 30, 1952, "But surely, a priori, one should expect the world to be chaotic."[84] But instead of the expectation of chaos, we expect the world to have a remarkable order. The laws of nature which science brings to light are the many patterns of regularity we detect in this orderly world. No wonder, Einstein also spoke of the "harmony of the Universe." He also said in one of his interviews about his formula $E = mc^2$, "If I hadn't an absolute faith in the harmony of creation, I wouldn't have tried for thirty years to express it in a mathematical formula."[85] Other scientists, such as Galileo, could have said something similar.

The order of the Universe is a fundamental assumption for science. When scientists study matter and energy, they see regular patterns of behavior. It is only due to the orderly design of the Universe that scientists can explain and predict—which would be impossible in a chaotic world of disorder and irregularity. In other words, order must come first before science can even get started. Order is not something scientists discovered after more and more successful searches revealed more and more cases of order. There is no way we can prove order by adding more and more confirming cases, like inductivists want us to think. In short, order is not a scientific discovery but rather a philosophical assumption that

---

[84] Albert Einstein, *Letters to Solovine*, trans. Wade Baskin (New York: Philosophical Library, 1987), 132–133.

[85] William Hermanns, *Einstein and the Poet: In Search of the Cosmic Man* (Wellesley, MA: Branden, 1983), 68.

enables science and propels scientific research. It is needed for science to come off the ground.

Apparently, there is no way we can scientifically prove there is order and uniformity in nature. The assumption of order and uniformity is a "prerequisite" for any scientific exploration. Even the principle or method of falsification is based on the assumption of order in the Universe. Without "law and order" in nature, there simply could not be any falsifying evidence. When we do find falsifying evidence, we do not take such a finding as proof that the Universe is not orderly, but instead as an indication that there is something wrong with the specific order we had conjectured up in our minds. Apparently, falsification itself is based on order and cannot be falsified by disorder. Hence, counterevidence does allow us to falsify theories, but not the principle of falsification itself, because it is necessarily based on an assumption of order.

If science keeps finding that there is order in the world, why do we still call it an assumption? The reason is that when scientists say they have found something chaotic, the search has not ended but just begun so as to uncover the order that is still eluding them. Mere chaos is unacceptable in science, as science by its nature is in search of order. Whatever may seem chaotic to laypeople will turn out to be very orderly when science advances. Those who reject order in the Universe have basically given up on science. If there were no order in the Universe, it would make no sense to search for laws of nature in physics, chemistry, biology, and other disciplines.

What seems to belie all of this is the fact that many scientists recently developed a strong interest in chaos and chaotic systems, as if these could falsify the existence of "law and order" in the Universe. They point out that some natural systems can only be described by non-linear mathematical equations with such complex solutions that we cannot exactly predict what the system will do in the near future. Or to take another example, our measurements of all the initial conditions of a particular system (for example, in meteorology) may be too numerous and/or too inaccurate to predict what exactly the outcome would be.

However, examples are not really cases of chaos, but only appear to us as chaos. As a matter of fact, these scientists are still looking for the very order behind seemingly chaotic phenomena, even if they are of a probabilistic nature. When the weather forecast is off the mark, we do not conclude that the weather is unpredictable. We just do not know enough to be perfectly accurate in our predictions. But that's not chaos!

Assumption #3: There Is Causality in the Universe

There is this simple and basic rule used in all sciences that says like causes have like effects. In translation: from causes which appear similar, scientists *expect* similar effects; if there are effects, then there must be certain causes involved; if the effects are different, then they must have had different causes.

The general idea behind this rule is the assumption that we live in a world of causality—nothing comes from nothing. This assumption is obviously order-related, but there is much more to it. You do not have to be a scientist to understand that like causes have like effects. All of us seem to know this rule almost "intuitively." But scientists in particular make it their "profession" to apply this rule methodically. In their research, they attempt to unveil what exactly the causality patterns are of this Universe.

But there is a potential problem here: We do not *see* causality—like the way we do not see gravity or electricity. It's true, we do not see causation in the same way in which we see colors and shapes and motion. So, what is causality then? Is it merely something we imagine in our minds? The skeptical philosopher David

Hume went that road. Since the supposed influence of a cause upon its effect is not directly evident to sense observation, Hume concluded that the connection between cause and effect is not an aspect of the real world, but only a habit of our thinking as we become accustomed to seeing one thing constantly conjoined to another. Thus, Hume reduced causality to some form of correlation at best—no longer as something real found in the world outside of us, but rather as a way of thinking about the world inside of us.

Does Hume have a point here? His view has certainly not been embraced by great physicists such as Max Planck and Albert Einstein, who all assume that physical laws describe a reality independent of ourselves, and that the theories of science show not only how nature behaves but also why it behaves as it does, and not otherwise. Besides, Hume's analysis would erase the important distinction between causation and correlation by having them both reduced to a series of mere subjective associations or generalizations. One of the first things you learn in a science class is that correlation doesn't imply causation.

So, where did Hume go wrong? When we see the sun rise each day, for instance, we know that there is not a different sun rising every morning. Although we know the world through sensations or sense impressions *à la* Hume, the truth of the matter is that they are just the media that give us access to reality. The Scottish philosopher John Haldane put it well when he said, "One only knows about cats and dogs through sensations, but they are not themselves sensations, any more than the players in a televised football game are color patterns on a flat screen."[86]

---

[86] John Haldane, "Hume's Destructive Genius," *First Things*, December 2011, https://www.firstthings.com/article/2011/12/humes-destructive-genius, 23–25.

How could Hume miss this point? He actually came to his view because he took causality as rooted not in the identity of acting *things*, but in a relationship between *events*, by assuming, as he puts it, that "All events seem entirely loose and separate. One event follows another; but we never can observe any tie between them. They seem *conjoined*, but never *connected*."[87]

Instead, it should be argued that the actions an entity can take are determined by what that entity *is*. When one billiard ball strikes another, it sends the other rolling because of the nature of the two balls and their surroundings. This entails the following: when we know that billiard balls are solid and when we see one ball moving toward another, then certain effects are quite impossible. The moving ball cannot, for example, just pass through the second ball and come out the other side continuing at the same speed; nor can the first ball stop at exactly the same place as the second ball; nor can one of the balls suddenly vanish, and so on and so forth. The qualities of the balls determine the kind of effect that the impulse of the first ball, as a cause, will have on the second ball, as an effect. In other words, when we see entities acting, we see causality and causation in terms of "like causes having like effects." The general statement, "Like causes have like effects," admits no exception.

This also means that nothing happens without a cause. One could even argue that it is logically impossible to prove that something has no cause at all, since searches like these never reveal the *absence* of their object. Causality can never be conclusively defeated by experiments since causality is the very foundation of

---

[87] David Hume, *An Enquiry Concerning Human Understanding and Selections from a Treatise of Human Nature* (Chicago: Open Court, 1907), 76.

all experiments. Since science can never prove there is causality in this Universe, it must *assume* there is. Science cannot get started without that assumption, and this very assumption can never be falsified.

Assumption #4: The World Is Comprehensible to Us

Albert Einstein had good reason to say that the most incomprehensible thing about the Universe is that it is comprehensible; he actually spoke of a mystery.[88] It is indeed incomprehensible that we can, at least in principle, comprehend the Universe the way it is. The Universe could as well have been a complete enigma to us—but fortunately, and apparently, it's not.

The idea that this Universe is comprehensible, or intelligible, certainly does not come from science itself. Scientists assume and know that the world can be understood and be taken as intelligible—otherwise there would be no reason for them to pursue science. They don't yet fully know what this intelligible world looks like, but they do know the world must be intelligible in principle. So, intelligibility is certainly not the outcome of intense and extensive scientific research: it is again a notion that must come first before science can even get started. It does not have to be confirmed over and over again, but it is a precondition for confirmation to work. We just *know* that this world is intelligible.

This knowledge is so basic to science that it easily eludes scientists. If you were told some scientists had discovered that certain physical phenomena are not intelligible, you would, or at least should, tell them to keep searching and come up with a better hypothesis or theory—based on this fundamental philosophical

---

[88] Albert Einstein, *Out of My Later Years*, (repr., New York: Gramercy, 1993), 64.

knowledge that says the Universe is fundamentally intelligible and comprehensible. Science calls for this assumption. It is only because of their trusting that nature is comprehensible in principle that scientists have reason to pursue any scientific research.

Earlier we talked about the use of *concepts* in science. It is thanks to those that we can study and think about electrons, atoms, molecules, cells, neurons, and the like. Concepts make the world intelligible for us and allow us to use them when talking to other scientists (or others). They make the world comprehensible to the human mind, and thus ultimately accessible to everyone. As said earlier, concepts play a central role in how we know the world by helping us see similarities that were not visible before we had them. And scientific statements, for their part, depend on concepts like these. Scientific statements about nuclear particles, genes, neurons, and the like may appear incomprehensible to people who do not know the concepts used in those statements, but they are essential for the scientists who speak about them and study them.

Assumption #5: The World Can Be Put to the Test

Scientists explore their field of study by using not only their "senses" (although often aided by observational devices) but also their "hands," typically extended by experimental tools. Indeed, most sciences are of an experimental nature. In a simple setting, scientists start with two variables, of which the independent variable is the one freely chosen and manipulated by the scientist so as to trace its effect on the other, so-called dependent, variable. The idea behind this is, again, that like causes have like effects. When changing the causes, the effects must change as well.

For modern minds, that is easily understood and even expected. Nowadays, we no longer accept that science should exclusively be

It is clear by now that experimental science has won the battle. Observational evidence proved itself more reliable, most of the time, than theoretical speculation. Experimentation is no longer seen as something foreign or unnatural to studying nature, but it has become the hallmark of most scientific studies. By using tests, scientists can experimentally change causes and find out how that changes the effects.

Obviously, there can be no science without the above-mentioned assumptions. Without the assumption that there is an objectively real world, science would not be possible. Without the assumption that there is order in nature, science would not be possible. Without the assumption of like causes having like effects, science would not be possible. Without the assumption that the world is comprehensible, science would not be possible. Without the assumption that nature can be put to the test, science would not be possible.

Science itself did not discover any of these assumptions. Instead, all of them combined are needed to make science possible the way we know it nowadays. Put in general terms, a science free from any assumptions simply does not exist. They are in essence the pillars on which science rests, preventing it from collapsing. Apparently, whatever science can do ultimately rests on what science *cannot* do—scientifically testing its own assumptions. To put it briefly, science needs reason to get any results, but it also needs faith to get started—that is, faith in its own assumptions.

Because of all the above, we must conclude that science is something you need to believe in before you can practice it. Strange as it may sound, practicing science requires faith.

c. Assumptions from Heaven

Now that we know that science cannot function without certain assumptions, we need to address an even more intriguing question: Does religion have anything to do with them? How do we know that the assumptions which science entertains are warranted and do not end up being mere inventions or conjectures? Certainly not so through science itself, so we found out, for science cannot scientifically prove or test its own assumptions — they come before science can even begin. Since science presupposes these assumptions, it cannot attempt to justify them without arguing in a circle. To break out of this circle, their validity and legitimacy must come from somewhere else. From where could that be?

Their definitive source is probably a surprise to many: these assumptions must have come ultimately from God and reside in Heaven, in a divine intellect. Scientists could not do their work without the silent, often forgotten assumption that God is the very foundation of their work. God is the ultimate source where all the above assumptions find their foundation. God is the First Cause behind all secondary causes. In other words, all these assumptions are in essence *religious* beliefs grounded in our faith of God's existence. How can that possibly be true? Let's find out for each assumption separately.

#1: Where does the assumption of a real world come from? Of course, the world is either real, or it is not. The world is not, and cannot be, real if we merely *believe* it is real. Beliefs don't create or change reality; believing the Earth is flat doesn't make the Earth flat. Besides, the world cannot give reality to itself—that would be bootstrap magic. The reality of the world must come from somewhere else—from a Creator, that is. The world is real, as its Maker is real and has created a real world. Only God, the First Cause, can call the world into existence and thus make the world real. Therefore, the world can only be real if its Maker is real.

Nevertheless, some scientists keep thinking that the Universe was caused, not by God, but by the big bang. The late cosmologist Stephen Hawking, for instance, spoke of a "spontaneous creation." He thought that the Universe could create and explain itself when he said, "Because there is a law such as gravity, the universe can and will create itself from nothing.... Spontaneous creation is the reason there is something rather than nothing."[91]

But how could that explanation ever be true? How could the Universe be the explanation of its own existence? First of all, the law of gravity cannot do the trick, for the laws of physics come with the Universe and are ultimately the set of laws which govern the existing Universe. Since the laws of nature presuppose the very existence of the Universe, they cannot be used to explain the existence of the Universe. So, Hawking is actually saying that laws which have meaning only in the context of an existing Universe can generate that Universe, including the laws of nature, all by themselves before either exists—which is not only a form of circular reasoning but also makes for an absurd conclusion.

Second, the laws of nature could have been other than they are—they could exist or not exist, they could be this or that. It is easy to think, for instance, about possible worlds in which the laws of nature are radically different from those that are operational right here and now in our Universe. The Universe could have been as much as "law-less." Physicist Paul C. Davies is right: "There are endless ways in which the universe might have been totally chaotic. It might have had no laws at all, or merely an incoherent jumble of laws that caused matter to behave in disorderly or

[91] "Stephen Hawking Says Universe Not Created by God," *The Guardian*, September 1, 2010, https://www.theguardian.com/science/2010/sep/02/stephen-hawking-big-bang-creator.

unstable ways."[92] Instead, we find in this Universe a very specific law and order.

Third, if there is no inherent necessity for the Universe to exist, then the Universe, including everything in it, is not self-explanatory and therefore must find an explanation outside of itself. Obviously, it cannot be explained by something finite, not necessary, and not self-explanatory—for that would lead to infinite regress, among other things. So, the Universe can only be explained by an unconditioned, infinite, and necessary Being. The physicist Paul Davies goes as far as to speak of "the mystery of … why there is a universe at all."[93] The mystery of why there is a real world can only be explained by the existence of a Creator God.

Therefore, we must conclude that the assumption of a real world can only be found in a First Cause, a Creator God. Without the creative power of God, the world could not have come into existence, and without the sustaining power of God, the world could not keep existing.

#2: Where does the assumption of order and regularity come from? Science keeps unveiling laws of nature and patterns of order and regularity. The Sun will never rise from the west, for example. However, in no way can regularity explain itself—it's not self-explanatory. John Stuart Mill said already in 1865, "the laws of nature cannot account for their own origin."[94] We could try to come up with another explanation—another "law," that is—to explain the existence

---

[92] Paul Davies, *The Mind of God: The Scientific Basis for a Rational World* (New York: Simon and Schuster, 1992), 195.

[93] Paul Davies, *God and the New Physics* ((New York: Simon and Schuster, 1983), 43.

[94] John Stuart Mill, *Auguste Comte and Positivism* (London: N. Trübner, 1865), 14.

of a certain regularity. But that move would open the gate for an unending appeal to more and more explanations—which amounts to an infinite regress that can never finish the job. Hence, ultimately, we cannot evade the idea of a Lawgiver, a First Cause, who gave us the laws of nature on which secondary causes are based.

This would not come as a surprise to religious believers, but even scientists come more and more to the awareness that the Universe does have an elegant, intelligible, and discoverable underlying physical and mathematical structure. The beauty and elegance of the laws of nature and the mathematical equations behind them point to the divine intellect of the one who created them. Albert Einstein, for one, had to acknowledge, "Everyone who is seriously involved in the pursuit of science becomes convinced that a Spirit is manifest in the laws of the Universe—a Spirit vastly superior to that of man."[95]

Steven Weinberg, a convinced atheist, had to admit that "sometimes nature seems more beautiful than strictly necessary."[96] However, he merely took it as a brute fact not in need of any further explanation.

Since laws of nature cannot explain themselves or their own existence, they must find their explanation and origin in a cosmic Lawgiver. Because there is a cosmic Lawgiver, it makes sense to search for laws in physics, chemistry, and the life sciences. Even the fact that they are typically called "laws" suggests there is a Lawgiver. As St. Thomas Aquinas puts it concisely, "Therefore some

[95] Albert Einstein, *Dear Professor Einstein: Albert Einstein's Letters to and from Children*, ed. Alice Calaprice (Amherst, NY: Prometheus Books, 2002), 129; also quoted in Max Jammer, *Einstein and Religion: Physics and Theology* (Princeton, NJ: Princeton University Press, 1999), 93.
[96] Steven Weinberg, *Dreams of a Final Theory* (New York: Pantheon Books, 1992), 250.

intelligent being exists by whom all natural things are directed to their end; and this being we call God."[97]

#3: Where does the assumption of causality come from? Obviously, causality is closely connected with the assumption of order and regularity in the Universe. If like causes do have like effects, there must be something in nature that makes this happen. There is something very real about cause-and-effect relationships. What is it then that makes them real? There must be an ultimate Cause that causes all secondary causes to be causes of their own and thus having the effect of making "like causes having like effects." This ultimate cause is the First Cause, God, who is the origin of all secondary causes and lets them be causes of their own.

The general statement, "Like causes have like effects," admits no exception. All things in this Universe were made in such way that like causes do have like effects. Earlier we mentioned the universal statement that all things that have come into existence need a cause that makes them exist. It is based on the assumption of universal causality, which means too that nothing can happen without a cause. That's the way God has made all things in this world to be based on law and order—that is, they all must follow laws. What is so peculiar about these laws is this: if they are true, then they are always true. If a certain law of nature is correct and true, then all entities covered by the law must exemplify that law.

Belief in a Divine Lawgiver is obviously part of our religious faith. This means, in more religious terms, that the Christian God is a reliable God, who is faithful to the covenant He made with His people. This God is infinitely different from capricious deities such as the Olympians in ancient Greece or the deities of paganism,

[97] Aquinas, *The Summa Theologiae of St. Thomas*, I, q. 2, art. 3.

who are all unpredictable in their actions. He is also different from the God of Islam, who is supposed to be entirely beyond human comprehension and entirely unlimited in his freedom to act. To assume, instead, that there are laws of nature would limit "Allah's freedom to act" whenever he wishes to act.

In contrast, our God has installed laws of nature in the Universe He created—gas laws, gravity laws, laws of thermodynamics, laws of genetics, and so on. Amazingly enough, these laws just are—there is no *scientific* explanation for the fact that the laws of nature are the way they are. Again, since the laws of nature cannot be used to explain the existence of the Universe, they must find their explanation in a Divine Lawgiver.

When John Stuart Mill said, "It is a law that every event depends on some law,"[98] he never wondered where that law itself then came from (other than from himself). As Dimitri Mendeleev, who discovered the periodic table of elements, put it: "It is the function of science to discover the existence of a general reign of order in nature and to find the causes governing this order."[99] Since science can never explain how the laws of nature came into existence and why they are the way they are, only a Divine Lawgiver can explain this enigma.

#4: Where does the assumption of intelligibility come from? If the world is indeed comprehensible and intelligible, as science assumes it is, then the world must be intelligible to the human intellect. Well, it is the *rationality* of the human intellect that makes the

---

[98] John Stuart Mill, A System of Logic: Ratiocinative and Inductive (London: Longmans, Green, 1884), 213.
[99] Dmitri Mendeleev, The Principles of Chemistry, vol. 1 (London: Longmans, Green, 1905), 240. Mendeleev on the Periodic Law: Selected Writings, 1869–1905.

world intelligible and understandable to us: it gives us the power to comprehend the Universe through reasoning and to discover truths about this world. To believe that nature, God's creation, is intelligible and that nature can be grasped and understood by human reason is a necessary assumption for science. If we do away with a rational God, we do away with a rational creation, and therefore with the rational enterprise of science.

It is the rationality of the human intellect that also gives us access to the divine intellect—to God, to the laws of nature, and to the structure of this Universe. In other words, not only is there rationality in the human intellect, but there is also rationality in the world itself—otherwise the two could never match and correspond. This raises the question as to where the rationality of the world comes from? The fact that the Universe has an elegant, intelligible, and discoverable underlying mathematical and physical structure calls for an explanation—or otherwise must be left unexplained. We said it several times: even scientists uphold the conviction—consciously or subconsciously—that there is an intelligible plan behind this Universe, a plan that is accessible to the human intellect through the natural light of reason. To think there is no explanation for this—things just are the way they are, as some say—is not a very satisfying explanation but is in fact an irrational position. We need to look for an answer somewhere, but certainly not in science.

As a matter of fact, more and more scientists are beginning to agree with this. Paul Davies once said, "There must be an unchanging rational ground in which the logical, orderly nature of the universe is rooted."[100] And the British physicist John Polkinghorne

---

[100] Paul Davies, "What Happened before the Big Bang?," in *God for the 21st Century*, ed. Russell Stannard (Philadelphia: Templeton Foundation Press, 2000), 12.

speaks of "pointers to the divine as the only totally adequate ground of intelligibility."[101] In other words, the Universe itself is loaded with reason and rationality. Only the rationality of the Creator can explain that the world is an orderly, rational entity accessible to the human mind because the mind, too, is an orderly, rational product of the divine intellect.

In short, there is rationality in the human intellect and there is rationality in the world around us. How come they match each other so beautifully? The only rational answer must run like this: they both derive from the reason we find in the Creator's intellect. That's exactly the answer religion gives us: we were created in God's image and likeness (Gen. 1:26). Only this can explain the power of reason both in the physical world and in the human intellect. The encyclical *Fides et Ratio* puts it this way, "It is the one and the same God who establishes and guarantees the intelligibility and reasonableness of the natural order of things upon which scientists confidently depend."[102]

The physicist Paul Davies once summarized this well:

[Even] the most atheistic scientist accepts as an act of faith that the Universe is not absurd, that there is a rational basis to physical existence manifested as lawlike order in nature that is at least in part comprehensible to us. So science can proceed only if the scientist adopts an essentially theological worldview.[103]

---

[101] John Polkinghorne, *Science and Creation: The Search for Understanding* (Philadelphia: Templeton Foundation Press, 2006), 19.

[102] John Paul II, *Fides et Ratio*, no. 34.

[103] Paul Davies, "Physics and the Mind of God: The Templeton Prize Address," *First Things*, August 1995, https://www.firstthings.com/article/1995/08/physics-and-the-mind-of-god-the-templeton-prize-address.

As we noticed earlier, somehow the rationality of the human intellect enables us to capture reality the way it *is*. Not only does the world of rationality in the human intellect appear to be amazingly "consistent," but so does the physical order we observe in this world. How could the world be comprehensible if its structure—its "law and order"—did not have some kind of "rationality" in it, making the world comprehensible for us? Again, our conclusion must be that the rationality present in the human intellect matches the rationality we find in the natural world.

Is there really any rationality in the physical world around us? Not in the literal sense, of course. But on further inspection, there are many "rational" elements in the structure and order of the physical world. They make the world look highly "consistent" —which is essentially a rational concept—and therefore, they make the world intelligible for us. Somehow the order we discover in the world is rational and intelligible, and that's why our scientific findings and theories can appear as rational and intelligible, too. This gave the late astrophysicist Sir James Jeans reason to say, "The Universe begins to look more like a great thought than a great machine."[104]

#5: Where does the assumption of testability come from? Again, it is an assumption based on the fact that all there is in the Universe comes from a Creator God, who is the First Cause of all secondary causes. The only God that can be proven to exist is a Creator of all there is. All other so-called gods, products of human invention, are unworthy of comparison to the true God. Even the Universe cannot be the cause of itself and therefore cannot be divine. So, there is no need to worship the world as if it were God. In contrast,

[104] Sir James Jeans, *The Mysterious Universe* (Cambridge, UK: Cambridge University Press, 1930), 137.

faith in a Creator God takes any divinity away from everything God has created. In short, God is divine, but the Universe is not.

This insight has quite some consequences. Only a world that has lost any divinity can be explored, investigated, and experimented upon. In the words of Bishop Robert Barron, "the world is not divine—and hence can be experimented upon rather than worshipped."[105] We are able and allowed to interrogate the Universe by investigation, exploration, and experiment, but also by using logic, reason, and philosophy. If the world itself were divine, we would not be permitted to "touch" the world, let alone put it to the test. Only a created world can be interrogated and explored.

It is hard, if not impossible, to deny that only this very Christian concept of a Creator God makes science possible. Belief in a Creator God entails that nature is not a divine but a created entity—which opens the door for scientific exploration. A created world, by definition, is not divine in itself: it is other than God, and in that very otherness, scientists find their freedom to act. A rational God has created a Universe that we can rely on with our rational minds, made in likeness of God's mind, and that we can put to the test in our experiments due to its built-in rationality.

The book of Wisdom says about God, "Thou hast arranged all things by measure and number and weight" (Wisd. 11:20). Hence the only way to find out what the Creator has actually done is to go out, look, and measure—which is a necessary condition for scientific exploration and experimentation. It's like putting the world to the test through "interrogation." It is through scientific experiments that we can "read" God's mind, so to speak. In contrast, if

[105] Bishop Robert Barron, "'Cosmos' and One More Telling of the Tired Myth," Word on Fire, March 18, 2014, https://www.wordonfire.org/articles/barron/cosmos-and-one-more-telling-of-the-tired-myth/.

the world itself is considered divine, then one would never allow oneself to analyze it, dissect it, or perform experiments upon it, and thus all incentives for doing science would be suppressed.

The general conclusion after all the above is that the assumptions science must entertain in order to do its work find their foundation in religious faith. Only religious faith can "prove" the very assumptions that science cannot prove on its own. In light of this, one might argue that all scientists keep living off Christian capital, whether they like to admit it or not. They borrow from Christianity what they themselves cannot provide.

d. Faith as the Cradle of Science

The previous section showed us that there would be no science without certain assumptions. It also showed that those assumptions could (at best) be explained as rooted in religious beliefs. As we found out, science cannot take credit for its own starting point. For science to get off the ground, it needs to make a series of assumptions that science itself cannot validate. It must assume that an external world exists, that it is both orderly and intelligible, that the human mind is reliable, and that scientific investigation, in the final analysis, will prove to be worth the effort.

One could even go much further than this and make the case that science could not have come forth at all without a belief in God. It is an essential part of the Christian view that the Universe is the creation of a rational intellect that is capable of being rationally interrogated by all human beings, including the scientists among them.

In contrast, nature remains an enigma so long as it is ruled by whimsical deities, chaotic powers, or our own man-made philosophical decrees and regulations. This view is detrimental for the rise of science. The physicist Fr. Stanley L. Jaki used the phrase "stillbirths of science" in reference to the ancient cultures of Egypt, China, India, Babylon, Greece, and Arabia.[106] Their cyclical worldviews—a "cosmic treadmill" in Jaki's words—prevented the breakthrough of science as a self-sustaining discipline. Jaki claimed that science—as a universal discipline where one discovery leads to another, and through which laws of physics and systems of laws were established—was born in the cradle of Christianity. In Jaki's words,

> Within the biblical world view it was ultimately possible to assume that the heavens and the earth are ruled by the same laws. But it was not possible to do this within the world vision that dominated all other ancient cultures. In all of them the heavens were divine.[107]

Although Aristotle, for example, did make a few significant discoveries, his classical Greek culture was unable to maintain and nurture further development. The ancient Greek world conceived of the Universe as a huge organism dominated by a pantheon of deities, and destined to go through endless cycles of birth, death, and rebirth. Aristotle taught that all things had a soul, so he thought that all motion is directed toward what the soul most desires. It was this animistic view of physics that led Aristotle to conclude that if two bodies were dropped from the same height on Earth, the one with twice the weight of the other one would fall twice as fast because it had twice the nature and twice the desire to seek its place.

The pagan culture Aristotle lived in obviously had taken its toll. If the world is controlled by the whim of animistic or pagan

---

[106] Stanley L. Jaki, A Mind's Matter: An Intellectual Autobiography (Grand Rapids, MI: Wm. B. Eerdmans, 2002), 51-52.

[107] Stanley L. Jaki, "The Biblical Basis of Western Science," Crisis 15, no. 9 (October 1997): 17-20.

powers, then there can be no real laws of nature to discover. The ancient ideas of an eternal, cycling, pantheistic, animistic world had to be abandoned before real science could emerge—and that was in Christian Europe. Only the Christian faith tells us that nature is to be investigated, not worshipped. Stanley Jaki again:

> Within the Greek ambiance it was impossible, in fact it would have been a sacrilege, to assume that the motion of the moon and the fall of an apple were governed by the same law. It was, however, possible for Newton, because he was the beneficiary of the age-old Christian faith.[108]

Something similar can be said about other non-Christian civilizations. When the first Jesuits went to China, they were amazed at the Asians' lack of progress in their understanding of the world and the heavens. These cultures did contribute talent and ingenuity, but scientific enterprise came to a standstill.

In the Muslim world, to use another example, Muslim mystics such as al-Ashari and al-Ghazali held that reference to laws of nature was a blasphemy against Allah's omnipotence.[109] Laws of nature would limit "Allah's freedom to act" whenever he wishes to act. Even the non-religious philosopher Bertrand Russell had to admit that Islamic science, while admirable in many technical ways, "was chiefly important as a preserver of ancient knowledge and transmitter to medieval Europe."[110] One could add to this that if Muslims did make some scientific discoveries, it was because they

---

[108]Jaki, "The Biblical Basis of Western Science."

[109]Stanley L. Jaki, *Science and Creation: From Eternal Cycles to an Oscillating Universe* (Edinburgh: Scottish Academic Press, 1986), chapter 9.

[110]Bertrand Russell, *History of Western Philosophy* (New York: Simon and Schuster, 1967), bk. 2, pt. 2, chap. 10.

had been influenced already by the Christian perception of the world during the centuries before Mohammed came along in the sixth and seventh centuries. Currently, they are still surrounded by Christian achievements in science.

There is more and more evidence that Christianity did indeed furnish the conceptual framework in which science could emerge and flourish. If that is true, then it would be dangerous for scientists to cut off the roots they came from. They would undermine their own foundation. Instead, they should respect and acknowledge where they came from. They should also be grateful for what the Catholic Church has done for science. Just as she patronized the arts, so did she vigorously support scientific research—perhaps not explicitly from the very beginning, but at least from the late Middle Ages on.

Many nowadays still have the false impression that the Catholic Middle Ages were "dark" ages that did not have any scientific activities. Nowadays it is common to distinguish the Dark Ages (ca. 500–ca. 1000) from the Middle Ages (ca. 1000–ca. 1500). The Dark Ages were certainly not "dark" because of the Catholic Church, but rather because of invading and rioting vandals. The only reason any science at all made it through these "dark" ages was because of the Catholic Church hiding all her textbooks from the rampaging and pillaging Huns, Vandals, Visigoths, and Vikings. Had it not been for the Catholic Church, all schools of learning would have perished during these Dark Ages.

During the Middle Ages, the positive influence of the Catholic Church would benefit the sciences even more. It is actually amazing how someone like the astronomer Carl Sagan, in one of his books, makes it look as if nothing happened in the natural sciences between AD 415 and AD 1543.[111] That can only be historical

---

[111] Especially in his book *Cosmos* (New York: Ballantine, 2013).

ignorance. It is becoming more and more evident, and has been accepted by a growing contingent of historians, that modern science was born in the Catholic cradle of the Middle Ages. The following list of some of its pioneer crafters testifies to this:

As early as the seventeenth century, the English Benedictine monk Bede studied the sea's tidal currents. At the end of the first millennium, Pope Sylvester II had already used advanced instruments of astronomical observation, driven by a passion for understanding the order of the Universe. He also endorsed and promoted study of mathematics and astronomy. All of these would be important tools for the advances of science.

During the Middle Ages, monasteries of that era, too, were very active in the study of medicine. As early as 633, the Council of Toledo required the establishment of a school in every diocese, teaching every branch of knowledge, including medicine. Then, around the year 800, the Emperor Charlemagne decreed that each monastery and cathedral chapter should establish a school; medicine was commonly taught in these schools. It was at one such school that the man who would become Pope Sylvester II taught medicine. Clergy were also active at the School of Salerno, the oldest medical school in Western Europe.

Famous physicians and medical researchers included the Abbot of Monte Cassino, Bertharius, the Abbot of Reichenau, Walafrid Strabo, and the bishop of Rennes, Marbodus of Angers. Notably, Hildegard of Bingen (1098–1179), a Doctor of the Church, is among the most distinguished of medieval Catholic women scientists. Hildegard wrote a text on the natural sciences, called *Physica*, as well as a text on *Causes and Cures* (*Causae et Curae*).

During this era, Bishop Robert Grosseteste introduced the scientific method, including the concept of falsification, while the Franciscan friar Roger Bacon established concepts such as hypothesis, experimentation, and verification. In other words, the scientific project, even the scientific method itself, was and is an invention of these Catholic pioneers.

Had it not been for the Catholic Church, the Scientific Revolution would most likely not have happened. After all, science did not take root in South America, Africa, the Middle East, or Asia—it took place in Christian Europe. It was during the Middle Ages that the first universities arose. The Middle Ages in Europe were of course Catholic, so these first universities of the world were Catholic universities. They were the hotbed for a period of great technological and scientific advancements, as well as achievements in nearly all other fields.

And more was coming. It is in fact revealing that the "Scientific Revolution" in the seventeenth century coincided with the period when Christian belief was at its strongest. It was in God that these scientists found reason to investigate nature and trust their own scientific reasoning. The founder of quantum physics, Max Planck, put it well: "It was not by accident that the greatest thinkers of all ages were deeply religious souls."[112]

Examples of such souls are Johannes Kepler, Isaac Newton, Blaise Pascal and, later, Fr. Gregor Mendel, Louis Pasteur, and Fr. George Lemaître. As argued before, science was born in the cradle of the Catholic Church, and could not have been born anywhere else—not in China, with its sophisticated society; not in India, with its philosophical schools; not in Arabia, with its advanced mathematics; not in Japan, with its dedicated craftsmen and technologies. It only flourished in Christian soil.

[112] Max Planck, "Religion and Natural Science," lecture given in 1937, in *Scientific Autobiography and Other Papers*, trans. Frank Gaynor (New York: Philosophical Library, 1949), 184.

No wonder many scientists have thanked the Catholic Church for this belief. The tweintieth-century physicist Pierre Duhem had to come to the conclusion that "the mechanics and physics of which modern times are justifiably proud ... [came] from doctrines professed in the heart of the medieval schools."[113] When the mathematician and philosopher Alfred North Whitehead told his Harvard audience in 1925 that modern science was a product of Christianity, they were surprised, out of mere ignorance. He pointed out to them, as he put it, that Christianity is the "mother of science" because of its "insistence on the rationality of God."[114]

The nuclear physicist J. Robert Oppenheimer, though not a Christian himself, also had to acknowledge that "Christianity was needed to give birth to modern science." The philosopher Alvin Plantinga agrees: "Modern science was conceived, and born, and flourished in the matrix of Christian theism."[115] Obviously, Christianity furnished the conceptual framework in which science could flourish. Even someone like the physicist Thomas Kuhn, who coined the term "paradigm shift," had to say about Europe that "No other place and time has supported the very special communities from with scientific productivity comes."[116]

[113] Quoted in David C. Lindbergh and Robert S. Westman, eds., *Reappraisals of the Scientific Revolution* (New York: Cambridge University Press, 1990), 14.

[114] Alfred North Whitehead, *Science and the Modern World: Lowell Lectures, 1925* (New York: Macmillan, 1947), 18.

[115] Alvin Plantinga, "Darwin, Mind and Meaning," Christian Faculty Forum, University of California Santa Barbara, May 1996, http://www.veritas-ucsb.org/library/plantinga/dennett.html.

[116] Thomas S. Kuhn, *The Structure of Scientific Revolutions* (Chicago: University of Chicago Press, 1962), 167.

A Catholic Scientist Harmonizes Science and Faith

After the Middle Ages, the Catholic Church became even more involved with the sciences, especially through the work of Jesuits. The historian Jonathan Wright, for instance, mentions the breadth of Jesuit involvement in the sciences. He says the Jesuits

> contributed to the development of pendulum clocks, pantographs, barometers, reflecting telescopes, and microscopes, to scientific fields as various as magnetism, optics, and electricity. They observed, in some cases before anyone else, the colored bands on Jupiter's surface, the Andromeda nebula and Saturn's rings. They theorized about the circulation of the blood (independently of Harvey), the theoretical possibility of flight, the way the moon effected the tides, and the wave-like nature of light. Star maps of the Southern Hemisphere, symbolic logic, flood-control measures on the Po and Adige rivers, introducing plus and minus signs into Italian mathematics—all were typical Jesuit achievements, and scientists as influential as Fermat, Huygens, Leibniz, and Newton were not alone in counting Jesuits among their most prized correspondents.[117]

To sum up this discussion, the creation of the university, the commitment to reason and rational argument, and the overall spirit of inquiry that characterized medieval intellectual life and had culminated in Aquinas's philosophy amounted to what the historian Edward Grant calls "a gift from the Latin Middle Ages to the modern world."[118] The modern world glories in its science

---

[117] Jonathan Wright, *God's Soldiers: Adventure, Politics, Intrigue, and Power—A History of the Jesuits* (New York: Image, 2004), 200.

[118] Edward Grant, *God and Reason in the Middle Ages* (New York: Cambridge University Press, 2001), 364.

which has allowed us to see to the very edge of the Universe, to the beginnings of time, and even to the invisible world that may be the very boundary marker between physics and metaphysics. It is this very gift St. Thomas Aquinas has given us that may in fact never be widely acknowledged. The evolutionary anthropologist and science writer Loren Eiseley summarizes this well:

> It is surely one of the curious paradoxes of history that science, which professionally has little to do with faith, owes its origins to an act of faith that the Universe can be rationally interpreted, and that science today is sustained by that assumption.[119]

When, in 1936, Pope Pius XI reestablished the Pontifical Academy of Sciences (originally founded in 1603) in order to support serious scientific study within the Catholic Church, he said in his *motu proprio,*

> Science, when it is real cognition, is never in contrast with the truth of the Christian faith. Indeed, as is well known to those who study the history of science, it must be recognized that the Roman Pontiffs and the Catholic Church have always fostered the research of the learned in the experimental field.[120]

The conclusion that science has Catholic roots has become hardly undeniable. After all we have seen, it should not take us by surprise anymore—as it did Whitehead's audience at Harvard—that

---

[119] Loren Eiseley, *Darwin's Century: Evolution and the Men Who Discovered It* (New York: Anchor, 1961), 62.
[120] Pius XI, *motu proprio In Multis Solaciis* (October 28, 1936), *Acta Apostolicae Sedis* 28, 1936, 427.

science could not have emerged without the impetus of religious faith. Yet it still seems to be the best kept secret for many people in modern society, including its scientists.

e. Scientific Knowledge Is Incomplete

Finally, we must point out that scientific knowledge is necessarily partial and incomplete. Not only is science unable to prove its own assumptions, but its scope is necessarily limited. Science can only tell us something about *one* aspect of the world: its scientific, material, quantifiable aspect. But that doesn't preclude the existence of other aspects and views. The domain of science is only one of the domains covered by what we know about ourselves and the world.

Even self-professed non-believers are aware of this fact. The positivistic philosopher Gilbert Ryle, for instance, had to acknowledge that there is a plurality of domains: "The nuclear physicist, the theologian, the historian, the lyric poet and the man in the street produce very different, yet compatible and even complementary pictures of one and the same 'world.'"[121] In other words, science provides only one of these pictures. Another "non-believer," the late University of California at Berkeley philosopher of science Paul Feyerabend, could say, "Science should be taught as one view among many and not as the one and only road to truth and reality."[122] Put in similar terms, science provides only one view and only one of the roads to truth and reality.

This is in stark contrast to what scientism claims, so we found out earlier. Science does not have answers to all our questions.

[121] Gilbert Ryle, *Dilemmas: The Tarner Lectures, 1953* (New York: Cambridge University Press, 1960), 68–69.
[122] Paul Feyerabend, *Against Method: Outline of an Anarchistic Theory of Knowledge* (New York: Verso Books, 1975), viii.

Many answers to our questions must come from somewhere else. Nevertheless, as Pope John Paul II put it, scientism "relegates religious, theological, ethical and aesthetic knowledge to the realm of mere fantasy."[123] What is crucial here in our discussion is that there is not only a domain of science but at least also a domain of religion and faith (and several others), which is certainly not a domain of mere fantasy. What we know through science is incomplete without what we know through religious faith.

That's a rather bold statement, many would reply. They perhaps do agree that science is (still) incomplete, as there are many scientific questions that have not been answered yet. But they will probably reject that there are questions science can never answer, and they certainly will rebuff questions about the *supernatural*. Their reason is most likely that the world is just a vast and complicated machine in which everything can be reduced to prior material and natural causes. Consequently, this calls for natural explanations, leaving no room for supernatural ones. This view declares, ahead of time, that there is nothing *outside* this system, so everything happening in this system must find its explanation *within* the system. However, that claim in itself is just something we do not *know* but can merely *believe*. It is a faith—scientism—which is a faith as much as any taught by religious believers. It is in fact a faith that is hostile to religious faith.

Even though many modern scientists are self-declared agnostics or atheists, a growing number of them are beginning to see that science does have a faith dimension, even up to the point of religious faith. One of them is the late nuclear physicist and Nobel laureate Werner Heisenberg, who once said: "The first drink from the cup of natural science makes atheistic but at the bottom of the cup,

---

[123] John Paul II, *Fides et Ratio*, no. 88.

God is waiting."[124] Remarkably enough, Pope Pius XII had said already in 1951 that "true science discovers God in an ever-increasing degree—as though God were waiting behind every door opened by science."[125] Indeed, in the words of G. K. Chesterton, science is racing toward the supernatural with the speed of an express train.[126]

And then there is Max Planck, who revolutionized physics with his quantum theory. It was his observation that "the greatest naturalists of all times, men like Kepler, Newton, Leibniz, were inspired by profound religiosity."[127] And then he goes on: "For the believer, God is the *beginning*, for the scientist He is the *end* of all reflections."[128] Interestingly enough, St. Thomas Aquinas had said something similar much earlier: "All our knowledge has its origin in sensation. But God is most remote from sensation. So he is not known to us first, but last."[129] Elsewhere, Planck says

All matter originates and exists only by virtue of a force which brings the particles of the atom to vibration. I must assume behind this force the existence of a conscious and intelligent mind. This mind is the matrix of all matter.[130]

[124]Quoted in Ulrich Hildebrand, "Das Universum—Hinweis auf Gott?," *Ethos* 10 (October 1988).

[125]Pius XII, Address to the Pontifical Academy of Sciences (November 22, 1951).

[126]Quoted in George Sim Johnston: "Belief and Unbelief I: Emile Zola at Lourdes." *Crisis*, December 1, 1989, https://www.crisismagazine.com/1989/belief-and-unbelief-i-emile-zola-at-lourdes/.

[127]Max Planck, *Religion und Example* (Leipzig: Joh. Ambrosius Barth, 1937), 332, my translation.

[128]Max Planck, "Religion and Natural Science," 184.

[129]Aquinas, *Disputed Questions on Truth*, q. 1, art. 11, my translation.

[130]Max Planck, "Das Wesen der Materie [The Nature of Matter]" (lecture, Florence, Italy, 1944), in *Archiv zur Geschichte der Max-Planck-Gesellschaft*, Abteilung Va, rep. 11 Planck, no. 1797.

The history of science shows us that in fact many scientists, through their belief in God, were inspired to investigate nature. Nicolaus Copernicus's achievements were heavily based on his religious belief that nothing was easier for God than to have the Earth move, if He so wished: "To know the mighty works of God, to comprehend His wisdom and majesty and power ... surely all this must be a pleasing and acceptable mode of worship to the Most High, to whom ignorance cannot be more grateful than knowledge."[131] Johannes Kepler's Christian faith told him God would not tolerate the inaccuracy of circular models of planetary movements in astronomy, so Kepler replaced circular orbits with elliptical orbits[132]—which made him exclaim, "Through my effort God is being celebrated in astronomy."[133] He also said, "God wanted us to recognize Him by creating us after His own image so that we could share in His own thoughts."[134]

More recently, Fr. George Lemaître spoke about the God of the big bang as the "One Who gave us the mind to understand him and to recognize a glimpse of his glory in our Universe which he has so wonderfully adjusted to the mental power with which he has endowed us."[135] Johannes Kepler had already beautifully summarized all of this, "The chief aim of all investigations of the external

---

[131] As quoted by Francis S. Collins, *The Language of God: A Scientist Presents Evidence for Belief* (New York: Free Press, 2006), 230-231.

[132] Johannes Kepler, *Astronomia Nova*, (Heidelberg: Gotthard Vögelin, 1609), chap. 19, 113-114.

[133] Johannes Kepler to Michael Maestlin, October 3, 1595.

[134] Johannes Kepler, Graz, April 9 and 10, 1599, in *Johannes Kepler Life and Letters*, ed. Carola Baumgardt (New York: Philosophical Library, 1953), 50.

[135] Georges Lemaître, *The Primeval Atom: An Essay on Cosmogony* (New York: D. Van Nostrand, 1950), 55.

world should be to discover the rational order and harmony which has been imposed on it by God."[136] Again, if the Creator can do whatever He likes, there is only one way to find out what God has actually done: interrogate nature by observation and experiment.

[136] Johannes Kepler, *De fundamentis astrologiae certioribus*, thesis 20.

5

Why Faith Needs Science

One cannot just believe anything one wishes to believe. Faith—even religious faith—requires scrutiny. It needs not only the test of reason but also the test of science. If science tells us that a certain belief cannot be true, we need to seriously question that belief, but obviously only after scrutinizing what science claims. If science is right on that issue, the belief one has as part of faith needs to be reassessed.

In other words, there are two sides to this. On the one hand, science can question the truth of certain religious beliefs. On the other hand, religious faith can question the truth of certain scientific claims as to whether they are indeed true. The reason for using this two-sided sword is rather simple: there is no such thing as "double truth." What do we mean by that?

a. No Double Truth

The issue of "double truth" has sometimes been caricaturized as living a "double life": honoring science and reason on weekdays, but faith and religion on Sundays. Of course, it's a travesty, as we said earlier, but it's widely popular among people who like to ridicule religious believers. The contrast painted in this parody is clear: religious believers live a schizophrenic life.

A Catholic Scientist Harmonizes Science and Faith

What's wrong with this picture? Well, the key question is this: Why should we believe *anything*—anything at all, whether it's in science or in faith or in philosophy or what have you? The only valid reason must be because it is *true*. Apparently, there are two key types of truth: religious truth as found in Scripture and scientific truth as found in nature. What unites both kinds of truth is truth itself. Truth is always true, whether you call it scientific or religious or philosophical or whatever.

Chesterton once made the assertion, "Truth exists whether we like it or not, and ... it is for us to accommodate ourselves to it."[137] It is beyond human control. Beliefs cannot change the truth. If the Earth is not flat, believing it is doesn't make it flat. Similarly, believing in a godless Universe cannot make God disappear. In either case we are dealing with truths and facts.

St. Thomas Aquinas explicitly dealt with this issue. He in fact rejected the idea of what Islamic philosophers had called "double truth," which meant that a notion could be true in faith and religion and, at the same time, false according to reason and science. Instead, Aquinas asserted that what we know through reason can never conflict with what we know through faith, and what we know through faith can never be in violation of what we know through reasoning. In his own words, "[The] truth that the human reason is naturally endowed to know cannot be opposed to the truth of the Christian faith."[138] These two sources of information can never contradict each other—so long as we understand them correctly.

---

[137] G. K. Chesterton, *Illustrated London News*, June 8, 1907.
[138] Thomas Aquinas, *Summa contra Gentiles, Book One: God*, trans. Anton C. Pegis, F.R.S.C. (Notre Dame, IN: University of Notre Dame Press, 1975), chap. 7.

This view must also be applied to the twosome of religion and science. What is true in science cannot be false in religion, and what is true in religion cannot be false in science. If there ever arises a conflict between these two, then one of them must be wrong, or perhaps both. It remains tempting, though, to mitigate this rule. It was tried by some, for instance, in speaking of a "lesser" truth, claiming that the Earth circled the Sun, as Copernicus claimed, and a "greater" truth, which says that when Joshua fought at Jericho it was the Sun, not the Earth, which stood still. However, even seen this way, we still have a case of double truth here, and therefore this solution must be rejected. One cannot claim that both "truths" are true in their own sphere, for that would still amount to a case of double truth.

Perhaps a few examples may demonstrate how important the rejection of "double truth" is. Since there are truths of science as well as truths of faith—which can never contradict each other—it cannot be that the Earth is flat according to faith and religion, but at the same time spherical according to reason and science, for that would create a contradiction. In a similar way, if science tells us that the Earth circles the Sun, it cannot be that faith has the Sun circle the Earth. But also, faith or Scripture cannot tell us that the plants were created on the third day before the Sun on the fourth day, whereas science tells us that plants cannot exist without light from the Sun. In all such cases we are dealing with contradictions which cannot both be true at the same time. Again, when we do detect a "double truth," either one or both must have been claimed in error and must be reevaluated.

One word of caution, though. Sometimes we might think we have a double-truth issue, when in fact we do not. For instance, creation as understood by faith and evolution as understood by science do not contradict each other. Creation is about how secondary causes are related to God, the First Cause, whereas evolution deals with how secondary causes are related to each other through reproduction and natural selection. No "double truth" here.

Something similar can be said about the big bang theory in science and the Creation account in faith. The big bang account is about how events are related to each other, whereas the Creation account is about how events are related to God. So, we do not need to make a choice between two truths in these cases because there is no problem of "double truth" here either. They are not in conflict with each other and do not contradict each other, and therefore can be true together.

How important the rejection of "double truth" is can be shown when we weigh it against contrary views. Some believers (like Martin Luther in his more excitable moments) claim that faith at all times trumps reason. Others have held—especially so nowadays—that science must always trump faith if religion is to apply in the modern world. Contrary to these views, St. Thomas claims that the truths of faith and religion must agree with the truths of reason and science, because God is the author of both, and so any apparent conflict shows that we have failed to understand one or the other or both.

Truth is truth, even if you do not accept it; and untruth is untruth, even if you claim it. Truth is truth—for everyone, anywhere, at any time, no matter whether it is in faith or in science. Knowledge is about reality, not about knowledge. To know is to know things in the real world, not to know mental abstractions in the mind. Either we conform our minds to reality, or we shape reality to conform to our thinking. St. Thomas tells us that we must choose the former, not the latter.

The *Catechism of the Catholic Church* summarizes all of this well: "Though faith is above reason, there can never be any real discrepancy between faith and reason. Since the same God who reveals mysteries and infuses faith has bestowed the light of reason on the human mind, God cannot deny himself, nor can truth ever contradict truth" (CCC 159).

In his address to a group of U.S. bishops visiting Rome, Pope John Paul II expressed very clearly that he wished to defend the capacity of human reason to know the truth:

> The result [of the closure of reason to objective truth] has been a pervasive skepticism and relativism, which have not led to a more 'mature' humanity but to much despair and irrationality.... Confidence in reason is an integral part of the Catholic intellectual tradition, but it needs reaffirming today in the face of widespread and doctrinaire doubt about our ability to answer the fundamental questions: Who am I? Where have I come from and where am I going? Why is there evil? What is there after this life?[139]

Cardinal Joseph Ratzinger, during a homily just before he became Pope Benedict XVI, spoke in the same vein when he declared the "dictatorship of relativism" to be the greatest problem of our time because of its claim that mutually opposed viewpoints can be equally legitimate.[140] This view elevates the will of individuals and their opinions over what reality tells us. It undermines reality as the determining factor of whether the Earth is flat or not, for instance. Not what we want reality to be but what reality *is*, that is the crux of the matter. If the Earth is not flat, then there is no way to legitimately claim that the Earth is *really* flat, not even in religion.

---

[139] John Paul II, Address to the Bishops of the Episcopal Conference of the United States of America (October 24, 1998), 5.

[140] Cardinal Joseph Ratzinger, Homily *Pro Eligendo Romano Pontifice*, Vatican Basilica (April 18, 2005).

b. Science Can Do What Faith Cannot

So far, we have tried to make it lucidly clear, and I hope convincingly clear, that the faith-alone approach is unsustainable as it eliminates the role of reason in religion. Fideism is unreasonable and irrational, we said earlier. St. Thomas Aquinas is very definite in defending that when something is against reason, God cannot create it.[141]

Aquinas is so adamant on this issue because God is reason himself, so He cannot go against His own nature by doing what is contradictory. He could not have written more clearly about what this entails when he wrote, "When anyone in the endeavor to prove the faith brings forward reasons which are not cogent, he falls under the ridicule of the unbelievers: since they suppose that we stand upon such reasons, and that we believe on such grounds."[142]

Not only did we find out that reason does and must play an important role in faith and religion, but we also discussed that it does and must play an equally important role in science. However, the role of reason is different in both cases. In faith and religion, on the one hand, reason is needed to ensure that religious beliefs are tested for not being false, irrational, illogical, or contradictory. Otherwise they cannot be true. In science, on the other hand, reason is needed specifically to ensure that hypotheses are tested for observational implications so they can lead us to confirmation or falsification. Otherwise they cannot be known to be true.

But there is one more issue that needs to be addressed in this context. Although faith requires reason, it also needs science in order to make sure that religion remains anchored in reality. Science tells us things we could never have discovered by faith alone.

[141] Aquinas, *De Aeternitate Mundi*, 1, 4.
[142] Aquinas, *The Summa Theologiae of St. Thomas*, I, q. 32, art. 1.

This raises the question as to what science can and must do for faith and religion. Let's discuss at least five reasons why faith needs science and should not live without it.

#1: Science Gives Faith Eyes

As Albert Einstein once said, "Religion without science is blind." How right he was. Without the "eyes" of science, faith may easily become detached from reality and lead to errors and superstition. Science must always question faith, so that faith doesn't become blind. This idea has been expressed in several ways.

The Catholic Faith should heed Augustine's warning that it is "dangerous to have an infidel hear a Christian ... talking nonsense."[143] St. Thomas Aquinas is often quoted as saying, "The faith is made ridiculous to the unbeliever when a simple-minded believer asserts as an article of faith that which is demonstrably false."[144] By "demonstrably false," he means false based on reason or false based on science (although science was still poorly developed at his time).

It is through the eyes of science that we know the Earth is not in the center of the Universe. It is through the eyes of science that we know the world is more than ten thousand years old. It is through the "eyes" of science that we know the world is made of atoms, molecules, and cells. To ignore or reject all of this in faith would change faith into a form of blind faith, which embarrasses believers and their creed.

There are also some branches of Christianity that one might call "blind" to reality. What comes to mind are certain forms of

---

[143] Augustine, *The Literal Meaning of Genesis*, bk. 1, chap. 20, my translation.
[144] Aquinas, *De Potentia Dei*, q. 4, art. 1, ad. 8.

fundamentalism that reject almost all commonly accepted scientific discoveries and insights on grounds we must consider highly questionable. To dispute the scientifically accepted age of the Universe based on religious grounds is basically a form of "blind faith" that comes close to fideism.

#2: Science Purifies Faith

As Pope John Paul II once said, "Science can purify religion from error and superstition."[145] It is rather obvious that science can protect us from superstition, for without science, religion may easily lead to superstitious beliefs in astrology, alchemy, horoscopes, and mediums. Science can be an important tool to protect religious people from such erroneous or dangerous beliefs that merely appear to be religious but are in fact mere irrational beliefs.

It is equally true that religion does not know anything about molecules, cells, hormones, enzymes, stars, brains, computers, and so on. Religion depends on science for discoveries like these, as it does not have the tools to learn more about these scientific issues. As a matter of fact, science and technology have given religious people the tools to be God's "co-workers" on earth. Without the input of science, religion could easily lose its anchor in this world. In other words, science keeps faith in its place—for that is where it belongs.

As a matter of fact, often it is in the very interaction between science and faith that we can discover what the true nature of either one is. A telling case is the conflict between Galileo and the

[145]John Paul II to George V. Coyne, S.J., Director of the Vatican Observatory, June 1, 1988, in Robert J. Russell, *John Paul II on Science and Religion: Reflections on the New View from Rome* (Rome: Vatican Observatory Publications, 1990), 82.

Church. There are several reasons why things went wrong between the Church and Galileo. Here are just a few.

Reason #1 for the ensuing conflict was that Galileo had become highly embroiled in various controversies with Jesuit astronomers. One dispute was with the eminent Jesuit mathematician and astronomer Fr. Horazio Grassi over the nature of comets. Although we now know that Galileo was on the wrong side of the argument, his irony and wit took their toll on his opponents. Another dispute he had was with Fr. Christopher Scheiner, about the priority of the discovery of sunspots. (Scholars now believe that neither man was the first.) Undoubtedly, controversies like these helped cement the Jesuits' opposition to Galileo. Initially, he had powerful friends among cardinals, Jesuits, and even popes, but in time, he would lose their support—not so much as a result of scientific disputes, but mostly because of the frequency and acidity of his attacks. All these factors played an important role in causing many Jesuits to withdraw their support of Galileo—which he later would need so badly. What irked Church officials was not so much *what* Galileo was saying, but *how* he was saying it.

Reason #2 for the upcoming conflict with the Church was Galileo's ideological intent on ramming heliocentrism down the throat of Christendom. The ideologist in him was so convinced of the truth of heliocentrism that he refused to present his theory as a tentative hypothesis at the time instead of established truth, until further proof could be given. He completely refused to even mention an equally viable alternative, Tycho Brahe's model. As a good scientist, he should at least have mentioned Tycho's alternative.

But Galileo did not. He was an early instance of that very modern type: the activist scientist. He had taken on a sacred mission and was determined that all of Europe should buy into his heliocentric model, starting with the Church.

The Church had no objection to the use of the heliocentric system as a *hypothesis* whose truth was not yet established. Most astronomers, at the time, saw the heliocentric system as just another way of doing astronomical calculations, not as a claim about which bodies in the heavens are in actual motion. Galileo, however, believed his model to be literally true, even though he lacked adequate evidence to support the physical truth of his theory at the time.

Perhaps the head of the Roman Inquisition, Cardinal Robert Bellarmine, expressed this best in a letter to Galileo's friend Foscarini,

> If there were a real proof that the Sun is in the center of the universe ... then we should have to proceed with great circumspection in explaining passages of Scripture which appear to teach the contrary.... But as for myself, I shall not believe that there are such proofs until they are shown to me.[146]

Reason #3 for the upcoming collision between Galileo and the Church was another important development. Despite the warnings of his friends in Rome, Galileo insisted on moving the debate from the scientific arena onto theological grounds. When certain theologians objected that his theory seemed contrary to Scripture, he entered, with no real expertise, into a theological discussion on the proper mode of interpreting Scripture. In those days, if you argued a new *scientific* theory, you would get the Church's attention and even support, because so many high-ranking churchmen were also men of science, so you would be arguing on equal footing.

On the other hand, if you ventured to argue a new *scriptural* interpretation, as Galileo did, you immediately got the whole Church

---

[146] James Brodrick, *The Life and Work of Blessed Robert Francis Cardinal Bellarmine. 1542–1621*, vol. 1 (New York: P. J. Kenedy, 1928), 267–297.

on her feet, and you would no longer be arguing on equal footing. We need to realize that, at the time, there was precious little elasticity in Catholic biblical theology, because the Church had just gone through the bruising battles of the Protestant Reformation. Times had changed: whereas Copernicus's heliocentrism, almost a century earlier, had hardly received any negative response from the Church, Galileo published his books at a time the Church was facing theological turbulence. One of the chief quarrels with the Protestants was over the private interpretation of Scripture—and here was another private interpretation, this time by a scientist. Galileo had taken it upon himself to interpret Scripture according to his own "private insights." His friend Cardinal Piero Dini warned him that he could write freely so long as he "kept out of the sacristy."[147]

How should we assess this conflict in hindsight? Without new developments in science, we would probably not have been able to get a clearer view of how science and religion each have a different approach in a case like this. When Pope John Paul II held a conference in 1983, celebrating the 350th anniversary of the publication of Galileo's *Dialogue Concerning the Two Chief World Systems*, he remarked that the experience of the Galileo case had led the Church "to a more mature attitude and a more accurate grasp of the authority proper to her," enabling her better to distinguish between "essentials of the faith" and the "scientific systems of a given age."[148] The pontiff called Galileo's run-in with the Church

---

[147] James Brodrick, *Robert Bellarmine—Saint and Scholar* (Westminster, MD: Newman Press, 1961), 373; see also Giorgio De Santillana, *Crime of Galileo* (Chicago: University of Chicago Press, 1955), 44.

[148] John Paul II, Address to an International Symposium on the Occasion of the 350th Anniversary of the Publication of Galileo's *Dialogue Concerning the Two Chief World Systems* (May 9, 1983).

a "tragic mutual incomprehension" in which both sides were at fault. Although both Galileo and the Church were at fault at the time, they also both learned from this experience.

#3: Science Lets God Be God

God created a world of secondary causes which follow God's laws of nature for their operation. The law of gravity, for instance, prevents us from falling off the Earth and makes sure planets revolve around the Sun in elliptical orbits. It does not require constant interventions by God to make all of this happen. The First Cause created secondary causes in such a way that they have become causes of their own. These secondary causes are the causes studied by science. Without science, we would hardly know anything about the laws of nature which regulate what we see happening in this world.

Well, the Universe is bound to follow its God-given laws of nature, for the laws of nature must operate as they do. As St. Thomas Aquinas put it, "It was in God's wisdom to ordain not to be responsible for all contingent events."[149] Because secondary causes follow laws of nature, their effects are the way they are. Most of the time, the outcome is good for us, but sometimes it's not—such as a falling stone hitting your head or an earthquake destroying your home.

The point we are making here is that, thanks to what science has discovered, God is no longer directly "responsible" for all effects caused by secondary causes. Apparently, these causes can have good or bad effects. As the philosopher Michael Augros puts it: "If secondary causes, unlike the Primary [First] Cause, are not infallible, if they are defective, then we might well blame them, rather

[149] *Summa Theologiae* I, q. 22, art. 2.

than the first cause, for any flaws we find (or think we find)."[150] Science takes God "off the hook," so to speak—it lets God be God, and lets secondary causes be causes of their own. Letting God be God prevents us from degrading God to a secondary cause directly responsible for its effects.

In this context, it's important to make a distinction between what God *wills* and what God *allows*. St. Thomas says that God "neither wills evil to be done, nor wills it not to be done, but wills to permit evil to be done."[151] God does not will earthquakes, but He allows them when they are a consequence of the laws of nature—in the same way as God does not will wars but allows them when humans use their free will to start them. In other words, there is God's positive or *providential* will, and then there is God's *permissive* will. Consequently, not everything that happens in this Universe is directly willed by God. To say that God "allows" or "permits" bad or evil effects does not mean that He sanctions them in the sense that He approves of them, let alone wants or directly causes them.

Doesn't this mean God is at the mercy of secondary causes and their laws of nature? Or is God still the God who oversees everything that happens in the world—all-powerful and all-knowing? Faith is very definite on this issue: God is the One in charge. How can this be if secondary causes come with their own law, their own order? Well, think of what we, as human beings, can do with secondary causes and their laws of nature. We can still manipulate them to our own needs and for our own purposes, without being at their mercy. We can't change or violate laws of nature, but we can still direct them in such a way that their outcome is as we intended.

---

[150] Augros, *Who Designed the Designer?*, 103.
[151] Aquinas, *The Summa Theologiae of St. Thomas*, I, q. 19, art. 9, reply to objection 3.

We do so constantly in life. We use our knowledge, obtained through science, to produce electricity, to make machines work for us, to vaccinate for infections, to make medications, and the list goes on and on. So, why couldn't God do something similar, but then in an even much more comprehensive way?

Science lets God be God. Ultimately, it is God who is the origin of everything that happens in this world.

#4: Science and Faith Challenge Each Other

Earlier we made a distinction between the truths of science and the truths of faith. Another way of distinguishing between these two kinds of truths is to follow Benedict XVI, who urged us to see "nature as a book whose author is God in the same way that Scripture has God as its author."[152] So, we have these two books before us: a book of Scripture, which holds the truths of faith, and a book of nature, which holds the truths of science.

The origin of this distinction can be found in the following words of St. Augustine: "It is the divine page that you must listen to; it is the book of the Universe that you must observe."[153] This conviction was a belief shared in the past by many other Christian thinkers: from early apologists and Fathers to St. Basil; from St. Gregory of Nyssa to St. Augustine, from St. Albert the Great to St. Thomas Aquinas, from Roger Bacon to William of Ockham.

How are we to read these two books? Science knows how to read the book of nature, whereas the Church knows how to read the book of Scripture. These two books complement each other, for they have the same Author—a match made in Heaven, so to speak. To set them up against each other creates a false dichotomy.

---

[152] Address to the Pontifical Academy of Science (October 31, 2008).
[153] Augustine, *Enarrationes in Psalmos*, 45, 7.

As Cardinal Baronius said to Galileo, "The Bible teaches us how to go to heaven, not how the heavens go."[154] In order to find out more about God, we need to read the book of Scripture; to find out more about the Universe, we need to read the book of nature. Scientific, natural truths can be found in the book of nature, whereas religious, supernatural truths come from the book of Scripture. Pope John Paul II makes a similar distinction:

> It may help, then, to turn briefly to the different modes of truth. Most of them depend upon immediate evidence or are confirmed by experimentation. This is the mode of truth proper to everyday life and to scientific research. At another level we find philosophical truth, attained by means of the speculative powers of the human intellect. Finally, there are religious truths which are to some degree grounded in philosophy, and which we find in the answers which the different religious traditions offer to the ultimate questions.[155]

There is an important caveat, however. We should never read the book of Scripture as if it were the book of nature, or vice-versa. Scientific discoveries and research have helped us enormously to get a better and better reading of the book of nature. But reading the book of Scripture does not tell us how the heavens go, nor does reading the book of nature tell us how to go to Heaven. As it turns out, science in itself is incomplete, and religion (as we use the word) doesn't offer a comprehensive compendium of all there

---

[154] This remark, which Baronius probably made in conversation with Galileo, was cited in Galileo's 1615 letter to the Grand Duchess Christina.

[155] John Paul II, *Fides et Ratio*, no. 30.

is to know. That's why we need both books together. We need faith *and* reason, religion *and* science.

In this discussion, we find an interesting case of how important terminology is. Faith tells us that God created the Universe out of nothing, whereas science tells us how God created the Universe. The "nothing" proclaimed by faith is meant to stress that God did not make the Universe out of something else. The Universe was nonexistent until God brought the Universe into existence. So, don't confuse the term "nothing" used in faith with similar-looking terms used in science, terms such as "vacuum," "emptiness," "annihilation," "vacuum fluctuation," or "quantum tunneling."

The best way to explain the difference between these two very distinct terminologies or vocabularies is using the distinction St. Thomas Aquinas makes between "producing" (*facere*) and "creating" (*creare*).[156] Most people use these two terms interchangeably, but Aquinas teaches us to clearly separate them, for clarity's sake and to avoid contradictions and conflicts. Science is about "producing" something from something else—it is about changes taking place in this Universe. Creation, on the other hand, is about "creating" something from nothing—which is not a change at all; certainly not a change from "nothing" to "something."

St. Thomas puts it this way: "To create is, properly speaking, to cause or produce the being of things."[157] In other words, God the Creator doesn't just take pre-existing stuff and fashion it, as does the Demiurge in Plato's *Timaeus*. Nor does He use some something called "nothing" and then create the Universe out of that. Rather, God calls the Universe into existence without using pre-existing

---

[156] Aquinas, *De Symbolo Apostolorum*, 33.
[157] Aquinas, *The Summa Theologiae of St. Thomas*, I, q. 45, art. 6.

space, matter, time, or anything else. Creation is about producing the very being and existence of things.

Therefore, we should keep in mind that the term "nothing" has a very specific philosophical and theological meaning. Someone like Woody Allen missed that point completely when he joked, "In the beginning, there was nothing. And God said, 'Let there be light.' And there was light. There was still nothing, but you could see it a lot better."

Now we should also be better equipped to avoid some common confusion. Whereas religion is about "creating" something from nothing, science is about "producing" something from something else. Consider the words of the English physicist and Anglican priest John C. Polkinghorne. "When quantum cosmologists gaily characterize their inflated vacuum fluctuation as being the scientific equivalent of *creatio ex nihilo*," Dr. Polkinghorne says, "a quantum vacuum is not *nihil*, for it is structured by the laws of quantum mechanics and the equations of the quantum fields involved."[158]

To explain the difference, Stephen Barr uses the analogy of having a bank account with no money in it: even if we have "nothing" in the bank, we still have a bank account, with all that comes with it, but it happens to be in a "no-money state" for us. This kind of "nothing" is different from having no bank account at all.[159] So we certainly don't have a double truth issue here—rather a very different, twofold terminology or conception.

What we can learn from this is that religion and science do need each other, because there are at least two sides to the story. The two sides are incomplete on their own. One cannot replace the other.

---

[158] John Polkinghorne, *Science and Theology* (Minneapolis: Fortress Press, 1998), 80.
[159] Barr, *Modern Physics and Ancient Faith*, 277–278.

On the one hand, science could never silence religion, for there's no scientific proof that science is the only way to prove things. On the other hand, religion could never silence science, for there is no religious proof that religion is the only way to prove things.

#5: Faith and Science: Two Different Accounts

When faith and science do seem to be in conflict with each other—I mean causing really contradictory claims, not only a matter of a different terminology—either one or both of them must be wrong as we found out earlier. This stand has quite some consequences. It means first of all that the book of Scripture cannot be read as a book of nature, nor reversed. Reading the book of nature as if it contradicts the book of Scripture makes for a serious conflict that should not be.

Take, for instance, what we said earlier: faith tells us *that* God is the Creator of the Universe, but it does not tell us *how* God created the Universe. To read Scripture as a description of *how* God created the world is bound to crash with the description science gives us based on reading the book of nature. That's a very common source of conflicts between science and faith.

Here is a striking example. Reading the book of Scripture as if it were the book of nature made James Ussher (1581–1656), the Anglican Archbishop of Armagh in the Church of Ireland, calculate a chronology of the history of the world based on data he had gathered from the book of Scripture. Based on a literal reading of the Old Testament, Ussher deduced that the first day of creation began at nightfall on Saturday, October 22, 4004 BC.[160]

Science has come up with an entirely different calculation and timescale. Astrophysics estimates the big bang happened

---

[160]James Ussher, *Annals of the World*, 1.

approximately 13.8 billion years ago, which is thus considered the age of the Universe. Astronomy tells us the age of the Earth is 4.5 billion years, based on evidence from radiometric age dating of meteorite material. Geology adds to this that we find on all of Earth's continents ancient rocks exceeding 3.5 billion years in age. And paleontology shows us that fossils range enormously in age, and can be up to 3.48 billion years old, or even as old as 4.1 billion years.

There is an enormous difference between these two accounts and their timescales. Which one is right? There is no way these two accounts can be reconciled for they tell us truths that conflict with each other. However, there is not a real conflict here because the book of Scripture is about the fact *that* God created this Universe, whereas the book of nature is about *how* God created the Universe. There is no conflict here, no double truth, because both "books" answer different questions, using a different vocabulary. Ussher didn't seem to realize that the book of Scripture is not a history book or a science textbook.

What can we learn from this? Because science can read the book of nature much better than religion can, science can tell us things that faith cannot tell us. St. Augustine could not have said it more clearly: "It not infrequently happens that something about the Earth, about the sky ... about the nature of animals, of fruits, of stones, and of other such things, may be known with the greatest certainty by reasoning or by experience, even by one who is not a Christian."[161] That's why scientists—even if they are not of the Christian faith—can tell us much more about the age of the Universe and the age of the Earth than the book of Scripture ever could achieve.

[161] Augustine, *The Literal Meaning of Genesis*, bk. 1, chap. 19.

In a case like this, the seeming conflict between the two books can easily be solved if both parties respect each other's authority. In the previous case, it was hard for religion, at least for some of its members, to accept the account given by science. Sometimes, the situation is reversed. A case in point is the distinction between body and soul. Reading the book of nature seems to suggest that the body regulates what we think and do, specifically through the working of the *brain*—that is, through genes, neurons, and the like.

However, that particular reading might be just one part of the story. The book of Scripture would add to this that our thinking and acting are also under control of the human soul, working through its intellectual part, the mind. Isn't that a conflict situation, you might ask—a conflict between body and soul, or mind and brain? Indeed, for many scientists it is. They claim that the soul is just another word for the body's vital processes, and that the mind is just another word for the brain. So, they basically solve the conflict by eliminating the role of the soul and its mind, and thus limiting themselves to one kind of terminology.

The problem is, though, that this "solution" obscures or ignores the fact that these terms come from two different perspectives, and therefore come with two different vocabularies. Studying the *body* makes perfect sense in the context of the book of nature. Science studies bodies and how they follow laws of nature—how they came along during evolution, how they come from genes, how they interact with the brain and its neurons, and so forth. But the *soul* doesn't do any of these; neither does the mind. Souls don't come from genes or evolution, and the mind doesn't come from the brain. True, matter can evolve. But the human soul is immaterial and therefore cannot evolve.

Consequently, we didn't inherit our souls from our parents or from some non-human ancestors, and our souls certainly didn't come with our DNA or through the umbilical cord. Science knows nothing about soul or mind, and religion on its own knows basically nothing about body or evolution. But together they tell us a more comprehensive story.

Because of all of this, science and religion tell us two different, yet equally important, stories about humanity and its history. For this reason, Chesterton once acknowledged the possibility that man's "body may have been evolved from the brutes," but he adds emphatically that "we know nothing of any such transition that throws the smallest light upon his soul as it has shown itself in history."[162] He says elsewhere, "There may be a broken trail of stones and bones faintly suggesting the development of the human body. There is nothing even faintly suggesting such a development of this human mind."[163] In other words, there is a deep divide between the two. In the words of Pope John Paul II, "The moment of passage into the spiritual realm is not something that can be observed with research in the fields of physics and chemistry."[164]

In other words, neither the soul nor the mind are part of the biological domain and vocabulary—or to put it briefly, the soul is not the body, and the mind is not the brain. If they were indeed identical, we would run into trouble. As the neurologist Viktor Frankl put it, while the brain conditions the mind, it does not give rise to it.[165] In plain words, the brain does not secrete thoughts

---

[162] G. K. Chesterton, *The Everlasting Man* (New York: Dodd, Mead, 1926), 28.

[163] Chesterton, *The Everlasting Man*, 22.

[164] John Paul II, Message to the Pontifical Academy of Sciences (October 22, 1996).

[165] Viktor Frankl, in a discussion of J. R. Smythies's paper, "Some Aspects of Consciousness," in *Beyond Reductionism*, ed. Arthur Koestler and J. R. Smythies (London: Hutchinson, 1969), 254.

like the pancreas secretes hormones. If thoughts were merely a product of the brain, then thoughts about the brain would also be merely a product of the brain. This inevitably leads us into a vicious circle. Therefore, the mind must be more than, or at least different from, the brain—there must be more to the mind, which is the intellectual part of the soul, than just the brain, which is merely a biological part of the body.

What we are using in this discussion again is the logical method of reasoning called *reductio ad absurdum*. The idea that the mind is "nothing other than," or identical to, the brain leads to absurd or contradictory consequences. First of all, the brain cannot study itself, but needs the mind to do so. It is hard to see how the brain could study itself; that would be like a camera taking a picture of itself on its own. Second, if the mind were the same as the brain, then thoughts could never be right or wrong and true or false. The brain on its own is not capable of telling false thoughts apart from true beliefs in the mind. Third, if the mind were just the brain, its thoughts would be as fragile as the molecules they are supposedly based on—it would be sitting on a "swamp of molecules," unable to pull itself up by its own bootstraps. Fourth, denying the existence of mental activities is in itself a mental activity, and thus would lead to contradiction. Ironically, one cannot deny the mental without somewhat affirming it. And there are probably more absurd or contradictory consequences to the idea that the mind is the same as the brain.

Now, what is the bottom line of all we discussed and discovered here? If we are looking for a key to understanding ourselves as human beings, then it will not only be in terms of matter and brain, but must also be in terms of mind and soul. The brain is governed by laws of physics, chemistry, and biology, but thoughts are not. As Stephen Barr pithily puts it, "We do not infer the existence *of* our minds, rather we infer the existence of everything else *with* our minds. To put it another way: the brain does not infer the existence of the mind, the mind infers the existence of the brain."[166]

So, put in more general terms, we are dealing here with two different kinds of truths—truths we know by "reading" the book of nature as well as truths we know by "reading" the book of Scripture. Together, these two different kinds of truths make for a more comprehensive story about this world. But what they both have in common is that they must go through the test of reason and cannot contradict each other.

However, we can only use reason and reasoning if we have *faith* that the world itself is open to reason and that there are laws of logic which correctly prescribe the correct chain of reasoning. Since laws of logic cannot be observed with the senses, our confidence in them is a form of faith—not necessarily a religious kind of faith, but faith it is. Besides, when we come to a logical conclusion by reasoning, we can only do so by starting with premises that we accept on faith, trust, or authority.

In short, people must *believe* something before they can *know* something. All human knowledge is dependent on some form of faith, so we found out: faith in our senses, faith in our premises, faith in in the power of reason, faith in our memories, and faith in the accounts of events we receive from others. Rejecting faith entirely undermines all that we claim to know. In other words, faith is at the basis of all our doing, thinking, and knowing. We could not live without faith. We could even argue that all forms of faith are ultimately based upon faith in God. Without faith in God, everything else would completely collapse.

[166] Barr, *Modern Physics and Ancient Faith*, 188.

If indeed we cannot live without faith, it is rather discomforting to see that some people have come to believe we can. They call themselves *agnostics* or *atheists*. So, we should ask them and ourselves as to how anyone could ever say no to faith in God. Let's find out.

6

Could Anyone Say No to Faith in God?

After all we have seen about how science and faith can live in harmony, the question becomes even more pressing: if there is indeed such a striking harmony between science and faith in God, then how can people say no to faith in God?

It is hard to accept that disbelief, for there are so many "pointers" to God in science, as we found out. Besides, the proofs of God's existence are extremely compelling and have never been seriously or conclusively invalidated or refuted. Yet, these proofs have been ignored or even rejected by those who say no to faith in God. It looks like a mindboggling inconsistency. But let's face it: you don't lose your faith overnight. It's usually a long process of growing farther and farther away from what you once believed in.

A relatively large group among these non-believers call themselves *agnostics*. They don't accept faith in God, but they do so in a rather cautious manner. There might be several reasons why these people decide to consider themselves agnostics. Perhaps some have studied the compelling proofs of God's existence only briefly or superficially, so they may have missed important conditions and wordings in the premises. Perhaps some have no interest in proofs of God's existence and therefore never felt the need to study the evidence that points to God. Of course, there might be other issues than religion one may not be interested in—for instance, when it comes to the existence of flying saucers or extraterrestrial life—because it takes time to study such issues or to weigh the arguments pro and con.

Whatever their reason is for ignoring the proofs of God's existence and the power of pointers to God, the fact remains that many people do lead a life without faith in God, don't know if God exists, don't want to know if God exists, or else vehemently deny that there is a God. How is that possible?

There is no meaning in a meaningless Universe—that is to say, in a Universe without God. If there is no God, then we are alone in this Universe. That's basically a view that all people who say no to God must accept. Our view of the Universe determines how we live our lives.

a. Can One Really Reject Faith in God?

If the arguments for God's existence are indeed so compelling and conclusive as we've suggested, then how can one deny or even reject them? The answer is that we are not only dealing here with reason and logic. There might very well be another player on the scene: it's the human *will*.

In other words, often agnosticism, and even more so atheism, may very well not be a rational conclusion but rather a matter of choice and preference. What we often see in the lives of agnostics and atheists is some kind of disconnect between what they know and what they choose to know. St. Thomas Aquinas was very aware of this disconnect: "Hence the cause of unbelief is in the will, while unbelief itself is in the intellect."[167]

---

[167] Aquinas, *The Summa Theologiae of St. Thomas*, II-II, q. 10, art. 2, reply to objection 2.

No matter how strong the empirical and rational evidence is in favor of God's existence, some atheists decide not to accept God's existence as a fact because they don't like the way the world looks to them with God in the picture. They are like those who know that certain habits of drinking, smoking, or eating are unhealthy, yet they don't want to acknowledge it and keep nursing their bad habits despite the ill effects to their health. It is the will, says Blaise Pascal, which "turns away the mind from considering the qualities of all that it does not like to see."[168] The Psalmist puts it this way: "O that today you would hearken to his voice! Harden not your hearts" (Ps. 95:7–8). Instead of worshipping the real God, people who say no to faith in God prefer to worship their own gods instead—gods such as materialism, scientism, evolutionism, and the like—and they dig into their position.

Even the best arguments won't work for those who are unwilling to listen to them. Atheists often do not will what they know, but they do know what they will. They are not willing to see what they don't like to see. Take the example of the British philosopher Anthony Flew, who seemed to be one of them. For more than fifty years, he scrutinized arguments for and against God before finally abandoning atheism in favor of theism.[169] One could say in general that if someone is not interested in whether God exists, or vehemently rejects God, it is almost impossible for such a person to be won over by any kind of empirical evidence or rational arguments.

Here is another example: the biologist Richard Lewontin, a self-proclaimed Marxist, who once wrote, "We cannot allow a Divine

[168] Blaise Pascal, *Pensées*, 2.99, quoted in "Pascal's Pensées," 99.
[169] Antony Flew, *There Is a God: How the World's Most Notorious Atheist Changed His Mind* (San Francisco: HarperOne, 2007), 121–122.

Foot in the door."[170] The keyword is "allow." Apparently, we are dealing here with a choice made before evidence is brought in. Atheists often invest a great deal of time and energy in fleeing the very God they deny or reject. But one might argue that the flight itself is the recognition that there must be something in reality from which to flee.

b. Atheists Come in Various Colors

What most atheists have in common is that they don't believe God exists. Their reasons for not accepting faith in God may be different, though. They can run a wide gamut, ranging from being unaware to undecided to narrowminded to brainwashed to militant to enslaved. They might even be transitioning into each other.

The New Paganism: Unaware Atheists

In the new paganism, the answer to the question of God's existence is just ignored and neglected. It has become irrelevant, a non-issue. People who fit in this line of atheism are those who no longer perceive anything spiritual or religious in their lives; they suffer from some kind of "spiritual amnesia"; they have completely lost their religious dimension. They are not so much atheists as they are heathens who have never thought about God, or never even heard of God. God has completely disappeared from their radar. These people live in a very noisy and busy world, filled with radio, TV, cellphones, loudspeakers, and earphones, which overpower and squash any other thoughts — thus turning them into "heathens."

Let's keep in mind that, for centuries, it was unthinkable in the Western world to even deny God's existence. Although atheists

[170] Richard Lewontin, "Billions and Billions of Demons," *New York Review*, January 9, 1997, 31.

are still a tiny, yet very vocal and growing minority in the Western World (approximately four percent of the U.S. population), our society is changing quickly. More and more people have no memory of the way life used to be — they live obliviously in complete religious ignorance. They are quietly leading a life of religious amnesia — aimless and clueless. It is a life of "heathens." The bottom has been taken out of their lives — and they don't even know it. They are spiritually illiterate. They never give God or religion any thought. When Aleksandr Solzhenitsyn, in his 1983 Templeton Prize lecture, tried to locate the root of the evils of the twentieth century — two world wars, three totalitarian regimes with death camps, and the Cold War — he discerned a profound truth: "Men have forgotten God."

It is not that many of these heathens explicitly dismiss any basic kind of faith in God. They do not dismiss it, for one cannot dismiss what one has never received. They just never heard of it or never thought of it. It never crossed their minds. They have no way of seeing the world through the eyes of religious faith because they were never given that opportunity. When schools create graduates that are illiterate, we normally protest, but somehow, we accept that schools, including the "school of family life," create "graduates" who are spiritually illiterate. As a matter of fact, children without faith not only become adults without faith, but adults who will pass that faithlessness on to their children too. Tradition means, literally, something we "pass" or "hand on." Unfortunately, our culture does not appreciate what has been handed on to us, because it is often considered secondhand.

In one of her novels, Flannery O'Connor gave a good description of what this kind of atheism leads to: "Where you come from is gone, where you thought you were going to never was there, and where you are is no good unless you can get away from it. Where is there a place for you to be? No place."[171] When C. S. Lewis was told about a gravestone inscription in Thurmont, Maryland, that read: "Here lies an atheist—all dressed up and nowhere to go," Lewis quietly replied, "I bet he wishes that were so." That's where life without God ends. It is a form of atheism that can be very explicit, but also very hidden underground at the same time.

The bottom line is this: there is no longer any need for us to protest or even deny God's existence, because we are completely absorbed by what we can see, feel, hear, and touch in our surroundings. As far as God is concerned, out of "sight" means out of mind. Since God is not someone to capture with our senses, God has become a "non-entity" in this world, making us blind to what cannot be seen as well as deaf to what cannot be heard. As St. Paul put it, "they exchanged the truth about God for a lie and worshiped and served the creature rather than the Creator" (Rom. 1:25).

What this leads to is the disappearance of God from our radar screen—or what the late Jewish philosopher Martin Buber more accurately called "the eclipse of God." A pagan society does not allow any mention of God in the public square. It denies there is any religious dimension to a human being. But when God disappears, we lose also all that comes with God. Both previous popes, John Paul II and Benedict XVI, mentioned the image of the eclipse of God—the disappearance of God from the human horizon—several times to describe what they saw as the single most serious and urgent problem of our time.

Calling this an "eclipse" of God expresses clearly that this does not make God Himself disappear the way the new paganism has it.

---

[171] Flannery O'Connor, *Wise Blood* (New York: Farrar, Straus and Giroux, 2007), 165.

Eclipses are only temporary, so the Sun can reclaim the day again. It is not the Sun that is in darkness during an eclipse, but the Earth is. Everything has lost the "shine" of God, but only temporarily.

Agnosticism: Undecided Atheists

Agnosticism is a form of unbelief in God that is rooted in doubts. The label of agnosticism may have been a recent invention, coined by the twentieth-century biologist Thomas H. Huxley, but the idea behind it is much older. Protagoras said already in the third century, "As to the gods, I have no means of knowing either that they exist or do not exist." Agnosticism nowadays applies this idea about "gods" in paganism to the Christian notion of God as well—which is quite a stretch. It asserts that we just do not know whether God exists or not, and what is worse, we presumably have no way of ever knowing in life one way or the other.

In that sense, agnosticism is not really atheism, as it also says that we have no way of knowing that God does not exist. It just keeps agnostics in limbo. They neither deny nor affirm God's existence. Agnostics think that they are not taking any stand pro-or-con at all and therefore that they are invulnerable to any attacks.

Are agnostics really atheists? Yes and no. The agnostic says, "I don't *know* that God exists." The atheist says, "I don't *believe* that God exists." You can say both things at the same time. Some agnostics are atheistic, some are theistic. Agnosticism is not a belief system the way atheism is. Rather, it is a theory of knowledge. An atheist denies the existence of God; an agnostic is not sure about God's existence. For the latter, God may exist, but in this view, reason can neither prove nor disprove it. So, agnosticism keeps its supporters undecided.

Agnostics do swear by reason and logic, but taken in a very truncated way. They claim that logic cannot demonstrate the falsity of a belief in God (it is said to be an unbeatable, unverifiable hypothesis), but neither can it demonstrate the truth of a belief in God (it is said to be a daring, undecided hypothesis). This led to the biologist Julian Huxley's famous exclamation, "We should be agnostic about those things for which there is no evidence." Agnostics often stress that they are not taking any stand pro-or-con God at all. This makes agnosticism look like a rather harmless form of atheism—it merely questions God's existence. But is it really harmless? Should we really remain undecided the way agnostics want us to? There are several reasons why we shouldn't.

First, agnostics often swear by the power of logic, but logic may not be a good tool to prove that God does not exist. G. K. Chesterton once said, "Atheism is indeed the most daring of all dogmas.... For it is the assertion of a universal negative; for a man to say that there is no God in the universe is like saying that there are no insects in any of the stars."[172] Chesterton is right; it is much easier to establish that there is a white swan somewhere on the earth than to prove that all swans are white.

Second, if you seriously honor the power of reason and logic the way agnostics do, then you cannot just ignore the famous proofs of God's existence which prove on compelling rational and metaphysical grounds that God must exist, as we discussed earlier. The power of these proofs cannot just be ignored or rejected without having strong arguments against them. But no one has come up with valid arguments to conclusively disprove those proofs of God's existence. Because one can certainly prove God's existence through reason and logic, we must conclude that agnostics are just misinformed or unwilling to be informed.

Third, agnosticism should be criticized as a limitation of the mind's capacity to know reality. It limits the mind's capacity to

---

[172] G. K. Chesterton, *Varied Types* (New York: Dodd, Mead, 1903), 86.

know reality to the narrow viewpoint of materialism, empiricism, scientism, and rationalism. It tends to stifle the religious sense engraved in the depths of our nature and thus it obscures God—similar to what a solar eclipse does to the Sun when it gets temporarily obscured by the Moon, so that nothing else on earth can reflect God's light.

Fourth, since agnosticism keeps us in limbo, it refuses to give God the honor and worship He deserves as our Maker. Agnostics just never give God their time to study the evidence that points to Him. As they say, if you are not interested in saucers, don't waste your time studying that subject. But when it comes to God, lack of interest is a much more serious case. We owe God our interest—but that assumes of course that God exists. That's why non-believers have no excuse, according to St. Paul, "for although they knew God they did not honor him as God or give thanks to him" (Rom. 1:21).

Fifth, Catholic philosophers such as Peter Kreeft point out that agnosticism's demand for evidence pro-or-con God's existence degrades God, the Supreme Being, to our own level. They argue that the question of God should be treated differently from other knowable objects in that this question regards not that which is below us, but that which is above us. For one thing, God is a first cause, not a secondary cause. The question "Does God exist?" is not like "Do neutrinos exist?" God cannot be "trapped" by some ingenious experiment, for God is not a secondary cause.

Sixth, while sitting on the fence, unsure if there is a God, agnostics often act as if they are instead very sure there is no God. They are theoretically agnostics, but practically atheists. But there is more that comes with agnosticism. Very often agnostics do have a rather negative and highly selective attitude toward religion and religious believers in particular. Agnostics think that their own logic is so compelling that everyone who disagrees with their agnostic conclusions must be misinformed or just brainless—which is rather an arrogant position. So, they often call religious people superstitious believers in something unknown and unprovable.

Empiricism: Narrow-Minded Atheists

These atheists claim that in order to prove there is a God, we need empirical proof for the existence of God. Stephen Hawking, for instance, thinks along these lines as he exclaims, "When people ask me if a god created the Universe, I tell them that the question itself makes no sense." Atheists in this category proclaim that there cannot be any empirical proof, because God is not accessible to our senses, so He is not measurable, quantifiable, or touchable. What this boils down to is that the faith of religion is belief based on insufficient empirical evidence, or even none. We recall that quote from Mark Twain: "A man is accepted into a church for what he believes, and he is turned out for what he knows."

Although atheism is commonly understood to be about the absence of belief in God, most atheists of this kind will say it is about the absence of God himself. They are "positively" sure that God does not exist, because they want proof, in particular empirical proof, for God's existence. Thus, God ends up as a "nothing," at best an illusion or delusion.

Because "God" is a concept that cannot be empirically or experimentally tested and verified, God-talk is ipso facto considered meaningless in atheism, not worth any further attention. In this view, there is no way of knowing with any degree of empirical certainty at all whether God exists, because we cannot find God in the world around us.

This explains why there is another dimension to this kind of atheism. The French philosopher Denis Diderot had said already during the Enlightenment era that God has come to rank among the most useless truths. In this kind of atheism, God is an unwanted and uncalled-for entity, at best a nuisance.

The late biochemist and popular science-fiction writer Isaac Asimov, for instance, expressed as his opinion: "I don't have the evidence to prove that God doesn't exist, but I so strongly suspect he doesn't that I don't want to waste my time." Belief in God has become a waste of time. The founder of Microsoft, Bill Gates, put it more directly: "Religion is not very efficient. There's a lot more I could be doing on a Sunday morning."

In this mix of atheists, we find also people who strongly hope there is no God. One of them is the philosopher Thomas Nagel: "It isn't just that I don't believe in God and, naturally, hope that I'm right in my belief. It's that I hope there is no God! I don't want there to be a God; I don't want the universe to be like that."[173] One could also say that these atheists do not like the way the world looks to them with God in the picture.

Scientism: Brainwashed Atheists

Scientism is a further attempt to force God out of the Universe using bad definitions and circular theories. Empiricism tried and failed to explain the Universe on purely material grounds. There was still much in existence that defied human understanding. So, atheists and agnostics began to endow science itself with godlike properties. It becomes the source and explanation of all that exists.

As we discussed earlier in this book, scientism confuses methodology with reality. If we try to find plastic cups on the beach

---

[173] Thomas Nagel, *The Last Word* (New York: Oxford University Press, 1997), 130.

with a metal detector, we will find out there are no plastic cups on the beach—but that doesn't mean they don't exist. So we should tell these atheists never to let methodology dictate what reality is like but, instead, to let reality dictate which methodology we need. This kind of atheism denies everything that can't be dissected, counted, measured, or quantified—and so that's the end of God. But, ironically, that viewpoint must also include its own claim. Science on its own cannot answer questions that are beyond the reach of its empirical and experimental techniques.

Yet, these atheists tend to (falsely) believe that modern science is on their side. They have been brainwashed by scientists and their successes. Science has become their "god." The idea is clear: atheism is based on scientific knowledge; religion is not, and therefore should be abandoned. When we look through our telescopes or microscopes, we never see God, so we know there is no God—on scientific grounds, they say. This view is probably best summarized by the title of one of Dawkins's books—*The God Delusion*. That's what God is according to this view—a delusion. Why? Because science tells us so! Of course, it is not science but *scientism* that tells us so.

Indeed, these atheists are right that science uses reason, but we discussed already that religious faith does so as well. If we try to find God with scientific tools, we will never find God, as it is the wrong instrument to detect God. You cannot expect a microscope to reveal the square root of sixteen. Just as reason gives us access to the existence of numbers, so it is reason that gives us access to the existence of God, as we found out in this book. Fortunately, it is not methodology that determines reality.

When these atheists speak of "blind faith" in religion, they seem to be "blind" to their own "blind faith" in science. As the late physicist and scholar of science and religion Ian Barbour aptly has an astounding answer to these questions. He noticed that the Communist press in his country "constantly reminds us of God while maintaining he does not exist." Then he wrote, "to hate God you must first have faith that there is a God."

What is going on here? The philosopher William Lane Craig gives us a plausible answer: "No one in the final analysis really fails to become a Christian because of lack of arguments; he fails to become a Christian because he loves darkness rather than light and wants nothing to do with God."[176] The key line here is that such a person "loves darkness": they want no part of the Light, but cherish the darkness instead. One could say in general that if someone deeply dislikes God, it is almost impossible for such a person to be won over by any kind of empirical evidence or rational arguments. So, the pivotal question is this: What is behind the deep-seated hatred that these atheists nurse against religion and against God?

Let's face it. There is only one force that hates God's creation more than anything else, and that force is Satan. Satan is not an atheist in the regular sense. Satan knows very well that God exists, he wants no part of God. Satan rejects God and refuses to acknowledge the honor due to Him. It is Satan's goal to demolish Christian elements in society and to damage the human image of God's image. Satan prowls about the world for the ruin His hatred of God revels in spreading atheism.

Satan be the real instigator of this aggressive form of atheism hard to deny it. As a matter of fact, destructive atheism well be part of a much larger picture—a cosmic warfare, between good and evil, between God and Satan. It is

ne Craig, *Reasonable Faith: Christian Truth and Apologetics*, heaton, IL: Crossway, 2008), 47.

put it, "Science is not as objective, nor religion as subjective, as had been assumed."

Science should never forget that it is "blind" to many other-than-scientific aspects of this world. The physicist Erwin Schrödinger once said about science, "It knows nothing of beautiful and ugly, good or bad, God and eternity. Science sometimes pretends to answer questions in these domains, but the answers are very often so silly that we are not inclined to take them seriously."[174]

Antitheism: Militant Atheists

It is often said lately that a new kind of atheism has emerged: atheists who don't believe in God because they actually detest to know if God exists. They do not just profess atheism but are actively involved in fighting theism with their own doctrine: antitheism. They consider theism, or belief in God, a real and dangerous threat to society, and they assert that it should therefore be rejected and attacked with all the tools we have at our disposal. This form of atheism is often referred to as *New Atheism*. We will call it what it is: antitheism.

The term *New Atheism* was coined in 2006 by the journalist Gary Wolf to describe the positions promoted by some atheists of the twenty-first century. This modern-day atheism is advanced by a group of thinkers and writers who advocate the view that superstition, religion, and irrationalism are interconnected and should not simply be tolerated but should be counteracted, combated, and exposed by rational argument wherever their influence arises in government, education, and politics, so that they can be eradicated.

[174] Erwin Schrödinger, *Nature and the Greeks and Science and Humanism* (Cambridge: Cambridge University Press, 1996), 95.

In 2009, starting in Britain, advocates of the New Atheism got behind a campaign to put pro-atheist ads on buses. They were in fact antitheism ads. Gradually, the group grew with authors of early twenty-first-century books promoting antitheism. These authors include Sam Harris, Richard Dawkins, Daniel Dennett, and Christopher Hitchens—sometimes called "The Four Horsemen of the New Atheism." New Atheists have sometimes been described in scornful terms as "evangelical atheists."

In their eyes, belief in God has turned into a danger for society. Based on this common belief, the New Atheists basically started a church of non-religious believers. They don't have common services or a common book, of course, but they do have a common creed and doctrine. They reject all religions, declare them all equally anti-intellectual, and challenge them as lacking evidence, particularly scientific evidence.

What unites them is a handful of charismatic "pastors," like Dawkins and Hitchens, who served much the same role as pastors of megachurches. They offered absurdly simple answers to complex problems. Ironically, the New Atheism quickly devolved into an irrationalist cult—one where the YouTube-based proclamations of antitheism's high priests were accepted as dogma, however absurd or small-minded.

The New Atheists think that a few deft blows to one of those religions, such as Islam, can disarm and destroy all of them as irrational. They mention weak arguments for the existence of "God"—a deity that bears little or no resemblance to the Christian God—and then tear them down. However, the New Atheist definition of faith is a straw man. Needless to say, a false idea of God can easily be refuted. The Chief Rabbi of the United Hebrew Congregations of Great Britain, Jonathan Sacks, could not have said it better: "The cure of bad religion is good religion, not no

religion, just as the cure of bad science is good science, not the abandonment of science."[175]

These antitheists want others to believe that believing in God is "evil" and needs to be attacked or even eradicated. They consider spreading this message to be their "holy war," their "sacred mission," a *jihad* against God. Ironically, it is the religious motivation behind *jihad* that made these atheists detest any belief in God and instigated them to eradicate religion. God has such a bad reputation, in their view, that he must be banished from the Unive...

Satanism: Enslaved Atheists

At the other end of the spectrum, we find mostly believ...
ologies such as communism. This is the atheism of...
vehemently detest or hate belief in God and who w...
believe that belief in God needs to be attacked or...
This form of atheism does not question God;...
God; it does not neglect God; but it plainly re...
George Orwell referred to this sort when...
scribed someone as "an embittered atheist...
does not so much disbelieve in God as...

There is something very peculiar a...
is a kind of hate speech that tries to...
while maintaining at the same ti...
could one dislike, let alone hate,...
would one persistently try to p...
a being that is not supposed...

Cardinal Stefan Wyszyń...
most of his life with the...

175 Rabbi Jonathan...
the Search for M...

176 William L...
3rd ed. (W...

God's aim for each one of us to attain Heaven after death, whereas Satan's aim is to ensure that as many people as possible miss that eternal goal. Obviously, Satan is a reality; and evil is something real to watch out for. God can do so much good when we let Him, whereas Satan can do so much evil when we let him.

It is only the religious "eye" that sees all of history as a cosmic, spiritual, and constant warfare between God and Satan, waged everywhere and daily, 24/7. It sees how life is more of a battleground than a playground. It sees how the power of evil did spellbind and enable Hitler, Stalin, Mao, bin Laden, and al-Baghdadi to enslave the minds and spirits of millions, creating little hells right here on earth. This explains how such people could have sold their souls by following "orders" that stem from sources far beyond their own resources. Only religious people can see this dimension in history which historians usually miss. They can uncover what is unseen behind all that is seen.

And now we witness again how the power of evil, the "light" of Satan, is enabling atheists to spellbind and enslave the minds and spirits of millions, creating havoc on earth with religious erosion and mudslides. These atheists have been happy to sell their souls to their new master. No wonder the reality of evil goes far beyond material and physical powers. It goes even far beyond what human beings can do on their own.

Aleksandr Solzhenitsyn is very adamant about the way atheistic communism operated in the former Soviet Union: "Militant atheism is not merely incidental or marginal to Communist policy; it is not a side effect, but the central pivot."[177] Whether it is Stalin

---

[177] Aleksandr Solzhenitsyn, *The Solzhenitsyn Reader: New and Essential Writings, 1947–2005*, ed. Edward E. Ericson Jr. and Daniel J. Mahoney (Wilmington, DE: ISI, 2006), 579.

or Mao or Hitler, the key question is this: Could they have ever done what they did relying on their own human power alone? The answer seems to be a definite *no*.

This explains also how such people can follow "orders" to churn out endless propaganda against God through books, mass media, and the internet. They are amazingly successful in doing so. The fuel behind all their toxic convictions is some satanic force engaged in a battle against God's creation—which is the role of Satan, the father of all lies, the great divider, who knows how to remain hidden from view.

Now, it is obvious that so many unbelievers have gone far beyond agnosticism, atheism, scientism, and antitheism to become followers of satanism.

c. Is Atheism a Wise Strategy?

Is it possible to reject faith in God? Obviously, it is, because we are free creatures who have the freedom to reject belief in God's existence. Sometimes atheists reject faith in God because they don't accept or understand the arguments for God's existence; sometimes, they do understand them but are not willing to accept them. We discussed these possibilities extensively. But no matter what, we should at least ask these atheists whether it is smart or wise to reject God's existence. Or is there a price to pay?

Even if atheists haven't been convinced by the arguments given in this book, they should at least heed the advice Blaise Pascal gave them in his so-called Wager, in which he shows us that the decision to reject faith in God is not a wise choice after all. This may look like a strange strategy, but Blaise Pascal argued in his Wager that belief in God is in fact a very smart strategy.

The Wager tells us that "sitting on the fence," the way agnostics do, or deliberately ignoring or rejecting God, as other kinds of atheists do, is not a smart strategy. For how long can one keep doing that? At the end of life, a coin is being spun that will come down heads (God) or tails (no God). How will you wager?

Peter Kreeft describes Pascal's Wager as follows: "If God does not exist, it does not matter how you wager, for there is nothing to win after death and nothing to lose after death. But if God does exist, your only chance of winning eternal happiness is to believe, and your only chance of losing it is to refuse to believe."[178] In other words, agnosticism and atheism are a terrible bet, for they give you no chance of winning. As Pascal said about belief in God, "If you gain, you gain all; if you lose, you lose nothing."[179]

Why are atheism and agnosticism impossible options to wager? The reason is simple, in the words of Peter Kreeft again: "Because we are moving. The ship of life is moving along the waters of time, and there comes a point of no return, when our fuel runs out, when it is too late. The Wager works because of the fact of death."[180] And mortal we all are!

The option of not to wager at all is out of the question; for each one of us has no choice but to wager in the face of death, given the possibility that we might be judged by God after death. So, by "sitting on the fence," agnostics wager against God—and something similar can be said about atheism in general. By refusing to choose in support of God, one has already chosen to wager on the idea that picking no religion is safer than accepting a false one.

In other words, the only way to win is believing in God. The only way to lose is not believing in God. That's perhaps a very

---

[178] Peter Kreeft, *Fundamentals of the Faith: Essays in Christian Apologetics* (San Francisco: Ignatius Press, 1988), 51.

[179] Blaise Pascal, *The Thoughts of Blaise Pascal*, trans. M. Auguste Molinier (London: Kegan Paul, Trench, 1885), 98.

[180] Kreeft, *Fundamentals of the Faith*, 50.

meager outcome—logical, impersonal, and dispassionate—but nevertheless something that is appropriate for the mindset of scientists and the like. Pascal's argument is that a rational person should live as though God exists and seek to believe in God. If God does not exist, such a person will have only a finite loss (some pleasures, for instance), whereas he stands to receive infinite gains (as represented by eternity in Heaven) and avoid infinite losses (eternity in Hell) if God does exist.

Is this a lethal blow to atheism in any form? Probably not, but at least it shows those who do not accept the arguments for the existence of God to at least consider one more argument, which says it's much wiser and smarter to believe in God than not to believe in God—at least live as if God exists. This is not another argument for the existence of God, but it is a strong reason for believing in God rather than not believing in God.

Isn't it strange to make arguments like these? It is indeed perplexing, for throughout the history of humanity some form of theism has been almost universal. Almost everybody has believed in God (or gods). Almost everybody has believed that some supernatural divine power (or powers) presides over the world. This explains why atheism has been rare and unnatural for so many centuries. Belief in God used to be the default, but nowadays disbelief in God is becoming the new norm. It is up to us to make a wise choice and turn the tide.

Conclusion

The Conflict That Wasn't

The idea that there is a conflict between science and faith is a rather recent development. For centuries, most scientists were ardent believers. As we discovered earlier, the history of science shows us that in fact many scientists, through their belief in God, were inspired to do their work and investigate nature. As a matter of fact, their Christian faith gave them the incentive and motivation to study and explore nature. Names that come to mind are Copernicus, Kepler, Galileo, Mendel, Pasteur, and Lemaître, and the list goes on and on.

So, where did the idea of a conflict come from? It is a myth that was born and conceived during the age of the Enlightenment in the seventeenth century. It was promoted and popularized by philosophers (who were not scientists!) such as John Locke, Montesquieu, and Voltaire. The so-called conflict theory is not the outcome of scientific research but rather the assumption of what some people like to believe about science and its relation to faith. It is not a "theory," but at best a "hypothesis"—and a poor one at that.

The truth is that science still allows ample of room for faith in God, which should leave the seeming conflict shattered. Let's wrap up this book by analyzing the following cases of what has been portrayed by some as a conflict.

A Catholic Scientist Harmonizes Science and Faith

a. Theism vs. Science

The conflict theory puts faith in opposition to science. It claims that science forces us to side with unbelief in God against belief in God. It makes us believe that we should defend atheism against theism. Undoubtedly, there is a real conflict between these two claims: either God exists, or He does not exist. You cannot have it both ways.

But then the question remains whether there is in fact a conflict between faith and science. Does science really tell us there is no God? There is no way to defend this claim. As we discovered in this book, science does not have the power to prove or claim that there is no God, because science only deals with material entities, whereas God is not one of them. Therefore, the idea that there is a conflict between faith and science has no foot to stand on. It's a myth, a conflict that wasn't.

At first sight, science may seem to side with atheism, but we showed extensively that this is a serious misconception. Atheism, in any form, does not have the competence to discredit belief in God. Nor does science. Therefore, in opposition to atheism, we should make the case for theism.

Theism is a cornerstone of the Catholic Faith. It is very different from deism. The God of *deism* is a god who once made the world, but He did so as a watchmaker who makes a watch, then abandons it to itself and lets it run its own course—the "hands-off" approach, so to speak, of an absent landlord. In contrast to deism, *theism* tells us that the Creator of this world remains actively involved with this world, not only by sustaining and preserving what He has created but also by guiding its course and history directly.

It is obvious that atheism rejects all that theism claims. It does so, frequently, in the name of science and with the authority of science. Whereas there is a real conflict between theism and atheism—they cannot both be true—there is no such conflict between theism and science. What theism claims is not in violation of what science claims.

b. First Cause versus Secondary Causes

There is no conflict between the secondary causes all of us are familiar with and the First Cause that seems to elude atheists. Yet, the difference between a first cause and secondary causes is crucial. Secondary causes can be studied by the sciences, but the First Cause is not something the sciences can study. As we showed repeatedly, without a first cause, secondary causes could not even exist.

Because God is the Primary Cause, God could never be discovered among the secondary causes of this Universe, for God is not one of them. Again, science is about secondary causes, not the Primary Cause. God is outside its scope, just as everything else that is unseen and cannot be dissected, measured, counted, or quantified is beyond its reach. God cannot be "seen" through telescopes or microscopes. As God is "everywhere," it only looks as if God is "nowhere." Theism tells us God is all-present, all-knowing, and all-powerful.

Therefore, God could never be called a working hypothesis that we stumbled upon or used in our scientific endeavors, because God is not another secondary cause. Hypotheses are always open to disproof and thus should only be tentatively held. God is not a hypothesis that we hold on to tentatively and provisionally until more evidence for or against it emerges. Laplace was right when he answered Napoleon—in an anecdotal, probably apocryphal account—that in science, "I had no need of that hypothesis." However, the fact that there is no need for God in science as a hypothesis cannot be a reason for Dawkins to claim there is no place for God at all. Dawkins's belief that God is a scientific hypothesis—a "god of the gaps"—is a misconception that obscures the real nature of theism. Therefore, it no longer makes sense to maintain, like Dawkins does, that "religions still make claims about the world which, on analysis, turn out to be scientific claims."[181]

That we are not dealing with a conflict here is also expressed by the popular distinction between the book of Scripture and the book of nature. Scientific truths come from the book of nature, and religious truths come from the book of Scripture. They are different answers to different questions. Yet, they come from the same Author, and therefore should be in harmony with each other.

Based on this distinction, the idea of "gaps" in scientific explanations is rather questionable. In the late Victorian period, the Scottish evangelist Henry Drummond raised concerns about this search for gaps: "There are reverent minds who ceaselessly scan the fields of Nature and the books of Science in search of gaps—gaps which they fill up with God. As if God lived in gaps?"[182] During his 1954 McNair Lecture at the University of North Carolina, the late chemist Charles Coulson said something similar: "Either God is in the whole of Nature, with no gaps, or He's not there at all."[183] So, the outcome of this discussion is again that there is no conflict between science dealing with secondary causes versus faith rooted in the First Cause.

c. Supernatural Truths versus Natural Truths

There is no conflict between the truths we know from our Catholic Faith and the truths science has uncovered for us. However,

---

[181] Richard Dawkins, A Devil's Chaplain: Refelections on Hope, Lies, Science, and Love (New York: Houghton Mifflin, 2003), 150.

[182] Henry Drummond, The Lowell Lectures on the Ascent of Man, 10th ed. (New York: James Pott, 1900), 333.

[183] C. A. Coulson, Science and Christian Belief (London: Fontana, 1955), 22.

they may be of a different nature. They differ, for instance, in the way we get to those truths. As a result, science and faith convey two different kinds of truth—let's call them "natural truths" versus "supernatural truths," or "earthly truths" versus "heavenly truths."

Many natural truths are based on human testimony; sometimes they are based on our own experience, but often they were received from hearsay—that is, from the experiences of others through education, formation, and the like. Supernatural truths, on the other hand, come from divine testimony, received through direct witnesses such as the apostles, or through prophets and saints. No matter how they came to us, they come ultimately from God. As St. Paul put it, "when you received the word of God which you heard from us, you accepted it not as the word of men but as what it really is, the word of God" (1 Thess. 2:13).

Take, for example, these two truths: the Crucifixion and the Resurrection. The Crucifixion of Jesus is a natural, earthly truth, whereas the Resurrection of Jesus is a supernatural, heavenly truth. Another example of a natural truth would be heliocentrism—in the sense of the Sun being the (gravitational) center of the solar system—whereas an example of a supernatural truth would be Christocentrism—in the sense of Christ being the (spiritual) center of the Universe. Natural truths we can often claim "in the name of science and with the authority of science"; supernatural truths, on the other hand, we claim "in the name of Jesus and with the authority of Jesus."

The distinction of natural truths, which we gain through obser-vation and experiment, versus supernatural truths, which we gain through revelation and faith, has some consequences. Science has *theories* to help our understanding, but they are subject to change, because we keep trying to capture the truth more and more, better and better. Therefore, let us not make science more than what it is—a work in progress.

The Catholic Faith, on the other hand, has *dogmas* to help our understanding, but they were revealed to us and tell us truths we would not know without them—so let us not make religion less than what it is. Science masquerading as religion is as unseemly as religion masquerading as science. Yet they both deal with truths and facts, no matter whether they are discovered or revealed. Science and religion are, in the words of Francis Collins, "like the two unshakable pillars, holding up a building called Truth."[184]

As a consequence, science cannot deny the existence of supernatural truths. Science doesn't have the power to explain the unexplainable by denying its existence. One can only conclude that supernatural truths are impossible by presuming beforehand that the supernatural world cannot or does not exist and thereby must be rejected. But that is a flawed logic; you assume already what you want to prove.

The fact remains that both kinds of truths have this in common: truth is truth, even if you do not accept it; and untruth is untruth, even if you claim it. In other words, there are not as many truths as there are different opinions. St. Augustine famously said, "All truth is God's truth."[185] As much as it is a matter of fact that the Earth is not flat—believing that it is flat does not make it flat—so it is also a matter of fact that God exists—believing that He doesn't exist does not make Him disappear. The belief that only science knows the truth is only held by a warped, misguided mind. Again, we must reject the conflict theory as a myth.

---

[184] Francis S. Collins, *The Language of God: A Scientist Presents Evidence for Belief* (New York: Free Press, 2006), 210.
[185] See Augustine, *On Christian Doctrine*, bk. 2.

d. Humans versus Animals

There is no conflict between what we know about animals and what we know about humans—which may seem amazing, as we do know more about humans than what science tells us about animals. Science will tell us that humans were made "in the image" of animals. Indeed, humans do share many characteristics with animals: they all breed, feed, bleed, and excrete.

So how can our Catholic Faith then tell us that humans were made "in the image of God"? Well, the supernatural truth is that humans have a *soul*, which comes with a mind as the intellectual part of the soul as well as a will as the voluntary part of the soul. In other words, the fact that all humans are mortal is a natural truth about their bodies, but the fact that they are also immortal is a supernatural truth that comes with their souls. Human beings do not simply cease to exist when they die, because they are made in God's image and their souls are immortal. Those are supernatural truths, which cannot come from science.

As a consequence, when we discuss what distinguishes humans from animals, we need to distinguish the notion of a creature which is "human" in a supernatural sense from that of a creature which is "human" merely in a natural sense. The biological creature would be to a certain degree like us in its bodily properties but would lack our spiritual powers. In short, it would lack a human soul and therefore a human mind and human will.

This may raise an uncomfortable question: When did such souls emerge in evolution or prehistory? Science cannot answer this question—for the simple reason that, as astronomer Owen Gingerich pithily puts it, "the transition to a spiritual being ... does not fossilize."[186]

---

[186] Owen Gingerich, *God's Planet* (Cambridge, MA: Harvard University Press, 2014), 91.

For this reason, Chesterton once acknowledged the possibility that man's "body may have been evolved from the brutes," but then he adds emphatically that "we know nothing of any such transition that throws the smallest light upon his soul as it has shown itself in history."[187] He also said, "There may be a broken trail of stones and bones faintly suggesting the development of the human body. There is nothing even faintly suggesting such a development of the human mind.... We can accept man as a fact, if we are content with an unexplained fact. We can accept him as an animal, if we can live with a fabulous animal."[188]

The Catholic Faith is very emphatic about this supernatural truth. The *Catechism of the Catholic Church* puts it this way: "The doctrine of the faith affirms that the spiritual and immortal soul is created immediately by God" (CCC 382). Or, in the words of Pope John Paul II, "The moment of passage into the spiritual realm is not something that can be observed with research in the fields of physics and chemistry."[189]

The notion of a supernatural truth beyond what meets the natural eye or is discovered by the scientific method may be hard to accept for many nowadays, but this in itself does not make that notion invalid. To use a distinction we used earlier, the book of nature may be about our biological roots, but the book of Scripture deals with our spiritual roots. That's where the assumed conflict ends.

e. Providence versus Chance

There is no conflict between God's providence and what happens by chance. The Catholic Church is very definite in maintaining

---

[187]Chesterton, *The Everlasting Man*, 28.
[188]Chesterton, *The Everlasting Man*, 22.
[189]John Paul II, Message to the Pontifical Academy of Sciences.

her position regarding immediate providence. The *Catechism of the Catholic Church* puts it this way: "The witness of Scripture is unanimous that the solicitude of divine providence is concrete and immediate; God cares for all, from the least things to the great events of the world and its history" (CCC 303).

On the other hand, science often talks about chance and randomness. For instance, radioactive decay is a process connected with randomness. And in biology and genetics, mutations in DNA have a random aspect to them. The word *random* is a scientific, actually a statistical or stochastic, concept. When people toss a coin, there is randomness involved because the outcome is independent of what the one who tosses the coin would like to see, and it is independent of previous and future tosses. Yet the outcome is predictable in terms of statistical probabilities.

Doesn't that create a conflict with God's providence? Doesn't this give us the impression that randomness has taken over the role of God's providence? How can a random outcome ever be connected to God, for randomness and God can hardly go together? As a matter of fact, many scientists think it has indeed replaced God who, if He exists, is only "playing dice." Do they have a point?

Not really. It depends on how we understand randomness and chance. Stephen Barr makes it clear that randomness is "a concept that fits within empirical science.... [Randomness is] because it can be tested for."[190] But that does not mean it can be used to replace the "role" of God's providence. Take, for instance, St. Thomas Aquinas, who once said, "Whoever believes that everything is a

---

[190]Stephen M. Barr, "Chance, by Design," *First Things*, December 2012, https://www.firstthings.com/article/2012/12/chance-by-design, 26.

matter of chance, does not believe that God exists."[191] According to William E. Carroll, Aquinas "argues that God causes chance and random events to be the chance and random events which they are, just as he causes the free acts of human beings to be free acts."[192]

Yet, randomness can still play a role in God's relationship to the world. Take St. Padre Pio, who was apt to say in various ways that it is God who arranges coincidences. Once he asked a man who claimed such-and-such an event had happened by chance, "And who, do you suppose, arranged the chances?"[193] Science has no answer to this question—not even the answer "nobody did." Anything that seems to be random from a scientific point of view may very well be included in God's eternal plan. Cardinal John Henry Newman wrote in an 1868 letter, "I do not [see] that 'the accidental evolution of organic beings' is inconsistent with divine design—it is accidental to us, not to God."[194]

This suggests that God and randomness are not in conflict with each other and do not exclude each other. The role of randomness concerns the relationship between secondary causes, whereas the "role" of God's providence is about the relationship of secondary causes to the First Cause. Therefore, anything that seems to be random from a scientific point of view may very well be related to God at the same time—which eliminates another conflict.

[191] Aquinas, *De Symbolo Apostolorum*, 4, 33.

[192] William Carroll, "Evolution, Creation, and the Catholic Church" (lecture, Williams College, Williamson, MA, October 19, 2006).

[193] Quoted in Mark Brumley, *The Catholic Answer*, January–February 2005.

[194] John Henry Newman, "Letter to J. Walker of Scarborough, May 22, 1868," in *The Letters and Diaries of John Henry Newman* (Oxford: Clarendon Press, 1973).

f. Miracles versus Laws of Nature

There is no conflict between what the laws of nature dictate and the miracles we hear about in the Catholic Faith. Miracles play a significant role in the Catholic Faith. They are at the core of the Christian message: the Incarnation of Jesus, His birth from the virgin Mary, His Resurrection from the dead, and His Ascension into Heaven. Miracles like these appear frequently in the book of Scripture. Miracles also play a common role in the lives of saints.

So, the question arises why some see a conflict here with what science tells us. The stock argument that skeptic philosophers such as David Hume use is that miracles are violations of the laws of nature. Do they have a point? To answer that question, we must clarify first how we understand miracles and the laws of nature. To begin with, we need a more concise definition of miracle. C. S. Lewis provides one: "I use the word *Miracle* to mean an interference with Nature by supernatural power."[195] The word *supernatural* is key here.

Second, we need to better understand what the laws of nature entail. We discussed them extensively in this book, but now we must stress that they are processes that naturally and consistently occur when all *extraneous* factors are held constant. For instance, the law of gravity tells us that a ball will fall to the ground every time we drop it, but that doesn't mean someone may stop this from happening by catching the ball before it hits the ground. Catching the ball is an interfering, extraneous factor.

The laws of nature manifest themselves only when certain conditions are met: put more technically, as we did before, they come with a clause of *ceteris paribus* (all things being equal). A

---

[195] C. S. Lewis, *Miracles: A Preliminary Study* (New York: HarperOne, 2001), 5.

law of nature states what happens if, and only if, all other factors are held constant. If that is the case, then we should also include supernatural factors based on God's interference. Those would obviously be intervening factors of the *supernatural* kind. That's basically the point Lewis is making: miracles are interventions of the supernatural world in the natural world. He argues that miracles go beyond natural law, yet they are consistent with nature.

This removes the assumed conflict between miracles and the laws of nature. If skeptics still protest, then they must hold at least one hidden assumption, which says that there is only one world: a natural world, and therefore, no supernatural world. This excludes miracles beforehand. You can only conclude that miracles are impossible if you presume beforehand that the supernatural world cannot or does not exist and thereby cannot intervene in the natural world. But isn't that the whole question in the first place? Apparently, the idea that miracles are impossible is based on the presupposition that what it is trying to prove is already true.

There is no way science can eliminate supernatural factors ahead of time. Accepting miracles simply indicates that there is a supernatural cause, based on religious faith, in addition to and beyond the natural causes, based on scientific laws of nature. Rather than breaking the laws of nature, God allows His miracles to transcend them. Pope Benedict XVI went even further when he rejected the modern notion that God is "allowed" to only act in the spiritual domain, but not in the material. In his own words, "God is God, and he does not operate merely on the level of ideas.... If God does not also have power over matter, then he simply is not God."[196]

---

[196] Joseph Ratzinger, *Jesus of Nazareth: The Infancy Narratives* (New York: Image, 2012), 56–57.

g. Magisterium of the Church versus Magisterium of Science

There is no conflict between these two magisteria. You probably know what the Magisterium of the Church represents. The *Catechism of the Catholic Church* says, "The task of interpreting the Word of God authentically has been entrusted solely to the Magisterium of the Church, that is, to the Pope and to the bishops in communion with him" (CCC 100; see 85). In other words, the Magisterium of the Church is a teaching authority.

But what is the "magisterium of science"? You might think that expression came from a philosopher or theologian, but the amazing answer is that it came from a scientist, the late evolutionary biologist Stephen J. Gould. He spoke of *two* separate magisteria, denying that there is a conflict between them. In his own words, "No such conflict should exist because each subject has a legitimate magisterium, or domain of teaching authority—and these magisteria do not overlap."[197]

Speaking of a Magisterium of the Church may be a familiar expression, but using the concept of a magisterium of science may raise eyebrows. Is there really a board or panel behind this magisterium? True, unlike the Magisterium of the Catholic Church which has a rather centralized authority—through the successors of St. Peter, ecumenical councils, Doctors of the Church, bishops, synods, and theologians—science's authority is rather diffuse, spread out over academies and societies of scientists, editorial boards of scientific journals, and teams of peer reviewers. Nevertheless, it still comes close to a magisterium. It also had, and still has, its extremely gifted and ingenious key players—scientists such as Galileo, Newton, Darwin, Mendel, Pasteur, and Einstein. Nowadays, we

[197] Stephen Jay Gould, "Nonoverlapping Magisteria," *Natural History* 106 (March 1997): 16–22.

wait every year to hear who the current key players are when the new Nobel laureates are announced.

In further analysis, there are some striking parallels between both magisteria. They each have their own distinctive authority, their own distinctive territory, their own distinctive questions, their own distinctive members, and their own distinctive limitations. The magisterium of science deals with natural, scientific truths, whereas the Magisterium of the Church relates to supernatural, religious truths. As a consequence, the magisterium of science can neither endorse nor reject what is beyond its reach—issues such as God's existence, creation, the existence of souls, divine revelation, or the sacredness of human life. Those are contained in dogmas that express the supernatural truths of the Catholic Faith.

Stephen Jay Gould was right when he said: "Science can work only with naturalistic explanations; it can neither affirm nor deny other types of actors (like God) in other spheres (the moral realm, for example)."[198] In that sense, both magisteria have their own "responsibilities." They cannot replace each other.

As repeatedly stressed, science may be separated from religion, but the two are not isolated from each other. Correctly understood, they both need each other in order to function best. In other words, there may be, and probably must be some interaction between the two. We see in the history of science again and again that scientists are guided by philosophical and religious notions, and that religious believers get better informed by scientists.

To sum up, religion must keep itself open to the findings of science, in the same way as science must respect what lies outside the boundaries surrounding its inquiries. So, though the two

---

[198] Stephen Jay Gould, "Impeaching a Self-Appointed Judge," *Scientific American* 267 (July 1992): 118–121.

domains are separate, they do interact by complementing each other. Together they make us whole, whereas on their own, they are incomplete and underperforming.

The truth of the matter is that faith and religion can coexist, they have coexisted, they coexist now, and they will continue to coexist in the future. They have the same goal of explaining *reality*—either the material part of reality or the immaterial part of reality. Science and religion are the two windows or the two ways that let humans look at the world they live in. Yet, there is only one world, and it is the same world these two windows try to make known. Closing off either window would make us partially blind.

h. The Conflicts That Never Were

All of the above cases have often been portrayed as conflicts. However, the idea of a conflict between science and faith is a *myth* that erroneously forces us to choose either one of them, as if we were dealing here with an either/or issue. And the same can be said about the other so-called conflicts shown above.

Since there is no conflict, our faith must keep itself open to the findings of science, in the same way as science must respect what faith has to tell us. So, though the two domains are separate, they do interact by complementing each other. Together they make us whole, whereas on their own, they are incomplete and underperforming. As stated repeatedly, they may live in separation, but they cannot live in isolation. Besides, they cannot but live together within the same person. We cannot live faith on Sundays alone, and science only on weekdays—that would be schizophrenic.

This conviction has been expressed in various ways by authorities in both science and religion. In the science camp, Albert Einstein used to say, "Science without religion is lame; religion without science is blind."[199] In the religious camp, Pope John Paul II said something similar: "Science can purify religion from error and superstition. Religion can purify science from idolatry and false absolutes."[200] The right-minded representatives of both camps agree that science and faith need each other.

Peter Kreeft's analogy, mentioned at the beginning, portrays science and faith as two rivals in a Western town who think one of them must leave, because the town isn't big enough for both of them. We can declare it now as a misconception, forced on us by atheists. Science and faith can perfectly live together — in the same home, in the same town, in the same world. They can live together and even should live together in the same person. God's creation is "big" enough for both of them — neither one is bound to leave, but both are bound to stay. Therefore, science and faith can certainly live together, and actually should.

---

[199] Albert Einstein, *Science, Philosophy and Religion: A Symposium.*
[200] John Paul II to George V. Coyne, S.J.

Index

About the Author

Gerard M. Verschuuren is a human geneticist who also earned a doctorate in the philosophy of science. He studied and worked at universities in Europe and the United States. Currently semi-retired, he spends most of his time as a writer, speaker, and consultant on the interface of science and religion, and of faith and reason. Here are some of his most recent books:

Darwin's Philosophical Legacy: The Good and the Not-So-Good (Lanham, MD: Lexington Books, 2012)

The Destiny of the Universe: In Pursuit of the Great Unknown (St. Paul, MN: Paragon House, 2014)

Five Anti-Catholic Myths: Slavery, Crusades, Inquisition, Galileo, and Holocaust (Kettering, OH: Angelico Press, 2015)

Life's Journey: A Guide from Conception to Growing Up, Growing Old, and Natural Death (Kettering, OH: Angelico Press, 2016)

St. Thomas and Modern Science: A Match Made in Heaven (Kettering, OH: Angelico Press, 2016)

Matters of Life & Death: A Catholic Guide to the Moral Dilemmas of Our Time (Kettering, OH: Angelico Press, 2017)

A Catholic Scientist Harmonizes Science and Faith

The Myth of an Anti-Science Church: Galileo, Darwin,
  Teilhard, Hawking, Dawkins. (Kettering, OH: Angelico
  Press, Spring 2018)

For more info, visit http://en.wikipedia.org/wiki/Gerard
_Verschuuren.

Gerard Verschuuren can be contacted at www.where-do-we-
come-from.com.

Sophia Institute

Sophia Institute is a nonprofit institution that seeks to nurture the spiritual, moral, and cultural life of souls and to spread the gospel of Christ in conformity with the authentic teachings of the Roman Catholic Church.

Sophia Institute Press fulfills this mission by offering translations, reprints, and new publications that afford readers a rich source of the enduring wisdom of mankind.

Sophia Institute also operates the popular online resource CatholicExchange.com. *Catholic Exchange* provides world news from a Catholic perspective as well as daily devotionals and articles that will help readers to grow in holiness and live a life consistent with the teachings of the Church.

In 2013, Sophia Institute launched Sophia Institute for Teachers to renew and rebuild Catholic culture through service to Catholic education. With the goal of nurturing the spiritual, moral, and cultural life of souls, and an abiding respect for the role and work of teachers, we strive to provide materials and programs that are at once enlightening to the mind and ennobling to the heart; faithful and complete, as well as useful and practical.

Sophia Institute gratefully recognizes the Solidarity Association for preserving and encouraging the growth of our apostolate over the course of many years. Without their generous and timely support, this book would not be in your hands.

www.SophiaInstitute.com
www.CatholicExchange.com
www.SophiaInstituteforTeachers.org

Sophia Institute Press is a registered trademark of Sophia Institute.
Sophia Institute is a tax-exempt institution as defined by the
Internal Revenue Code, Section 501(c)(3). Tax ID 22-2548708.